STOCKHOLM

A NOVEL

NOA YEDLIN

Translated by Jessica Cohen

HARPERVIA

An Imprint of HarperCollinsPublishers

English translation copyright © 2023 by Jessica Cohen. With support from Am Ha-Sefer—Hebrew Books, the Cultural Administration, Israel Ministry of Culture and Sport.

HarperCollins books may be purchased for educational, business, or sales promotional use. For information, please email the Special Markets Department at SPsales@harpercollins.com.

Originally published as שטוקהולם in Israel in 2016 by Zmora-Bitan Dvir, Ḥevel Modi'in.

FIRST HARPERVIA EDITION PUBLISHED IN 2023

Designed by Terry McGrath

Library of Congress Cataloging-in-Publication Data has been applied for.

ISBN 978-0-06-331081-0

23 24 25 26 27 LBC 5 4 3 2 1

For Doron

From a premature obituary of
Alfred Nobel in a French newspaper:

"Le marchand de la mort est mort."
("The merchant of death is dead.")

Wednesday

Zohara

1

Never choose a job that depends on young people's taste. Doesn't matter if it's music or clothes, beauty or food. Not that they don't have good taste—a lot of them actually do. But you don't want to be trying to guess what it is when you're in your sixties. You want to forget that they exist.

She thought back to that piece of advice, which her father had given her, while she drove to Avishay's. She'd arranged to meet him in the evening for a consultation. The truth was, there was no consultation necessary; she just wanted to spend some time with him. But with her and Avishay that was not an option. Even after twenty years, or a little more now, she was still obliged to give every meeting a label: picking up the second volume of *The Man Without Qualities*, watching the last season of *Breaking Bad*, learning something, asking something, fixing, organizing, dropping off. If the meeting had no label, that meant they were having sex. Of the two of them, only Avishay was permitted to exchange one kind of meeting for the other, to demote it, and even though she repeatedly swore that next time she would say she wasn't in the mood, if only for her token self-respect, she always ended up saying yes.

But the accountant she'd met with that morning had given her the perfect excuse: she'd discovered that she wasn't making much money, especially if you factored in a mortgage, and even without that things weren't great, and had been particularly bad in the past three or four years, which wasn't surprising given the internet and all that. There was no shortage of make-your-own-family-memoir-dot-com rackets, and generally a glut of writers willing to work for insulting fees, who devalued the industry and made a cruel mockery of her refined business model ("Zohara Zack: Personalized Biographies for Families and Institutions"). Gone were the days when she'd had the luxury of not taking every gig that came her way, with all due respect. It wasn't that she hadn't listened to her father, yet here she was at sixty-eight still forced to accommodate these young people, the grandchildren, who could always find someone to do Daddy's book for a lot cheaper. But still, Zohara thought happily, though later sorrowfully, she was gladder to have the excuse to meet Avishay than saddened by her possible poverty.

Nili claimed that any two people's romantic destiny was determined immediately after the first time they fucked—at that very moment, as soon as their backs hit the bed and they lay there, even before they knew it. "It's something I can't explain," she said, "but I know they want me, and I know they want me because of that fuck, and just so you understand—it has nothing to do with the sex, right?" "Then what the hell *does* it have to do with?" Zohara wondered, and Nili said, "It has to do with power relations. It's about something men need that I can give them. It's not even giving them what they want, it's making them feel that what I have is exactly what they need." Zohara was exasperated: "That means nothing to me, Nili. I can't use that information at all, don't you see?" Nili said, "Never mind, forget it, I'm just saying that next time you start something new, try to make a tiny change in how you approach it. I mean in the smallest things."

Having learned her lesson, Zohara did not ask: Who exactly am I going to start something new with? Because Nili actually did have some good men to offer on occasion, not just doctors like her. But they were all part of a package deal, a contract Zohara had signed years ago in a moment of weakness. "You know what, Zohara?" Nili had said back then, "I'll make a deal with you. You know how you always want to know the real truth, the truth no one tells you? Well, if I set you up with someone, I promise to tell you everything he says afterwards. I won't hold anything back. That way, we can really delve into it, we can understand things, so you can get something out of it." Zohara had liked the idea, she'd liked it a lot, both as a way to paper over Nili's insulting assumption that the guy in question wouldn't want her, before she even knew who he was, and because it was the kind of idea you couldn't refuse: Who doesn't want to know the truth, theoretically, in principle? The kind of truth that obeys the unwritten agreement between friends to protect each other's feelings: You can demand the truth, you can beg for it, but I'll keep it to myself and I won't really give it to you.

Except that with Nili it was different: "You're sure you want to know what he said, right? It's helpful, isn't it?" she would say. And what could Zohara do? Particularly since there *was* something to know, the truth was already sitting there, a neatly gift-wrapped package of poison on the table in the café, between the salt shaker and the packets of sweetener. And so then she was forced to find out that he'd said, "I don't know," or, "She's nice, she's interesting, and she's pretty attractive, too, but something just wasn't right, I don't know . . ." Lots of *I don't know*, lots of *not quite right*, and Nili reported all these things simply, casually, because she found them encouraging: It's not that there's anything wrong with you; there's nothing wrong at all. Until one day Zohara said to Nili, "I don't understand what you thought they'd say—did you think they'd say my armpits stink and I should use more deodorant?" Nili burst out laughing, but to Zohara the things she said were horrible, as horrible as anything could be, because there was nothing specific, it was just as she'd always suspected, you couldn't put your finger on it, she was just somehow damaged.

Above all she envied Nili for the normality. She wasn't jealous
of that caveman Nili was dating—Zohara was not attracted to
bearded men at all, and considered them members of a parallel species, unmateable, romantically transparent. What she envied was
the fact that Nili had completed one cycle of love and couplehood,
marriage and divorce, children and grandchildren, everything you
were supposed to have achieved at sixty-something, and could now
allow herself to engage in the anomalous, having proved her ex-
pertise in the normal. Whereas she, Zohara, was still struggling at
sixty-eight to find her first love, the kind that should have come by
sixteen at the latest, and if not sixteen then twenty-six, and at some
point even thirty-six sounded fine.

Once, about fifteen years ago, when the whole group was having dinner at Varda and Amos's place, Zohara had walked into their
daughter Hagar's bedroom to look for the cat. On a bookshelf, next
to some completely ordinary items, was a blister pack of contra-
ceptive pills, left out quite naturally, with a few missing. And even
though there was nothing secretive about the way it sat there like
something perfectly normal, or in fact precisely because of that, Zohara stood there and thought: Amos's seventeen-year-old daughter
has already found love. Amos's daughter. And to think that Zohara
herself should have had a daughter who would catch up with her in
that realm, and that Zohara would forgive her because she had her
own love.

Not that she was particularly interested in meeting someone else.
That wasn't what was supposed to happen—her and some Modi,
or Motti, whom she'd have to sit in a café with and endlessly get to
know, grudgingly hacking a tortuous path through to his soul. She
wanted Avishay. They were a couple anyway, in many respects. They
slept together sometimes and were best friends, and you couldn't
even say that about most of the married couples she knew. Avishay

simply needed to understand what could not possibly be misunderstood.

There seemed to be only one tiny step between her and all the love, all the happiness. Between her and the life she should have been living, in which all the defects had been magically erased. Yet the passing years gnawed away at the riverbanks, pushing them farther away from each other, because it did not happen, over and over again. And Zohara's soul was being eroded too, and her joy, and even, just slightly, her love, which although willing to perk up when given a sign, for the time being simply had to make way so that she could live without completely losing her mind.

She'd been in love with him more when he was available, more when he'd come back to Israel, more toward age forty, and less when she'd realized she would not have children. She'd been in love with other people, too, loving more urgently, more freshly, and whenever those affairs shattered she settled back into their old non-couplehood like the comforting vessel that it was.

———

She often wondered how Nili and Yehuda and Amos would have responded if they'd known that the man she was sleeping with was Avishay, their best friend, everyone's, including her own. Yehuda didn't know she was sleeping with anyone at all, nor did Amos, even though in some ways it was his fault that she was sleeping with Avishay.

They'd met in Jerusalem, she and Amos, at an event organized by Matzpen, the leftist student group. She was studying English literature and history, he was doing economics, of course, and together they discovered that there was always something they felt like doing more than fomenting a socialist revolution, with all due respect. She suspected that Amos was one of the men she didn't want but who wanted her very much—there were a few of those—but it was only a vague feeling, so she slept with him just to be on the safe side. After the sex it was suddenly clear to her that she did want him, but then a faint breeze of lack-of-desire began wafting from Amos's direction, and Zohara quickly adapted herself to the changing circumstances without having to be humiliated, a modus operandi she started cultivating at the time.

She had since killed off any trace of that affection, burying it in her heart alongside countless embryos of tiny affections. Amos became her best friend, and always encouraged her: You'll find him, you'll find him, you'll see, Zohara. She clung to his reassurances although logic demanded that she believe in them less and less, and she therefore challenged him more and more: But I'm not finding him! Look, Amos, this is the situation, these are the facts. She hurled this riddle that she herself had invented at him, forcing him to turn up the volume.

=====

Why hadn't she told them? At nights, when she contemplated various dynamics between her and Avishay and they floated around, disconnected, some long gone and some that existed only in her imagination, she would list the reasons: She didn't want to destroy the delicate fabric of their pentagonal friendship—to hurt them, to betray them, with a twenty-year-old secret; she didn't want to ruin things between her and Amos, who spoke to her so openly, confiding in her about how desperately he also wanted to be considered for the Nobel, burning with desire—if only he'd known she was lying naked next to Avishay; it would be a pity to ruin things for Yehuda, too, who was certain that there was nothing in the world Avishay didn't share with him. Besides, it would be wrong to build up expectations. The others were liable to seriously think there was a chance that Avishay and Zohara could be together, and they'd push for it, they'd demand it, only half-jokingly. When in fact there was no chance.

As the nights deepened, they darkened her sharp senses and her alertness, and then she would wonder about the meaning of this ritual she conducted every night, reciting carefully worded responses even though no one was listening, disciplining her mind as it threatened to ramble under cover of darkness. As though if she repeated it often enough and with sufficiently powerful inner conviction, she would finally merge with the things she wanted to want, first convincing the audience and finally herself.

Only one thing had any real significance: Avishay didn't want to tell. He didn't want to tell because of all those reasons, which they had declaimed together, first him and then her, almost at the same time, in that way she had learned to tell other men with only a split second's delay: It's funny that you're not interested because I'm not really interested either. But Zohara knew that none of these were the real reasons. He just didn't want to tell. That was all.

And just as she knew that she would betray the four-decade-long friendship right this minute, and would joylessly toss aside the trust Amos had placed in her, if she could only tell the world about her and Avishay, tell them that she was normal, or two-thirds normal, and had been for more than twenty years, she also knew that Avishay would tell everything without a second thought if he wanted to. But he didn't.

Why didn't he? Zohara tried not to think about that. She was not very successful, but the futile thought finally wore down and faded away, awakening and breathing in the darkness, in the silence, only when Zohara looked at the women Avishay dated, who introduced pauses of various durations between her and him. They were usually quite good-looking, but that in and of itself did not bother Zohara. It was actually the less beautiful ones, the ones who must have had something under the surface, who disquieted her. He never said where he met them. He did not make a habit of relating such things and they never asked, the assumption being that people like him simply met women; that women emerged from some unknown source, bumps in the road that could not be avoided. Some of his girlfriends had children, but although this made no chronological sense, Zohara had the impression that the children were always independent, mature enough to release their mothers to their own affairs, even twenty or thirty years ago. Or perhaps their neediness had never been loud enough to break through to Avishay, and therefore did not reach Zohara either.

Avishay took no interest in children. Three of his four closest friends—Yehuda, Nili, and Amos—had children, and now grandchildren, too. Avishay was there when they were born and when they grew up and when they married and had their own children, just a short drive away, in some cases walking distance, and he saw their parents often, usually at dinners held in their homes, yet still he managed to limit his contact with them to birthday parties. Zohara was always astonished by how he made it through entire events, which were at times extremely noisy, even screechy, with total serenity, skipping effortlessly over cute voices, little jokes, painful falls, and tearful tantrums. He seemed to refuse any acknowledgment of these offshoots that had grown out of his friends after the original contract between him and them was signed.

While Avishay conducted his relationships, Zohara had no choice but to wait patiently. Over time, she learned to play the game. She not only responded swiftly—"Oh yes, I have a thing going on now, too"—but also sometimes headed him off by reporting on her own developments. And if nothing was going on, she borrowed stories from her clients. In those moments she slightly envied her father for his imagination, even though she'd never wanted to be a writer herself. On the contrary, she'd always felt it was important to emphasize that she was not an author, that ghostwriting other people's life stories was a completely unrelated profession, like comparing a land appraiser to a writer, even though deep down inside she knew the analogy was slightly far-fetched.

_____

She planned to leave the house at eight, eight thirty. Maybe she'd pick up some ice cream on the way—she really shouldn't, because of the sugar, but Avishay only liked sorbet anyway, which she didn't find very hard to resist. There was a message from the real estate agent in her inbox. The subject line said: "2 more apts, note the 2nd (ground flr) has a grdn, lmk if interested." She googled the address. It was four blocks away. She had not spent seven years searching just to end up stuck in the same suburb.

She was living in that location temporarily, designating her years there as the moment before, as preparatory. She was there as someone on whom inadequate homeownership had been imposed, a wish that someone had hastily granted without listening all the way to the end. But when she finally tried to get out, something odd happened: practically overnight, she stopped being wealthy and became poor. She'd lived in the apartment, which had belonged to her parents, for years, her worries lubricated by the awareness of ownership and prosperity. But when she contacted real estate agents, whose faces were never unsmiling—*of course you can, there's a huge selection, even at your budget, there's no doubt at all,* they all recited politely, like a greeting one has to get through before reaching the point—she suddenly realized that she was a woman with no money: she had the apartment and nothing else. She would not, in her dotage, live in Paris or London; it was doubtful she could even afford Tel Aviv. So Zohara straggled after the agents from garden-level studios in reasonable neighborhoods to two-bedroom apartments in unreasonable ones, and found herself thinking: This is the apartment I will die in; this is what the end of the horizon looks like, the place from which nothing else branches off. And she would have to host guests in these places, too.

Zohara began to think of it as going through a particular kind of diminishment—that's what she would call it—because she was not poor, there was no need to get carried away. Lower middle class? Could it be that? Of the sort that had become modish? People who owned nothing yet kept up decent apartments and jobs until the day when it was so willed, or not willed, that one tiny, arbitrary movement should expose the truth with a deafening boom.

Still she kept looking, and she looked only in Tel Aviv—she had become one of those people who need the city to protect them from their abnormality, to dilute it, like all the oddballs and weirdos who simply cannot live in the suburbs—as though if she abandoned the search she would be forced to abandon too many other things. She thought she would one day find an apartment and also find happiness, and beneath the layers of contempt she did believe all the real estate agents.

She flipped through the photos of the apartment. The living room was rectangular, exactly the kind she disliked. She tried to imagine her and Avishay sitting there drinking strong Turkish coffee. Then she cropped him out of the picture, but she still couldn't see it.

2

She climbed up to the second floor and knocked on the door; Avishay didn't like it when people rang the bell. She waited too long before knocking again, and suddenly became furious. There she was, all sweaty, holding her heavy bag and a pound of sorbet and Avishay wasn't letting her in, even though they'd arranged for nine and it was almost nine fifteen. Yet she was so reluctant to ring the bell—as if *she'd* installed it secretly—when it was right there, the damned thing, precisely for this purpose, so screw him: she gave the bell a long, irritable press, like a repairman in a hurry to check the address off his list: I tried and tried but they weren't home.

No one came to the door. She put her ear against it, wondering if he had loud music on, in which case she'd forgive him, but she couldn't hear anything.

It suddenly occurred to her that he might be dead. It was childish, like those women who'd rather believe their man was dead than just not calling them back, but the staging seemed perfect: in a moment she would open the door with the key she'd been given on their parallel track, the friendship track, when she and Yehuda had each been given a copy at the same time, so there wouldn't be any misunderstandings, and what else could a person expect to find upon entering someone's apartment, after knocking and knocking, and then yelling, Avishay, Avishay, if not a dead Avishay? In another sort of film she would find him hanging in the shower, but that wasn't their film. Or spread-eagled on the bed with blood-soaked sheets. But that was a death from a different TV series. For a moment she amused herself with the notion that Amos had murdered Avishay, ten days or however long it was before the Nobel announcement—murdered him rather than watch him get the prize. Rather than kill himself.

How else could a man die? He could have died while having sex, but only with a younger woman. The woman had fled, shut the door behind her, and Zohara would find him in bed with a peculiar expression on his face and maybe an erection—or was that just television nonsense? But he wouldn't have been sleeping with anyone on the day she was visiting, and that thought suddenly made her sad—why couldn't it have ended in the middle?

She sat down on the steps, slightly hunched, planning to straighten up and restore her good spirits before she knocked again. She carefully opened the Styrofoam lid of the sorbet container and dug one finger into the white sheet, and it sunk in too quickly, too deeply. She dialed his number and heard the phone ringing from inside the apartment. He must be in the shower, he felt comfortable doing that, he considered her a member of the household. She was flooded with anger again, but the anger seemed lower merely because she was stooped, so she stood up, pulled out a bunch of keys from her bag, and searched for Avishay's. It had to be the green one, it was the green one, she knew it was, and she rang the bell again and waited another moment before she put it into the keyhole.

———

The apartment was quiet, with its blond laminate flooring and white metal bookcases custom-made for Avishay by a commercial furniture maker, grounded only by the sounds from the street, as if they were keeping it from floating away above the Levant.

"Avishay?" she said, and moved toward the big bathroom. But

when she walked past the bedroom she saw him: he was lying on his back in bed, wearing pants one does not sleep in, with his chest bare and his eyes partially open.

For a moment she considered calling someone, maybe those neighbors of his, so they could be with her, so she wouldn't be scared, but who were they compared to her and Avishay? How could these people be with her in this moment, sullying it? She felt her heart pounding as though she was on the precipice of a critical moment.

She knew he was dead. She knew she wouldn't have to shake him: Avishay, Avishay, wake up! He was dead, he was really dead, Avishay was dead. A flicker of relief just had time to cross her mind at the speed of light—the idea that Avishay wouldn't let her in, wouldn't take her arrival seriously, was clearly ridiculous—before it was banished by a torrent of thoughts, an impassioned mob that burst into her consciousness and began swinging batons in all directions, exploiting the moment to loot anything it could get its hands on: she would meet someone else, no, it was too late, but it wasn't too late for Nili, yes, but she wasn't Nili, nothing would ever change, maybe it would, she could tell everyone now, who would get the apartment, she mustn't think about that, he had a sister, what was her name, Ruthi, as if she really couldn't remember.

She took a step toward the bed. She'd seen dead people before— her father, her mother, and there were others, with proper farewells— but she'd never been with a dead person alone, and how did she even know he was dead? She looked at him from above in an unnatural close-up: no one looked at anyone like that. He didn't look green- ish or gray—what else was it they said in books?—maybe just a lit- tle pale, that was all. But she knew he was dead even though she couldn't say why. He looked like someone who was lying on the bed thanks to a particularly powerful gravitational pull, trying to cleave his way through to the ground. He looked like someone who would never get up again, not even to protest, no matter which of his many rules she violated in his presence.

She sat down on the bed. She touched his shoulder with one finger, as if fearing frostbite, but also perhaps to wake him up after all. Feeling nothing, she put her hand on his chest. For a moment she was unable to gauge it—she had never considered the temperature before; she thought he felt lukewarm. She scratched the skin with her fingernail; he did not resist and she stopped. She had to call an ambulance. *That's what one did*, she thought: *they take away the body, and it somehow ends up at the cemetery*. She imagined making the call: *There's a dead man here, I think he had a heart attack, please come.* She opened her mouth as if to rehearse, and said out loud, "There's a dead man here," just to see how it sounded and if anyone would believe her. But why wouldn't they?

She imagined the paramedics arriving, a chubby guy and a woman with a ponytail. They'd think she was his wife. Maybe they'd treat her with compassion and tenderness, if they even concerned themselves with such things. The apartment would fill with a hubbub, a stretcher would be brought up the stairs and an ambulance would be parked out front, Yehuda and Nili and Amos would arrive, and they'd have to call Ruthi, too.

One more moment. Five more. She ran her finger over his cheek but it did not feel pleasant, and she stood up.

She mechanically walked to the bathroom to pee, just in case, but when she stood by the toilet she couldn't be bothered.

She went into the study and turned on the light; the computer screen looked dead. She touched the mouse and the desktop lit up green, almost bare. But that was too much for her now.

She turned the light off and went into the kitchen, opened a couple of cabinets without knowing what she was looking for, then sat down at the dining table. How she had dreamed of seeing this life of his from inside, of being in this home without him: that was the ultimate sign of intimacy, when someone allowed you to be in their home on your own, when it truly became shared. It was too bad he had to die for this to happen. Then she thought: Over my dead body. This was the definition of *over my dead body*. It was the height of pathetic, the embodiment of pitiful. You think you can be my partner? Over my dead body!

She took a deep breath to make herself stop thinking about it. But when she exhaled, the air stuck to her lungs and instead it was tears that exited her eyes. Zohara looked down her face in surprise, having failed to recognize the tears even though they'd been weighing down her breath all this time: Avishay was dead. There was no Avishay. Things would have to change.

Thursday

Yehuda

3

Smoke, smoke, smoke, smoke. Just one cigarette, dear God. He briefly considered coming clean, confessing right then and there. The cigarette would be worth the humiliation. He'd need half a pack by the time they finished yakking. Just a second, he could say, just stop for a second, I have to tell you something: I'm not a vegan anymore, and I've taken up smoking again, okay? And when they recovered from the shock—that was the part he really couldn't face, the shocked silence, the righteous horror he would inflict upon humanity, the *But when? But why?* Big deal, so a guy starts smoking again and having a bit of meat once in a while, why can't we just move on?—he would say: Avishay is lying dead in the next room, shouldn't we be focused on that?

Perhaps that was what might be called a cynical exploitation of the deceased, but Avishay would have forgiven him. And he would have laughed. Right after he forgave him and laughed about his betrayal of their shared obsession with veganism, or nutritarianism—Yehuda had slightly lost track of which one it was, but he kept up a very convincing act: he sent Avishay links to online recipes (that was the easy part) for things like seitan goulash with leek puree and lentil dal, or buckwheat with minted peas; he reported at length on his disillusionment with conventional medicine as he sought to cure his bum knee so that he could finally resume exercising with Avishay; and every few weeks, when he had no choice, he let Avishay drag him to that punishment of a restaurant with the mosquito-infested patio and the "cheese" cake (quotes in the original) for dessert, which was somehow the course that made his heart sink the deepest.

But if Avishay would have been so forgiving and amused, why hadn't he simply come clean? Perhaps because he was ashamed to have abandoned yet another idea, afraid to be caught fleeing from another project that for a long time he had planned to devote his life to, wary of providing their smirking friends with yet more unnecessary proof—Yes, well, that's Yehuda for you, there's nothing you can do, that's how he is. But there *was* something you could do, and there was no reason to smirk, because that *wasn't* how he was, and he couldn't stand it any longer.

That was why he kept sitting through the half-vegan dinners that Varda and Idit hosted, where he would eat from the wrong half, listen to Avishay go overboard about his improving health, and finally remark, *I have to admit that I actually don't feel any dramatic physical change, I know that's what they always say, but no, at least not anything extreme, I just do it because it's the right thing to do*, and feel as though he were lying less by saying that.

No, he would bite his tongue. Besides, he had to admit that this wasn't really the right time. He would hold strong and not smoke. Cancer-cancer-cancer-cancer, agonizing death, remorse and regret for not quitting in time, not seeing grandchildren from Daria, not seeing Daniella through her pregnancy, seeing Daniella through her pregnancy and then dying the minute the boy starts talking, they won't bring him to see me because I'll be coughing up blood and I'll look like a corpse. Cancer-cancer-cancer-cancer.

He had to focus.

"She's completely lucid, at least as far as I know. Isn't she, Yehuda?" It was Nili speaking: "His mother's pretty much fine, except she can't walk much, right?"

Yehuda said, "For a woman in her late nineties she's fine. A bit less with it the past few months."

"Can she even make it to the funeral?"

"I don't know," Yehuda said.

He thought about Penina, Avishay's mother Penina, whom he'd hardly seen since she'd moved into the care home and stopped going out. When they were kids he'd envied Avishay because of her: there were rumors that Yehuda's own mother, who was a high school AP math teacher, was having an affair with the remedial math teacher—which always struck Yehuda as somewhat demeaning, like she'd been forced to make do with that—and Yehuda had no choice but to feign collaboration with his friends' attempts to spy on them; the only other option was to be humiliated, which was never an option.

After his mother died, long after, he sometimes toyed with the idea of asking his father about it. He would do it in a bemused tone, like it was an anecdote from ancient history, giving him the perfect opportunity to repudiate it if he wanted to. He used to sit there in the retirement home, desperately seeking topics, accomplishments, pieces of the sparse medley of life that he could somehow fish out to pass the time with, to fill the obligatory ninety minutes, and the question always sat in his mouth. Right here, right now, he would just open his mouth and ask. His father might even be glad. But he couldn't take the step, he couldn't utter those few words that might have moved the whole room into a different dimension, sixty-odd years of a certain kind of parenting fundamentally altered in an instant. Afterward his father was moved into nursing care and eventually developed Alzheimer's, and it was too late. It was just like they warned on all those *Dr. Phil*–type shows: in the end people die without tying up loose ends and you discover with sadness that it's too late. But what Yehuda discovered was that he was relieved.

Zohara said, "Well, anyway, Ruthi will tell her, won't she?" Yehuda said, "I guess so," and Amos asked if he would call Ruthi. Yehuda agreed, and Amos said, "We have to do it now, it's been a while," and Yehuda said, "You know what? I'll run out to get us something to drink and I'll call her on the way. I don't feel comfortable having that conversation in front of you anyway." Amos said, "Whatever you're getting, bring us back a large bottle of Coke Zero," and Yehuda said, "It might interest you to know that in the United States the police use that stuff you drink to clean bloodstains off asphalt." Zohara said, "It's not for cleaning blood, it's to disinfect bodies," and Amos quipped, "Then by all means, bring a six-pack." "Very funny," said Yehuda. "I'm really sorry to rain on your parade," Nili interjected, "but both of those are urban legends. Now please go out for some Diet Coke and stop messing around."

———

He turned right, then right again, and after making sure the C-shaped route wasn't leading him around to the back of the same building where someone might look out of Avishay's bathroom window and see the bench, he sat down and lit a cigarette.

He felt irritated instead of sad, or perhaps in addition; his foul mood overshadowed everything and he wasn't sure what was hiding underneath it.

How had they even ended up in this situation? He'd said right from the start, "Let's call an ambulance. Why do we need to wait for Nili, or for Amos? What is Nili going do? Resuscitate him?"

But Zohara said, "It's not a question of resuscitating, Yehuda, there are extremely delicate decisions that need to be made."

"What delicate decisions? Honestly, Zohara, we have to call an ambulance and arrange things with the cemetery. The only decision we need to make is who's doing what, that's all, and once we do that I can go home and cry in peace."

"I don't know, that crazy sister of his, maybe she'll want to see him in his home."

"What difference does it make? She should be thankful her brother has sane friends so she can just turn up at the funeral when we tell her to. And by the way, I don't have any illusions that she's going to pay for it. Not that I care, I'm stoked to pay for Avishay's funeral, you know that." Zohara made a little face meant to project a special sense of humor alongside a proficiency in the nuances of colloquial language. Yehuda couldn't stand that face. "All right, you know what I mean."

"Yehuda, how about a little compassion? Poor woman, she is his sister, and with all due respect, we are not relatives. Her brother died today!"

"Yesterday," Yehuda clarified.

"Okay."

"Or the day before yesterday. I have no idea how long he's been lying here."

"Okay, then all the more so—she doesn't even know about it, so I think she has the right to do what she wants and the right to decide what she wants to do, and I don't think she's going to be all that thrilled to go and see him in a freezer drawer in a morgue, that's all I'm saying."

"Come on, then, let's call Ruthi now. We can't keep drawing it out."

"Amos and Nili are on their way, Yehuda, give it another five minutes. At least Nili can have a look at him, so we'll have a little bit more information for Ruthi. She can be here in two minutes, she lives a few feet away. They asked us to wait for them."

So they sat in Avishay's living room and waited for Nili and Amos. It was a good thing they had death to keep them company. Every so often Zohara walked over to Avishay's room, apparently to make sure nothing had changed; she was a little preoccupied by it. Yehuda sat on the couch with his head between his hands, a position he considered legitimate in a state of mourning, even though he couldn't touch his pain at all in these conditions—for that he needed quiet and a cigarette.

=====

There was a time when they were the solid pair in this fivesome. She was available and he was also pretty available, Idit was busy with a million things and wasn't bothered by it—Zohara was like a sister. They would go to movies at the art-house cinema, no matter what was showing, from Croatian watchmakers to Korean orphans, they saw it all, nothing was disqualified, they didn't read the reviews first or anything, and afterward they'd have dinner at an Italian restaurant.

They'd gossip a little, within the boundaries they'd demarcated over thousands of conversations, aware of what was gossipable and what was not: they were allowed to talk about the women Avishay was seeing, but not about the men Nili was dating; they were allowed to ask anything about Yehuda and Idit, nothing at all about Amos and Varda; and every so often they gingerly touched on a fresh topic, feeling around with their toes to find out how solid the ground was. Like the time they discussed Varda's new legal career, which no one could stand to hear about anymore, but it still took an impatient puff from Zohara for Yehuda to finally say, "It is a little tedious, isn't it?"

Zohara had endless patience, of the kind that has no visible limits on the horizon; the kind of patience typical of people who don't have children. Yehuda told her about his ideas and his plans, examining all the angles over and over again even when they were the same angles, and the uselessness was the same uselessness, and he was grateful for her fresh ears, for the way she didn't nod impatiently as if to say, Yes, you can skip that bit, we've already talked about it, don't you remember, but rather she herself repeated the same arguments and reasons, the same "on one hand, but on the other hand," nobly shouldering her share of the burden.

Only on one occasion did she near the end of her tether. They had just had dinner at Varda and Amos's, and Zohara said there was something pitiful about the way Varda made such a clumsy effort to compensate for her feelings of inferiority. To which Yehuda said, "What are all of our lives if not one big effort to compensate for feelings of inferiority?"

"Mine isn't," Zohara insisted. "Not at all. I don't even know what inferiority is. I mean, I know what the word means, but I don't think I've ever experienced anything like it. I can't relate to the notion of standing next to someone and feeling inferior to them."

"Oh, come on, don't you feel inferior compared to people who are more successful than you?"

"Yehuda, *you* feel inferior around people who are more successful. That's your problem, not mine."

"That's not true at all. You could say that I feel inferior compared to people who've found their purpose in life, people who've achieved greatness, that may be true."

"What on earth is greatness? I don't even understand what that is."

"People who've achieved international, unequivocal recognition of their accomplishments, okay?"

"So wait, do you consider Avishay someone who's achieved greatness?" she asked.

"You know what? If Avishay really does get the Nobel, then yes, I'll be happy for him and I'll be thrilled and all that, but—you know what, not but, *and*—yes, I suppose I'll also feel a tiny bit inferior around him. And to tell you the truth, I can't imagine anyone in the world who wouldn't."

"I must say, I find that a very provincial perspective, and also pretty surprising, to be honest. I mean, you're Yehuda Harlap, an incredibly successful, wealthy man, with a family, and *this* is going to make you feel small? Someone getting a prize in Sweden, in a field you have nothing to do with? I mean it's not like it's your area, it's not like academia was something that ever interested you."

"In my opinion you're being naïve, Zohara. It's the greatest honor in Western culture, it's like an Oscar. Everyone envies Israelis who win an Oscar, even if they've never seen a movie in their lives. Why? Because. Because if success is relative—and what is success anyway, and who decides and all that—then there are two things that put an end to the whole debate because they amount to absolute, incontrovertible proof of success: Oscars and Nobels. And Nobels even more than Oscars. So all right, we're lucky enough to have a friend who might be about to get one, and if it happens it'll be . . . I don't even know what to call it . . . It'll be a truly great thing. But to tell you it's going to make *me* feel better?"

"But the fact that you know him so well, that you know all his problems and his issues and his weaknesses, doesn't that make a difference? Doesn't it show you exactly the opposite? That the minute you know these people we're supposed to feel inferior to, you realize that everything's complicated, that everyone has their own inferiority complex, that it all balances out?"

"You know what," Yehuda said, "let me ask you this: When you meet Tirzah, and she tells you about all her trips overseas and her prizes and everything . . ."

"Yes?"

"And let's say you tell her about how you've just finished writing a jubilee book for some factory, right? Don't you say to yourself: Wow, we're the same age, but look at her and look at me. Even though I never wanted to be a writer and I'm really successful and good at what I do and all that, still, I've achieved less. Objectively, in this world, I've achieved less, and because—unfortunately—I'm not dumb, in fact I'm really smart, I understand these things. I'm aware of them. But there's nothing I can do."

"I don't understand, are you trying to convince me to have an inferiority complex?"

"God forbid, I think you're amazingly smart and beautiful and successful, that goes without saying, doesn't it? Otherwise I wouldn't get into this at all."

"Yehuda, the fact that there are people who've achieved more than I have is obvious. The question is, how do you feel when you're around them? And when I'm with Tirzah, I'm telling you honestly, Yehuda, first of all I hear a lot of things from her that you don't, so if you think everything's always easy and fun and goes smoothly for her then you are very much mistaken—she spends half her life dealing with hardships and failures, at least the way she sees it, and I'm not even talking about personal stuff."

He hesitated for a moment, but a very short one, because he was convinced that this was an interesting debate, that honesty was the whole thing here, which justified him, and so he said, "But see? On a personal level, too, when she tells you about her problems, it's not like you can offer anything better as so-called consolation."

"What's that supposed to mean? That because I don't have children I'm supposed to feel even more inferior?"

"You're not offended or anything, right?"

"Of course not, I'm saying hurtful things, too."

"If we're not being politically correct, and we're not, then yes, I would think that when you live alone in the world, surrounded by people with families, then yes, that's something that has to . . . that affects you, that makes you examine yourself relative to others. It seems only natural."

"Of course it's something that affects you, it's not something that can't have an effect, the question is *how* it affects you. And I have to say that these days, when half the people we know are divorced, and their kids are grown and have their own problems—I mean look around us, how many of the children, including your girls, don't have issues? They're not cute little three-year-olds anymore. But me? I have a slightly different life, that's all—so you know what, I don't know if things are as absolute as your Oscars and Nobels."

"Yes, *mine*, like I'm the only one who cares," Yehuda commented.

"I have to tell you, I've known you for almost fifty years and I consider you an extremely sophisticated person, and it's like all of a sudden this side of you comes out that I've never seen before."

"If you're completely untarnished by this feeling then I'm happy for you. What can I say, it must be fun to live like that. The question is whether you really feel that way or if it's a story you tell yourself. And only you can answer that."

"Well, maybe I do need to do some soul-searching."

"You're not offended or anything, are you? You know it's all meant in the tone I said it in."

"Offended by what? By the fact that you suspect I have no self-awareness?"

"I don't know, by this whole conversation."

"It's all good, Yehuda."

═══

Not long afterward, he decided to ask for her help with the book. She'd always said: If you ever want to do something with it, let me know, I'll give you whatever advice I can. And Yehuda had always said: It's not there yet, I'm sad to say, but thanks.

Nothing had changed: the file still sat there, untouched since the day he'd finished writing. But he didn't know whom to give it to, which of his close friends was the right person to read something like that. Definitely not Idit, she was completely opposed to the whole writing project, and this kind of book wasn't her style anyway. Zohara seemed too limited in her aspirations. The natural thing would have been to show it to Nili. She was very familiar with his dilemmas about it, and always took them seriously. But Nili was dangerous, knotty, the complete opposite of how she looked, deconstructing and analyzing everything until there was nothing left of it. He felt a need to protect the book from her, and perhaps to protect the two of them, too, as though if she lopped off that foot, they'd have nothing left.

At some point he considered Amos, of all people, with all his stuff about the economics of happiness. He had an unconventional mind, Amos. Yehuda felt he would be able to appreciate *The Courage to Invent*, that he would enjoy reading it and maybe even get something out of it. But Avishay might be offended—he'd never understand why Yehuda would show it to Amos before he showed it to him, and he wasn't about to keep things from Avishay.

Of course he could let Avishay read it, too, but he didn't want to. He told himself he was saving Avishay for last, that Avishay was not someone you could show a draft to. That was true, but the real reason was that Yehuda was afraid of something, although he himself wasn't sure exactly what. Even before he showed Zohara the book, before anything happened, he sensed an undercurrent of dread: as though the book were designed to destroy friendships, to decimate them with a flip of the page. In retrospect it was the smartest decision he'd ever made, because Avishay did read the book in the end, after it was edited and proofread, and then Yehuda got a foreword—written by Avishay himself.

He hadn't thought of Tirzah Bar-Ness, even though he knew very well that she was a friend of Zohara's; after all, he was the one who'd mentioned her in their infamous inferiority-complex argument. She had seemed inaccessible because she was so well known and successful, but when Zohara mentioned her distresses and failures—and she wasn't even talking about personal stuff—he suddenly had the feeling she would like him, that they were actually quite similar.

One evening at a restaurant, Yehuda told Zohara where things stood: He'd basically finished writing but he couldn't decide whom to show it to, and then he'd remembered her friend, Tirzah, and he wasn't sure why but she seemed like the perfect reader. Zohara looked surprised, which put a dent in Yehuda's certainty: maybe he was exaggerating, maybe it was inappropriate.

Zohara said, "It's a sort of self-help book, if I understand correctly, isn't it?"

That was when Yehuda knew that he wasn't exaggerating and it *was* appropriate, because to call a book like his self-help showed a complete misunderstanding. There was a thread stretching between him and Tirzah, and it ran right over Zohara's head.

Zohara continued: "Look, this is a woman who writes serious novels." Then she corrected herself: "She writes novels, I don't know if she's the right person for a book like this, about training your brain. Who exactly would she be reading it as?"

Yehuda said, "First of all, it's not a book about training your brain. Or rather, it's not only about that. There are lots of personal parts in it too, about our childhood, my life story, insights. It doesn't matter . . ."

"It does matter, of course it does."

"And secondly, what do you mean, 'who would she read it as?' She'd read it as a smart woman, as a woman, as a writer, as someone who travels the world, who knows the market, or just as someone who might enjoy it. Isn't that enough?"

"Have you read her books?"

"I read the first one."

"*Perks and Recreation*?"

"Yes."

"That wasn't the first one."

"What difference does it make? You knew what I meant."

"It's just that she published it twenty-five years ago. I didn't realize you were such a Tirzah Bar-Ness fanboy."

"Look, if you're not into it then let's drop it, I can contact her myself if you don't feel comfortable doing it."

"No, it's fine, send me the book and I'll get it to her. Just tell me what to tell her, what sort of criticism you're looking for."

"I want her to say whatever she thinks, without holding back. For all I care she can jot down anything that goes through her mind." He meant it, he really did want the absolute truth, but try as he might to acknowledge his own limitations, to recognize that there was a distinct possibility that he was partially blind when it came to his own writing, he still could not conceive of a truth other than that his book was good. He knew there could be any number of responses, but his heart was stronger than his mind, and despite his attempts to exercise self-restraint, he was preparing to celebrate.

Three weeks later, Zohara forwarded him Tirzah's message:

Dear Yehuda,
Thank you for the manuscript and for the pleasure of reading it.
First, I would like to say that you certainly do walk the talk: your quick thinking and originality are evident in almost every line of the book's many lines, and reading it is an enjoyable and at times entertaining experience.

However, to my mind, the book requires extensive work before it can be published. First and foremost, there is a problem of focus. The idea of combining a sort of "practical guide for the inventor" together with the biography of an inventor is interesting, yet at least at this point it seems we are dealing with two separate works that have been combined somewhat artificially and do not illuminate each other in any new light. The current structure seems almost associative, drawing the reader's attention, demanding that he make an effort, rather than allowing him to focus on the stories and exercises and enjoy them.

As an example, when you tell your personal story about how you invented the bag opener (and by the way, this is probably the time to thank you for that—I have only just discovered that you are the person who changed my life, and if I were not someone who studiously avoids doing so, I would add a smiley at this point) the story comes across as completely arbitrary. Even if that really was how things happened and the depiction is realistic, it does somehow pull the rug out from under the entire story. The reader is left struggling to understand how he might learn anything from this story, or what he might apply to his own life from it, other than to pray that such a thing might happen to him too.

Practically speaking, various exercises to sharpen one's brain have been distributed online for years, and these days, in the Facebook era, even more so. Do you have anything new to offer in this area? These are questions that must be considered, perhaps with the help of a professional editor.

Another point worth mentioning is the writing. The biographical sections represent the lion's share of the book, and some of the stories are touching. However, I would

suggest shortening the sentences and ke
the reader is positioned outside your min
you must therefore mediate the content f
possible way.

  I thank you, again, for the opportunity to
and fascinating world, and I send you my h
success,

Tirzah

He didn't call Zohara for a week. He didn't know if she'd read the email before forwarding it, and even if she hadn't, Tirzah might have told her. Either way, he couldn't risk not telling her the truth. At first he thought she wasn't calling either because she knew—she was smart enough to understand that humiliation wants no company. But the thought of all that criticism settling into Zohara's mind just as it was, without any mediating factors, drove him even madder than the letter, and so he finally phoned her.

She didn't say anything about it, so after a while he said, "She didn't like my book, your friend."

"Oh, didn't she?"

"Didn't she say anything to you about it?"

"Of course not, she'd a very discreet person."

He felt helpless, humiliated to a degree he was unable to gauge, unable to gauge what ammo he would have to enlist and where he should aim it, so he simply threw up his hands, and to his great surprise and without having intended to do so, he said to Zohara, "Would you be willing to read it?"

"If you'd like me to. It's just that the whole brain-training thing and all that isn't my area, so bear that in mind."

"It's okay, I trust you, and I want you to read what she wrote, too. I'm specifically interested in your opinion about what she said."

blem, but resend her email to me, I deleted it right after I
ded it to you."

At that moment, Yehuda knew she was lying.

====

The next time they met, when they sat down for dinner after a movie,
she pulled the manuscript out of her bag. Yehuda couldn't believe
she'd kept him hanging through an entire movie and was now choosing such casual timing, a minute before the eggplant pizza arrived.
But he was willing to forgive anything.

"Look," she began. "I think you write very, very well."

And Yehuda said, "But?"

"Why but? I think you write very, very well and that it's an ex-
traordinarily original book. Seriously, I've never read anything like
it, and I've read a lot."

"Okay," he said gingerly.

"I also think it's full of humor. I could almost hear you writing-
reading it to me. It's totally you, this book."

"Okay, thank you."

"You're welcome, I'm just telling you what I think. But I will say—"

"Go on."

"It's precisely because it's such a lovely idea, this combination,
the whole thing about inventiveness and all that, that it's a shame
that it isn't seen through all the way. Do you see what I mean? It
comes off more as a book about lots of things that preoccupy you,
all sorts of thoughts and ideas and contemplations, and that's totally
fine if that's what you want to write, but right now it's posing as a
different book."

"What do you mean, thoughts and ideas and contemplations?
This is my life story, Zohara, that's the whole idea here. I'm not in-

terested in putting out another self-help book or brain training or I don't know what, that's exactly what I was trying *not* to do."

"Okay, then maybe I really did miss that. But right now, my sense is that the personal sections are not quite as powerful."

"But the personal sections are most of the book! They *are* they book."

"Not at all, I did not read it that way at all."

"How can you say you didn't read it that way? This kills me—it's like if something doesn't have a clear title, you people can't understand it!"

"Which people? What do you want from me?"

"I don't know, I'm starting to feel like it's not coming through at all."

"What isn't?" Zohara asked.

"Everything. I don't know. The whole idea of the book."

"Why don't you tell me in your own words what the idea is? Give me your elevator pitch."

"It's the coming-of-age story of a Tel Aviv boy who grows up to be an inventor, so it also shows that aspect, his insights from that."

"Good, then that's completely clear."

"But you just said it wasn't clear!"

"Forget what I said. What I'm talking about is simply a question of proportions, that's all."

"Well, all right," Yehuda said. "What else?"

"No, now I'm afraid to say anything."

"Go on, go on, tell me."

"All right. About the exercises. Some of them are great, honestly. I did a few and their effect is amazing. But some of them seem a little bit like something you'd do at circle time in elementary school—and again, I'm just saying this about certain parts. In other parts I would just leave them as is, don't get me wrong."

"So bottom line, you agree with your friend Tirzah."

"About what?"

"Let's do it this way: is there anything she wrote that you disagree with?"

"Yehuda, don't start court-martialing me here."

"So basically, the book is no good."

"At this point in time, the book is not as good as it could be. And it's a shame, because you do have the talent to turn it into a great book."

"Okay, but is it worth working on? That's the question. Is it worth doing the work?"

"Of course it is! I mean, not that I'd ever tell anyone to shelve their book. Unrelated to you, not that this has nothing to do with you. But it's a fantastic book."

"Okay, I get the point," Yehuda said.

"Don't get all insulted now, because that's unfair, Yehuda, that's the most unfair thing you could do."

"My feelings are not hurt at all. On the contrary. And I don't want you to soften the blow, I want you to tell me everything."

"I did tell you everything. If I have anything else to say it's only good things, but now you won't believe anything I tell you."

"Tell me, feel free, go on, like what?"

"Like I think you're one of the most brilliant people I know."

"Stop it, Zohara, I'm not a five-year-old."

She gave him another compliment or two and he harped on the insults a while longer, squeezing out alternative versions from her that were by turns softer and more extreme, and finally they said, "Okay," as if mutually agreeing to shake off the conversation in favor of the time they had left to enjoy and in favor of their friendship and in favor of their mental health, and they spent the rest of the long evening in an excessively lively talk about a guy Zohara was dating.

"Are you ready to hear this? Is it the right time?" she asked.

Yehuda said, "If I get any readier than this I'll be overdone."

Zohara talked and Yehuda listened and nodded yes even though his heart was saying no.

They said goodbye with a particularly firm hug in the car outside Yehuda's house. Zohara said, "You know I love you and I think you're super-talented," and Yehuda said, "Okay, okay, let's drop the melodrama," and he kissed her on the cheek and affectionately rubbed her leather-jacket-clad arm, and that was the last time they saw each other alone.

———

From the other side of the street, a fifty-something-year-old man was heading toward him. He was bald and wore clothes that looked slightly too young for him, like the guys you sometimes see on Rothschild Boulevard, pushing an afterthought-baby in a stroller, compensating their younger wives by letting them sleep in on a Friday morning. He reminded Yehuda of Yossi, Professor Yossi Vital, Daniella's fifty-four-year-old husband, who was seventeen years older than her and treated Yehuda like a comrade in old age when he came over to their place for dinner, as if the two of them had seen it all and heard it all, as if their lives were behind them, which drove Yehuda crazy. Yossi and Daniella were going to have a baby soon, and all at once Yehuda was flooded with thoughts of the dead Avishay. They would not live together in this world, Avishay and the baby—an old human and a new human.

He scrolled through his phone for Ruthi's number. Maybe he didn't have it? But then he found it. He should be nicer to her. He should be nicer in general.

If Avishay had won the Nobel, the baby would know who he was. But now what could Yehuda say about him? Anything else would just sound like a pestering old grandpa: I had this friend, want to hear about him? It wouldn't interest him. Yehuda started to have the feeling that the baby was already alive and kicking, a complete human being inside his mother's belly, perfecting the contempt and lack of interest.

He had to call his editor, too. The author of his foreword was dead. They were going to need a new cover, something with "the late" added in.

He wondered if you could get a Nobel after you were dead. Probably not. Maybe in special cases, but what was special about this case? Nothing.

He opened Wikipedia. Nobel Prize. Alfred Nobel's will, prize ceremony, candidacy and selection, late recognition of achievements. What about dead people, where did they write about dead people?

"The prohibition against awarding the prize to deceased recipients has prevented recognition of members of a research team who died before the prize was awarded." There. "The recognition withheld by the prize committee is often bestowed by the winners themselves: at the ceremony where the Nobel Prize in Economics was awarded to Daniel Kahneman, he noted the role of his research colleague, Amos Tversky, who had died before the prize was announced." That wasn't any help.

He kept reading. Alfred Nobel, a chemist and industrialist who invented dynamite, had left the money in his will. Nobel's inventions were directly related to the development and manufacturing of explosives, and he felt increasing distress at the military uses of his inventions. It is said that one of the causes of his final will was a premature obituary of him mistakenly published in a French newspaper, after his brother Ludwig died. The erroneous notice of Nobel's death appeared under the headline "*Le marchand de la mort est mort*" ("The merchant of death is dead").

What would they write about Yehuda when he died? They might call him the bag man. "The Bag Man Is Dead." No: "The inventor of the bag opener has died." Something like that. Forty years and they still couldn't come up with a good name for that product. It was like a garlic press, as Idit liked to console him: the best products are simply what they are, witty slogans are for fleeting novelties. But who would write "bag man" about him? No one would, because no one would write about him at all. Maybe, on an especially slow news day, in the lower right corner of the financial supplement you read when you were grabbing a falafel for lunch and there was nothing else around.

The announcement of the economics prize was next week, on the sixteenth. Or had they moved it forward? He checked the Nobel Prize's imposing website. Physics, chemistry, peace, economics. October 16. What was today's date?

4

He walked into Avishay's apartment with a two-liter bottle of Coke Zero and a packet of cappuccino-flavored wafers—he needed his friends placated—and from the doorway, before they could even ask about Ruthi, he said, "Listen, I thought about something on the way."

"Did you talk to Ruthi?" Amos asked.

"Just listen for a sec." He put the Zero and wafers on the table and sat down in an armchair and closed his eyes, instead of lighting a cigarette, and then he opened them and said, "Next Thursday is the Nobel, when they announce the winner of the Nobel for economics."

Amos said, "It's on Wednesday."

"I just checked, it's on the sixteenth."

"Yeah, the sixteenth is Wednesday."

"Okay then, Wednesday, even better," Yehuda said. "You know this was supposed to be Avishay's year, right? There's not even a question about it."

"No one can predict these things, it's a total hypothetical, there's no official list of candidates," Amos said.

Nili said, "Okay, but he did know that unofficially he was a strong candidate—remember he was at that conference in Sweden last year? The what's-it-called?"

"You mean the Nobel Symposium?"

"Yes, that's it. According to Avishay, they only invite candidates—isn't that right, Amos?"

"But still, you can be a supposed candidate for years and never win. People are invited to the symposium and then they wait and wait and never get it—can you imagine the torture?"

Yehuda struggled to contain his impatience. "He also knows they had that assessment done about him."

"What assessment?" Nili asked.

Amos said: "When someone makes it onto the short list—you know 'short' could mean dozens of candidates, yes?—then they ask an expert in the field to write an assessment."

Yehuda added, "And they wrote one about Avishay, he was explicitly told that."

"Okay, I'm not saying they didn't, I'm sure he is a candidate and apparently he is on the short list."

Zohara said, "What difference does it make now? Why does it even matter? Why are we having this conversation?"

"It really doesn't matter," Nili agreed.

"Okay, so why bring it up?"

"It's just a way of not thinking about it."

"He's right here in the next room, dead, so how can we not think about it?"

Amos said, "It's not a question of not thinking about it, Zohara, do you understand what I'm saying? It's just frustrating, that's all, this whole . . ."

And Yehuda thought: This is it, this is my chance. As he skirted the words, about to aim straight at them, Amos continued, as if on cue: "His odds on the sites were really good."

"What sites?" Nili asked.

Yehuda jumped in: "The online betting sites for the Nobel. They have them, like the lottery. I had a look and I saw these long discussions there, with people from all over the world weighing in, experts in the various fields, and Avishay was definitely a strong contender for this year."

"Well, he could still win, couldn't he? Or not?" Nili asked.

"Only living candidates can win, there's no such thing as a posthumous award," Amos said.

"Are you telling me if they find out he died a few days earlier, they're going to disqualify him? That doesn't make sense to me, and it's not fair either," said Zohara.

Yehuda picked up the thread: "Wait a second, wait, just listen to me for a sec, I just did all the research while I was out. You can't give the prize to a dead candidate, that's true. Or rather, the candidate has to be alive when the announcement is made, meaning now. But there's no problem if they die in between the announcement and the ceremony, which is in December. Right, Amos?"

"I have no idea."

Nili said, "Okay, but he *will* be dead at the time of the announcement."

"Yes," Yehuda conceded, "but there have been cases when the committee announced a winner without knowing that he'd died a few days earlier. It was an innocent mistake, and the win was still valid. I just read about it."

"But they *will* know about Avishay. Everyone will know," Amos said.

"That's just it. Now listen to me for a minute and keep an open mind, I know it sounds outlandish but I'll never forgive myself if I don't bring it up." Yehuda looked at their expectant faces like a suicide examining the ground from the roof of a skyscraper. "What if we keep him quote-unquote alive until next week?"

Nili smiled. "Oh, I don't believe it."

Feeling buoyed, Yehuda said, "Think about it for a second. There are two options: either he died yesterday and is buried today, just a nice, single professor of economics—"

"A nice, *divorced* professor," Zohara interrupted.

"Zohara, if you wouldn't mind concentrating on the main issue here," Yehuda said, but he immediately regretted it and corrected himself: "A nice, divorced professor of economics who had a few friends who liked him, who will also die not long from now. Or, he dies seven days from now as the winner of the Nobel Prize in Economics, a man who will be immortalized, remembered forever, whose entire life's work was not in vain, who will receive the greatest honor bestowed by humanity, and I'm not even talking about the million dollars, or krona, or whatever it is."

"And what exactly is he going to do with that million dollars?" Nili wondered. "Pad his grave with it? He has no kids, no nothing."

"Excuse me, but his having no kids, that doesn't mean he has nothing," Zohara said.

"I meant in terms of heirs, you know what I meant. What does he need a million dollars for now?"

"That doesn't matter, it can go to research, charity, whatever. The million dollars is the marginal issue here, to my mind," said Yehuda.

Amos said, "Well, this whole conversation is hypothetical anyway, isn't it? It's not like we have a million dollars to give out."

Nili said, "Obviously not, but you have to admit that it's an amusing idea."

"For sure, very amusing."

"Oh, I thought Yehuda was being serious," Zohara said.

"I'm not sure. It's something I thought of five minutes ago, but it seems to me that we should give it some serious thought before dismissing it. There's a very significant issue at stake here."

"First of all," said Amos, "I'm not sure how significant it is and to whom: the man is dead, he doesn't care."

"See, that's where I disagree with you," Zohara said.

"On whose behalf are you doing this? He's dead. Avishay is dead. It's not for him, because he won't get to enjoy it."

"He won't enjoy it in the sense of drinking champagne when they make the announcement, but you would be ensuring something that you know was very, very important to him. I mean, come on, wasn't it important to Avishay how he'd be remembered? What he'd be remembered for? Giving back to humanity and all that? You'd be helping to implement something you know was important to him, maybe even the most important thing."

"Do you know what this is like?" Amos said. "It's like someone . . . I don't know, let's say Yehuda, really wants to have grandchildren from Daria, it's his life's dream, okay?"

Yehuda nodded vigorously even though the example was alien to him.

"And after he dies, she finally goes out of her way to make him happy and has a child. Once he's dead."

"So? What's wrong with that?" asked Zohara. "And anyway, it's not the same thing at all. In this case you're talking about a man who was motivated in his lifetime by his afterlife, by the question of what he would leave behind."

"He's dead," Amos repeated, "he doesn't care about anything anymore and nothing is going to make him happy now. I can't understand how that isn't the point of departure here. But even if we put aside the philosophical question for now—"

"I don't view it as philosophical at all," Yehuda interjected.

"Forget it, it's just not relevant anyway because it's simply impossible. You can't keep someone alive, not in quotes and not *not* in quotes. How are you going to do it? It's a technical impossibility."

Yehuda wanted to respond, but when he looked at Amos he noticed that his cheeks looked strange, or perhaps it was his lips, as if someone had removed something from his face or maybe added to it. It looked either flushed or pale, and he wasn't sure if Amos had always looked that way, or had for some time, or whether he'd slowly grown old or aged right at that minute, and if so, shouldn't he be pitied? He looked around in a panic but no one else seemed to see it, and maybe there was nothing to see.

Nili said, "Wait a sec, I'm trying to understand what you're talking about here. What do you mean 'keep him alive'? You mean simply not tell anyone he's dead, right?"

"No, we do tell everyone he's dead, but only seven or eight days from now, after we find out if he's won," Yehuda answered.

Amos said, "It's not 'simply not tell anyone he's dead.' There's nothing simple about it, and not telling would be the easy part, which would actually be very difficult, by the way, because you don't just have to not tell, you have to actually hide his death actively, and lie to a great deal of people."

"How many people would it be? He lives alone, which is an advantage in this case."

"How many people? His mother, his sister, his students, his colleagues, a million people who call and email him? And that's the easy part, like I said. What are you going to do with his body? Leave it here on the bed, where it'll start to stink up the whole building in a couple of hours? And I'm not even talking about the fact that it's illegal."

"That's true, it's not legal," Nili said.

Yehuda pressed on: "What exactly is illegal about it? I mean, we're not the ones who killed him."

"Not reporting a body, or harboring a body, or god knows what, and for such a long time? That can't be legal. I have no doubt that it breaks at least one law."

"First of all, no one's going to know that we didn't report it: he could have been lying here without anyone knowing. And also, if someone does find out, what are they going to do? Arrest us all for failing to call the police when someone has a heart attack? Are they going to throw us in jail—a professor of economics, a memoirist, a businessman, and a pediatrician in their seventies? Are we going to spend the rest of our lives in prison for reporting a death a few days late? Nonsense. There may be reasons not to do it, but that's not one of them."

Zohara said, "But what *would* we do with his body?"

"What do you mean, what would we do with his body?" Amos said. "We're going to bury his body, that's what we'll do, Zohara. I mean, you understand the dimension of this discussion, right?"

Nili said, "Hold on, let's think about this logically for a minute. Let's try to understand what would be involved in doing something like this. Let's break it down into concrete steps, so we'll know what we're even talking about. We can always dismiss it later."

Yehuda said, "The way I see it, it's mostly a question of keeping up all his communications for a few days, answering emails, text messages, that sort of thing. It's not very complicated, but someone does need to be here the whole time to take care of it. We could also set up an out-of-office reply—'I'll be unavailable until the 17th' or whatever. Maybe we could do something like that on his phone, too."

Zohara said, "There's no such thing as unavailable these days— people are available wherever they are."

"A, not necessarily, and B, that seems solvable to me. People from his work will buy anything: I'm at a conference, I'm in the Carpathians, I've disconnected for a while to finish writing a book, there are plenty of reasons. And we can tell his mother he's going away for a few days."

"Would she even comprehend that?" Nili asked.

"I think so, she's in the early stages of dementia but she's basically still okay. I know she talks with Avishay regularly. Talked, I mean."

Zohara said, "So are you going to pose as Avishay? Lie to his mother? I don't think, when push comes to shove, that you'll be capable of doing that. That's one of those ideas that sounds exciting and sexy and whatever, but in practice, I mean, are you going to lie to a hundred-year-old woman about how her son went overseas when in fact he's lying here dead and she has no idea? I don't know, it just seems . . . I don't know."

Yehuda tried to imagine himself googling the retirement home's phone number, calling, asking for Penina. Maybe visiting. He hadn't talked to her for ages. Zohara was right: All it took was the crude outline, just the chapter headings, to bring a preamble of tears to his eyes. But maybe someone else could do it.

Nili said, "I have to say, I don't find the idea so terrible either. Just think about the *naches* his mother would get if she could see him win a Nobel before she completely loses her marbles. It could really comfort her around his death."

"I don't think that after Avishay dies she'll care what prizes he got," Zohara argued.

"The Nobel? Somehow I think she'll care about that one."

"Well, I don't know. I don't care, whatever you decide."

"You don't care?"

"It's not that I don't care, I just can't think about it now. I feel like I'm in some kind of hallucination, this whole conversation seems . . . I just can't judge it in any reasonable way. I trust you, whatever you decide. But I'm not touching the body, I'm telling you that right now."

"Why would you touch the body? Who's touching the body? We shut the door to his room, end of story," Nili said.

Yehuda could almost hear the sound of that door moving, the uneven way it brushed over the carpeting, and he suddenly regretted the whole thing. It was his idea but now he didn't want to do it, not really. He couldn't do it. He was like Zohara—he couldn't be in this apartment with Avishay in it. He already couldn't be here. He took a deep, loud breath, without meaning to—perhaps he was about to drop dead himself—but no one paid any attention. It was as though death had expanded the range of reasonable behaviors.

"Okay, so what reason do we have, in fact, not to do it? What are the cons?" Zohara asked.

Nili said, "If we're talking seriously for a minute, then what Amos said is true: It would not be simple, there are quite a lot of things we'd need to think about, and think seriously. It would be very easy to miss something."

"Go ahead, then, let's think. Now's the time."

Yehuda could feel it slowly passing, vanishing as abruptly as it had appeared: their indifference was helping him regain his senses, pushing him to demand his rights as the deceased's best friend.

Amos said, "Here's something, for example: What are you going to do when you finally report that he died—I assume we will eventually report him dead, right? Or is there some other prize we're waiting for?"

"Go on, go on," Nili urged him.

"No, I mean maybe we should wait for him to get the Israel Prize, too. Then he can make a political statement by refusing to accept it, and then he'll die even more ballsy."

"All right, Amos, we get the point," said Yehuda.

"So what do you do when you report him dead and the police notice that he's actually been dead for a while? That he didn't just die two hours ago. Where exactly has he been hanging out all those two weeks?"

"It'll be eight days, tops. Maybe nine. It won't get to two weeks," Yehuda assured him.

"Whatever. Believe me, even our police can tell the difference between someone who's been dead for eight days and someone who's been dead for two hours."

"Haven't we already covered this? The man lived alone, so it took a while to find out he was dead. No one has to know how many friends he has and how frequently they see him, that's irrelevant. He died in his apartment, and eight days later one of us found him. Problem solved."

"Okay, but if I understand the plan correctly, we're going to be sending emails in his name, and text messages, and maybe we're saying he's overseas. He can't text *and* be dead. I assume there's no argument about that?"

"By the way," Nili commented, "I'm not sure we have to get the police involved at all."

"What do you mean?" Amos exclaimed. "You call the emergency number and they call the police, that's the law."

"So don't call the emergency number. Just call a private ambulance, pay the three thousand shekels, end of story. I actually think I can sign the death certificate. I have to check but I'm almost sure I can. We might even be able to download it from the Web."

Yehuda said, "Listen, obviously we haven't thought it all the way through yet, but these are technicalities. We just have to decide what the smartest story is, the best way to go about this, and then go from there. It doesn't seem impossible to me. The question is a principled one: Are we going for it? Are we doing this? If the answer is yes then we'll figure out the details. These don't seem like issues beyond our capacity—we have a room full of smart people here."

Nili remarked, "I must say that I really connect with what Yehuda said before. We're a group of people in our late sixties, early seventies—what are they going to do to us?"

"That depends on what we do," Amos answered.

"I don't know, we're not doing anything malicious, it's all well-intentioned. Avishay wouldn't have cared if his body was harbored or not harbored or anything else, but he absolutely would have cared about the Nobel, we know that. It was his life's dream, that thing, he would have been thrilled for us to do something like this for him. So what'll happen to us, even if we assume for a moment that everything comes out? I mean everything, all the stuff we hid and lied about. What'll they do to us? No one's going to do anything. I say, let's do it. Also, it seems like a nice way to celebrate Avishay's life, an appropriate finale, like in the movies, when all the friends get together and celebrate their friend's death in a special way. *The Big Chill* or something."

Yehuda knew he couldn't stand that movie, even though he hardly remembered any of it. That and *Breaking the Waves*, two supposed hallmarks of good taste. He wondered if he should consider it a warning sign: Were they seriously invoking *The Big Chill*, of all things? He reminded himself, with some effort, that he was a rationalist.

Zohara said, "If anything, it's like *Waking Ned Devine*."

"What's that?" Nili asked her.

Zohara looked at Yehuda and Amos: "Did you see it?"

Amos said, "It rings a bell. That's the one with the old people who win the lottery in Scotland, right?"

"Ireland."

"This is so not *Waking Ned Devine*," Yehuda insisted.

"But why? Remember how they win the lottery? They don't tell anyone that he died!"

Yehuda felt surprisingly irate: his idea was so original, so brilliant—why was she trying to take that away from him? "What do you mean they don't tell anyone he died? They pose as Ned, to get his lottery money!"

"Exactly!" Zohara proclaimed triumphantly.

"Can someone explain to me what the hell *Waking Ned Devine* is?" Nili pleaded.

Yehuda said, "It's a sting operation that the whole village is in on, to get rich."

"But Ned is dead, that's the whole point," Zohara clarified.

"Okay, but it's not about keeping him alive, it's just posing as him and using his name and his National Insurance number to get the money. Kind of like the Ultra-Orthodox who vote after they're dead." He looked to Amos for backup.

"All I remember is that they ride a motorcycle naked," Amos said apologetically.

Peering at her phone, Nili said, "Based on what I'm seeing on Wikipedia, it's not the same thing at all."

"I didn't say it was the same thing, I just said it was more like that than *The Big Chill*," Zohara argued.

Yehuda's patience was wearing thin. "Look, what difference does it make now?"

Amos said, "We're not a gang of Scottish villagers anyway, so it's not exactly a valid reference point."

"Irish! Irish!" Zohara repeated.

"A gang of Irish villagers in a movie, okay? We're real people. Unfortunately."

"That's too bad," Nili commented, "because in the movie they actually do get the money in the end."

"I thought you hadn't seen it"

Nili waved her phone: "Wikipedia."

"Well, yes, but things always turn out better in the movies," Zohara said, sulking.

They sat quietly for a moment and then Yehuda said, "Amos, the other thing is you don't have to be a part of it if you don't feel comfortable. It's really not obligatory for us all to take part, even though of course it would be better if we did, both in terms of brainstorming and in terms of manpower."

"And in terms of numbers, because the more good people are involved, the less they'll be able to do anything to us," Nili added.

"Come on, do you really think they could do something to us for this?"

Yehuda said, "They're not going to do anything to us, Zohara. And besides, I doubt we're even going to do anything. We'll probably get up tomorrow morning and this whole idea will seem ridiculous and we'll bury him in the afternoon. But all I'm saying is, why not start? Let's give it a shot, maybe it'll turn out to be easy."

Nili said, "Amos, you really don't have to."

Picking up on his abandoned monologue, Yehuda repeated, "You absolutely do not."

"You don't have to, but I mean, are you going to let us do it alone? Will you just go home? We'd have to kill you anyway, so you don't tell anyone," Nili quipped.

"But wait, what if he doesn't end up winning?" Amos wondered.

"If he doesn't win, then we've been really, really good friends," Yehuda declared.

Nili said, "He will win, he will. How could he possibly not win, Amos? He's Avishay."

5

When he tried to reconstruct their conversation later, he couldn't do it: he felt as though his memory was trying to protect him.

It had worked. He hadn't believed it would work. On another day, at another time, it might not have; maybe if the seats had been arranged differently. He had simply tossed the idea into the air, entirely willing to resheathe it—I was just joking, he'd say. But then the thing became possible. How slippery was normalcy, how eager to accommodate. Someone suggests an idea—is it reasonable? No one knows. How could they? People don't know what to believe. They think they have opinions, but those can be suspended with the flick of a tail. All it takes is a nanosecond to give a sideways glance, to understand what works.

Keeping a person alive, just like that—is that a good idea? Where does one find the answer to such a question? Who can offer a precedent, a relevant anecdote? And how can you say no, really, if it's for someone else, for a friend? How violent altruism was, he realized, decimating its objectors, shutting mouths.

No one wants to be a naysayer; certainly not his friends. That was what had helped him, too.

═══

A few minutes after he and Zohara had finished that horrible, infamous conversation, something she'd said began to spread through his veins like poison: *Not that I'd ever tell anyone to shelve their book. Unrelated to you.*

This had nothing to do with him. It was unrelated, and Yehuda had calmed down enough to somehow get through the evening, to survive the conversation. But the moment he was on his own, free to concentrate, he was forced to admit that there was a limit to how dumb he could be: If it had nothing to do with him, then why had she said it? What were those words if not a flashing red light: Even if I thought differently, I wouldn't say so.

He turned it over and over and kept reaching the same conclusion: She thought he should shelve the book. She thought it was unpublishable, irredeemable. Yet he still couldn't accept it. It wasn't possible, he couldn't live with it. It couldn't be a genuine, lucid thought. What came to mind were the reality shows he watched—he was a bit of an addict—with the bikini-clad girls who faced the cameras and made their excuses for getting booted off. *They were threatened by me. They were jealous. They knew I was going to win.* Yehuda always scoffed when he listened to these pathetic, imbecilic, shallow women. Who could possibly be jealous of them? Why would anyone? But now he thought: Wasn't this the same thing? Wouldn't an observer mock him just as cruelly? Someone just told you to shelve your book—can't you hear what you're being told? They're telling you to shelve it not because they're jealous, but because it's bad.

But it wasn't the same thing. It just wasn't, if only because he was aware of that possibility and had considered it thoroughly. He and Zohara had a long-standing, complicated relationship: her criticism had a history. He remembered once again something that he did not like to remember: Zohara's body touched Avishay's. She was beating Yehuda in an unfair competition. Sometimes he wished Avishay hadn't told him. And he'd done it as if he were giving Yehuda a gift, as if Yehuda were a child: *I'm only telling you, Yehuda.* Knocking him down and lifting him up at the same time.

He asked himself if he would have forgiven her if she'd said simply: Shelve it. He had to admit that he wouldn't have. Never. He would have hated her for the rest of their lives. What did he want, then? What was he accusing her of? He had asked her to tell him the truth. He'd warned her again and again: I'm telling you, Zohara, you have to give me the truth, don't go easy on me. Hadn't he meant it? He had, with all his heart. He'd wanted the truth, it just hadn't occurred to him that *this* was the truth. It still didn't.

At the age of sixty-something, he sensed something unacknowledged about the nature of truth itself: no one wants it, no friendship can withstand it. Yet he marveled at how flexible the soul could be in order to survive, to protect itself, making countless maneuvers and manipulations that all led to one conclusion: The unpleasant truth that has been uttered is, quite simply, not the real truth.

"You should shelve the book" was an empty recommendation; no one would ever accept it. No one would acknowledge either its veracity or its meaning. And so—should he shelve it? Was that the conclusion? Absolutely not. With all due respect to Zohara, she was just one individual, with numerous weaknesses. Besides, she had her own motives, which he didn't even want to get into.

He asked around and found out which was the biggest publisher, and sent it the manuscript. The reply came soon: "Dear Yehuda, thank you for submitting your manuscript. Our editors read *The Courage to Invent* with interest. Regretfully, the current uncertainty in the book industry prevents us from publishing it. We wish you the best of luck."

His body went slack with disappointment. Then he reread the answer. The book was good, they were not questioning that. But it wasn't commercial, or not commercial enough, or it was risky—the word

sent a thrill through Yehuda and immediately galvanized him: it was
practically a compliment. He thought of other rejections—Proust,
maybe? Or Salinger? At least one of them, he was almost certain, had
been rejected repeatedly. Not that he was comparing, of course.

That night he had an idea: What if he indemnified them for the
risk? If that was the problem, then it wasn't a problem at all. It was
inconceivable that the book would go unpublished merely because
of the publishers' dire financial straits. Finally, a worthy cause for his
money.

═══

Only once during his long months of work with Hadass, the editor assigned to him by the publisher, did he suddenly remember the
sum of the indemnification, which he'd forgotten about as soon as it
had vanished into thin air out of the two bank accounts, the sender's
and the recipient's.

The book was almost ready, and after she'd canceled twice, the
publicist finally met with him. She was businesslike, too businesslike, very different from all the others he'd met, who were extremely
friendly—80,000 shekels friendly—and in an instant the artist's
state of mind that had padded him like cotton wool switched to that
of an unsatisfied customer. He felt like reporting her to the boss:
Just so you know, she's not behaving appropriately. But he resisted and
listened to her when she said he wasn't a familiar name and they had
to be very realistic, the chances for a newspaper article were virtu-
ally nonexistent, she was telling him that right off the bat. Yehuda
wanted to remind her where things stood, so he said, "What about
radio? Or newspaper ads, stuff like that?"

The publicist said, "We don't do that kind of thing, it costs a
fortune."

So then Yehuda said, "What if I'm paying?"

And all at once her face softened and her patience lengthened, as though he were buying her, not the newspaper inches. "Well," she said, "that's different. But you should know that it's a lot of money."

"Can you set it up for me?" he asked.

"What—radio? Papers?"

"Yes, all of it."

"It's really expensive."

"I don't care. Will it sell the book? Will it help?"

"There's nothing like radio," she said, "it's just that it's a lot of money, so people don't usually do it."

Yehuda suddenly felt like he could buy anything: the whole world was in his wallet. "What about an article in the paper? Can you buy that?"

"No," she replied firmly. But her tone was starting to sound slightly more commiserating, and a moment later she said, "But let's think for a second. There might be something in your life story, something we can work with. Family, career, I don't know what."

"There's the bag opener."

"Yes . . . Explain to me again what that is?"

Yehuda understood then that she hadn't read the book, that she had no idea what it was about, had no idea who he even was, nor was she interested. "I invented that thing that opens bags, you know?"

"What thing?"

"That thing that separates the bag when it's closed."

"What do you mean, separates the bag? I don't get it. Separates it from what?"

"I mean, like, opens it." He made the movement with his fingers.

"You mean, like, for the handicapped?"

"Handicapped . . . ? No, it's just for people."

"But you open bags with your fingers," the publicist insisted.

"Well, twenty million people all over the world no longer open them with their fingers."

"Okay, but that doesn't really do anything for us in terms of the book. It might help us get you into the financial press, though."

"I've already been in the financial press," Yehuda said.

"Okay. Well, anyway, that doesn't sell books."

"What about Avishay Sar-Shalom?" Yehuda asked her.

"What about him?"

"He's my best friend."

"Okay . . ."

"And he's in the book, too. He's my childhood friend. The story his theory is based on is in the book: I'm the original class king."

"What do you mean?"

"You know, the most popular kid in the class. Class king. That's the concept he used for his whole theory of economics. Could we do something with that?"

"Will he agree to blurb the book? Maybe give a cover quote?"

"I think so."

"Actually, now that I think about it, why doesn't he write you a foreword? A preface? Not that I want to interfere in your work with Hadass, she's the editor, so consult with her, but if he's mentioned in the book, if it's his childhood too, plus he's a professor of economics, game theory and all that, then it's perfect for a book about inventions."

"He doesn't do game theory at all, actually," Yehuda clarified.

"Never mind, I'm sure we can find an angle."

"And he might be getting a Nobel any minute now."

Her distracted attention now lasered in on Yehuda, as if to say, *Don't give me a heart attack for no reason.*

"He really might get it this year, he has a really good chance," Yehuda continued.

"You mean, like, a *Nobel* Nobel? *The* Nobel Prize?" she said, gaping.

"I'm not familiar with any other Nobels." Upon seeing the look on her face, he added, "Yes, *the* Nobel Prize."

"If you have a foreword by a Nobel Prize winner, Yehuda"—that was the first time she'd said his name—"then we're in a whole different league. In publicity, in rights for foreign editions, in buzz around the book, you name it. It's an ace in the hole. Definitely with a brand-new winner, a hot name that everyone remembers."

"Well," Yehuda backtracked, "he could also not win, you know. But in any case it would be good for me to have his foreword, right? It's a familiar name."

"Let's just say that the Nobel is pretty much key here."

He thought about it for a moment. Avishay hadn't read the book yet. But the deal was already sealed in that room the minute the idea was mentioned. Avishay was trapped. He would write the foreword and he would win the Nobel, because otherwise—Yehuda had no book.

6

In the end he found the charger in the bathroom, on top of the washing machine. He'd invested a great deal of energy searching for it outside the bedroom where Avishay lay, covered, as though the effort could change the results by moving the charger away from where it was. And although he was well aware of how foolish the method was, to his surprise it worked.

He connected the iPhone to the charger and the charger to the outlet in the bathroom. It was better that way, he'd answer it from in there, so they wouldn't all be breathing down his neck. It's too bad Avishay couldn't be recharged—5 percent, 7 percent, one more conversation, perhaps another dinner. The device drank thirstily and began to expose its activities over the past day: three missed calls, including two from Zohara, the first part of a text message—or was it a WhatsApp message? Yes, that's what it was—and a series of blue Fs: he'd completely forgotten about Facebook.

He felt a panic similar to the one he experienced when he himself had been away from the phone for too long and found, upon his return, that people had been trying to get hold of him. But when he ran his finger over the slider it asked for a password. He'd known it once, he knew he had, if he wasn't mistaken it was Avishay's birthday. He tapped in two-three-one-two but the screen shuddered its refusal. Yehuda yelled at the study: "Zohara, what's the password? Isn't it twenty-three twelve?" Zohara shouted back, "Try one-two-two-three." Yes, one-two-two-three, he knew that. He pressed the numbers and the iPhone surrendered—two text messages, seven Facebook updates, three missed calls—revealing all the decrees, the bombs that would have to be neutralized, one by one.

He started with the calls. Two were from Zohara, he'd already seen that. He looked at the other number: 052-3112168, yesterday at 3:30 p.m. Did that mean he was already dead then, or that he simply hadn't answered? Then a third possibility occurred to him: Avishay before his death, Avishay before his death in pain, Avishay lying in bed.

The unidentified caller had tried only once, which was a good sign: he didn't want to bother Avishay, probably wasn't even expecting him to call back. Yehuda was about to exempt himself from the task, there was nothing to do about it anyway, when he realized the same person had sent a text message. So he was a bother after all.

Dear Avishay, we'd like to reschedule the event from March 1 to March 12, same time. Please confirm asap if that works for you. Thanks. Yoad, Institute for Socio-Economic Development.

It works, of course it works. He typed out a message:

Confirming. Thanks, Avishay.

Then he erased the period—did he use periods at the end of text messages?—and read it again. The message looked suspiciously businesslike. He deleted it and wrote:

No problem, updating my calendar. Thanks, Avishay.

He tried to erase "calendar" and replace it with "schedule," but he clicked on "Paste" by mistake, which always happened to him when he tried to select text on the iPhone, and the short message suddenly expanded into three more lines, which must have been the last thing Avishay had ever copied:

Me too! I arranged with Dan two days ago that I'd talk with Roni and she'd let us know when to come over. There are some times that work."

Yehuda reread the text before erasing it, in case it was hiding some-thing. But what could it be hiding? He wasn't looking for anything. Who was Dan? Who was Roni? He suddenly felt that this mission was too much for him—for them. It was impossible, just as Amos had said. For a brief moment he also thought that Avishay didn't deserve it, that he wasn't worthy of all this effort, that he should be punished for these suddenly revealed expanses of his life that were previously untouristed. He erased the extra text with a long, vio-lent press, until he accidentally erased part of the "updating," too. He reinstated the "ing"—"updating my calendar," whatever, it didn't matter—and pressed "Send."

He felt exhausted, and this was just one text message—would he really be able to get through this week? But when he looked back at the screen before putting down the iPhone and finally leaving the bathroom, a little number on the green-and-white icon reminded him that there was one more message. It was from "Liat," no last name:

Keep your fingers crossed for us!!!

It had been sent almost three hours earlier.

He thought of calling someone from the study—they'd agreed that if they weren't 1,000 percent sure about something, they would consult. But he couldn't be bothered, he just couldn't. He could hear them in there, arguing about the email inbox, and he simply didn't have the patience for it. He wondered if he was starting to slack off too soon, because of course it was too soon, but after quickly scanning the risks he decided it couldn't do any harm.

Crossed!!! ☺

he texted, with a smiley face. He made sure the charger was properly connected and started walking away, but the phone chirped again.

Smiley face?!

Perhaps this was their real mission: to send Avishay into a better place only after scattering smiles around on his behalf, after making everyone more fond of him.

He texted:

I'm full of surprises.

No smiley face.

He looked at the screen for a while longer, but Liat didn't answer.

═══

Zohara and Amos were sitting close together at Avishay's desk, while Nili stood by the window. "We wrote all the things we talked about," she updated Yehuda, "now they're answering all the emails that piled up."

"What did you write?" Yehuda asked. "Show me." But Nili shook her head as if to warn him against reopening that can of worms, so he tried to dismiss his previous request with a new one: "We have to come up with something to tell his mother. I mean, she's not going to email him and see the autoreply."

"But do they talk every day? Do you know?" Zohara wondered. "It's so awful, just thinking about it."

"Her hearing is bad, she can barely talk on the phone," Yehuda said, "but he visits her every Saturday, or almost every Saturday. Someone has to call the home and tell them he won't be there this weekend." A strange scoff came out of his mouth when he added, "He won't be there any weekend." He thought he sounded like a pig.

Nili said, "But what will we say? Why isn't he coming?"

"We can say he's sick, or that he has to go somewhere on Saturday, it's not a problem. I mean, whoever phones could even pretend to be Avishay. It's the staff you talk to, not her, you just leave a message."

"It's best not to say he's sick," Zohara opined, "that might just worry her and then she might send Ruthi over to check on him or something."

Nili said, "But actually if we say he's sick it'll make sense afterwards for him to die. It'll seem somehow logical to her."

"Besides," Yehuda added, "there's no risk of Ruthi turning up, believe me. You think that nutcase is going to come all the way from Tivon to bring her brother some soup? She can barely afford the bus fare."

"Is it that bad? Poor woman," Nili said.

"She's not a poor woman at all," Yehuda said dismissively, but as the words came out it occurred to him that perhaps she was, and he realized with some surprise that he'd forgotten to update his grudges and replace Avishay's big sister from when they were kids with a seventy-something-year-old woman.

"Isn't she the one who got mixed up in some pyramid scheme?" Nili asked.

"Oh yes, but that was ages ago. It wasn't exactly a pyramid scheme, but something similar. That was in her business days," Yehuda said, pronouncing the word *business* with a disdain he could not relinquish.

Zohara said, "Now she's a nutritional therapist or something, isn't she?"

"She weans people off sugar," Yehuda said.

"Dear God," Nili exclaimed.

"Oh, you have no idea."

"She weans people off sugar?" Amos asked incredulously.

"Yes, she weans them off sugar," Yehuda repeated.

"You mean that's a profession?"

"No."

"Guys," Amos said, "let's focus for a minute, okay? Have you finished with the phone, Yehuda?"

"I saw some Facebook messages there, but we'll do that on the computer, right?"

Nili said, "Facebook is less urgent, we just have to make sure he's not logged on."

"He isn't, we checked," Zohara said.

"Then it's irrelevant anyway. Besides, we don't have his password, do we?"

Yehuda said, "Let's not worry about that, he's not very active on there anyway."

"Okay," Amos said, "but other than that?"

"I think that's everything," Yehuda said. "By the way, who's Liat? Do any of you know Liat?"

"What do you mean?" Nili said. "Know her how?"

"A Liat who has something to do with Avishay. She texted him— wish me luck or something like that."

"Didn't you look back on what they'd texted before that?"

"I didn't think about that, to be honest. Yes, that would have been the smart thing to do."

"Wait, what did you text back?" Amos asked.

"Good luck or something."

"Then never mind," Amos said.

———

Yehuda wondered whether the idea had occurred to them; he felt it must be written all over his face. *Listen to this, I thought of something on the way*, he'd said, sounding so casual but actually burning with guilt, secretly writing his own defense statement, willing to be subjected to a barrage of insults and perhaps even penalties: *So basically, you're trying to make sure you have a Nobel laureate for your book's foreword. At least be honest, Yehuda.*

They knew, of course, that Avishay had written his foreword; that was one of the ordinary topics that came up among them in phone calls and meetings, floating on the surface, at times remembered and at other times forgotten, because after all it wasn't theirs, it was Yehuda's. He marveled again at the chasm between *ours* and *not ours*, which had worked in his favor this time: We do take an interest in things that are not part of us, it's not that we don't, but we care only so much.

They did not know, for example, and why would they, about the two covers that were proofread and ready to go at the publisher: "Send to Print" was all it would take. They'd told him it was unnecessary, that it would take only two seconds for a redesign the minute they knew if he'd won; his editor thought he was mad, she claimed it was bad luck to write "Nobel Laureate" before the man had even won. He remembered that now. But he hadn't wanted to draw things out any longer—they'd already postponed the release until after the announcement. He wasn't superstitious, thank God—or at least he didn't used to be—and money certainly wasn't an issue. So it'll cost another thousand shekels, another two thousand: he'd already lost all awareness of money. Anything that could not be purchased just made him angry these days. So he bought more and more of the graphic designer's time, greedily and gleefully stealing him away from Zeruya Shalev or David Grossman or God knows who, until they had a perfectly designed pair: one that said "Foreword by Professor Avishay Sar-Shalom" in white typeface across the bottom, and a second one with the text repositioned higher up, closer to his own name, in plumped-up letters: "Foreword by Nobel Prize Laureate in Economics Avishay Sar-Shalom." As soon as he'd laid eyes on the second cover, an ugly hole had opened up in the first one: something had been ripped out of it, it was no longer acceptable, its publication would be an admission of defeat.

But only when they sat there in the living room, considering his proposal and deliberating in that strange tone that was both dreadfully serious yet derisively dismissive—only then did he suddenly grasp that it was not their indifference that protected him, but their friendship. To express the suspicion out loud would be a betrayal of the purity of that friendship, because who if not a mentally insane person could even consider such a thing? If someone were to raise the suspicion, who would they be casting aspersions on if not themselves? It was just like when they were kids: he who smelt it, dealt it. *Do you really think I would hide Avishay's body for a week to promote my book? Do you really think that is the likely scenario, and not, say, that I just care about him?* Yehuda clung to this speech, which was loaded in his magazine, ready to be discharged. He even thought he believed in it, that it wasn't for show at all, that he himself was protected by the power of that very same friendship, incapable of being a villain. He wanted only good

things for Avishay, just as he'd said; so what if he had something
to gain from it?

━━━

They sat in the living room. Avishay's bedroom door was shut, but
still it seemed to Yehuda that they'd turned the TV on only to mask
the silence coming from that room.

"We have to think about the smell," Nili said.

"Think what about the smell?" Zohara asked.

"I don't know, there's going to be a smell at some point."

"Good God."

Yehuda said, "It's just another few days. Do you know what kind
of smell there'd have to be in here for it to get out? It would have
to reek."

Nili said, "And if he starts to reek?" When Zohara made a disgusted face, she added, "It's gross, I get it, but if we're doing this seriously then we have to be prepared."

They sat quietly. Yehuda imaganed them all filling their nostrils, as
he was, with imaginary smells, barely staying seated. "I believe it'll
be all right," he said finally.

"All right in what sense?" Zohara wondered.

"It's not like we're in desert conditions here and the buzzards are
circling. I don't know, I can't smell anything at the moment."

"Maybe we should just drop it?" Zohara suggested out of nowhere.

Yehuda turned to look at her like an actor in a daytime soap. Her
line was uncoordinated, its pacing so off, jabbed into the conversation. He had an urge to rebuke her and reject her objection on that
basis alone. She thinks she's the widow, he realized. That's what she
thinks. That she's sadder. He wanted to remind her that she wasn't,
perhaps on behalf of his dead friend.

"I don't know," Zohara said, "I just don't feel I have the strength for this. I'm not up for it."

"I really sympathize with you," Nili said comfortingly.

"I keep thinking about the hours before, I can't stop thinking about it."

"That what? What about them?" Amos asked.

But Nili interfered: "Enough, I don't want to hear this. I haven't thought about it and I don't want to."

"He had a heart attack," Amos said, "it couldn't have been prevented."

Nili ran her tongue around her mouth slowly, dubiously. "Well, I mean, we can't know for sure. That's the truth."

"You mean, what if I'd got here two hours earlier?" Zohara asked.

"Forget it, Zohara, this is never going to be resolved. He lived alone, what can you do? Even people who don't live alone die of heart attacks," Nili said.

Amos asked, "Does it hurt? A heart attack?"

"I don't even know if it was a heart attack," Nili replied. "We don't know exactly what happened."

"Because he looked normal. He didn't look, you know, like his body had been through anything."

"I have no idea, to be honest," Nili admitted.

Zohara was still unsettled. "I don't know, doesn't he deserve to be allowed to be dead for a while? We're in such a hurry to jump ahead, we didn't even . . . It's like we're not mourning."

"But what is mourning, really?" Nili said. "There are lots of different ways to mourn."

"But this whole idea, it's like it doesn't give us any time to, I don't know . . ."

"To be sad?"

"Yes, to be sad."

Amos made a face that Yehuda could not interpret, and apparently neither could Zohara, because she said, "What?"

"It's very difficult to be sad together," Amos replied. "There's something terribly artificial about it."

"Difficult?" Nili asked. "Being sad together is the easiest—it brings relief."

"Well, I guess that comes down to personal preference," Amos said.

"I don't know," said Zohara, "this is a man we really loved. And he's dead. So we'll get him his Nobel. Let's say we get it for him. He's still dead."

Yehuda felt protected behind a transparent wall, the sorrow banging its fists on the reinforced glass. "I'll tell you what helps me," he said, and everyone looked at him. "That he will keep on living. As far as I'm concerned, he keeps on living. If this works, right? If this succeeds then in some sense he will still be in this world, he will remain and he'll leave something in it, just like he would have wanted to."

"But he won't really still be in it, Yehuda," Zohara said. "For me and for you he won't be here anymore. He'll always be in the annals of economics or history or whatever—great. A lot of good that does me."

Nili said, "You're absolutely right, Zohara, it's just that it's not a zero sum, it's not like if we devote ourselves to mourning exclusively it'll be less sad, or more sad, whatever. It is what it is, it's as sad as it is, the only question is whether you're going to do this gesture for Avishay, like Yehuda says."

"Gesture?" Amos repeated. But no one paid any attention.

"Okay, you're right, but it's just difficult for me to psych myself up for this thing right now, to kick myself into action," Zohara said.

"It's difficult for everyone," Nili told her.

"Although the way I understand it, there's not much to do at this point."

"Bottom line, we've done most of it already. We just have to decide about the smell. What do we do about it?"

Yehuda inhaled again, but he detected nothing except the sweet, sweet aroma of a cigarette. He was slightly surprised at Nili's eagerness. He hadn't expect anything from Amos, who would obviously be against it, and Zohara herself didn't know what she wanted; she might not be much help, but she wouldn't ruin things either. No, she wouldn't ruin things for him, Yehuda thought, awkwardly overcome with an unsummoned wave of affection. But Nili was unpredictable, especially in this context, which lacked any context, and when he'd realized she was in favor he'd been relieved, but only briefly, because the next moment he got it into his head that she might also have something to gain from it, maybe even something bigger, and his guilt mounted and with it his anger. "I don't smell anything," he said, "but we have to take into account that we've been sitting here continuously, so I don't know if we can trust ourselves to notice a difference. We might just be used to it."

"When does a body start to decompose, in theory?" Amos asked Nili.

"I don't know exactly, but just making an educated guess, it's a cold October, I assume if we shut the windows and the door and keep the room cool, then it'll take a good few days for him to start to smell, but I can't say exactly how many."

"What good is it for us to have a doctor on staff, then?" Zohara said.

"My dear, I'm a pediatrician. I *was* a pediatrician. Not anymore, thank God."

Yehuda didn't want to end up being the guy who based his intellectual world on Wikipedia—he was dangerously close to that status anyway—but more than that, he wanted to smoke. He said, "Listen, I'm reading the Wiki on body decomposition." Zohara said, "Yuck," but he went on: "Hospital morgues maintain a temperature that prevents the initial stages of decomposition." He stopped reading. "There's an A/C unit in his room, isn't there?"

Zohara said, "Yes, but I don't think it's on. That was dumb of us . . ."

"It's not on? You didn't turn on the A/C?" Nili exclaimed.

Amos went to the room, opened the door and shouted back, "How low? Fifty degrees? Sixty?"

Nili yelled back, "As low as possible. I don't know—forty, even less."

Zohara said, "Nili, we'll die of cold in here!"

"Well, what can I do? We'll put on extra layers. Hospitals are a lot colder than that."

Amos came back to the living room and said, "Sixty is as low as it goes."

"That can't be right," Yehuda insisted.

"Of course it can—who sets the A/C to fifty degrees? Think about it."

"It's an electrical appliance, it doesn't make those decisions for you," Yehuda countered, and he went into the bedroom and tried to walk over resolutely to the remote control and the mission ahead, but the remote was on the bureau next to Avishay.

He had a sheet pulled up over his head, sparing them the sight of his skin, but that was precisely what made him look even more dead to Yehuda; even more like someone who could not change his mind and decide to come back and breathe again. He reached out quickly and grabbed the remote, then pressed it against his stomach as if hoping to deceive Avishay, to swipe something without him knowing, perhaps fearing he might reach out an all-knowing hand and grip his arm as it moved away. He pressed the button a few times, discharging his duty, but it was pointless: He'd known Amos was right even before he'd entered the room. He walked out, shut the door, and sat back down in the living room.

Zohara was holding his iPhone, which irritated him, but he bit his tongue and said to Nili, "But is sixty enough, do you think?"

"What do you mean? Enough for what? It's all a question of how long it takes for—"

"It says here," Zohara read, "'decomposition—disintegration resulting from bacterial activity.'"

"Obviously, yes, that's exactly why I said we have to seal off his room so flies don't come in and lay larvae. That would go rotten really quickly."

"You mean seal it off, or just shut the door and the window?" Amos asked.

"I think shutting them is enough, it's just so flies can't get in and lay eggs."

"You see, you *do* know something after all."

"Trust me, it's all from *Dexter*."

Zohara said, "All right, the window's shut, but I'm trying to see if there's anything other than keeping it cold. Is there anything else we can control?"

Nili said, "You know who would know?"

"Who would know what?" Yehuda asked.

"How to keep a body in good condition, to control humidity, that kind of thing."

"Well?"

"Nathan."

It took Yehuda a minute to figure out who Nathan was, and then Zohara said, "I thought he was an Egyptologist." And that's when Yehuda remembered: Nathan, the character Nili was seeing.

"He is an Egyptologist, but he specializes in mummies, which is exactly what this is. This is what he deals with all day, exactly these questions."

Amos said, "But that's all on a theoretical level. Don't tell me he's actually mummified someone."

"I'm not suggesting we mummify Avishay, but if there's something we can do, I don't know, humidity, salt, then he'll know. It's his PhD dissertation."

"His dissertation is on preserving bodies?" Amos asked.

"What is this, a job talk at Princeton? How should I know what his dissertation is about? But if there's anyone in this world who knows how to preserve a body in field conditions, it's someone who's dedicated his life to mummification. Wouldn't you agree?"

Amos said, "I'd actually put my money on a pathologist."

"All right, then this is second place," Nili conceded.

The idea that someone else, someone other than them, would appear in this living room, in this world, in this little tomb they were now designing, aroused terror in Yehuda. He felt like the leader of a small cult when one of the members suddenly invites his parents over. He wanted to say something but did not trust his own voice or his words; he didn't trust himself at all, he now realized. For an instant he was gripped by fresh loneliness, but he shook it off before he could decipher its meaning or seriously give himself over to the idea of a whole new life spent in its presence.

Zohara said, "Well, we're not going to ask over someone you've known for a month and have him start messing around with Avishay's body."

"First of all, we've been together for almost six months, and second, we don't have to ask him over. I can just get his advice over the phone. If that's what you're worried about, then it's not a problem."

"What are you going to tell him? For what purpose exactly do you need to preserve a body?"

"What am I going to tell him? I'll tell him the truth: we want optimal conditions for preserving a body, in terms of temperature and humidity, something effective but realistic, nothing with formaldehyde and jars. This isn't just some theoretical game here, he has to know what we're talking about."

"Do you trust him enough to tell him what we're doing? What if you break up tomorrow?"

"What kind of a question is that? He's my partner, who am I going to trust if not him?"

"Nili," Amos said, "he's been your partner for all of five minutes. Seriously, we have to be on the same page about these things. No one apart from the five of us—the four of us—can know anything about this. Honestly, I mean isn't that obvious?"

"Okay, Amos, it's not . . ."

"It's not what? What is it not? This cannot get out, whether we pull it off or not. This is something that could destroy people's lives, destroy careers."

"Oh, come on," Nili said.

"You know what? I take that back: it could destroy *my* career. If people think I was trying to play games with the Nobel Prize? What's the matter with you? They'd boot me out of the university without a second thought."

"So you mean you're not going to tell Varda?" Nili asked.

"Nili, Varda and I have been married for thirty-seven, thirty-eight years, how can you compare? And you know what? No. I'm not going to tell her. She has her bar exam soon, she's stressed out, I don't want to burden her."

Zohara said, "How is this burdening her? It's not like she has to do anything about it."

"It is absolutely adding to her burden. Both the fact that Avishay died, and then a body on top of everything. She's already under a lot of pressure not to break any laws—you think she needs this to worry about? What for? So that I can have someone to talk to? I'll talk to you."

"Okay," Nili said, "but what if she wasn't taking the bar now?"

Amos said, "Nili . . ."

"I'm not telling Idit, I can tell you that for sure," Yehuda inter-vened.

"There you go," Amos said.

Yehuda envied Amos for the automatic way he leaped to his wife's defense, her welfare, which seemed so natural to him that he didn't even have to think about it. He also envied Amos's reason: he didn't want to be a burden on Varda, to stress her out, but he trusted her completely to be with them, to be with him.

He wondered what would have happened if Idit weren't going overseas in two days, if she were here with him all week—would he tell her? He could tell her now, after all, before she left, but he didn't. It didn't occur to him. He could also argue that with Idit's job at the newspaper it was better for her not to know things like this, not to get mixed up in anything shady. There was no shortage of politi-cians trying to trip her up, and nonpoliticians, no shortage at all. She had to be squeaky clean. But all those lines sounded foreign on his tongue, like the recitations at Holocaust Memorial Day ceremonies in school.

He'd been married to one of the most senior political commen-tators in the country for forty years, and for at least twenty of them he'd been busy arguing with her over whether there was any point in those commentaries, in all the "on one hand, but on the other hand." When had that ever changed anything? A self-perpetuating cycle of words meant to feed the job and the jobholder, and the ultimate proof was Idit, who'd been ruminating on the same three positions for twenty-five years, as he told her time and time again even though he knew it annoyed her. She always said, "There are exactly two is-sues in this country. Everything else is nuances, derivations. So what do you expect me to write about? What other positions exactly do you expect me to come up with? It's a ridiculous argument, what you're claiming." Yehuda knew she was right, in principle, but only because there was a piece of data she lacked, a winning card he held but could not show: he never told her what she looked like when she watched the news, when she was searching for a topic for her column, in a panic, with a deadline in four hours, mulling over the possibilities out loud, debating which issue to take on, like a rich woman in an orphanage, as if she had the power to save someone. Sometimes he thought that the day he stopped holding back would be the day they separated, the day he decided he'd had enough. Other people revealed affairs, confessed to secret loves, but he wouldn't manage to be grandiose even in that moment: he would simply describe to her what she looked like when she was trying to pick a topic to write about. He knew it would sound mean, he'd been refining the speech for too long, and he also knew she would not forgive him.

Meanwhile he'd been developing a theory whereby this whole opinion thing was generally overrated. They never reached a conclusion anyway. He used to be quite fond of it, impressed by it, but now it just seemed childish to believe in opinions when you were seventy, like believing in God or fairies.

Anyway, paper or no paper, he couldn't tell her. She might not sabotage the project—even though it didn't take much for him to imagine that—but she certainly wouldn't collaborate with anything meant to glorify Avishay's name. Yehuda usually attributed that to the fact that they'd briefly been separated before they got married. Avishay was thrilled when that happened, and he'd suddenly come out with a whole, carefully worded, terrible analysis of Idit. Perhaps that speech was why Yehuda was subsequently so afraid of well-rehearsed speeches that suddenly gain an audience. They got back together eventually, and in his surge of renewed love for Idit, he'd betrayed Avishay and told her more or less what he'd said. They had disliked each other ever since: Idit thought Avishay was a blathering, self-focused windbag, he thought roughly the same about her, and neither of them was entirely wrong.

Yehuda sometimes tried to remember what had happened before the breakup, and if that was where it had started. But he couldn't, perhaps because he was unable to untangle that one thought from the knot of thoughts in those days, when he had considered the possibility that perhaps she wasn't right for him. Either way, Idit and Avishay's relationship since then had been kept artificially alive only thanks to this gang, which had enough warmth to cover over the occasional cold spot.

He recalled something he'd once read, or heard, he couldn't remember where, but he clearly remembered the content, and it kept coming back to him, more and more convincing each time: everything in this world has only one reason. One real reason, for every choice and every decision and every fear or desire. All the other explanations were merely latecomers, backtrackers, rationalizations, so that things would seem less decisive, less arbitrary, less changeable. Idit's relationship with Avishay, her newspaper articles—none of that really mattered. The real reason he wasn't telling Idit and never would was simply that she'd be on to him in five seconds: *You want the Nobel imprimatur on your book.* Simple as that.

"What bothers me," Nili harped on, "is that you don't take Nathan seriously." Her voice grew high-pitched for emphasis. "You don't take my relationship with him seriously, it's been that way right from the start, and it bugs me. I'm telling you honestly, it gets on my nerves."

"Please, Nili," Zohara said, "this has nothing to do with Nathan. Everyone here is very fond of him. I know I am. But still, it is a new relationship, you know how long it's been since any of us went out with someone for six whole months. Everyone here is either married or on their own, we're not used to this kind of thing."

"You're exaggerating a little, don't you think? Avishay dated women, you've gone out with men. You're making out as if I brought some alien in here."

"Right, but did any of the women Avishay went out with last? Any guy I've gone out with? Just imagine if one of them knew about something like this. I mean, this is the kind of thing that could be exposed even years later. It'll still be something the whole world will pay attention to."

"Right, so here we are again at the main point, which is that you don't believe Nathan and I are going to last. Because he's attractive and I'm fat, or I don't know what."

Amos said, "Oh, really."

"Amos, I'm not insulted, I know he's thin and I'm fat."

"I think you're being a little oversensitive, Nili. You're taking this the wrong way. Everyone is happy for you and Nathan, we're just trying to think practically about how to get this whole production off the ground in the most discreet and logical way. We're not even telling our own children."

Yehuda tried to imagine her telling all this to Nathan, the way he remembered him from a dinner party he'd hosted at his home in Pardes Hanna. He lived in a big house, too big for a man like that, and his living there just seemed like a real-estate malfunction. The house was designed in that clean sort of aesthetic, Yehuda wasn't sure what it was called—maybe Zen?—with lots of black and white. He couldn't remember the details, but that was the general impression. At first he thought Nathan was renting, but Zohara said he'd bought a house, torn it down, and had an architect design a new one on the lot. When Nili told them he was an Egyptologist, Yehuda was stunned. He was convinced the guy was either an engineer or a pimp.

Nathan had an exaggerated beard that completely hid his lips, from which his voice erupted like a ventriloquist. But he was nice, and pretty funny, and when Yehuda was finally forced to acknowledge this, his plans went awry and he became filled with disquiet. Nathan seemed at least as put-together as the rest of them, and Yehuda needed a real flaw in order to forgive him for that. Not to mention that he had to be a little strange to explain his relationship with Nili. If Yehuda had still been meeting with Zohara, just the two of them, he would surely have walked down that delicate path with her. Nili was a sixty-six-year-old woman. A successful bachelor, even at Nathan's age, could have gone out with women in their fifties, even mid-forties. He was sure of it, he wasn't imagining things. His daughter Daria was thirty-eight, and she had trouble finding guys to date. Now she was looking for someone to have a child with; Idit told Yehuda, after Daria told her, that even for that purpose most men preferred younger women, so they would be free to think about another child in a few years, and also—Yehuda was shocked when he heard this—as insurance, so that if the dad died, the child would be left with a relatively young mother, instead of turning into a ticking bomb of orphanhood.

He wanted to protect his daughter from the injustice, in the world at large and particularly on this point, but he had the vague sense that it didn't gel with Nili's situation, with what he secretly thought to himself: How could Nathan want her? She was older, and very overweight, things you may not be allowed to say but you can think. Who *wouldn't* think that? Who would look at her and not think that? And again that thing happened to him that sometimes happened when he tried to adapt himself to the zeitgeist, because he really did try to be open-minded, yet still he couldn't understand it: if there's something here that everyone sees and everyone thinks—and he was willing to bet money that they did—then why is it so terrible to say it? Not to mention that Nili was sixty-six but Daria was only thirty-eight; it wasn't the same thing at all.

He felt that all this was grating on his nerves for another reason, a more important reason than the others, but before he could trap it in its hasty flight, Nili said, "Okay, I won't tell him anything."

"But are you going to be mad at us?" Zohara asked.

"No." When she heard her own tone, she added, "Really, I won't. My relationship with Nathan and the world's relationship with me and Nathan is a different story, it's not right to mix it up in our business here. You're right about that, okay? I can see that, now let's move on. So we're not consulting with anyone. I mean, it's not that I really thought we would."

"Unless something extreme develops," Yehuda said.

Amos summed up: "All right. I suggest that for now we concentrate on dealing with the current extreme scenario. It's not as though we lack for problems."

"But what about the preservation and all that? Have we dropped that?" Zohara asked.

"I'll dig around online a bit," Yehuda said, "see if I come up with anything. But either way, I believe it'll work out."

"Either it will or it won't," Nili observed.

7

On Sunday he would turn seventy. Two months and three days before Avishay. When they were nine they decided to switch birthdays: Avishay would now celebrate his in October and Yehuda two months later. They felt they were entering a pact, mingling blood without having to prick their fingers. On October 13, 1952, Yehuda spent the day declining salutations and insisting that it was not his birthday. He gave the present he received from his brother—it was a book; he gave Yehuda a book every year, to this day—to Avishay, as if offloading stolen goods. But by the time December 23 rolled around the prank had faded, and so Avishay ended up celebrating twice that year and got two presents, while Yehuda got nothing at all.

This year Avishay would not be celebrating his birthday. It had taken sixty years for the wrong to be righted, but the whole stupid joke was worthless without Avishay. Yehuda brushed away the thought aggressively, practically swatting it. He felt propelled by a feverish engine, his mind focused on one thing, and he feared that if it stopped rattling he would suddenly hear the sadness, just like in the cartoons, when the hero plunges into the abyss the second he stops scuttling in midair above it.

The big seven-oh. At least Idit wouldn't be there. She thought he was upset but he wasn't. She had an overseas trip she couldn't get out of—something for the newspaper, a seminar in Washington, DC, she'd explained at length even though he wasn't really listening. She promised they'd celebrate on Friday, after she got back, with the girls and maybe his brother Shuki and his family. She'd make it up to him, big-time. But Yehuda did not need compensation: as far as he was concerned they could skip the whole thing. In fact he had to tell the others that he wouldn't be there on Sunday; he was going to be unavailable at least from midday onward, it was unavoidable, force majeure. But he would not tell them where he was going; if it were up to him, Idit wouldn't have known either.

But Idit had been there when he got the call: "Hello, is this Mr. Yehuda Harlap?" "Yes," he'd answered. "Hi, this is Tirzah Bar-Ness." Then she'd clarified: "The writer." But Yehuda needed no reminder: Tirzah, Tirzah Bar-Ness from *requires extensive work before it can be published*. Tirzah Bar-Ness who should have changed her mind and here she was, apparently, doing just that. Yet right after their phone call he hurried to Google to remind himself exactly what she'd written and which prizes she'd won, so that he could explain how momentous this occasion was to Idit, and mostly to himself, and also in preparation for Sunday.

"I hope I'm not disturbing you," Tirzah continued, and Yehuda said, "No, not at all," and wondered whether to add something about being honored. "Did you end up doing anything with the book?" she wondered, and Yehuda said, "Actually, it's about to be published." Tirzah said, "That's great! I'm glad to hear I didn't discourage you." Yehuda made some sort of snickering sound instead of saying, "You did, you discouraged the heck out of me, you ruined my life." Tirzah went on: "Anyway, I'm sort of working on that whole subject now, about inventors and inventions. From a literary perspective, of course. I'd be interested to hear a little more about it. Is there any way we could meet?" Yehuda said, "Of course, I'd be honored and delighted," and Tirzah said, "I'm so happy to hear that." "Could you just explain what exactly you'd like to know about? So that I can prepare?" he asked, but Tirzah replied, "There's no need to prepare anything. It's for a book

I'm writing. If I could just chat with you it would be wonderful." Yehuda said, "Of course, with pleasure."

"About the logistics," she continued, "if it's not too much to ask, would it be possible for you to come to Alonei Aba?" Yehuda said, "Of course," even though he had no idea where that was. "It's just that I'm not mobile," she explained, and Yehuda reassured her, "No need to explain, I'm completely mobile and it's no trouble at all." "What's your schedule like on Sunday?" she asked, and he said, "Immaculate," and was quite pleased with himself. "Around six thirty or seven?" she said. "In the morning?" he asked fearfully. "No, no, evening," she said quickly, and Yehuda briefly wondered if she was single—he'd have to google that, too. "Friday at six thirty p.m. is perfect. I'm writing it down. What's the address?" "Four-A Ha'Haruv Street," she said, "it's a street that turns off Alonim." "Don't worry," Yehuda said, "I'll use GPS."

═══

He put the phone back in its cradle even though Idit claimed it was more carcinogenic when it was charging, just to prolong the sweet moment before telling her.

"Well? Well?" she immediately said.

"Do you know who that was?"

"Go on."

"Tirzah Bar-Ness."

"Tirzah Bar-Ness the writer?" Idit exclaimed.

"She and none other. She wants to meet me."

"You don't say! Why?"

"Not clear. She's interested in the whole topic of inventions. Something for a book she's writing. I don't know, I guess she'll tell me. But it's pretty amazing, isn't it? And maybe she read the book again, who knows."

"Absolutely," Idit said, but her enthusiastic momentum had screeched to a halt by the end of the last syllable. She paused for a moment, and Yehuda knew she wanted to say something else but was biting her tongue. Eventually she added, "Maybe she is just doing research for a book or something."

"So?"

"So nothing, it's still a big honor and it could be an amazing experience. But I'm not sure if it's going to make a difference in terms of the book's fate. Your book, I mean. Maybe she'll give you an acknowledgment in her book or something, but that doesn't mean it'll do any good. Don't forget that she did write you some pretty serious things. I mean, I just don't want you to get disappointed. And on your birthday."

He looked at her. They slept together once every couple of weeks, jerked each other off a little more frequently. He did not understand her. He did not understand the things she took seriously, the things she valued. He did not understand what she wasn't understanding, why she made that little face every time he mentioned the book, like it was unnecessary, like there was no chance that he, at his age, could become an author. Not that he really cared about the end of that sentence, but he cared about the beginning: he wasn't prepared to accept that there could be no chance at his age of being something.

———

They stood at the door without moving, feeling guilty for leaving Nili there, or perhaps unsure whom they should say goodbye to: the living or the dead.

"Go on already, leave," Nili urged them.

"We've been standing here for so long I have to pee again," Zohara said.

"Then go pee."

"I'm so sick of myself already." Zohara disappeared down the hall-way to the bathroom.

"Poor woman," Nili said.

Just as Amos made a scolding *shhhh*, Zohara reappeared in the living room: "Did you know his phone's on silent?" She was holding the device as evidence.

"Then turn the volume on," Amos said.

Zohara slid the little button on the side, and just then the phone started ringing.

"Give it to me, it might be urgent," Yehuda said, and she handed him the phone. "I'm answering."

"Are you crazy?" Nili said.

"We have to know who it is."

"Okay, but answer it like you're Avishay."

Yehuda took a deep breath. "Hello?"

A woman's voice on the other end of the line said, "Thank God! I thought you were dead."

"Put it on speakerphone," Nili whispered.

"One sec," Yehuda said, "I'm putting you on speakerphone."

"Speakerphone? Why? Avishay, where are you?" The woman's loud voice filled the room.

"I'm home sick."

Zohara made a puzzled face at him, but Nili shushed her with a wave, as if to say, That's good, that's good.

The woman continued: "I've got three hundred people waiting for you here!"

"Where?" He was so busy trying to make his voice sound deeper that it came out as a sort of squawk.

"What?" the woman said. "I can't hear anything."

"Where are there three hundred people?" Yehuda asked.

"Where?! At the university!"

"For a lecture?" Yehuda croaked, and Zohara grimaced as if to say, What on earth?! But he had no choice—he didn't know whether this woman knew Avishay and would recognize his voice.

"Avishay?" she said. "Are you okay? What's wrong?"

"I'm sick, I'm running a high fever."

"Can't you make it? I'm sending a cab, he'll bring you and take you back, I'll set you up an armchair, a cup of tea, whatever you need."

"I really can't do it."

"Avishay, I'm begging you, they've been sitting here in the auditorium for ten minutes." Then she lowered her voice: "The donors are here, too. I've told them maybe five times that you called from the road, that you'll be here any minute."

"I can't move, I can barely speak."

"This is such a screw-up, I want to die. I'm going to kill you, Avishay, I will murder you with my own two hands."

Yehuda was wracked with guilt, as though he really were Avishay, as though he himself had destroyed this woman's evening and maybe just slightly her life, too, and he suddenly realized they were not going to be able to do this. It was too much for them. It was too much for anyone: no one could lie like this. He made a throat-slitting gesture at them: *I'm telling her, I can't do this.* Zohara looked at Nili, but Nili was too slow, and the woman said impatiently, "Avishay?" Nili screamed silently: *No!* and wagged her finger: *No, no, no, you're sick, that's it, say goodbye.* She made a little wave with her hand, like a baby, but Amos looked at him and signaled: *It's enough, just tell her.* And then Yehuda realized: Amos. Amos! He looked at Amos and pointed into the phone, but Amos furrowed his brow uncomprehendingly. Yehuda motioned at him again and whispered, "Can you?" But Amos still didn't understand, and the woman said, "Avishay!" again, and Nili whispered, "Goodbye, say goodbye," and Yehuda said, "Listen,

I'm sending you another professor of economics, okay?" Amos gave him a terrified look, and the woman asked dubiously, "Who?" Yehuda touched Amos's arm to reassure him and said, "He's a big name in economic happiness." Zohara whispered, "Happiness economics," and Amos whispered, "No, Yehuda, stop it," and Yehuda said, "It's Amos Barzani, he's also a Nobel candidate." Amos gave him a "this is not funny" glare. Yehuda closed his eyes and held up his hand as if to say: It's on me, Amos. "He'll be there in ten minutes," he said into the phone.

———

"I'm not going," Amos declared.

Yehuda was prepared for this. "That's the reason, Amos, why Avishay will get a Nobel Prize and you won't. I just want you to know that it's because of exactly this kind of thing, not because he's more talented."

"What kind of thing?"

"Because you don't know how to grab opportunities, you don't know how to recognize an opportunity when it jumps out at you. What do I always tell you?"

"I don't even know what the lecture is about!"

Zohara asked, "What difference does it make? I mean it's obvious to them that you're not going to speak about the same thing, you're just a substitute."

Amos gave Yehuda a reproachful look. "Substitute. Did you hear that? Opportunities?! You don't know what you're talking about, Yehuda."

"How do you know who's going to be there? Who these donors are?"

"Go on, Amos," Nili said, "you really need to leave."

"You're putting me in an unfair situation," Amos protested.

"We'll make it up to you," Yehuda promised.

"Anyway," Zohara started, "in general—"

But Avishay's phone rang at that moment, and everyone tensed up except Yehuda, who answered it and said, "He'll be down in a minute." Then he explained: "I ordered a cab on Avishay's app, so he can pay for it." But he wasn't convinced it had sounded like a joke, and indeed, no one was smiling.

"Wasn't it on his calendar?" Nili asked.

Yehuda waited indifferently for someone to answer, until he realized she was looking at him. Was he responsible for the calendar? He felt the same kind of panic he'd been getting for months: he repeatedly had the feeling he'd forgotten something important, something critical, and if he didn't remember it soon disaster may strike—perhaps it already had. "I don't know," he admitted.

Zohara slid her finger over the phone's screen. "You know what happened?"

"What?"

"He had it written down for next Thursday."

"Oops," said Nili.

"See?" Zohara held up the screen but Yehuda couldn't see anything without his glasses on.

═══

People? Those, he could never remember. He liked to brag about his terrible memory and discuss it more than was necessary. He secretly believed that it was to his credit, proof that the world took more of an interest in him than he did in it. But the things he'd been forgetting recently were of a different species: not people or dates, nothing that could be verified or restored, just a vague sense that something was deficient. Things he wanted to forget, though—he remembered. Every so often he made sure, but no. Not yet. On the contrary: the more he tried to convince himself that he no longer remembered exactly what had happened on that day that ruined his life, the sharper and more voluminous the details became. Sometimes he thought it would be his very last memory, the final thing he'd have left.

He was in his third year of law school at the time. He hadn't chosen law for any particular reason—perhaps just to show Avishay that he was also interested in something, something different, not economics, something he had chosen completely on his own. He could imagine himself roaming the courthouse hallways, he could envision the power he would wield, and his twenty-seven-year-old mind even reluctantly added on a potbelly to his fifty- or sixty-something self. But it was justice itself that he could not envisage, not when it was parsed out into its individual components. And the insides of those big halls: they seemed too much for him to take on, or perhaps too little. Either way, he was not especially interested.

And then one Thursday, in winter, he invented it. It wasn't much of a Eureka moment, there was no anecdote, nothing to console him over the long years to come, all of which would be lived in the shadow of those two little pieces of metal that Yehuda had come to loathe, blaming them for everything that was wrong in the world, or in his world. All that happened was that he was struggling with a trash bag, trying to find the opening, which would have been aggravating enough even if they hadn't smoked a little pot, and he thought—that was the first and last time in his life he'd had this kind of thought—how convenient it would be if there was something that could quickly and simply open bags.

He went into the living room. Avishay, Amos, Nili, and Hemi, a guy they were friendly with, were sitting there. Only Zohara was missing; it was before she'd moved to Tel Aviv, and none of them except Amos knew her yet. He held up the trash bag and told them about his idea. During the seconds it took him to cover the distance between the little kitchen and the living room, he came to believe the idea was ingenious. It shouldn't be too difficult to build something like that, he could see it materializing in his mind's eye, and he skipped ahead to the various imaginary high points in his future. But they sniggered, the way one does in that obligatory way, not contemptuously or dismissively, but indifferently—who cares about a bag opener?— because they had to make some sound, a minor tax to keep the conversation moving, and all at once Yehuda lost the will.

That night he couldn't fall asleep. Not because of the bag; if that had been the reason, it might have made the story a little better. If only he'd fallen asleep that night; if only a tiny tip of a stray thought hadn't diverted his sleep from its usual course, he would have been a different man today.

But he didn't fall asleep. He lay with his eyes shut, and behind the eyelids was that terrible, total awakeness of those struggling in vain to fall asleep, and finally he got up and tried to put together the opener. He couldn't do it—all he had at home were little pieces of wood that had somehow ended up there, but he couldn't cut them, and in any case, wood wasn't the right material. He went back to sleep, dissatisfied. He knew exactly what he needed but he couldn't get it at two a.m., and the next morning he woke up full of resentment, the principled resentment of someone with unsated hunger. He went to the store, bought a few things—he clearly remembered the thought that went through this mind: what a waste of money— and by Saturday he had a prototype.

When he realized he was onto something—people said so, friends said so, their curiosity aroused in the light of day—he set up a tiny company that operated out of the apartment on Bezalel Yaffe Street as a legal entity without any real substance, except for two and a half pieces of metal that were now slightly stronger, which sat on his desk watching him and Idit while they had their collegiate sex, which was far more interesting to him, and continued to be even after they made him a millionaire, by which time it had all but ceased entirely.

A little more than two years later, he sold the company and the patent to Pe'er Industries for a fortune. He quit law school—he hated it anyway—and, delighted with his wealth, he married Idit, as if the money could buy all the opportunities in the world, even the opportunity for remorse.

And that was how the bag opener was born: a tool that had barely changed for more than forty years, which could now be found in almost every kitchen in the world, in one of two models: the kind you could attach to the wall and simply insert the bag into (39–59 shekels or $7.90–$11.90, depending on the size), and the kind that looked like a garlic-press, small and compact, which you might keep in your drawer.

———

He was free to pursue his dreams. He had the time and the money. But now that he was able to make them come true, he was no longer sure what they were.

He knew what he didn't want to be: a lawyer, a businessman. Perhaps an inventor? He spent hours upon hours trying to come up with another thing, another idea that would sprout from the same hidden wellspring he hadn't been aware of, another stroke of genius. Chain-smoking on the balcony, gazing out at the view, then lounging in the yard, he waited for something to strike. A ray of light or perhaps a trail of unicorns—who knows what inspiration looks like? But the landscape was boring, you could stare at it for ten minutes before your thoughts began to wander, and how long could one concentrate without doing anything but waiting?

Sometimes he heard people say: Ideas are cheap. When he grumbled about this, infrequently and only to people he felt close to, he was surprised to discover that they didn't know what he was talking about. Not everyone heard that line shouted out in cafés or on the street, mocking him: *ideas are cheap, ideas are cheap*. Maybe people only bothered reciting it to him, seeing as he was the great inventor, the prodigy. He felt they were apologizing: I have ideas too, ideas come cheap, the problem is—and here they would sigh as if to say: You know as well as I do what the problem is, right? Yehuda would nod wearily to signal feigned acknowledgment of camaraderie between the dreamy loser and the big success story, which was him—he had to remind himself of that. He guessed they were referring to free time, or money, and his heart sank with envy and a scream tried to get out of his throat: Where? Where do you get them? How do they just come to you, the ideas? How do they come to you so cheaply? If only I lacked for time and money—I'd give anything.

For a while he tried to simply enjoy the money. He explored the idea of making that his focal point in this life, doing what so very few could, simply thanks to the money. But he soon discovered that there really wasn't that much to do. Mostly traveling: more often, farther away, more expensive, better. But that was it. There weren't many things rich people could buy, apart from houses maybe, and how many houses could one person want, especially if he didn't need more money? Yachts, too, and private jets, which were mainly used to travel to even more places. He'd never really been that interested in traveling, and the more he traveled, the less interested he became. Beautiful, wonderful, spectacular . . . Whatever. Sometimes he longed for a little piece of ugly among all that wonderfully, perfectly picturesque beauty—something for the soul.

In general he began to suspect that at a certain echelon, and it wasn't even very high, the differences between wealth levels ceased to matter. They were no longer meaningful. There was a limit to how big a house one could buy, especially if one had good taste, normal taste, and there was a limit to how much fun one could have. His brother, Shuki, who'd been a traffic court judge his whole life and was now something in small claims court, was not particularly rich, only as rich as a judge could be—he had gained respectable affluence—but Yehuda had the impression that Shuki's life was a lot more enjoyable than his own. And it wasn't, God forbid, because of some profound moral lesson. It wasn't because Shuki had learned what really mattered in life—not money but inner peace, family, and good health—but rather because of what he used his money for. Unlike Yehuda, he had been blessed with the levelheaded hedonism of people who truly enjoy things that are appropriate for their age and economic status. Shuki could not understand why his wealthy brother did not get excited about a 5,500-euros-a-night hotel where you could look out the window and see the Northern Lights.

Sometimes Yehuda envied inventors in the movies, whose inventions were stolen by evil corporations and they had to set off on exhausting battles that lasted years, using up all their money, time, and energy to achieve justice. If he had that kind of struggle, at least his life would have a purpose. But he'd received the money he was owed and the recognition he deserved—too much recognition.

Eventually he got addicted to the "how to get rich working for four hours a month" genre of books: *How Wealthy People Think, The Complete Guide to Getting Rich, How to Get Rich Working from Home, Wealth in Ten Easy Steps, Wealth in Eight Easy Steps, Shark vs. Sardines, How to Get Rich Quick, How to Get Rich on eBay, How to Get Rich Easily, How Come That Idiot Is Rich and I'm Not, The Guide to Avoiding Guides to Getting Rich, How Older Women Can Get Rich,* and so forth. He even owned a copy of *How to Make Money Using Secrets from the Kabbalah.* These books filled him with temporary comfort and relief, because they prescribed all the actions one had to do, whereas he hadn't had to do anything at all. Everything in the book's title, everything people were trying so hard to get, everything that made hundreds of these books bestsellers—he already had.

When his self-satisfaction allowance was finally exceeded, he decided to write a book himself: *How to Invent the Inventor in You.* That was the original title; *The Courage to Invent* came later. He was aware of the irony and knew the old saying: Those who can't do, teach. But he alone was aware of it, and so he decided it could be ignored. Everyone around him always treated him like a sort of MacGyver, the worldly man, the inventor, the great improviser, the man who could build a tent out of two tin cans and a spool of thread if he had to. Maybe that was why he hated traveling so much.

The manuscript soon roamed into other territories when he found that he enjoyed writing about his childhood, about Tel Aviv in the 1950s, even when the writing lead nowhere, certainly not to his Big Bang, his invention, which nothing really led to because it had just happened. But Yehuda continued to cling to it desperately—the courage to invent, the story of an inventor, inventing yourself—because without it he was just another guy. He had nothing.

He himself still opened plastic bags exactly the way he had in the sixties: he rubbed the sides of the bag together until they gave in and separated. And while he did so, with a passionate practicality, he always thought to himself: *They can all go fuck themselves.*

Friday

Nili

8

Lately she'd developed a real hostility to the sound of the phone ringing: that soft jangle, like a sort of pre-yawn, a second before it woke up for good and startled the whole room. It scratched her skin from the inside, pinched her brain, imposed sharpness and swiftness precisely when she wanted to be slow and languid.

Whenever it rang, her first thought was: What's my excuse? What am I doing now? Or in an hour or two, or this evening if it's a babysitter they need? Or tomorrow morning, if one of them's sick? So many time slots and so many factors—how many perfect lies could she come up with in an instant? How many excuses could be invented by a sixty-six-year-old retired woman with no asterisk—no conferences, no private clinic, no training days, no hobbies, not even a husband—whose days stretched out vacantly before her and who they believed had moved to Tel Aviv precisely to be near her children and take care of her grandchildren.

And so many grandchildren, good lord. It was a horrible thought, and she had to remind herself over and over again that no one could read her mind, that she was allowed to think whatever she wanted. Still, she kept insisting to an imaginary audience that she loved them, her grandchildren and her children, as if the declaration were a password that gained her entry into another room.

Besides, it was true: they were all lovely and wonderful, as lovely and wonderful as children in their forties should be, and her grandchildren, the toddler versions of their adult parents, were also perfect and talented. So could they please just leave her in peace now? She'd done her job, and she'd clearly done it well—exceedingly well. If they were so successful and wonderful, shouldn't she get something out of it too? If they were so successful and wonderful, wasn't she allowed to expect them to get along on their own once in a while? To be successful and wonderful among themselves and leave her out of it?

She carefully calculated the minutes of fertility her daughter and daughters-in-law still had left. They started late with kids these days, basking in an illusion of liberalism, individualism, freedom, but then at the last minute they all caught up in just a few years, closing the gaps in their middle-class conventionality by having two, three, four kids when they were in their late thirties and into their early forties. And they enslaved themselves to the endeavor, throwing everything else away, especially the women, as if to say: We've had our careers, that's it, it's enough to last us a lifetime. Whereas Nili and her friends, and even their mothers, had at least had their children in a normal way, with proper gaps, and not so many of them.

When Shelly told her she was pregnant again, Nili was stunned: Yanai was only eleven months old, and Shelly had spent all of those months in a harried state, and seemed even more harried when she made the announcement. Nili was sure it was an accident. "You know," she pointed out, "you could have an abortion. No one's going to blame you, and any committee would approve it. Have another kid in a couple of years, when the time is right, with a gap." But Shelly stared at her like a Mormon virgin looking at a drag queen, all horror and sanctity, and eight months later Yoel was born.

———

She knew what the problem was: the problem was that she was a pediatrician. Or rather, that she used to be. She was both fat and a children's doctor, and what did those two things make her if not some kind of Mary Poppins? How could someone like her not be crazy about children? How could she not press them to her huge bosom and send the parents off, admonishing them cheerfully: *For all I care, you don't need to come back! We're going to have the time of our lives!*

They were convinced, for example, that because she was a pediatrician she'd be thrilled to watch the kids when they were sick—they seemed to have confused physician with kindergarten teacher. They didn't know that pediatricians hated sick kids more than anyone else, just like they say that gynecologists . . . Well, people say a lot of stupid things about doctors, but that one happened to be true.

They knew, of course, that she didn't love her job. Everyone knew it. In the early years, when she'd just started at the clinic, she might not have hated it quite so much—she couldn't exactly remember anymore, she didn't trust her memory much, and she trusted the girl she'd been back then even less. That was why she was reluctant to recommend books she'd read long ago: How could you trust your twenty-year-old-self's taste? But at the time she'd been ambitious, possessing that formulaic drive that needed only to be filled with content, any content, which characterized very young people. She'd skipped two grades, she was a genius, and that was what geniuses were supposed to study. She'd started medical school at sixteen, the minute she graduated from high school, God help her. It horrified her to think that her fate had been sealed at sixteen—that her life had been somewhat terminated.

She could have done so many interesting and exciting things with that brain instead of dividing it up among parents clamoring for antibiotics (the first thirty years) and parents who filed police charges if she insisted their child needed antibiotics (the fourth decade). Once—this was already in the Tel Aviv clinic, by which time she was really miserable—she told a couple that their daughter was being slightly dramatic, which was true: the girl put on an off-Broadway show before Nili could even touch her, and besides, it was a funny thing to say, at least in her opinion. It went all the way to the regional director of the HMO and Nili was accused of "labeling" the child and summoned for a talk with management, who admonished her for pigeonholing a ten-month-old.

Perhaps that was why she had limited patience, even though everyone told her it would be different with her own grandchildren. She was not impatient with the kids themselves, who were usually healthy and sweet, but with their parents, her own children, who reminded her of the parents at the clinic because they tried to force her into a tangled, tiresome, multifarious parental galaxy. The kids weren't allowed to watch TV but they could have half an hour of YouTube, which was called "screen time"; it was rude to offer candy to friends without asking their parents first; *Hello Daddy* was a chauvinistic book—or was it racist? She couldn't remember, but either way she had to take it back to the store. In her role as an active grandmother, she was expected to obey the laws of this galaxy down to the last detail, under the watchful eyes of three sets of parents, each with its own rules, and she had to keep track of who deducted points for which transgression. Just like the clinic, except worse.

Anyway, she had done her job, she'd taken advantage of her brains, in a manner of speaking, as much as doctors could, which wasn't all that much, as she well knew. That might have been one advantage in her chosen profession: a doctor was considered enough, she didn't have to reinvent herself later in life the way many of her friends did. Dear God, what a horrible expression: not only invent yourself, as if that weren't bad enough, but then you had to *re*invent yourself, too. You had to find meaning not only for Life No. 1 but for the second phase. Even then there was no exemption, even then you couldn't just patiently, idly wait to drop dead like a normal person in their late sixties.

Well, thank you very much, but she'd had enough. She wasn't about to do interior design or coaching, conferences or consultancies, and certainly not private practice. She hung a "Retired" sign around her neck, by which she meant: Do not disturb. But her children thought it said: Do disturb! Completely at your disposal! When all she wanted was to be left alone. All she wanted was for her children to be just a little bit estranged from her, for her ex-husband to stop speaking to her, the way exes did in the movies or in normal families, and to be allowed to sleep with her new boyfriend in peace.

The kids, of course, were convinced that she and her ex were still doing it: that they were one of *those* couples. They insisted on peppering family events with winks and nods and raised eyebrows, all of which Nili found appalling. They treated her ex-husband's girlfriend and her own Nathan very patiently, like necessary twists in a romantic comedy.

＝＝

But this time the phone was ringing and it wasn't any of her children or children-in-law; it was Zohara, to ask if she was all right—she felt bad about leaving Nili alone in the apartment.

When she'd volunteered, they protested feebly, for politeness's sake—none of them felt like being the first person to be left there alone, not to mention that the more time went by, the greater the chances that their shift would be canceled because the whole project would collapse. But Nili knew what they were thinking: she was the doctor, after all, and if she hadn't contributed much in the way of clinical information—which she hadn't, she was the first to admit it—at least they could take advantage of whatever experience she had with corpses. Pediatrician or not, this could not be the first dead body she'd seen in her life.

Zohara was worried about her. Nili had had too much death in her life. Maybe Zohara was afraid to leave her alone with it, as though there were no telling what she might do to it—to death, that is—if given the chance. Or perhaps what it might do to her, even just out of habit.

But Nili didn't care, she really didn't. On the contrary: she was happy to have a job to volunteer for, an unpopular task that she could take off their hands. She'd jumped at Yehuda's proposal gleefully, naturally, good-naturedly, and these traits were to her credit and would testify on her behalf if needed. Granted, she hadn't believed they would really go through with it, but she'd liked the possibility that they might.

Only later in the conversation, when details started peeking through the dust of the settling idea, had she discovered that it was her and Yehuda against the others. It was one of those moments that demanded inescapable decisions, demanded to make its mark. And at that moment, in that test, they needed no persuasion; it was a pop quiz in friendship, in altruism, in love for the deceased, which she and Yehuda passed with flying colors, unmaliciously exposing all the hesitators in the room.

She felt shame then, and it curtailed her presence, her enthusiasm, like those enormous raincoats that miraculously fold up into a ball: Was she really preoccupied by this stuff? Was this really what she was thinking about? But at the same time a certain excitement seeped into her veins, which seemed to have emerged from a different source: This was the moment that would fuse her into this group, flatten her into the concrete.

She didn't usually think about that. Her friends were who they were, her life was what it was. But when they talked about Nathan,

for example, she had to wonder: If Zohara had brought in someone after all these years, would they have been so stingy with their
happiness? There were five of them, there always had been, an even-
sided pentagon for all those years. Yet still she sometimes thought,
in the bad moments, that she was hanging loose, sewn on with crude
stitches that could easily be pulled out. A child's stitches. She didn't
think about it much, as if the thought had the power to seed life in
the possibility, to turn it from foolishness into truth. Yet still she had
a stash of answers prepared for the question of why: Why was it that
way, this thing that actually wasn't that way?

Because she'd joined the group by chance. She hadn't been chosen. And maybe it was not that she'd joined by chance so much as
that she'd been brought in for the drugs—how ridiculous it sounded
now, how implausible, but yes, that's why they'd sought her out, invited her, kept on inviting her, even after she broke up with their
friend Eli. Forty years had passed since then, during which none of
them smoked at all, but a tiny sense of inferiority still lived inside
her, a sense that she was always wanted for something.

Above all, she felt she hadn't been able to find her role. Zohara
was connected to Avishay through sex, and she had a connection
with Amos, too, an old one, stemming from their college friendship as well as an ancient fling, and, whatever the reason, he always
owed her. Yehuda was a childhood friend: *the* childhood friend. And
Amos and Avishay had their strange, private world of economics and
they had their competition, which was contagious, which wouldn't
let you go once you got caught up in it. And her? She was a friend,
she was nice, she was—smart? But nice girls were a dime a dozen.
Sometimes she thought this was the reason she was doing things:
to be more exceptional. But then she reminded herself that that was
childish, and she was a grown woman.

It came easily for her, at any rate. So she'd stay alone with Avishay.

She didn't see what the big deal was. The dead didn't scare her; the living did. She disliked that burden, that imperative to live well and enjoy yourself in case death arrived before you'd really done it. In case you hadn't been concentrating, in case you'd dozed off, in case you'd assumed there would be time, opportunities. But once you were dead—you were dead.

———

In fact Nili only had one dead person, officially: her sister Shlomit. She was four years younger than Nili. When she died of breast cancer, at forty-four, her husband, Michael, and her son, Itai, had left their home in Hod Hasharon and moved to live near Nili and Ram in Jerusalem. It had been Nili's idea, a genuine one, but she was surprised when Michael took her up on it.

Itai grew up in their home, like a fourth child, and so did Michael. Nili guided him from death back to life, the opposite of the usual track, date after date after date. He'd been on dozens of them since Shlomit's death, maybe hundreds, but even after all those years he still seemed like that semi-virgin who'd only just been widowed. Shlomit had sheltered him from this life, from these women; she'd been a once-in-a-lifetime stroke of luck, an unrecurring miracle.

A few years ago Nili heard Itai telling someone that his mother had been a social worker. She listened in amazement, the way she used to listen to parents telling little children basic things about nature—this tree is called that, this is how bees reproduce, that's called a bougainvillea—and she understood nothing of it. The information was new to her. She seemed to have forgotten that her sister had ever been anything except dead.

Nili had another younger sister, Shlomit's twin Smadar. She sometimes tried to remember the two girls at the same age and the same height, just the way they were born. But Smadar had grown constantly, without ever pausing, until she looked like Nili's twin. Sometimes, before Smadar got ill, Nili thought the day would come when Smadar turned into her older sister.

Smadar also had breast cancer, which she'd been living with for seven years without any treatment: no Herceptin and certainly no chemo. She had, however, completely changed her diet. But it wasn't veganism—oh no, she insisted, offended on behalf of the method. The method had been developed by a man named Hanan: *Hanansmethod,* as Smadar always said reverentially, as though if she separated the phrase into its components the method would stop working. Hanan had been cured of cancer thirty-something years ago, and had cured . . . At this point Smadar would simply gasp and spread her arms to indicate the multitude of people.

Smadar presented herself as evidence. She would hold her arms out to display her body, pointing her hands in to its center, as if to say: *Do I look like a sick woman to you?* The rhetorical display further implied: *And I haven't done a single one of the treatments they recommended. I told the doctors thanks but no thanks, I took care of myself through nutrition, and now look at me. See? See?* But to Nili it seemed that Smadar was fading away. Her body, her face, everything looked diseased, everything seemed to be progressing according to the clinical procedure, by the book, the conventional hospital book.

But she wasn't sure if she was imagining it, and she had no one to ask, no one to talk to. She certainly couldn't talk to Smadar, who behaved as if she'd been cured, as if she were walking proof of something. She was going to die, and so Nili felt she couldn't say anything to her, even though Smadar herself believed she was not going to die. So she couldn't treat her as if she were going to die and she couldn't treat her as if she were going to live.

Nili hadn't taken the test, the one with that cancer gene, even though the doctors had recommended it. She was a doctor, too, and she knew full well that if you go looking for something, you find it. No one at her age emerged unscathed from tests. In return, or perhaps as compensation for the irresponsibility, she simply assumed she was ill: with breast cancer, passive or active, that she had now or would have next year, and if not that then another cancer. That was how she granted herself permission to enter the world of the dying, the world of those who no longer have to give a crap.

———

She opened the door to Avishay's room tentatively, as though he were sleeping. She remembered the pile of newspapers next to his bed; Zohara had taken the paper delivered outside the front door that morning. "Take it, take it," Nili had told her, "I won't have the patience to read." But now she did. She could hear a faint sound of banging in the background—someone hanging a picture next door, trying hard not to make too much noise, or maybe gently knocking on a door because of a sleeping child.

She pulled the sheet slightly down off Avishay's face; it was one of those things one simply couldn't avoid doing. He looked like Avishay, not empty or hollow. He looked like someone who even in death had not relinquished his personality or facial expression. But there was nothing inside. *There's nothing*, she thought. You could burn it and nothing would happen to Avishay. Like a shirt that someone took off and threw on the bed.

Where was he, then? Where was the whole Avishay, with the mom and the dad and the love they gave him, or didn't? That really bothered her now, for some reason: the mother and the father and their imprint on his soul that was now gone, vanished into thin air upon his death. Maybe if he'd had children it would have remained, but he didn't. Or maybe if he'd had children it still wouldn't have existed anywhere anymore. Perhaps that was the real cruelty of death, the profound meaning of its finality: that it eradicates the child you once were.

Her back hurt. She sat down carefully on the edge of the bed. Avishay's lips were slightly parted. Zohara had slept with him. Other women had too. It suddenly seemed ridiculous, the whole business of sex. Two people moving and moving, and then what? Maybe this was the secret to self-confidence: instead of imagining your audience naked, imagine them dead. Imagine everyone dead, especially men, if you want them.

She looked at him. He wasn't particularly good-looking, but in a way that by this age ceases to matter, swallowed up in the general, all-encompassing aging. And he had another deceptive quality, which Nili had never encountered in anyone else: he was so charming and full of anecdotes and so knowledgeable about everything and so sharp and clever, that he was considered an extremely amusing man despite having no sense of humor whatsoever.

In this area, too, she sometimes felt a certain self-righteousness that she was not proud of, a sort of urge to correct inaccuracies even though they did no harm to her and anyway what did she care—on the contrary, let him enjoy it, she was on his side. But when she heard it once from Zohara—they were enumerating Avishay's positive qualities while discussing his ever-intriguing bachelorhood—she couldn't resist saying: "Amusing? Oh, come on, you can't be serious. He has enough lovely things about him that you don't have to stick that in there, too."

But Zohara said, "Not amusing ha-ha, but amusing in the sense of, you know, being charming."

"Charming is charming, amusing is amusing. They're not the same thing."

"Why are you so annoyed by this?" Zohara asked.

"I don't know, it's just like we're all this sticky mass of charming-ness and amusingness and cleverness just because we're friends. Like we're all the same thing. And we're not." She paused. "I don't know why it annoys me. Maybe because of the dating sites. It's this fad, where everyone has the same qualities, like we're done with the era when all the qualities were divided up among the population."

"Is everything okay, Nili?"

"Everything's fine, I just needed to vent."

She peeked under the sheet, and when she saw his stomach she re-moved the covers completely: a disgusting green patina had started to climb up from his lower right abdomen, and it was bloated, prob-ably from gas. She discovered that she remembered more than she'd thought from those days when she was a twenty-year-old medical student, and a surprising taste came to her mouth. She took a deep breath to inspect it, suddenly curious—had she been happy back then?—but instead of the campus in Jerusalem, what filled her nos-trils was an unpleasant odor, and she turned her attention back to Avishay's discoloring stomach. He was starting to smell a little. She inhaled deeply, to gauge the severity. It felt as though her nose were filling not with the smell itself but with the potential it held. With its destination. She felt nauseated.

She covered him up again and went back to the living room without a newspaper. She wished the apartment had a balcony. She really felt like sitting out on a balcony. She stood in the living room, unable to decide where to sit or what to do. The banging next door started up again. She looked at her watch and wondered what was on TV. But halfway to the television set she stopped abruptly, turned around, and faced the door: it was Avishay's. Someone was knocking on his door.

9

This was probably what it felt like in a horror film: no way out, the killer getting closer. Or maybe she was the killer in this scenario, the one people should flee, even though she'd done nothing wrong.

She wondered if it was one of the others, but they would have called or texted, or at the very least rung the doorbell.

She went halfway to the door and stopped. If she looked through the peephole she would have to open up, no matter who was there: she knew herself, she'd feel caught out just by touching the door, holding her breath up too close to it. What had they decided about visitors? They'd thrown out and dismissed so many ideas, they'd spent so much time deliberating and figuring out what was best, that she couldn't remember what they'd said about what. She didn't think they'd even discussed this possibility; they'd only considered emails and text messages. But that couldn't be right. Or was it? Who could be coming to visit a sixty-nine-year-old bachelor in the middle of the day, unannounced? Who visits people at all these days? No one even makes phone calls anymore.

She could simply not open the door. They'd think he was out. Quick—which was better? Pretend he wasn't home, or find out who wanted him? Because after all, whoever it was would try him again. And if she didn't know who it was, they wouldn't be able to prepare.

A ring of the doorbell muddled her thoughts, and she walked to the door. As she opened it she just had time to think: This is not smart. What if it's a rapist or a burglar? You don't just open the door even on a normal day. At least ask who it is first. Then she also thought: Fine, if it's a rapist, let him come in and catch sight of Avishay's room. But standing outside the door was a girl, a young woman, who looked at Nili in surprise as Nili looked back at her.

"Hello," she said.

Nili said, "Hello," and reminded herself that she was allowed to be there, she was the adult, she was the friend, she had to act like she belonged there, it was all up to her now.

"Is Avishay home?"

"No. I'm Nili, his friend." As she said it, she thought: Why are you telling her your name?

"You're Nili?"

"Yes."

"Oh!" Liat exclaimed. "I've heard so much about you."

And then Nili didn't care about anything anymore, and she asked, "From Avishay?" Which was a stupid question, so she added, "Only good things, I hope."

Liat said, "Yes," but she could have put more effort into it, for sure. "I'm Liat."

Nili thought quickly: Liat. They'd mentioned that name yester-day, or today. She'd texted Avishay, but what had the message said? She couldn't remember. She felt she was supposed to say, *I've heard a lot about you too*, but it wasn't true, and besides, this girl deserved to be punished a little, so she said, "Pleased to meet you, too. You must be looking for Avishay."

"Is he here?"

"Actually, no. Why, were you supposed to meet?"

That came out more accusatory than she'd intended, and Liat said awkwardly, "Um, no. We said I'd come by sometime on Friday, he might have forgotten."

"I'll tell you what, then," Nili said, aware that she was gradually coming into focus, albeit not very elegantly. "Avishay had to leave urgently for a few days to work on something, it just came up on very short notice, and I'm watching his apartment. But he's available by text or email, or you could send him a WhatsApp message, he's available the whole time."

"But he's not answering the phone?"

"No, just WhatsApp and text messages, you know. I think the idea was to minimize the disturbances." Then she heard herself say, "I was just reading an interview with Jonathan Franzen—have you read him?"

"Haven't had the chance," Liat said.

"Doesn't matter. But read *Freedom* first," Nili continued—she was getting good at this, more confident. "Anyway, he was saying that he plugs up the internet cable port on his computer so he won't even be able to get online while he's writing."

Liat said, "But everything's Wi-Fi, what port does he plug up?"

Nili remembered what Ram always said: You can spot a liar by the redundant information; liars try to cover up the lie with verbal excess. She threw her hands up in surrender and said, "I'm just quoting."

Liat looked like she was still standing there just to be polite, to avoid offending this overweight and probably unhappy woman, Avishay's friend, who was going off on a tangent about Jonathan Franzen.

Nili looked at her: they must be sleeping together. What other option could there be? It was either that or she was his long-lost daughter. But that wasn't exactly the type of drama people like them had in their lives. She could have been his student—but even then, they were still sleeping together. It was a Friday afternoon, although she wouldn't have thought any differently even if it was Sunday morning.

She looked about thirty-seven, thirty-eight. Not only could she have been Avishay's daughter, she could have been Nili's. She looked just like their kids, hers and Yehuda's and Amos's, some of whom were around that age. She was well-dressed and pretty attractive, all shored up by that final moment in which one could still be suspected of being in one's thirties, a second before something cracks and that's it—this person is forty. Her brown hair was held back with a barrette and she had a small face. She reminded Nili of an animal of some kind, even though she was quite good-looking. Nili couldn't think which one.

She wondered what this woman did for a living. Women of her age, these days, didn't usually do much: they made designer cloth diapers, baked vegan cakes. They used to have PhDs from the Weizmann Institute and a company car. Big deal. Now they were moms. But this Liat was no mom, there was no doubt about that—this girl was single, for sure, and all of a sudden Nili had an urgent need to find out what she did, to understand who she was. But asking would be like inviting her in. She had a moment of terror: Had she shut the door to Avishay's room? Liat was about to leave, but Nili still felt her body stiffen, trying to expand even more, perhaps for the first time in her life, to cover up the doorway. "Send him a message, it's fine, I'm sure he'll be happy."

"I will," Liat said. "Thanks anyway, great to meet you."

Nili called out, "Bye-bye, see you," and shut the door.

She wondered whether to call Zohara from her cell phone or from the landline. She hated talking on the cell but calling from Avishay's home phone might be leaving tracks. When she decided to do it anyway, because in fact Avishay phoning his friend Zohara from home was a sign of life, which was good, she heard Avishay's cell phone make a brief typewriter sound to signal an incoming message. It was probably from Liat, and then Nili worried—what if Liat was standing outside texting him? What if she heard his phone? She rushed to the bathroom, disconnected the phone from the charger, and punched in the password. *You have a picture from Liat.* Nili looked and saw fingers with bright green nail polish holding something. She held the phone away and squinted: What was it? She went to the living room and came back with her glasses, then enlarged the picture: two pink stripes on a pregnancy stick.

She'd never really seen one of those: in her day they didn't have them, and her kids had no good reason to show them to her. She'd seen them only in movies. But this wasn't real either, she thought; this was also just a picture, like on TV. Still, she felt embarrassed, as though she'd seen them having sex, real sex between two people having unphotogenic intercourse. She was alone with that stick, with only the iPhone screen between her and the smell of urine.

She felt old. Old and fat. And she realized it was not only embarrassment that made her body contract, it was also her giantness that she wanted to reduce. She was too crude for this moment, which was all fresh and pure, even though Avishay was dead.

She ran her finger over the screen, scrolling back through the conversation, trying to drown her thoughts in nosiness, in curiosity, in some quality that might be ugly but was universally human and not unique to her in any way. But the exchanges were impenetrable: "I'm full of surprises." "Smiley face?!" "Crossed," with three exclamation points and a smiley face. Who was saying what? Which was Avishay and which was Liat? And some of it was Yehuda, too, she remembered. She was too agitated to follow, searching in a panic for an unequivocal message or a solution, but none of that existed, people didn't talk that way on the phone, they talked the way they talked.

She took the phone to the living room and called Zohara from the landline. She just had time to think: Maybe I'd better not. But the need to gossip outweighed the compassion, and besides, it was better for Zohara to hear it from her.

"You're not going to believe this," she said.

"What?" Zohara asked.

"No, you will not believe it. I'm still in shock. You won't believe what I just went through."

"Nili, you're scaring me!"

"No, no, no one died or anything. I mean, no one else died." She wondered if she should skip to the end or give Zohara the full account. "I'm here in Avishay's living room," she began.

"Yes?"

"And suddenly there's a knock at the door."

"No!" Zohara cried.

"Yes. And I'm stunned! I'm like, what do I do now?"

"So? So?"

"So I open the door, and there's a girl standing there. She's maybe thirty-eight, something like that, and she's looking for Avishay."

"Who was it? Did she say?"

"Hang on. So I start giving her some story—he's not here, he's writing a paper, I'm watching his apartment, don't ask."

"Did she say why she wanted him?"

"Hang on. So anyway, I told her to text him, that he's getting text messages, and the second I shut the door I hear his phone beep, she sent him a message. And you know what the message was?"

"Go on!"

"A photo of a pregnancy test. With two stripes."

"What do you mean?" Zohara asked.

"What do you mean, what do I mean? What do you think I mean?"

"Okay, but whose is it? His?"

"What do you think?" Nili said.

"I don't know! Who is this girl anyway? Why would she be pregnant by Avishay?"

"Why would she be pregnant by Avishay? Because she slept with Avishay, that's why. In that sense it's not the most shocking thing I've ever heard. Did he want it? That's a different question. Probably not."

"I'm in shock," Zohara said.

"Although," Nili mused, "you don't send someone a picture of a pregnancy test if you think it will upset the other person, do you?"

"I don't think we can assume it's Avishay's."

"Well, look, we're not going to give this baby the million kronor before we make sure, right? But what other reason could she have to send him a picture of a pregnancy test? He's not her father."

"Maybe he's a friend of hers?" Zohara wondered.

"Maybe . . ."

"Look, I'm about to go into a meeting, I'll call you later, okay?"

"A meeting? Now?"

"What can I do, this woman can only meet on Fridays. I'll talk to you afterwards, okay?"

"Wait a minute," Nili said, "what am I going to tell her? You have to help me."

"Nili, she's already here, talk to Yehuda or something. I have to go."

Nili stood in the living room cradling the phone under her neck, unsatisfied. It was too bad Zohara wouldn't tell her the truth. She could have come over, they could have talked. More than anyone else, she wanted to talk with Zohara.

Maybe she wasn't sensitive enough. Maybe. But Zohara hadn't told her anything about it, not ever. And that was annoying. Still, she deserved compassion. Precisely because of that, she deserved it. She probably didn't want to mull over another loss with her friend, to give form and volume and validity to yet another failure. Nili had to go easy on her, not keep score.

She wondered whom to call: Yehuda or Amos? Or maybe Nathan?

Just to talk, to offload some guilt and tension. She felt like calling Amos, who had kids and a wife and a normal family, whom you could talk to about something like this and he would know what to say. Certainly more than Yehuda, who she sometimes thought was stuck in his family like a shipwrecked survivor on a desert island, waving at his previous life, or perhaps at the next one. But she suspected this wasn't about Amos being the right man for the job: she was sheltering under a feeble excuse to squeeze out an intimate conversation with him, just to restore a little of her dignity. Not that Amos treated her disrespectfully, of course. On the contrary: he gave her too much respect. With Yehuda, with Zohara, with Avishay, he had real relationships. And only she sat there untouched, like garnish, a piece of scaffolding on the pentagon and no more.

She was actually fond of Amos. Very fond. He had a dry, witty sense of humor, the same sense of humor mistakenly attributed to Avishay and never to him, as though it had been stolen away from him and given to his friend, as though there couldn't be two of them. It made Nili want to see justice done in this regard, precisely because Amos accepted his fate with such resignation. Also, they'd met just after his little brother, Arnon, had been killed in the Six-Day War, and Nili could never forget that. Even though he never talked about his brother, not even when he named his son after him.

She used to think he would sense her affection and that would be enough. But it wasn't, and Nili wasn't used to that. She didn't understand why not, but all her attempts to find out led nowhere, only buried her deeper and deeper. She voiced the suspicion that it was because he was attracted to her, but she secretly suspected something different: she tried to win him over with a sort of shared bourgeois sensibility, precisely the sensibility she mocked herself for at every opportunity. But in his company she allowed herself to shed a layer, admitting—with relief—its pleasures, and Nili thought he saw through her, that he saw what he wrongly perceived as hypocrisy or dishonesty, even though in fact it was just complexity.

Sometimes she thought he suspected her—as she herself did—of having snuck into this gang because of their kindness, by mistake. That she had to prove herself, to pass a test whose nature she could only guess at—and she hadn't guessed, and she hadn't passed it.

She found Yehuda's number in the iPhone and dialed it from the landline. He said, "Woah, you have no idea what it's like to get a phone call from Avishay's number," and Nili said, "I'm sorry, I didn't mean to give you a heart attack."

"What's up? How's it going?"

"You're not going to believe this."

"What happened?"

"No, you seriously won't believe this. I'm still in shock. You will not believe what I just went through."

"Tell me already."

———

"Yehuda?" she said.

"I don't know what to say. Is this sinking in for you?"

"It's starting to."

"What are we going to do?"

"First of all, I think we have reply to her message. It's been . . . twenty-one minutes."

"It took you twenty-one minutes to call me?" Yehuda said.

"I was in shock, what do you expect."

"So what do we say? I'm not good at these things. I spent an hour phrasing a text message about the dates for a conference I had to get back to someone about."

"All right," Nili said, "we'll figure this out together, it's not that complicated. What if we just say 'Congratulations' with three exclamation points? Keep it simple. Simple might be the best route here."

"But if it's his, it'll sound a little ridiculous for him to say congratulations, won't it? When you told Ram you were pregnant, did he say congratulations?"

"*If* it's his?"

"Well, we can't be sure. What do we know? We don't know the first thing about this girl."

"Even so," Nili insisted.

"All right, I agree with you, don't get me wrong, chances are it's his. But still."

"Okay, so what did Ram say when I told him I was pregnant . . . ?"

"No, forget it, that's no help. I just thought back to what I said to Idit, it's not the same as a pregnancy test by text message."

Neither of them spoke for a moment. Finally Nili said, "Could you come over here? We'll look at it on the screen together, it's easier to find the right words that way. Also, I could use the company."

"I can't, Nili, I'm sorry. Idit's going away tomorrow and the girls are coming over. But we'll solve this in two seconds, don't worry. Why don't we write, 'You've made me happy'? That's not bad, I think."

"Not bad. Not bad at all. But I'll tell you the problem: if it's not his, or if somehow this ends up in litigation—and if he wins the prize, that could happen—then I think saying something like that is like acknowledging paternity. It's tricky, this whole business, we have to be very careful."

"Nili, you're a genius."

"Thank you, thank you."

"Maybe 'Amazing'?" Yehuda suggested.

"Um, no. You know what? Okay, this is it, I have it."

"Nili, I love you, go on."

"Wow, I really am a genius."

"Go on already!"

"I won't write anything. I'll just put a whole bunch of those emoticons—party, celebration, fireworks, all that. From the iPhone. It doesn't mean anything anyway, I use them all the time."

"It doesn't mean he's happy?"

"It means he's happy in a general sense, it attests to a noncommittal sort of cheerfulness. I don't think a court would award paternity based on an emoticon of a clown hat with confetti."

"That's it, then."

"Okay, I'm going to send it. Wish me luck. But if she writes back, I'm calling you again, I'm telling you that right now."

"Good luck," Yehuda said, "and it's fine, I'm available all day."

10

She sat down in the TV armchair, iPhone in hand and landline beside her, ready to advance any scenario without having to get up. But Liat didn't respond, even though Nili stared at the screen for several minutes.

It would probably be her only child, she thought. She wouldn't have time to have others, she'd be too busy bringing him up. Too busy bringing him up alone. At least he was Avishay's—one could certainly do worse, Nobel or no Nobel.

Perhaps they should help raise him? Like the grandparents when the father is killed at war. She tried to figure out how that would work, how it would assimilate in their lives. Another grandchild. Good God. They wouldn't take him to the movies or that kind of thing—that would be too weird, and they didn't have time anyway, with all their personal grandchildren. Maybe Zohara? She could be a sort of paternal grandmother. She might like that. The question was whether Liat would like it. If she'd agree. They seemed so peculiar now, she and Zohara and Amos and Yehuda, with this whole week they'd put together, all the bizarre conversations they were having, that she found it hard to believe a healthy young woman would want them in her life. But the truth is that they were perfect grandparents. The best. They didn't shove candy at the kids and drag them to the public square to play. And they were good people, educated, completely normal. That was something she had to remember: only good, educated, normal people would embark on this adventure, daring to do something abnormal for ten days.

She tried to drop the job in Zohara's lap, to let everyone else off the hook, but it didn't look right. This boy needed a slightly more mischievous influence than Zohara in his life, and she could see herself volunteering: *I'm here whenever you need me, Liat.* Maybe even: *Liat, to me this boy is like another grandchild. You can count on me, even if you just want to spend an afternoon out with a friend; that's a no-less-sacred purpose to me than working or grocery shopping. You know what? Even more so.* She was bothered by how naturally this monologue came to her, the strange honesty it embodied as soon as it was uttered, even though she wanted nothing of all that. It was a good thing she'd found the text message alone, that she had time to control the situation, to practice.

She'd like the child to come to their lunches every so often. Yes, that would be nice. She wanted to be invited to his bar mitzvah. She wanted to know what this person Avishay had created was like, what interested him and what he liked, but without working hard at it. She wanted to be invited to class plays, to his polished performances. And she'd be willing to give him the occasional piece of advice, especially when he got older.

She thought about Nathan. He'd once said something similar: If you could get the child ready-made, cooked through, talking and with a personality, then he might want children. But you couldn't.

That reassured her at certain moments and to a certain extent: he didn't want children, he'd never wanted them, and so he could allow himself to date a woman his own age. A fat woman his own age. He was confident, that was true. He had the self-confidence of good kids. She knew them well, she remembered them from her youth: nice young Jerusalem kids, smart ones, who didn't give a fuck; who looked at her and immediately saw the groovy Nili. Was that even something people said anymore—*groovy*? But she didn't care, she wouldn't say it out loud anyway. It was thanks to those kids that she'd done well even though she was slightly fat. She used to repeat the word back then: *fat*. And she still did it, to preempt the slanderers, and to accentuate a certain quality she possessed, a charm that could not be named but which overpowered any physical attribute.

After the divorce she'd headed out into the world with measured confidence. It had been almost forty years since—well, since anything, really. But people didn't change, she knew that, and she always said, especially to Zohara: *It has nothing to do with wrinkles or the outer shell. Attraction is like a piece of your personality. People are as attracted as they are and as attractive as they are until the day they die, or as unattractive as they are. In that sense I'm glad I've always been a bit fat, that I've never depended on that side of things, you see?* And when she felt anxious—not about being naked, lying next to a new man, and all that, but anxious about herself when she was fully dressed, living as she did, eating as she did—she thought she may never eat with a man again the way she ate with herself.

Here and there it got to sex, albeit bad sex, but mostly it didn't work out. She was surprised to discover that it was generally easy to get to sex, even with men who probably didn't think she was their type, and if truth be told they weren't hers either. And from the moment she understood that, she stopped. And she started acting like a prudish aunt, the female equivalent of the serious, moralistic, horny men who looked at her indifferently.

She fell upon any article that dealt with the topic: advice columns, confessionals in women's magazines, documentary films and even romantic comedies, all of which discussed how difficult it was to find a second—or third—love after divorce. And how much harder it was after a certain age. She read and watched all these very deliberately, as if wanting to give them her own voice, to seek shelter in the crowd of ordinary, normal women who were no better at it than she was. Besides, sometimes she didn't even want it. More than sometimes. There were men who wanted her, or might have wanted her, but she explicitly did not want them.

Yet still she had the feeling that everyone around her thought it was because of her weight. They didn't say anything, they weren't crazy, but that only incensed her: she couldn't even brush them off and correct their mistake. And the more she herself suspected that perhaps her weight was the problem, the angrier she became at the people who didn't believe her, who didn't buy it—men with confidence wanted her, they always had, despite her weight—and the burden of proof became heavier, more urgent. Nili found herself sometimes telling only fragments of things, keeping some of the puzzle pieces to herself. The main gist was still there and that's what mattered: Had anything come out of it or not? It's not like she was lying.

The evidence was in Nathan, who turned up at the end, like a blunder, like an alien. He simply wanted her, period, as if they'd forgotten to tell him the rules—*Oh, you're supposed to not want her? I didn't know that. But why not?* And ever since, she'd been searching and searching: Was he a good boy? Yes or no? And if not, what was his problem?

She interrogated him a little, or a lot, about other women he'd been with. She tried to disguise it as the usual line of questioning rather than an attempt to uncover the only thing she was interested in: Were they fat? Her secret was her confidence, and she knew that if she exposed her weakness she wouldn't be able to hide it again, but she wasn't used to these investigations—*tell me something about your previous relationships*—and felt like a character on TV, childish and silly, and so eventually she just asked and it all came out.

He didn't like thin women, he said. She already knew that, and she believed it, but his other women had been reasonably sized. Maybe a little overweight, but not as fat as she was. She was troubled by the idea that she was the extreme version of his fetish. Why did he want her, she wondered. And when she answered, *Because I'm stunning, because I'm amazing, why wouldn't he want me, anyone who doesn't want me is an idiot*, she felt like a photocopied note in a fortune cookie. She didn't believe herself, only him. Still, she was reluctant to ask too much, so as not to give him any ideas.

Sometimes she thought: Maybe I'm just really good at sex. It was true, she knew she was, but how good could she be—good enough to make up for an extra seventy pounds? What did someone have to do in bed to make up for seventy pounds? Whatever it was, she definitely wasn't doing it.

He might still want kids, too. Avishay hadn't wanted them, and now look. If you gave things enough time they sometimes changed. Or maybe Avishay had always wanted children? She couldn't remember if they'd ever talked about it. She felt very guilty, realizing they might not have. Had she been too self-centered? Had she not listened to him? She'd always treated him like the mature Don Juan who'd escaped all that—the diapers and the worries and the burden and the heaviness, even though it was slightly put on, of course, because only someone who had all that could describe it as a burden. She started to feel that she was a horrible person, completely lacking in self-awareness. The way she put on that show every time one of her kids rang: *Believe me, Avishay, you should be counting your lucky stars.*

For the first time since he'd died, she felt genuine panic. She wanted to talk to him, to find out if she really had been like that, even only sometimes, and if so, to ask for his forgiveness, to show him she knew, that she'd figured it out herself before being reprimanded, before being reproved—and now she would never know. Or he would never know.

More than anything else, she wanted him to comfort her. She wanted him to say: *What nonsense, Nili, seriously, stop rambling. What are we friends for? To pat each other on the back or to really talk? You keep saying whatever you want to say, and I'll keep saying whatever I want to say, and if you take that away from me and start analyzing our relationship I'll walk away, understood?* And Nili would smile through the tears that might be rolling down her cheeks, and she would feel delicate and vindicated, and she would say, *Understood.*

═══

For a brief, terrible moment after they got divorced, it seemed as though Avishay might be about to become a close friend of her ex-husband. Ram was a sound engineer who consulted for opera houses around the world, and he was always brimming with irresistible stories. Since retiring, he was very proud of the work he did, sometimes pro bono, in third-world countries, and when he talked about it he got very serious. This always made Nili laugh, or at least it made her laugh as much as one was allowed to laugh at such things: the way he presented himself as a savior of the underdeveloped continent, when in fact no one gave a crap about an opera house in Sudan.

Avishay had always liked Ram, probably because of the sound engineering and the opera stuff. Avishay admired people who had managed to beat him at having a good life and a sense of mystique. But at some point he caught on to the fact that Ram was a bit of a good boy, which happened when Nili told him about her affair, maybe ten years after the fact.

She was working at a clinic in Beit Ha'Kerem at the time. She and Ram had a good relationship, a friendly one, with minor crushes once in a while that they did nothing about, without any attraction at all and with almost no sex. No-attraction-and-no-sex which they

made fun of for a while, slathered it over with self-awareness, and
remembered it mostly when they saw older couples talking about
sex or having it on TV, at which point they would disappear into the
kitchen to get a snack.

The truth was, Nili couldn't exactly say if that was the way it
was then, when she was forty-eight or forty-nine and had the affair, but that's the way it was afterward, for so many years, until
the divorce. The only period Nili could clearly distinguish from
that silt of no-sex was their first five years together, when they'd
smoked a lot of pot and not done much else—or at least that's
how she remembered things. Then the children were born, and in
the thirty-eight years since then she'd smoked pot twice and said
"pot" maybe ten times, on each of which she'd felt like a ridiculous
ten-thousand-year-old great aunt.

Anyway, it was at the Beit Ha'Kerem clinic where she met Avi. He
was around her age, a divorced father of a five-year-old autistic boy.
She liked him immediately, it was one of those things. He sat in her
office for ten minutes and that's all it took: she knew she was done
for. He was from her production line, limited edition, the kind that
if you're lucky you find more than once in a lifetime—or maybe if
you're unlucky.

She felt immature and spoiled, and spent a whole day feeling terribly guilty: of course she, with her healthy children and her perfect
life, could afford to fantasize about a love like that. But he had other
things to worry about. He clearly had a difficult life. When you have
an autistic child, you don't think about things like that.

But the next day he came back, alone, and it turned out she was
wrong; it turned out you do. She remembered that lesson very
clearly for the rest of her life: you *always* think about things like that.

———

Ten years later, when she picked Ram up at the airport, even before they'd left the parking lot, he told her he was in love with a
costume designer from the Luxembourg National Theatre. He said
they hadn't done anything—that went without saying—and they
wouldn't until after the divorce. And then it dawned on her that he'd
never cheated on her, in all those trips and all the opera houses, all
the long years of no-sex, he'd just gone without.

She was convinced they'd had an unspoken agreement, on the
basis of which she had assuaged her horrible guilt about Avi—it
had been short, she didn't really want to live with the father of an
autistic child, but it had happened—and about the long years of
not-telling that had followed. Ten years of tempered shame filled
her all at once, as well as intense anger at Ram. To get back at herself, and at him, she told him about Avi. "I thought you were sleeping around too," she explained defensively, and he said, "What sort
of reason is that? What sort of relationship is it when everyone as-
sumes everyone is lying?" And she didn't know what to say.

Afterward, the Luxembourger didn't want him anymore, but they
felt too empty with each other, too embarrassed to keep going even
if they'd wanted to. They separated unconfidently, clumsily, like two
pimply teenagers who break up instead of going to the movies. Their
children simply could not understand what was happening and what
they wanted, and even though Nili used to mock them for being too
conventional, in this case they couldn't be blamed.

———

She knew Avishay so well: when she told him she had cheated on
Ram, a long time ago, she could actually see the minuscule change
flickering in his eye as he suddenly came to understand something
about her that he hadn't before, about her power relations with this

world, about how she was the one putting herself out there, searching, not settling, and not only with Ram but generally in life, even
though she was fat.

That was when Avishay and Ram were starting to get friendly,
right after the divorce. Nili didn't object—not that anyone asked
her—because she was afraid of Ram being lonely, especially after
he'd been rejected by the Luxemburg costumer designer and seemed
so helpless. She knew it would be good for Avishay: he needed an
audience, but a high-quality one, and Ram was perfect. So she did
everything she could to encourage the friendship, but it didn't take,
maybe because it was hard to start a new friendship at sixty. When
it dwindled, she was so grateful that she compensated Avishay with
her own friendship.

It worked well for her: Avishay was the only one she could talk to
properly about relationships, the only one who was, like her, completely available. Zohara was available too, but she was the eternal
advice-seeker, and Nili had been trapped in the role of adviser for
too many years.

Of the four of them, Avishay was the only one who believed
her. That was how she felt. The only one who believed that people
wanted her, who believed that Nathan wanted her. Maybe because
he had it too, that thing that draws people to you regardless of how
you look. She thought they were similar thanks to that, maybe the
most similar of the five, and that they were better than the others
because of it. Not that Avishay would have dreamed of going near a
fat woman, nor did he pretend he would. But he got it, he felt it, he
knew there was something he might not understand but it clearly
existed, a parallel universe of attraction. Sometimes it seemed to her
that everyone else was just waiting for Nathan to be exposed as a
pervert.

She felt comfortable with Avishay when she was eating, too,

even though he was a vegan; not like with Yehuda, who glared at her food as though he couldn't look away from the horror. Perhaps because she and Avishay judged each other only by one criterion—love, relationships, sex—and in that domain she could always deliver the goods. It followed that, according to their rules, she was allowed to eat freely. She had earned the right.

Only occasionally, when Avishay hotly denounced another rejection she'd been dealt, did she consider the strange nature of their friendship: endless empathy for the unwanted one, even though in fact you were endlessly sympathetic toward the one who didn't want.

Sometimes she felt like asking him about Zohara. Not that she needed explanations; that relationship was so transparent, so obvious as to be insulting, to everyone except Zohara—or maybe to her, too. But she had a desire to conquer that stronghold, which Avishay shared only with Yehuda. True, Yehuda had told her, but it had left a bad taste in her mouth; she wanted Avishay to tell her everything. She wanted him to be unable, in that respect, to resist her.

Sometimes, when she spent time with Zohara, she felt like asking Avishay: Why not? What was wrong with Zohara? Why did he think he was better than that? She thought he was wrong, that he gave himself the wrong reasons. But when she moved back into his orbit she would get infected by the cheerfulness again, by the feverishness— the two of us understand these things better than anyone else—and betray Zohara without anyone knowing.

———

Ram ended up doing fine. He didn't say anything—he was discreet even when there was nothing to tell, which might have been what misled her, and he remained discreet now, when there was something to tell—but she picked up on it. She had the impression that she had opened up his sex chakra herself when she'd been so astonished to learn that he hadn't done anything. It hadn't even occurred to him that it was possible, that he was attractive. For the past few months he'd been dating someone, she knew this from the kids. She was a woman named Talia, she thought, who went by Tul-Tul, and she sounded quite a bit younger than him—Nili was pretty sure the kids were rounding up.

It drove her crazy to hear her children talking about Tul-Tul in her presence, as if forcing Nili to like her. Anyway, Ram and this Tutu woman were now opening a vegan gelateria, of all things— apparently she'd brought him into that fold. Too many people around her were suddenly turning vegan, which was getting on her nerves, but mostly she hoped Ram wasn't putting any money in it— her kids' inheritance—although she strongly suspected he was. Anyway, she reported to Avishay and Yehuda that there would soon be a vegan gelateria so they could stop whining, even though the truth was that they didn't whine at all, and to be honest they didn't seem all that thrilled by the news.

Avishay's iPhone jumped on the armrest. The screen turned on, displaying the message she'd sent. It took her a minute to realize there was another one. Liat had answered: a pair of young women dancing in black ballet clothes, twice; a girl in a red dress baring her leg, twice; the obligatory confetti hat; two hands high-fiving each other; three hand-claps.

Good God, she thought, *I hope the boy doesn't come out a moron.*

11

She felt like ordering some food, but she didn't want anyone to ring the doorbell again. She went into the kitchen. On the edge of the countertop was the open bag of cookies Yehuda had bought yesterday, standing upright. But when her hand invaded it, the bag surrendered and flopped onto its belly like an obedient dog, or a corpse.

She opened the fridge and was struck by its contents: red, green, and yellow peppers, beets, custard apples, eggplants, grapes, and cherry tomatoes, all uncovered and inviting, obviously washed, not like at her place, where vegetables went to die. They seemed impudently alive, defiantly so. Like a public service announcement for healthy nutrition, with its five, or nine—she'd stopped counting—colors. Like those posters they used to put up at the children's clinic in the seventies. The opposite of a bachelor's fridge—or rather, a childless divorcé's. Avishay would not be eating those vegetables, unfortunately for them. Or fortunately.

She leaned over into the light and cold of the refrigerator and just stood there for a moment or two, the way she sometimes fell asleep on the toilet in the middle of the night. She felt as though the chill were coming from the apartment while the open fridge blew a living, tropical warmth on her, and if she closed it she would be permanently sucked back into the world of the dead.

She was hungry. She tried to focus on that, roused herself, and slammed the door shut. She moved on to the cabinet drawers: the

top ones held silverware, parchment paper and sandwich bags,
sealed packets of tissues, dish towels, and batteries. Next came
plates, bowls, dishes, and mugs. She roamed down to the dry
goods. She'd almost lost hope, but then she opened the bottom
drawer, next to the Tupperware. Every kid's favorite junk food
was in there: snack-size bags of Bamba, chocolate bars, packets of
lemon-flavored wafers, a family-size bag of Bugles, all looking back
at her with the satisfied glee of a child hiding from his parents: *Did
you really think we wouldn't be here?*

She fished out a Kit Kat, peeled off the wrapping, and ate it standing up, hurriedly, not breaking it into fingers but just biting straight
into it, like food. When she'd finished, she shoved the wrapper in her
pocket. She looked at the open drawer. There was another Kit Kat,
but she didn't want it.

She discovered that she was breathing deeply, that she was happy.
She tried to isolate her pleasure at the unexpected company offered
by that drawer, to push it aside. She was almost full just from the
comforting discovery: Avishay was like her. Sometimes he needed
it, it couldn't be helped, that's how human beings were. He caged
his vice in a little drawer, he obviously snacked alone, in secret, but
he did snack, because that's how it had to be—a little outlet, a tiny
blemish, a faded stain of trans fat, tracked like fingerprints.

She felt like calling someone to share the exciting discovery,
but she quickly realized that all she would expose was her own
greediness—what was she so excited about? So she shut the drawer
with her foot. She didn't need any more now; she could resist. A
strange feeling came over her, a sort of condescending toward the
dead: at this particular moment she was better than him, that was
a fact. Her life was spread out before her, she could still change, she
could be bad if she felt like it, or good.

She leaned against the counter and tried to study this insight.

She had the feeling, again, that something was slipping between her fingers. Since Avishay's death, she'd felt gripped by a sense of urgency to learn from it about his life, and about her own. A sense that she should not be left without him yet with nothing else. That she should live a better life from now on, for his sake, or on his behalf, and not repeat his mistakes. That she should get the message. But every avenue for doing that seemed even more pathetic than the last, like those empowering interviews with terminally ill patients. What was she supposed to learn—that life was short? She knew that. Or maybe she didn't. She knew it as well as anyone could, and more than that was impossible. That you should live each day as if it were your last? She could not conceive of anything worth doing on her last day other than eating well. And she was already doing that, thereby assiduously diminishing the number of days she had left.

She let her head fall onto the counter and the thoughts fall like dandruff. Then she straightened up, stretched out her arms, and looked around for something to focus on. In the corner, where the marble met the wooden counter, lay a stack of mail. There was a large brown envelope at the bottom, which she pulled out. She suddenly knew she was about to discover something about Avishay; something that had to do with sex, because what else was there? They did talk about sex a fair amount, but not in that way, not like that, they talked about it theoretically. She carefully opened the envelope and pulled out a colorful catalog. She was so prepared that it took her a moment to understand: it was a Lego catalog. He's a pedophile, she thought. Avishay is a pedophile. Why else would a seventy-year-old man order a Lego catalog? She pictured a cellar full of Lego, a torture cellar of Lego. But Avishay didn't have a cellar, and then she understood: it's for his sister's grandchildren. He wasn't a pedophile, he was just a normal great-uncle. That was the momentous discovery. She almost laughed, but a moment later she felt surprisingly insulted: He was a normal uncle who bought Lego, gave gifts, planned ahead, ordered things, except he didn't do it for *their* kids. He hadn't when they were little, and he didn't do it now, for the grandchildren—they barely existed for him. But Ruthi's grandkids did. So what if she was his sister? Then another insult hit her: he was closer to Ruthi than he'd told them. She was taking up space, at their expense. At hers—who else's?

She opened the drawer and took out the Bugles—she didn't even know they came in a family-size bag. The drawer was less crowded with the bag gone, and the scene now looked familiar: chocolate bars, wafers, lots of snack-size Bamba. It was the snack drawer. For the grandkids.

=====

She raked over the rest of the mail, as if wishing to dilute her insult in bills, but the print looked so small, and then she realized it was dark. She opened the blinds but the darkness remained: it was evening. What time was it?

She turned on the lights in the kitchen and then moved to the living room, turning on every light she could find, hunting for switches under unnecessary lampshades. She went into the hallway and stopped outside Avishay's closed bedroom door. What was best in there—light or dark?

She opened the door a crack but immediately shut it as if bit by the darkness. She couldn't sleep there. Where would she sleep? In the living room? The study? Could she sleep in this apartment at all, with Avishay's body? She'd never fall asleep. She couldn't. No one could. What would she do all night? She felt like going out, to a café or maybe even to catch a movie. She felt like staying in a hotel. Being a stranger in the city, a tourist. But she couldn't. She mustn't. It would be irresponsible. She had to stay.

She felt imprisoned: her friends had locked her in there, precisely because of such thoughts. What could she have to do out there, anyway? Then what did she care? And now it was her and Avishay, the living against the dead, a duel that would be decided by morning.

She got up and headed to the front door. On the way she remembered that she had opened it today, for Liat—she wasn't trapped at all. Still, she walked over and opened it and shut it, opened and shut it again, then another time, as though greasing an axle, or perhaps hoping for a passerby. Finally she shut the door quickly and turned the latch to lock it.

She sat down in the living room with her back to the wall, her eyes roaming over the expanse, the dining area and the living room and the front door. No one could enter Avishay's room without her noticing, or leave it.

She went into the kitchen again and opened the drawer. She took out two little packets of Bamba, and pretzels, and Cheetos, even though she hated them—anything crunchy. She left the quiet, sweet things in the drawer.

She went back to the couch. She opened the pretzels and rummaged wildly inside the bag, her hand hitting the sides, the way one wouldn't even eat alone at home, hoping the plastic rustle had the power to banish someone, or perhaps to confirm her existence.

She picked up the cell phone, flipped through messages and emails and unanswered calls. Someone probably needed her, but no one was waiting for her to respond, to finally pick up.

Her eyes fell on the last message from Liat: dancing girls in black ballet clothes, a woman in a red dress with a bared leg, a confetti hat, high-fiving hands. She scrolled up through the thread. Her message was there, and the picture of the pregnancy test, and then, "I'm full of surprises." Who wrote that? Avishay; green was Avishay. And then "Smiley face?!"—that was Liat—and "Fingers crossed!!! ☺," and she wondered if all text message threads sounded so odd when they were read backwards, or maybe when they were read at all. She wondered what hers and Nathan's looked like. But she and Nathan didn't text, it was all on WhatsApp. Avishay wasn't on WhatsApp with anyone except them, he thought it was beneath him, that it was vulgar, and it suddenly occurred to her to check the date. October 10. So all of that had been sent by Yehuda—honestly, what an idiot he was, or what an idiot she was. She flipped to the end of another thread: "I'm outside"—Avishay. "Tomorrow at 3, Café Landwer. He was plotting to get us into his office, but I insisted politely on Tel Aviv"—that was Avishay too, it sounded like him. She scrolled further. Liat said, "Let's drop tomorrow morning," and then, "Wait—I might have a solution," and then, "Can you do Tuesday at 12:30?" What a bore. Avishay wrote, "Yes, let him know we've set a time and that's it. Don't give him a way out."

Was this how a couple in love corresponded? Did a couple in love correspond at all? She went into her and Nathan's WhatsApp thread. "Cilantro and parsley?" "Yes" "Ff" "???" "Mistake" "At least I took back the sauce." She scrolled up, looking for some small sign of affection, which had suddenly become important, in between the "I'll call soon" and "He's not taking the kids" and "Take a pic for Yehuda to make him happy" and "Never mind, we'll wait, no point going up" and "Should I use the famous joke? Then come alone . . ." She was suddenly filled with a deep sense of meaninglessness by these pieces of sentences and fragments of jokes. This was something one should not be allowed to read that way, it should be illegal, it was a fun-house mirror of relationships.

She scrolled all the way through Liat and Avishay, dancing girls in black ballet clothes, a woman in a red dress baring her leg, confetti hat. And besides, who said they were a couple in love? It was more likely that they'd entered a co-parenting agreement, and the office they'd mentioned was probably a lawyer's.

Maybe Liat was waiting for an answer?

Nili tapped the box and the keyboard popped up. She wrote:

"Are you happy?" Then she erased it. "Excited?" She erased that, too. She twisted her body into an impossible angle to make sure Avishay's door was still shut, as though sending messages in his name might tickle him out of death.

You free now?

she typed, and hit "Send." Liat answered immediately:

Yes!

And a second later,

Didn't want to disturb before, I understand you're disconnected for work. Should I call?

Nili panicked:

Can't talk now, only text.

Liat replied:

No problem. So what do you say? We did well, right?

We did well. Maybe she was just an old soul. "Definitely," she wrote, and then changed it to, "Absolutely," but she erased that, too. They were supposed to not admit to paternity or something—it had all been so clear to her just a few hours ago: they would tell her this, but not that, all sharp and correct, she'd cover his body with her own if she had to. But now it all seemed so pointless, the night had diluted her determination, restrained her logic, or perhaps lack thereof. "We did well? You did—" but before she could finish, another message came in from Liat:

Not that we have time to think about it. I'm telling you already, it's too late.

Then another one:

Nothing in the second part changed, so I didn't send it.

What the hell was she talking about? Nili waited, maybe she would just text back and forth with herself, this Liat, text and text and text, that would be the most convenient. But Liat was silent for a while, and then she sent a "?" Nili quickly typed: "We did it? You did it!" but that seemed so stupid that she erased it and inserted a smiley face and sent it without thinking. Maybe Yehuda wasn't so dumb after all. Liat wrote back: "I'm glad to see you're in a good mood," and Nili wrote, "Why not?" but then changed it to "Why wouldn't I be?" and then changed it to "Aren't you?" and sent it. A moment later Liat answered: "Super stressed and super excited." Nili wrote back, "Obviously," and Liat wrote, "Anyway, I'm saying this again: if you change your mind, at any stage, that won't be a problem for me," and a moment later she added, "For us." Nili waited: if she didn't send something else now she'd kill herself, and Liat was silent and Nili thought that was it, but after a few moments she sent a long message: "The money is one thing, but the whole thing about down the line feeling that you want to be involved—feel free. Worst case, we don't accept your opinion, no harm done. Forget the contract, you know we're not going by contracts here. As far as we're concerned, the contract doesn't exist. Honestly. Irrelevant."

So he'd made a child by contract. At least she knew that now. But what contract? What should she say now? Did he want to be involved or didn't he? How should she know? And really, what difference did it make? Involved was not something he could be anymore.

She simply had to write like Avishay would. That's all she had to do now. Other than that, she could say anything. But how did Avishay write? She tried to picture him lying in the next room, for inspiration. Then she tried to bring him alive. But the Avishay she managed to erect, with some effort, was slightly feeble, and he looked at her indifferently.

She felt suddenly furious. He'd abandoned her. He'd simply abandoned her. Not in his death, but much earlier. He was supposed to be her mentor in this next life of hers, the second one, the one after kids and births. He was supposed to take her in his hand and lead her into his life, the good life she wanted to have. They'd made a deal, and he'd reneged: he'd let her talk and tell him things, he'd laughed and nodded and told her some things about himself, but all that time he was digging a tunnel in the opposite direction, to escape from this life, to have a child at the age of seventy, for God's sake.

Maybe that was the message, the thing he'd bequeathed her when he'd died: that it was all about that. That children were the thing. They were the thing and nothing could replace it, and there was no getting around it in the end. Kids were the point of life.

Was that it? she wanted to ask, but Avishay's expression shifted around in her mind like that magic sand kids play with, and it finally steadied into mockery. Do you really think so?

Two chirps announced a new message: "Okay." Nili had almost forgotten about Liat. Okay what? She read her last message again, the one she hadn't answered, but it was still impenetrable. Was it an "Okay" to start wrapping up the conversation? Or was it an "Okay?" She liked communicating this way, on WhatsApp, or text messaging, with everyone. She never called anyone anymore, and she bad-mouthed people who called her—it was practically rude to call someone these days, a real invasion of privacy. Yet now she felt completely alien to this thing, as though she'd been dead for a hundred years and woken up in a new universe, with no punctuation or tone and without ever knowing if someone had finished talking or was only starting. Anyway, she had to write something back.

What would Avishay write? But she couldn't write like him. Texting like someone else was like imitating someone else masturbating. She didn't have to write like Avishay, she suddenly realized. What's the worst that could happen? Would Liat think that Avishay was dead and they were hiding it? They were completely protected, at least in that respect. They were protected by the logic, by the normalcy, of every other person, and in fact their own, too. She could write anything, whatever she felt like. So she wrote: "I want to be more involved, you know, I think I do." Why not? What did she care? What test did this have to pass? If ever there were such a thing as idle talk, this was it—why not make Liat happy? So she'd think the child would really have a father, if only for a brief moment. So she could tell him when he grew up: Your father wanted to be involved. Liat wrote, "???!" and a second later, "Since when?!" Then, "Not that it matters, I'm so happy!!!!" Nili wrote, "Me too," and added a smiley face with a little heart in the corner of its mouth, and Liat wrote, "Would you maybe like to come to the opening?" Why not, Nili thought. He could go to the opening, of course he could. "Gladly," she typed, and Liat said, "Great," and then, "Do you want to bring Nili and Yehuda and Amos, or is it not right yet?"

At the sight of her own name she tensed up, paused, and started calculating again: Was there something here she wasn't taking into account? Maybe it could be harmful after all? Perhaps not to their plans, but to this woman? Wasn't this a terrible injustice, to make her happy for no reason? And what later—not tell her that her son's father had died? How could she even be fooling around with something like this? But before she could reply, Liat sent another message: "By the way, I saw her today," and Nili was confused: for a minute she thought they'd seen the baby on an ultrasound, and maybe they somehow already knew it was a girl. "Who?" she wrote, and Liat wrote back: "Your Nili." The words made her smile. *Your Nili.* She was *his* Nili. He was her Avishay, too. Even if he didn't tell her everything, he did talk about her, and she would forgive him, she couldn't even remember for what, and she started writing, "Oh right! She told . . ." when another message popped up: "WTF is up with that?" Nili stopped. She didn't erase anything or write anything or send anything. Liat continued: "I mean, I'm sorry . . ." Nili still didn't answer, and Liat wrote: "She seems lovely . . ." Nili waited for a *but*, but Liat didn't write anything. Nili struggled and finally wrote: "She really is lovely." But as soon as she sent the message, almost instantly, another one came in: "But I mean, it's sick. She looks like a 70 yr old woman but 9 months pregnant. Like a medical miracle." Nili didn't write anything, just fretted that while Liat had been typing she might have missed the writ of defense: *She really is lovely.* A minute later, Liat sent a smiley face.

Saturday

Amos

12

He walked into the bathroom mechanically, even though he didn't need to pee. He opened the medicine cabinet. He was fairly sure he'd never done that before, he'd just seen it in movies. He poked around behind the throat lozenges and Nyquil, but the most interesting thing he could find was Ambien. Something was giving Avishay insomnia, and Amos wondered what it could be. Then again, he took a pill once in a while himself—melatonin, not Ambien—and he didn't have any interesting troubles. That's just the way it was, sometimes people couldn't fall asleep.

Soon he would. Soon Avishay would fall asleep good and proper: there was no better cure for insomnia than a child standing in the way of one's sleep. He was going to start raising a child now. It was inconceivable. Poor man. Life was complicated enough as it was, even after that, even without that, so to start now?

Except that Avishay wasn't going to be a parent. He was dead. Amos almost laughed out loud—a strange, uncoordinated laughter—when he realized he was imagining Avishay alive, helpless but alive, running around being a parent. He'd completely forgotten that Avishay was dead. He'd died just in the nick of time, there was no question.

He rewound the movie to the point where it had frozen in time. What had happened before that? What had happened in their previous life, the one they'd lived with him, before they'd been separated into the dead and the waiting? He would have to

reconsider it: Avishay had wanted children. Definitely. It had preoccupied him. If he'd consulted with Amos, Amos would have
given him an authoritative answer: children do not increase one's
happiness ranking, as any novice researcher of happiness economics could tell him. In fact, according to some studies, they
decrease it. Still, it had clearly bothered him; their absence was
bothersome, no less than their presence.

Amos had children, Avishay didn't. He would have to take comfort in that. But he couldn't.

He'd been planning to talk about it in the lecture. Happiness and
children was a winning topic, always of interest to everyone, certainly at this type of lecture—on the way, in the cab, he looked up
the event listing on the university's website. He reminded himself
not to say anything about Avishay. Nothing about him "sending his
deepest regrets for not being able to be here," nothing about "that
horrible flu that's going around"—he couldn't publicly incriminate
himself. That was what worried him more than anything: the possibility that the day would come, perhaps even tomorrow, when
everything would come out and they would all be a laughingstock.
It would be best if Avishay really did get the Nobel and then they'd
be home free. But when he finally got to the podium and stood there
with three hundred pairs of eyes upon him, and felt the power in
his hands, he had a sudden urge to rebel against the role he'd been
assigned and break all the rules, like a hostage who suddenly spots a
UN force. And so he decided to talk about death. Death and happiness. He decided to scratch the surface of danger, even if it was only
in his own little mind.

He talked about his research, about the uncertainty index, and
offered death as a clear example of the way uncertainty contrib-
utes to the happiness index, allowing all of us to somehow live
even though there is nothing more certain than death itself. "But

let's talk for a moment about what happens after death," he said, "about the certainty and the uncertainty—not of the dead person, at this point"—the audience chuckled—"but of his environment. There seems to be a reversal here, so that while we would expect the finality of death to provide comfort, to be the first step towards recovery, and so forth, in fact that is not the case. Here I refer, among other things, to a relatively new study by Achenbach, who is currently at the center of a very serious polemic among researchers of happiness economics, as well as other fields, because this question naturally concerns issues that are relevant to a great many economic questions today, including on the international level of conflict resolution and so forth. In any case, Achenbach shows that the death of a loved one has an extremely negative effect on the PUI—the Personal Uncertainty Index—and that is despite the certainty of death, right? There's nothing more certain than death . . ."

All at once his own words entered his ears: death is certain. It was as though they'd been picking that lock all this time and had finally managed to break in, fuming over the delay, ready to punch anything they came across, and Amos sensed the same chill he'd felt in Avishay's apartment, and it threatened to kill him, demanding that he disappear or shrink into a corner, that he stop for a moment, that he recognize something. But Amos didn't know what he was supposed to recognize and he didn't want to think about it. Nevertheless, he felt the same tears come to his eyes unwillingly, under duress. No one would suspect anything now, though, and so he said, "Excuse me," and took a sip from the water bottle that had been put out for him, and he cleared his throat even though his voice had been lucid, and he skipped ahead, knowingly creating a hole in the lecture's plotline, but he didn't care because the words in the middle posed a danger. "The question," he said, "is how it affects uncertainty indices in other areas of individual life. Areas that would appear to be unconnected to loss, such as employment, leisure, and even political security and freedom of religion. Surprisingly, certainty increases in these areas, too, with a correlated *decrease* in happiness. That is the paradox of uncertainty. Yes. Now, let us try to explain it." Amos talked on and on, restoring his wits by launching into a marathon of words, and as he spoke he began to wonder if it was even true. He thought he'd been given a unique opportunity in the form of this strange death of Avishay's, which was both certain and uncertain at the same time, a death in serial chapters which would end who-knows-where, a once-in-a-lifetime test case, and he tried to think about his own happiness, or lack thereof, but he couldn't or wouldn't, perhaps in the same way that a doctor or barber were better off not treating themselves.

He closed the medicine cabinet and felt intrusive, even though he hadn't touched anything. He sensed that Avishay knew the truth, that he was following him through his shut eyes but not kicking him out only because he was dead.

He really did not think this whole thing was a good idea. It wasn't "adventurous," it was childish. It was unfeasible, a little stupid, and, if he was being honest, it was dangerous. That's what he thought, honest to God. But at some point during the whole businesslike debate, they'd all been a little bit against it and a little bit for it, and he'd suddenly felt as though all eyes were upon him: he was naked, completely exposed, transparently pathetic, and a bad friend. Do you want Avishay to get the Nobel or not? Or rather: Okay, you want him to, we all do, but how hard are you willing to try to make it happen? That's the question. Yes, that sounds more like it: We all want him to get the Nobel, that goes without saying. But friendship is measured by effort, by creativity, by hard work. It's easy to just want something. And whether or not he was imagining it, Amos became determined at that moment to compensate, to compensate urgently, excessively, and to prove—mostly to himself—that he wasn't like that. Because he wasn't. Not at all.

He realized, too late, that in his rush to compensate, to disprove his culpability, he'd missed the easy way out that had been right in front of his eyes the whole time: he had something to lose and they didn't. He was an academic, the Nobel was a part of his life. He wasn't a bored retiree or a bored millionaire. In fact, he wasn't bored at all. He'd chosen the wrong line of defense. But by the time he came to his senses the decision had been made. Any late attempt to retreat, any hint of opposition or evidence of sabotage, would weigh down the wrong side of the scales and tip them over.

His cell phone was on the kitchen shelf, in a strange location next to a jar of rice; he had to call it from the landline to find it, and even then he had trouble remembering when he'd put it down there, next to Avishay's phone. He'd moved around the apartment all day with the two phones on him at all times, permeated with a sense of ministerial responsibility, and now he wondered when he'd abdicated it and how he could have done it so easily.

He had one unanswered call, from Varda. He tapped in his password to call her back and meanwhile gave Avishay's phone a cursory glance, like a babysitter looking at a sleeping child. But then a loud noise came from the living room, as though someone were trying to open a door, and Amos walked out with the phone, prepared for his suspicion to be disproved, as it had countless times, but the door to Avishay's apartment was open and in the entryway stood a woman. Amos couldn't see her face because she was looking back over her shoulder into her bag, and then she looked up and jumped, let out a quick gasp, and said, "Good God!" with a slight delay, already recognizing him. She closed her eyes as if to settle her nerves, put her hand to her chest, and said, "You scared the hell out of me."

"Ruthi . . ." Amos said. His voice was toneless.

"Amos! I haven't seen you in ages!" She came over to him, patted his belly, and declared, "You should switch to a wheat-free diet."

Amos immediately hated her, and he slightly hated her brother, too, for whom he was doing this whole thing. But he needed her on his side, and all he could think to say was, "Sit down, Ruthi." He watched her march into the depths of the apartment, diminishing the distance between her and her dead brother—*warm, hot, getting hotter, boiling!*—but then she sat down on the couch and said, "What's up? Is everything okay?"

"Yes." He didn't even feel like he was lying. In his imagination, Avishay lying on his bed was fine, absolutely fine, he was taken care of.

"Want to make us some coffee?"

Amos quickly scanned the apartment, although he wasn't sure which incriminating evidence he was looking for and of what—apart from Avishay himself, of course. But the whole place suddenly seemed incriminating, burning with a crude mockery of their dumb plan. He almost wished she would find out, that was the truth. That she would find out and release them from this burden. But he didn't want it to happen on his watch. He didn't feel like defending all this, and it wouldn't work anyway, he knew himself too well. All she'd have to do was ask—but why? How?—and he'd jump into her arms and snitch without a second thought: *I know, I know, I kept telling them.* "So you just dropped by to see Avishay?" he asked.

"I'm spending the night here," she said, as though it were obvious.

Barely concealing his astonishment, Amos asked, "You're spending the night at Avishay's?"

"Every Saturday night. I have my class on Sundays."

Now Amos fully remembered how annoying she was. He'd started to remember it when she'd said his name that way, and now it was stronger: she was one of those people who would say "my class" and assume you'd done nothing since they'd told you about the class fifteen years ago. "Oh yes," he said, "of course, Avishay told me, it's just that . . ."

"Where is he?" Ruthi asked.

"Avishay?"

Since the question sounded rhetorical, Ruthi said nothing, and Amos realized it was all over, he wouldn't be able to get through it, and no one would blame him. But that wasn't true, and he knew it. It's just that they might not blame him out loud. Purely so that he would be able to defend himself later, he opened his mouth and somehow uttered: "He needed a few days to finish up an article, he was on a deadline, so he just went away to disconnect somewhere."

"Where?" Ruthi asked.

"What?"

"Where did he go?"

"I don't remember," Amos said, and when he realized how that sounded, he added, "To tell you the truth, I wasn't paying attention." He thought that sounded genius.

"What a dummy. Why didn't he tell me?" As she spoke, she pulled out her phone and put it up to her ear, and that's when the phone in Amos's hand rang. He looked at the screen, which said, "Ruthi," but she didn't realize what was going on—it never even occurred to her: Why would Amos have Avishay's phone? Amos was pretty sure he could get out of it, but he didn't know how. He waved the iPhone at her and said, "He left his phone with me."

Ruthi said, "He lent you his iPhone?"

Without considering if it would be worth it, Amos jumped at the opportunity: "Yes, he wanted to disconnect, and my phone just happened to be broken, so he lent me his. You can only get hold of him by email, and even that I doubt he's checking more than a couple of times a day, unless he can't resist it. Or at least that was the plan." He counted his efforts, his strokes of genius, one, two, three, like someone racking up points in a battle he was about to lose, so that he could prove to Mommy that he did try.

"Oh, that's why he wasn't texting me back, I couldn't figure it out."

"Exactly," he said, unlocking Avishay's phone as he spoke. Texting her back? What was she talking about? But there were three fresh green balloons waiting there, from two hours ago. Three of them, telling the story in reverse, poking fun of people as usual: "If you're not home I'll use my key," "?," "Getting on the 843 bus now."

Amos sat down on the couch opposite her and they smiled at each other, she naturally and he effortfully, although perhaps it was an effort for her, too, who knows. For a moment it looked as though they were waiting for Avishay to finish getting ready in the bedroom and walk out and confess to everything.

Her white hair was cropped short and its sparseness was disguised by gelled spikes that made her seem taller than she was. She was wearing gray slacks and a white blouse, and only the enormous fabric tote beside her disclosed the fact that she was not a lawyer. All in all, she looked quite normal. She looked exactly like Avishay, in fact, but slightly thinner, and the resemblance filled Amos with guilt: about Avishay, to whom he wasn't giving enough thought, wasn't sad enough about, because he was too busy with other things that might have been important but were pathetic, and Avishay didn't deserve that. But also guilt about Ruthi: they hadn't seen her for so long that she'd become a parody in their discourse, and here she was, a real person, now bereaved of practically her whole family.

Amos remembered that she'd once been Miss Charm or Miss Israel or something, in the early sixties, before they'd all met, and that she'd always been very beautiful. He tried to detect whether she still was, but he couldn't say; that saddened him, too. He felt like someone whose system had been scrambled and he was being sad about the wrong things.

Ruthi was old now. How old? Older than Avishay—she had to be seventy-something, maybe seventy-three or -four. Perhaps that's why she looked normal, thanks to the natural aging process, which assiduously moderated both ugliness and beauty.

She just sat there without saying a word. And while Amos waited for it to somehow end, spontaneously, and soon, imagining her reaction, which he would have to bear alone, it suddenly occurred to him that he did not know who this woman really was. He remembered things he'd heard the day before yesterday: emotional blackmailer, crazy, dirt-poor. What else had they said about her? The magnitude of the trouble he was in became apparent, and it was greater than Yehuda's and greater than Nili's, exponentially greater than any justification he might have to make. Because this woman, if she found out what they'd done, could destroy his life. He wasn't sure exactly how; people like him didn't know that kind of thing. And he was seized by panic, the kind of panic that was the closest thing to initiative in those who lacked it, but he didn't know what to do with it or where to direct it.

"So what are you doing here?" Ruthi asked.

The question was uttered casually, unsuspectingly, so much so that Amos could barely understand the syntax. When he finally did, he said, "You wanted coffee, didn't you?"

"I did and I still do."

"Then let's make some and I'll tell you everything." But as he moved toward the kitchen he realized it would be irresponsible to leave her there, outside his field of vision, like a baby. He poked his head back into the living room but Ruthi hadn't moved. She looked up questioningly, and Amos said, "Turkish okay? 'Cause there's no milk."

"Then tea," Ruthi replied.

"D'you take sugar?"

Ruthi widened her eyes into an expression he could not comprehend. "What?" he asked fearfully. He felt so guilty, for so many things, that he no longer trusted his antennae to warn him of danger.

"Do I take *sugar*?" she repeated reproachfully.

"Oh right, I forgot." He kept looking at her for another moment. This was ridiculous: she wasn't going anywhere. He went back into the kitchen and quickly made some tea. As he carried the boiling-hot mugs into the living room, taking small steps, Ruthi stood up. He thought she was coming to get the tea, but instead she turned to the hallway, and Amos exclaimed, "No!"

"What's the problem?"

"Oh, I just thought I was about to spill the tea."

"Am I allowed to pee?"

"Of course," Amos said. He put the tea on the table and leaned against the wall outside Avishay's room, trying to look casual. He probably looked like John Travolta, that's how casual it looked, and Ruthi gave him a bemused look. It occurred to Amos that she might think he was into her—Good God, that's what she thought.

Moving slowly while still staring at him, as if she were flirting with a suitor, Ruthi said, "I'll just put my bag down," and she turned left out of the bathroom door and reached out for the handle of Avishay's bedroom door. Amos clutched her hand and stood up against the door, protecting it with his body, and he suddenly realized they were going to kiss. She was going to kiss him—what else could happen here? He felt alarmed and unsettled and excited. He hadn't kissed anyone except Varda since 1974, and hadn't wanted to, hadn't even thought of it, no other lips had ever made themselves available to him. He looked at them, at these lips, in fact not at them but at the skin around them, which quivered slightly, and it seemed to him that that's where the passion was concentrated, dispatching tiny supersonic messages across the little wrinkles to the skin, and he felt his innards being sucked up, the fear and the guilt and the urge and the desire, as though someone had shoved a vacuum cleaner down his throat, but before he had time to think or do anything, Ruthi said, "I knew it!" Amos had no idea what she meant but he felt as though he'd been caught red-handed: she'd been testing him and he'd failed, he'd been made a fool of, he was trapped. Ruthi said, "You naughty boy!" and Amos felt as though he'd suddenly been transported to a parallel universe, a universe of adulterers and lip-kissers. This must be how people talked there, but he needed a dictionary. "What?" he said.

"You're not alone! That's why you're being so secretive," Ruthi whispered. Amos said nothing, and Ruthi said, "You don't need to be embarrassed, you know I'm as discreet as they come." And then Amos finally understood, limping behind the conversation: She thinks I have a woman in the room. That's what she thinks. The exit route had fallen into his lap, and Amos felt that he was supposed to be glad, but he wasn't, the price was too high. But why? Why not go with it? Whose honor was he protecting? What fictional morality? Who cared what he made up now? Who cared if Ruthi Sar-Shalom, Avishay's sister, thought for twenty-four hours or even for a week that he was cheating on Varda, or had left her? Except it wasn't twenty-four hours, and it wasn't a week: if they pulled it off, she'd think it forever. Before he could calculate which was the worse option, Ruthi said, "Will two hours be enough?"

"For what?" he mumbled.

Ruthi stared at him with feigned innocence and said, "That's none of my business."

Amos felt disgusted. "Why, what's happening in two hours?"

"I'm going to my meeting soon, we'll probably be done at around ten."

Amos didn't even ask which meeting she was talking about as if it were so obvious. "Any chance you could draw it out a little longer?"

he asked, and he felt filthy, as though the mere suggestion meant that he had been fucking someone for two whole hours.

"Is twelve okay?" Ruthi said.

"Twelve p.m.? Midnight?"

"I'll tell you what, I wouldn't mind coming back even later, it's just that my last bus is at midnight."

And that's when the Ruthi who stood opposite him merged with the pieces of Ruthi that floated around, high up above their lives. He suddenly understood something about her, or at least he felt he did, and he was touched by the understanding. "Ruthi, a bus? Take a cab, it's on me. Both ways."

"Don't be crazy, Amos, that's unnecessary."

Amos kept playing his role in the ritual: "There's no argument, Ruthi. You're taking a cab, end of discussion. I'm the one who embarrassed myself, so let me at least feel a little less bad about things."

Ruthi acquiesced. "There's no arguing with you, is there?"

"Hang on, I'll get my wallet."

He knew exactly where Avishay's wallet was, having stumbled across it too many times that day—on the bureau in the entryway. As he opened it for the first time, he felt like a thief. There was no doubt that it would have been more elegant to pay for this cab with his own money, however much it ended up costing, but he didn't want to. For the sake of symbolism, he didn't want to do it: it seemed too unfair for Avishay to emerge unscathed from this whole story, while they danced around him and paid the price.

He felt petty again, niggling, not so much with money but with friendship, because surely friendship should mean generosity, certainly at a time of death. *Oh no, tell me what I can do to help, anything at all.* That's the sort of thing you were supposed to say, but you had to mean it, otherwise it was disgusting. And yet he *was* doing anything at all—he was doing everything he possibly could to help.

Would Avishay have acted differently if it were Amos's body lying in there? He tried to consider the question candidly, but in order for the comparison to work Amos would have had to be a Nobel candidate, a mentioned-as Nobel candidate, and so the whole exercise collapsed. It was easier for him to imagine himself dead than getting a Nobel, that was his conclusion, and he wondered if he should let that depress him. After all, everyone died eventually, not least him, a potbellied sixty-nine-year-old smoker. But not everyone got an award.

Then a new thought depressed him: He would die before everyone, or almost everyone. He would die prematurely, it would happen, it simply would, maybe even in a few minutes if he didn't stop smoking and do something about that gut. He wasn't sure which of the two was more urgent, and it didn't matter anyway because he was incapable of either one. A rational man, a professor of economics, a recipient of the Dan David Prize, the American Academy of Arts and Sciences's Talcott Parsons Prize, the Society of Experimental Economics's Syms Warren Medal, the Decision Analysis Society's Frank P. Ramsey Medal, and a lifetime achievement award from the Society for Medical Decision Making. He had so much decision-making coming out of his ears that he couldn't make one logical decision: to not eat chocolate-covered carbs every morning. To not finish off a giant bag of potato chips that gave him a stomachache anyway. To not act like a five-year-old with nothing but his parents standing between him and heaps of ice cream, white sugar, simple carbs, and junk. On this topic, Nili had said one of the smartest things she may ever have said: Every person, she explained, has to be undisciplined in something. And people like them, who were successful in everything they did, let their discipline slide in this one area, in the fats they consumed without any elegance at all, without any proportion, the wild little siblings of all the other areas in their lives.

It was true and he knew it immediately, the way you recognize the correct interpretation of a dream, and he was amazed that he hadn't thought of it himself, long before the age of sixty. Still, he found it irritating to hear it from Nili, who insisted on lumping them together, as though it were even possible to compare her dimensions with his potbelly, which, granted, was large and growing larger, but it hadn't been born with him, it wasn't part of him. They were not the same kind of person.

At first, when they met, Nili had just broken up with Yehuda and Avishay's roommate, but she kept hanging around their apartment, and Amos couldn't stand her. She seemed phony, like she was trying too hard, with all her recreational drugs and endless stories about medical school, which were intended to transmit some profound truth about the profession—and maybe about life—but mostly to differentiate her from everyone else in the field, to show she wasn't as naïve as they were. Over time, he learned to like her and believe her, and he was forced to admit that she had pretty good stories, mostly about the parents who came to her clinic, but also about the children; the way she talked about them released a tightly shut pressure valve inside them all. And what's more, she went out of her way to help Amos when his son Achinoam had that ear problem. She treated him then as if he were her brother, rather than a tenuous friend of friends.

Afterward she tried to promote the friendship a little, based on the fact that—as he discovered—she felt they were fellow sufferers, two family people living dreary lives. He did not like that at all, and he gently rejected her overtures, finding that he had to dilute her with the rest of the group. If the two of them ever arrived first, they were always slightly embarrassed—Nili because of Amos's embarrassment, and Amos because he was made uneasy by the way her eyes demanded honesty, the way they seemingly penetrated the depths of mediocrity. When she was restrained in her boundaries, in her proportion—20 percent of the group, or a fifth, if that sounded warmer—he liked her and enjoyed her company. Only one thing continued to drive him crazy: she always rolled around laughing whenever she said something funny. Varda was the one who noticed it, not him, but ever since she casually pointed it out, Amos could feel Nili's laughter tumbling straight out of her mouth onto his nerves and grating on them deliberately.

—————

Avishay had four credit cards in his wallet, and Amos paused before deciding it didn't matter which one he used. He was investing thought and effort in this: no one could say he wasn't. Would Avishay have gone out of his way to arrange a Nobel for Amos? The scenes Amos staged with some effort and the images he put together laboriously were all defeated by one single truth, to which he remained faithful: that Avishay and he were similar, and that if there were one reliable test, it was this—if this was how he acted, that would be how Avishay would have acted, too. Would Avishay really have wanted Amos to win a Nobel? The idea was ridiculous and the answer was obvious.

He wondered if Avishay would have signed off on that test, too, on that similarity between them. When they were younger it was certainly true. They'd met in their post-army service backpacking trip, in the United States. They called it a trip, but they didn't really get off their asses much, just sat around with ten or twelve other people in a little apartment in New York, came and went, smoked and drank and fucked a fair amount, at least some of them did. Amos had ended up there somehow, and Avishay came later—it was the only place in his life where Amos had arrived before Avishay—and they gradually became friends, two foreign implants in that tiny apartment, acting too serious, more serious than the others even though they all had promising careers waiting, temporary guests in that way of life, grown old before their time.

Amos was the one who brought Avishay to economics in the first place. Avishay had no idea what to study, and then suddenly he agreed: economics, all right, good, great idea, he'd combine it with sociology, that would be his twist. Amos instinctively ran the other way, to Jerusalem—studying alongside Avishay was not a good idea, although at the age of twenty-something it was hard to know why. Then they both became successful: Avishay specialized in economics and sociology, his research field in the past few years was the economics of power, with his famous "class king" model, whereas Amos, after many years of working on welfare economics, had recently made a name for himself in the increasingly popular field of happiness economics and was mentioned in the same breath as names like Richard Easterlin, Bruno Frey, and Richard Layard.

Amos's research dealt primarily with the influence of uncertainty on happiness levels. In his most cited work, he had developed (together with Frey and Andrew Oswald) the Personal Uncertainty Index (known as PUI), which was designed to quantify the uncertainty that characterizes an individual's life and its influence on individual well-being. In his paper, "The Uncertain Way to Happiness: The Economic Puzzle of Personal Choices," Amos showed that high rates of uncertainty had a marked effect not only on elements considered essential for the Happy Planet Index (HPI), such as income, personal freedom, a sense of control, employment, leisure, and so forth, but also a direct influence on happiness itself: as uncertainty increases, Amos argued, so does happiness ("the uncertainty paradox"). Although his many critics viewed his work as just another layer in a controversial field, he earned an excellent reputation. His research was cited in multiple disciplines and was considered applicable to various aspects of national and global economic policy; the index he developed had already been adopted by sixteen countries.

When he chose to focus on this—both out of genuine interest, since he was pretty tired of the narrow, neoclassical interpretations of welfare economics, but also out of a desire to dominate in a field, to finally find a place where he could say something new—he was certain that it was a sexy field. If he was going to be an economist, what could be sexier than the economics of happiness? What could be hotter than risk-taking? But then he learned that you can't plan sexiness: he, with his personality, managed to paint the red-hot discipline in a starchy tone, while Avishay, with his false power discrepancies, became a real superstar, who almost by accident was even dealing with economics.

How did this happen? Amos didn't have the answer, though no other question in the world preoccupied him more. But one thing he was forced to admit: if you were to ask anyone—with the possible exception of Varda—which of them was funnier, wittier, more entertaining, or any adjective that had to do with sharpness, no one would even hesitate. And that was how he learned another lesson: that personal charm of a certain kind goes along with humor, and that people imagine humor easily, even where there is none. God knows Avishay had none: people found him alluring, and so he had acquired a halo of lightheartedness, but from close up he was positively humorless.

More than anything else, it drove Amos mad to see how this worked on young people. It was one thing for Avishay to have power over people his own age, people who were more patient, or perhaps jaded, irredeemably damaged themselves, dozing off in ancient friendships. But Avishay had earned a large piece of his fame owing to his status as the cool professor, the one who held meetings at coffee shops, even with undergrads, and who gave extra credit questions about *Game of Thrones*, using trendiness to soften the impossibility of ever answering them. He always wore jeans, donning a suit only on special occasions. And year after year he made the list of favorite professors.

Amos couldn't understand how they missed the fawning. He'd known Avishay for so many years, and he was astonished again and again by the weakness that overcame him when a young person invaded his surroundings: the confident, slightly arrogant, righteous Avishay would melt in an instant, grow tense and unquiet, try to win him or her over with a touching, pitiful urgency, as though it were a matter of life or death. That was where he was the weak one, the blind one; he couldn't control it. Perhaps that was what made him human. But them? The twenty- or thirty-somethings? What was their problem? Did they really need so little? So he'd met Paul Auster once in a bookshop in New Haven—how many times could you hear that story?

Couldn't he, Amos, have made a connection between economics and sociology, like Avishay had? Couldn't he have invented a name for it? What was so brilliant about "The Economics of Power"? If he'd come up with it himself he would have rejected it for being so obvious. But he hadn't come up with it himself, and once again he felt a mounting resentment at the thin line between genius and trivial, which always seemed to work against people like him. He suspected that this was the real virtue that earned people Nobel Prizes: not luck, as he used to think, and certainly not talent, as he'd stupidly believed early on, and not even the keen sense of smell that led someone to sniff out the next important problem like a model scout sniffs out a lanky young beauty. No, it was the simple ability to trust in your achievements, not to scrutinize them too much but to shout them out loudly, crudely, because you never knew what would stick.

Early on, things had actually gone well. Both their careers had flourished, and there were advantages to working in the same field: no one understood them as well as they understood each other, like two survivors of the same disaster. And if one of them was ahead from time to time, it was always by single digits: Avishay got his PhD from MIT, Amos from Stanford; Avishay published his first article in *The Journal of Political Economy*, Amos in *The Review of Economic Studies*. Their relationship revolved around economics, career, academic life, but through that they connected in other areas too, personal ones, although they rarely discussed their real intimate troubles, as if that might end up as a strike against one of them in the race.

But there came a moment when Avishay suddenly left Amos in the dust. The race had been so close for so long, so evenly matched, that it seemed to have crossed into another dimension, one where there were no winners or losers—just like the lie kids are told: in this game, everyone's a winner. Amos was almost driven mad by his futile attempts to identify the precise moment at which he must have blinked, the moment when things went wrong. He scoured it endlessly, constantly, every award and every medal, every conference and every association, and finally narrowed it down to 1984 through 1986. In 1984, Avishay was invited to be a guest lecturer at the University of Chicago, but that was also a great year for Amos: he got an article accepted by the *Quarterly Journal of Economics*, and later that year his second book, *Between Well and Fair: Policy and Anti-Policy in Post-Eisenhower America*, was published by Oxford University Press. But in 1985, Avishay was appointed editor of *American Economic Review*, and roughly a year later he published "The Dollhouse Bargain," which was the last nail in Amos's coffin. More than four thousand citations, that damn article had already racked up. Amos, meanwhile, had almost eleven hundred citations for "The Asymmetry Dilemma," a phenomenal accomplishment by all opinions—except of course Avishay's.

In 2003, a Wikipedia entry about Avishay popped up. They were at Zohara's and Avishay casually mentioned it: "Someone put a Wiki up about me." He sounded amused in the way only someone who has a Wikipedia entry can be.

"So, what does it say?" Zohara asked.

"Oh, you know, just a bit about my research, the awards, nothing interesting. Nothing personal, let's put it that way. And no picture."

"You should send them one, it would be nice to have," Nili suggested.

"First of all, who's *them*?"

"Oh, so you don't know who wrote it?" Zohara asked.

"It's the Wikipedia editors who put things up, they do the research and everything, don't they, Avishay?" Nili wondered.

"I have no idea, I didn't even know about it until a student of mine told me."

Amos did not attribute any particular importance to this development, just as he had failed to recognize his setback in 1986 or even before. He didn't even think much of it when Nili asked, "Amos, do you have one too?"

"I have no idea, I don't think so," he said, but then he thought maybe he did; he'd have to check when he got home. He still didn't twig when he checked at home and found that he didn't have an entry.

Avishay's entry said: "Avishay Sar-Shalom (born Dec. 23, 1943) is a professor of economics at Tel Aviv University and an internationally renowned scholar in the field of Power Economics. Sar-Shalom is the recipient of an Israel Prize in Economics for 2000. In 1992 he was awarded the Distinguished Scientific Contributions Award from the Society for Industrial and Organizational Psychology, in 2003 he received the Distinguished Fellow award from the American Economics Association, and in 2006 he won the Society of Experimental

Economics' Syms Warren Medal. In 1997 he was appointed to the Israeli National Academy of Sciences, and in 2002 to the United States National Academy of Sciences. He has also been awarded several honorary doctorates, among others by the University of Pennsylvania (2001), Ben-Gurion University of the Negev (2002), University of British Columbia (2002), Northwestern University (2003), and Haifa University (2006). In the 1990s he was a member of a think tank working on negotiations with the Palestinians.

"Sar-Shalom is considered a ground-breaking theoretician in the combination of economics with sociology, and a harbinger of 'power economics,' a subfield in economic research that deals with market failures generated by both hidden and visible power discrepancies, which has led in the past three decades to a revolution in the theoretical conception of corporate finance as well as in other areas. Sar-Shalom's article 'The Dollhouse Bargain' serves as a basis for economic theories accepted by scholars around the world, including in the fields of political economics, political science, government and sociology.

"In his most famous work, Sar-Shalom proposed the 'Class King' model, which seeks to predict power relation changes within groups. Sar-Shalom equates the group to a school class, in which one 'king' presides and is recognized and unchallenged by all members, and those classmates who are closest to him function as 'deputies' of various ranks. He portrays the events that unfold when a new child joins the class, who is interested in and capable of being a leader: while the existing 'class king' will immediately be relegated to the bottom of the social ladder, those who served beneath him have a high chance of retaining their status under the new king; at most, they will lose a fraction of their status. It derives that it is in fact the most powerful figure who has the lowest chance of surviving in the long term in a group, and of preserving his status and enjoying the tokens of respect and assets it provides. Counter-intuitively, it is the king's 'servants,' the secondary figures with less prominent status, who have the highest chance of retaining their status in the long term.

"Sar-Shalom employs a historical perspective to show that an identical process has been occurring since the dawn of humanity, and that the only change is in the punishment visited upon the deposed king: from cutting off limbs in biblical times, to dismissal in the modern business world, where the CEO is the first to be fired and robbed of his status in the group. In this context, Sar-Shalom also discusses 'optimism as a predictor of defeat.' He shows, among other things, that an optimistic assessment of one's status, resources and power—the kind of assessment necessary in order to go to battle, for example, or to attempt to enter a new line of business that is controlled by an existing monopoly—increases one's chances of experiencing total defeat in that battle, whether in the short term or the long term.

"In recent years, with the uptick in exposures of government corruption, Sar-Shalom has made frequent pronouncements supported by his academic work: he argues that the very ambition to reach senior positions in the current political climate requires a great deal of optimism and even hubris, because very few public figures are untarnished by transgressions, even if they occurred in their distant past. Thus, while prominent figures are highly likely to have their misdeeds exposed and be totally and permanently condemned by the public system, it is actually those serving in lower positions, those who relinquished the race to the top of the pyramid a priori, who will be able to maintain not only their jobs and status, but also a certain degree of maneuverability regarding law abidance. For further reading…"

Over time the entry grew more voluminous. It was expanded to include "Family and Background" ("His parents, Penina, née Brida,

and Aharon Sar-Shalom, were both psychiatrists, and his father
served as the Chief Psychiatrist in the Ministry of Health"); "Publi-
cations" ("Sar-Shalom has published close to 150 peer-reviewed articles, as well as the following books:"); and "External Links."

By this time, Amos was addicted to the page, and he came to
believe that even if Avishay had not been active in the original initiative, there was no shadow of a doubt that he was now collaborating
with it generously and willingly. Amos felt this was wrong, although
he could not exactly say why, and he made a great effort to use this
feeling to assuage his pain just a little. He knew it was childish: Who
the hell cared about some silly Wikipedia entry? It was provincial,
it didn't interest anyone, it was beneath him. What's more, he could
write an entry on himself if it was so important to him, not that it
would even have occurred to him to do something like that—after
all, that would miss the whole point. But much as he tried, and Varda
tried too—"It's just a web page, it's something overseen by fifteen-
year-old kids, it's here today gone tomorrow"—the entry "Professor
Avishay Sar-Shalom" acquired mythic proportions in Amos's mind.
He viewed it as the essence of Avishay's unshakeable victory, a concrete symbol of a plethora of elusive moments: one moment it was
a miserable honorary doctorate, and the next moment only one of
them was a Nobel candidate, or "mentioned in recent years as a leading candidate for the Nobel Prize in Economics," which was the language that turned up on the Wikipedia page at some point, though
Amos had stupidly stopped combing over the "Economic Thought"
section, thinking nothing could possibly change there, and so he
missed the new addition for days, perhaps even weeks. It happened
long before Avishay was invited to that bloody Nobel Symposium,
that was sure; Amos would not have missed that.

He secretly hoped, perhaps even planned, to be the first economist
to get a Nobel in the field of happiness economics; in his mind's eye

he would receive the prize with two colleagues, Frey and Oswald, and this made the wish attainable, even modest. In one of their endless conversations about the topic, when Varda said, "Look how much you have that he doesn't," Amos was both embarrassed and annoyed when he realized she was talking about her and the kids, not the Frank P. Ramsey Medal. It was the sort of statement you couldn't disagree with, but it did nothing to console Amos.

When Avishay was invited to that conference in Sweden last September, Amos grumbled to Varda. In the absence of another culprit, he demanded that she take the blame. She had softened him and softened him with false claims all these years, arguments a woman voices to a man, all made up of irrelevant love. It would have been better for him to reach this day in a sober, more resilient state of mind. Clearly, once Avishay was invited to the Nobel Symposium, he was a real candidate. Not officially, but very concretely. They were seriously considering him.

When Avishay came back, after five or six days that were absolute torture for Amos—because it was simply cruel, but mainly because he had to hide his suffering under a veneer of normalcy—Avishay shared his experiences in a lighthearted, anecdotal tone. He talked as if all this had nothing to do with him, like an observer, a promising doctoral candidate or a member of the judging committee. *How smart Avishay was*, Amos thought. What an elegant way to convey to them that things had gone well, that he wasn't worried and wasn't deluded. And he realized that must have been how they'd all started, all the worried and deluded ones: they'd all once been promising graduates of the Nobel Symposium who came back from Stockholm in high spirits, and Avishay was still young and had many years ahead of him.

═══

Ruthi sat smoking on the couch, and Amos felt a short, strong burst of happiness, the kind he always felt when he found out about someone else who smoked, someone else who was dumb. And this was someone older than him, and she was a sugar-rehab specialist to boot.

He really felt like bumming a cigarette from her, and he weighed the desire against the price: it might cost him seven minutes of conversation. He was surprised to discover that he wasn't at all fearful of exposing their plan, and the death, of giving it away, but only of her invasive, nocturnal, nicotinic questions, which were covered by a thin film of hasty intimacy like spit: *So, Amos, how's it going? What's up with you, Amos?* The kind of questions that demanded truth. He was also surprised to discover that if any such questions were posed to him, he might cry.

He held out a 200-shekel bill and felt dirty again. She waved the bill up in the air and said, "I'll bring you the change."

13

The four of them sat in Avishay's living room. He felt like the host, but he soon realized that was wrong: everyone could get up and make their own coffee.

Yehuda said, "I'm borrowing Shuki's van."

"Won't he fit in a regular car?" Nili wondered.

"We're better off using a van from the get-go, we don't have time for experiments."

"No, I'm just saying, so we don't get Shuki messed up in this business."

"He doesn't know what it's for, and he doesn't care either."

Zohara said, "So that's it, we're moving him?"

"Do we have a choice?" Yehuda responded.

"I don't know, shouldn't we just think about what to tell Ruthi for a second?"

Yehuda looked around as if seeking conformation that he was being sensible. "I don't understand—didn't we agree we were hiding him until Wednesday?"

"Okay, Yehuda, but that was before we had to start moving a body around, with all due respect."

"Then what are you suggesting, Zohara?" At the sight of her vexed expression, Yehuda added, "No, I'm asking seriously. Suggest something and we'll consider it."

"I don't know, we have to think," Zohara said.

"Okay then, let's think. But fast. We have another . . ."

Amos could tell Yehuda needed help, so he stepped in: "Let's say two hours," even though the correct answer, the precise one, was one hour and forty-five minutes; that was the upper limit, and only if they trusted Ruthi. He felt once again as though he were straddling two sides of a very thin borderline, wobbling with one foot on either side: on one hand, there could be no sabotaging, no lying; that was very much forbidden. On the other hand, he just wanted her to come back. To save them from this. He didn't want her to find out about the plan, God forbid, not with her big mouth. But a lot of things could happen in two hours. They could have just found out he was dead, and then they'd let her know: *Ruthi, Avishay is dead. Yes, of course, we have to start thinking about arrangements.* He would have to find the right minute to bring it up.

Nili said, "I gather letting her in on it is out of the question."

"What do you mean? Letting her in on it and going on with the plan?" Amos said.

"Of course."

That was when he realized it was an option, which he hadn't considered at all when he'd been alone. The way he'd seen it, the minute Ruthi found out her brother was dead, the whole thing would be canceled and they'd be free. A plethora of horrifying possibilities suddenly besieged his imagination. That was all he needed, for this whole nightmare to continue *and* for Ruthi to bring them all down with her blathering, her frivolousness, with what she thought she knew about what Amos had supposedly been doing in Avishay's room. "No, no, no, no, no," he exclaimed, "do me a favor. Absolutely not. I just saw her, and now I remember what sort of woman we're talking about. This is not a person you can trust."

Yehuda quickly backed him up: "No, no, really, no."

"So do you want to give up?" Nili asked.

The question landed unsoftened, rudely premature. Amos

looked at them looking at her with what seemed to him like hope-
fulness.

"Give up?" Zohara said. "You mean, just call it off?"

"I don't know, I mean if you think it's too much," Nili said.

"I don't understand," Yehuda insisted, "what were you thinking?
That we'd just answer his text messages and that would be it? That's
what we're sacrificing for him?"

"What is this, Masada? Are we in some sort of heroism contest?"
Zohara retorted.

"No, but I mean, if we've come this far, why stop now?"

"It's not like we've done all that much, with all due respect,"
Zohara claimed.

"We have, Zohara, we have. Maybe you haven't because it hasn't
been your shift yet," Nili replied.

"Okay then," Zohara relented.

"To me it just seems like a waste," Yehuda said.

"Okay, I don't know," Nili said, "maybe we've all been imagining
this week slightly differently, each of us has different red lines. That's
okay, too, we just have to make a decision."

Amos felt as though he were watching a tennis match, or a horse
race he'd bet on—not that he'd ever been to either of those, but his
eyes were tracking the ball, or the pair of horses in the lead, and his
fate depended on luck, on split seconds, completely at the mercy of
arbitrary hands.

Zohara went on: "I don't know, are we seriously going to move
him? Actually carry a dead man on our shoulders? Are we going to
pick him up, dead, and carry him to the car, or what? I'm telling you
honestly, that's where my imaginative powers end. I can't see us doing something like that."

"*You* won't have to carry anyone on your shoulders," Yehuda said,
"calm down."

"And then we have to bring him back, too!"

"Well yes, obviously we'll have to bring him back, what did you think? You think they're going to send his flowers for the Nobel to Amos's house?"

Amos felt like someone had shoved him onstage from the aisles: *Amos's house?*

"By the way," Nili said, "he could also die in Amos's house. I mean, it could be that he simply died at Amos's."

"At Amos's house?" he ventured.

Yehuda said, "He can't die at Amos's house, because then he'd have to be lying dead at Amos's without anyone from Amos's family noticing."

"Oh, right."

Amos reiterated: "I'm asking again: at Amos's house?"

Nili explained: "It has to be a single-family residence, so it's either your place or Yehuda's, and somehow yours makes more sense to me, I'm not sure why."

Amos knew very well why: because Idit was at Yehuda's. He had his own weapon, his own woman, but before he could decide where to aim it, Yehuda said, "We can put him at my place, it's not a problem, Idit's away."

"Are you sure?" Nili asked.

"I have no problem with it."

Amos said, "I'm not sure if we should drop this on Yehuda, either. What I'm saying, again, is that we need a creative solution." But he knew he didn't mean that.

"What if the girls come over?" Zohara asked.

"Why would they suddenly turn up on a Sunday?" Yehuda wondered.

"I don't know."

"Don't worry," Yehuda said, and Amos knew it was over, the

opportunity had passed. From the moment Yehuda had offered his house he would not be able to suggest anything else, certainly not a defeatist plan that meant a funeral tomorrow.

They sat quietly for a moment, and then Zohara said, "So you're getting the van from Shuki?"

Amos wondered why she was so eager all of sudden, and Yehuda said, "I'll go over there now. The question is how we get him to the van. From here, I mean."

Nili said, "I've just realized why in the movies they . . . I mean, they cut them up."

"Why?" Yehuda asked.

"Because it's much easier to carry them that way."

"Well, obviously," Yehuda said.

"Guys, I'm pretty sure we're not going to cut Avishay into pieces," Amos commented.

"I wasn't planning to," said Nili.

Amos took a deep breath, so unintendedly loudly that he was afraid his insides had been exposed. They were moving Avishay. They were moving a body. He had to start accepting it. He had to pull himself together. It had to go off without a hitch, this thing. It couldn't be found out. "I just think we're trying to think like criminals, but that's a mistake. We look like normal people, that's our winning card. No one's going to suspect us, it doesn't matter what we do. We'll carry him on our back, like he's drunk or asleep or something. We'll walk fast but confident, and we'll put him in the car." He felt like someone gaining points on the way to a pardon.

Yehuda wasn't sure. "One person can't carry him on their back, he's too heavy. You need at least two people to hold him by the arms and legs. The question is whether he'll still look like he's sleeping or drunk that way."

"And whether we'll still look like normal people," Nili added.

"Generally speaking," Zohara said, "I think we're slightly overestimating our normality. All this stuff about 'no one's going to do anything to us because we're normal, a doctor and a businessman and a professor,' and all that."

"That's not what he said," Yehuda insisted.

"Not now, I mean when he died. And now, too. Yes, we're normal and we look normal, but only because we *act* normal. It's not some innate quality that's in our DNA. If we stop behaving normally—for example, by carrying a body down the street in the middle of the night—then we probably won't look so normal anymore."

"Do you think he smells at all?" Amos wondered. "Has anyone checked?"

"I certainly haven't," Zohara said.

"Because I haven't been in the bedroom," Amos added.

"There's a slight smell," Nili said, "I went in yesterday to get the paper, but it's only when you stand really close. On the other hand, that was yesterday."

"I just don't want us stinking up the whole of Bar Kochva Street."

"I personally can't smell anything, but maybe it's different in the room," Zohara said.

Amos tried to quickly calculate all the possible scenarios: What did he prefer to happen at this point? What would lead to what? But the flowchart faded in his mind as though someone had poured water on it, or poured panic on it: they mustn't get caught, no matter what.

"I haven't been here since Thursday," Yehuda said, "I have no idea."

"All right, then," Amos said finally, but he didn't know what he meant.

———

They stood in line outside Avishay's room. Nili went first—Amos made way for her with a gallant flourish that made them both laugh, and she said, "Ladies first, huh?" and ruined the joke. Amos was next, then Zohara, and Yehuda at the rear. Before she opened the door, Nili looked back as if to confirm they were all there, and Amos said, "What is this, a surprise party? Go in already." Nili opened the door gingerly and walked in and immediately moved left, into the corner, to make room for them, and they all went in and stood in a row at the foot of Avishay's bed.

Amos looked at them. Their nostrils widened and their pupils flicked from side to side as they tilted their heads up in a universal gesture of sniffing and concentrating, their awkwardness hanging in their darting eyes. It felt embarrassing to sniff but embarrassing not to.

"Nothing all that strong, is there?" Nili said, at the same exact moment as Zohara said, "I completely forgot he was covered up." Nili said, "What?" and Zohara repeated, "I forgot he was covered, it's a good thing he's covered, I wouldn't have been able to take it."

"But we're taking it off," Yehuda reminded them, "at least for a minute, we have to see what it smells like underneath."

"But why?" Zohara asked. "If there's no smell and we're carrying him covered up?"

"You're going to carry him covered up?! Are you mad? Besides, I just think we should know, so Yehuda knows what to expect. I'm assuming the smell inside is a day or two ahead of the smell in the room, isn't it, Nili?"

"I'm sorry, I just can't resist: it's like farting under a blanket, isn't it?" Nili answered.

"I'm glad to see you find this amusing."

"What do you want me to do, cry?"

"That's one option," Zohara commented.

"I don't know," Nili said, "for some reason I have this feeling of action in the apartment. Like we can still fight death. Don't you think so, Amos? Like doing hospital shifts when someone's sick."

"I actually felt kind of dumb sitting here," Amos confessed, "completely useless."

"Maybe because I had that Liat woman turn up, so I had a real job to do."

"Oh, and I didn't?"

"He got Ruthi, poor guy," Yehuda said. "There is a slight something, I can smell it now."

"Slight, I told you. But nothing dramatic. I don't think you can smell it from outside," Nili said.

"I smell it a little, I have to admit," Amos said. "It's not a stench, but there's definitely something in the air." He walked around the bed and stood next to the bureau. "I'm taking off the sheet."

"Maybe I should leave?" Zohara said.

"Amos, take a quick look before you remove it, tell us if he looks normal," Yehuda said.

"He does not look one hundred percent normal, I can already tell you that," Nili said, "so I hope you're not expecting a pretty sight."

Amos took a deep breath without meaning to—how had he become the hero here?—and lifted the sheet a little.

He pulled back for a second but there was no reason: the face was slightly puffy, but Avishay looked like Avishay. He pulled the sheet down a little further.

From her safe distance, Zohara pointed to the bottom of his back: "What's that?"

Nili bent over and put her glasses on. "It looks like livor mortis. The blood just flows downwards because there's no circulation, and it fills up the blood vessels." She threw off the sheet and said, "That's the worst there is, okay? There, that green on his stomach, there's nothing worse hiding here."

"What is that, is it like decomposition?" Yehuda wondered.

"It *is* decomposition," Nili confirmed.

Amos tried to focus on the green patina spreading in the middle of Avishay's body. He tried to be grossed out like the others, but what drew his attention was the bare chest, posing as alive: the gray hairs and the slight mound of a nascent potbelly; it seemed to him that that's where his weak spot had been hiding the whole time. He suddenly felt embarrassed by Zohara's presence, her gaze on him as he gazed at the almost-naked Avishay, as though she'd invited him into their bed. He tried not to look at her. Avishay looked dead, but not much more so than on the day they'd found him; and still, there he was, lying there, a real man. Amos was embarrassed the way he had been only a few hours earlier, when he'd remembered that Ruthi was real, not a joke or a notion. What was it about this family?

Yehuda finally spoke. "There is a smell, there's no doubt about that, but I don't think it's much more pronounced than in the room. I'm not sure, it's hard to tell."

"So what does that mean, that we're moving him like this?" Nili asked.

"Either way we have to move him like this, I don't think there's any way out of that," Yehuda said.

They stood there, Amos and Nili, next to Avishay's bed, like a pair of doctors with their heads bowed, sympathizing with the grieving family. Yehuda stood at the foot of the bed, arms crossed, and Zohara next to the wardrobe in the corner.

"We'll have to put some clothes on him," Zohara said.

14

Amos looked at the clock: ten forty. Maybe he should phone Ye-huda to find out how things were going, whether they'd finished with the van, when they were getting back. There wasn't much time left. Moving a body was not something you did under pressure. On the other hand, it wasn't something you did *not* under pressure either—it just wasn't something you did, period. But suddenly he completely believed in it. They were too successful, too businesslike, too rational to fail. Strangely, they were too square to fail at moving a body.

Varda texted him: "Going to bed." What did she think they were doing exactly, all Saturday long at Avishay's? Fortunately, she wasn't particularly interested and so he didn't particularly lie. But he had lied, of course: Avishay had been dead for three days and he hadn't told her.

On Wednesday she had her bar exam, and what she needed was a quiet house, without kids or grandkids, and preferably without Amos. Without distractions. But as the days went by, and the more he repeated the reason over and over again to his friends, the feebler it seemed, so much so that he could barely remember it at all, even though it used to be true; of that, he was sure.

Still, he didn't tell her, and not only because he needed the excuse to protect their house—their lives—from a corpse. Why was it, then? He wasn't sure. He felt like someone who'd wandered away from his personality these past few days, or maybe it was the opposite: he had been fully exposed, wearing a cancerous outburst of

qualities on his face. If he told Varda the truth, she would have to live
with a leper.

———

At the age of sixty-two, five days after retiring from her job as a human
resources manager at Sano, Varda had informed Amos that she was
going to law school. He thought she was joking. Why had she retired
when she was still young and in excellent health, if not to enjoy life a
little, before the cancer, before the Alzheimer's? And law? Where had
that come from? He'd known her for forty years, she'd never taken
an interest in law. She said, "I've always had a strong sense of justice,"
but Amos had no idea what she was talking about: Varda liked to
have fun, she liked to party. Unlike his friends, she knew how to enjoy
herself without any complications. Justice had never bothered her,
and that was one thing, but a judge? Because now that's what Varda
wanted to be. A judge had more influence, she explained, and when
Amos asked, "On what? What does she have more influence on?"
Varda replied, "On the world," and Amos missed his human resources
manager, even though she was sitting on the other side of the table.

She'd been in great spirits when she first retired. She had endless
plans, and not a single one of them included justice. In fact, most
were based on that vague injustice that enabled one to live a good
life—meaning, money. But the weekend after her retirement party,
Varda read an interview in the paper with a judge in her sixties, who'd
gone to law school at age forty, with four kids, one of them still a
baby. The judge said it was the only way to change the world, especially when it came to ageism. "To what?" Amos asked, and Varda
gave him a disappointed look, as if the question had proved the ne-
cessity of a revolution. "Age-based discrimination," she explained,
"ageism." And Amos said, "Oh."

He was continuously amazed by this new world they were living in, an impermeable maze without windows or doors, in which he was obliged to nod and smile and not to point out, for example, that her plan didn't make sense when you considered the appointment and retirement age of judges: she'd have all of two seconds to be a judge, at most, and even that was only if she was really fast. Because that was something one mustn't say, one was not allowed to, because it was ageism, or maybe something worse than that, with a name he didn't even know yet.

=====

Irrationally and unwillingly, Amos discovered that one lie begets another, that no sin dwells alone: he hadn't lied to her for thirty years, he couldn't lie to her, even if he saw a beautiful woman, even if he wanted her, he told Varda everything; and here he was, heaping lie upon lie.

He didn't tell her that he hated her new career, that he despised everything about it: the way she'd signed up for law school like a death row inmate in a Hollywood movie; the way she pronounced the word ageism; the obsessive conversations at the dinner table, especially with friends. He hated it so much that he felt like being an ageist himself, which would make him a self-hating old man. But still he could not bring himself to say anything to her, not a word, lest the entire truth leak out, lest he be exposed in his prolonged dishonesty, lest he break her heart.

And now he was lying to her about Avishay, too. He would have preferred to lie quietly, without witnesses, but they knew, the three others, and he felt that his betrayal of her was double, or triple. He'd lost count.

15

He lay down on the couch, just to rest his eyes a little. He thought about his last trip with Avishay, perhaps because it almost felt like he was about to go overseas: invading the wrong hours of the night, trying to outsmart the proper order of things, the faint shadow of adventure.

There'd been two trips, not counting the post-army US stay. In '97 the five of them had gone to Wales for ten days, without partners or kids. And three years ago, he and Avishay were at the same conference at Uppsala University. They arrived separately, Avishay from Israel and Amos straight from some other place, but they flew back together after the conference: Uppsala–Stockholm–Copenhagen–Tel Aviv, with a half-day layover in Stockholm.

Avishay had never been to Stockholm and Amos had been once, many years before, and they were both happy to have the chance to spend several hours there and didn't even look into other options, which would certainly have been more expensive. They were in a good mood all the way downtown on the train. Until it suddenly occurred to Amos: Stockholm. The Nobel city. He hadn't even thought of it.

It was too late by then, and he anxiously flipped through other options, but they didn't have much time, and the palace beckoned from every direction. It was a done deal: they would go to see the Royal Palace, where they give out the Nobel Prizes every December. Amos was about to spend half a day wandering through reconstructed halls and manicured gardens and capacious staircases, all in the company of a potential laureate.

When they bought water and some snacks for the road, he desperately scanned his mind and his surroundings: there had to be a way out. But when he left Avishay to pay and wandered off to examine a promising green sign from up close, the letters came into focus: "To the Nobel Museum." He hurried back to the snack bar in horror.

He dredged down the lanes with Avishay like a prisoner, trying to look as though he were deciphering the map they'd been given at the tourist information center, to disguise his subversiveness. They crossed a bridge and strolled up a few narrow streets until all at once the palace came into view, the way monuments overseas always do—one minute nothing, and the next a spectacular monstrosity. Avishay said, "It burned down once and they rebuilt it, that's why it's a little gray on the outside." Amos looked at his hands to see if they were still holding the map or whether it, along with its anecdotes and exegeses, had wandered over to Avishay. But no, he still had it, and he felt another grudge mounting at the fact that Avishay knew this, that he'd been planning, that he'd bothered to read up.

They paid a hundred and fifty kronor and went inside. Amos wouldn't have minded walking around this place with Avishay for a month, as long as he could be convinced with absolute certainly that the whole Nobel matter wasn't going through Avishay's mind. But he knew Avishay too well, because he knew himself, and as they made their way through the labyrinthine palace, through voluminous halls with gilded walls and ornate ceilings, velvet-lined corridors and massive chandeliers—for some reason he'd thought the Swedes had slightly better taste—the chances diminished: the palace seemed fictional, exaggerated, a parody of royalty or affluence. But the image of the well-groomed, stern-faced committee members standing in an ellipsis around the laureates, with the king in the background, inevitably sneaked into one's imagination, making a mockery of the mockers, running a chill down the spine of the mere mortals, those who paid a hundred and fifty kronor.

He remembered what Yehuda used to say sometimes about overseas: It's too pretty. It's disgusting how pretty everything is. That always struck Amos as the kind of nonsense uttered by someone who was too rich and too bored, a little bit like the veganism. Or maybe it was the opposite: an attempt by Yehuda to come off as an ordinary man despite his wealth, a barefoot kid from old-time Tel Aviv who hadn't changed much. But now he understood exactly what he'd meant: the palace seemed nauseating with its endlessly sprawling wings, its layer upon layer of beauty.

They ambled silently through the rooms. There were informational plaques on the walls, and Amos feared the moment when one of them would announce that here, right in this spot . . . The two of them would stop and read it curiously, perhaps even out loud, and from that moment on everything would be even more terrible. But the plaque never came, and when they walked out into the stone courtyard—a drab, mortal reprieve, at whose far end waited yet another wing—Amos could no longer stand it, and he said: "Shouldn't we be getting back? So we don't get stuck in traffic on the way to the airport or anything?" Avishay said, "Traffic? You're in Stockholm, not Tel Aviv." Amos tried again: "To tell you the truth, I'm pretty exhausted." Avishay said, "Actually, me too," and Amos almost hugged him with relief and gratitude. They started searching for the exit, going against the foot traffic's direction, crossing long lines, like two adolescents cutting class, cheerful and light-footed.

In the smoking room at the airport, while Avishay waited in the seating area, Amos flipped indifferently through the flyers stacked on a shelf next to the chairs. "Stockholm City Hall Nobel Tour," one of them announced, and Amos read: "Visit Stockholm's marvelous

City Hall, famed for its annual Nobel Banquet in honor of the Nobel Laureates. The ceremony takes place in the Concert Hall, followed by dinner in the Blue Hall and dancing in the Golden Hall, which is covered with a beautiful mosaic made of millions of golden tiles."

There was no getting around it: he was an idiot.

16

He expected them to be jovial when they came back, having cheered themselves up in his absence. But there was an air of restraint when they entered, and his resentment had no outlet.

"Have you heard from her?" Zohara asked.

"She's not answering, but she texted me. She'll tell me when she leaves," Amos said, and they all came in without sitting down or taking off their coats, as if to limit the duration of the pause.

"Did you know he's at nine to one?" Zohara said.

"What? What are you talking about?" Yehuda asked.

"His odds for the prize. On those betting sites."

"Oh, right."

"As of today it's nine to one."

"Isn't that a lot?" Nili wondered.

"I don't know how it works," Zohara admitted, "but I see other names there who are at four to one, five to one."

"Whatever, it doesn't mean anything," Yehuda dismissed.

Amos concurred: "Nine to one isn't very high, in theory, but it doesn't mean anything, it's just gambling, no one really has any clue who's going to win. Also, it depends which site you're looking at. Some sites have bets on horse races or I don't know what. And besides, in economics it's often two or three winners in the same year, so the chances are actually higher." He was suddenly filled with generosity, willing to be genuinely supportive of Avishay. Nine to one—that really wasn't very high. Not that it meant anything. Not that anyone took it seriously. He remembered how when he'd taught at MIT everyone in the department had bet on the next Nobel winner; apparently they did it every year, an office diversion, half-jokingly. Amos lost ten dollars.

Nine to one or not, Avishay might not win. Amos realized that Avishay's Nobel had turned into an irrefutable fact in his mind, which only a twist of fate or a tremor of randomness could take away from him. Their decision to do it, to hide him, had replaced the real question of whether he was going to win with a different one: whether they could pull it off.

"You keep trying to come up with reasons not to do it," Yehuda told Zohara.

"Me? I was the most cooperative one from the get-go, what are you talking about?"

Amos agreed—what was he talking about?

"I mean specifically this," Yehuda replied, "the idea of moving Avishay. First it was about normal people, how we're not going to look normal, and now you're saying maybe he won't win."

"That's not fair, Yehuda," Nili protested, "she does have a point."

"I think that if I, who with all due respect am about to host a dead man in my house for almost a week, am willing to do it, then there's really not much else to say. And if he doesn't win, then he doesn't win, it can't be helped. But maybe he will win, right? So that's that. You're not giving up anything, either way."

"No problem, Yehuda, we'll do it," Zohara said, "just let me get a word in without you getting annoyed, let me just explain to you why I'm bringing it up."

"Well?"

"I was totally supportive of it, I still am, but even so, this is an escalation, a tipping point, an I-don't-know-what. It's not the same anymore, babysitting an apartment versus moving a body in the middle of Tel Aviv at night. It's . . . I'm not saying we shouldn't do it, but it's not the same thing, that's all I'm saying."

"But that's not all you're saying," Yehuda protested. "What are you suggesting, then? I'm not getting annoyed, I'm just asking. Are you suggesting we leave him here?"

"No. I don't know. That's why I was waiting to ask Amos, because he knows more about it than the rest of us do, with the whole Nobel cliques and all that. I don't know, I'm just bringing up the topic."

Amos said, "I don't think anything's changed. This business of nine to one doesn't really change anything, if that's what you're asking. It's nonsense, the whole betting thing. There's a chance he'll win, there's a chance he won't, we knew that from the beginning, there's nothing new here. The question is what's guiding us."

They didn't respond. This was his chance: he had analyzed the odds in a truly virtuous fashion, he'd earned the right to say something. *Let's just tell Ruthi he's dead; let's get it over with.*

Yehuda finally said, "You decide. You know where I stand."

Amos strained his eyes in Nili and Zohara's direction, trying to influence them through the power of his furrowed brow.

Zohara said, "Okay. I say let's move him, stick with the plan. We're going ahead with doing everything we can to make sure he wins."

———

They went into the room and Yehuda said, "Shit, we still have to get him dressed, I told you we were being too blasé about timing."

"But Amos talked with Ruthi—didn't you, Amos?" Nili said. "She said she'd let you know."

"What if she decides to leave twenty minutes early? What if she doesn't let me know? You can't count on that."

"Okay, give me a minute."

Zohara opened the closet and lingered between the doors. "T-shirt or button-down?"

"Doesn't matter," Yehuda said. "It really, really, doesn't matter."

Nili said, "T-shirt, definitely."

Zohara pulled out a green shirt with a picture of a boat and seemed unsure whom to hand it to. She finally gave it to Yehuda, who said, "Hold him up for a sec." Zohara looked at Nili, who gave her a grimace of embarrassment, and Amos went over to the bed, mostly to put an end to all these fragments of shirking and exchanges of gestures, and started lifting Avishay's upper body. He was heavier than Amos had expected and the contact with his skin was disgusting, but he overcame it and forged ahead. Except that Avishay's skin peeled off under his fingers and he removed them and held Avishay with his sleeved arms so that he would have no skin-on-skin contact, no dead-skin-on-healthy-skin. But Avishay was heavy and Amos dropped him back onto the bed and looked at his fingers. He instinctively wiped them off on Avishay, but his skin only peeled off more. Nili said, "It can't be helped, that's what happens. It's these kind of blisters that come out sometimes afterwards." Yehuda came to his aid and put the shirt in Nili's hands and helped him hoist up Avishay, who was now sitting up in bed, one shoulder in Yehuda's hand and the other under three of Amos's fingers, as he tried to figure out how many fingers he could remove from the body without it collapsing.

Zohara said, "Dear God, what a terrible thing . . . Look at his back, look at that purple."

"Put it on him, put the shirt on," Yehuda said to Nili, and she came closer to Avishay with the neck-hole held wide open between her fists, the way you dress a baby. She tried to lift his drooping head with her elbow but she couldn't do it, and Amos said to Zohara, "Help her out." Zohara came closer to the bed and tried to lift Avishay's head, first with one finger, then with two, the opposite path of the one Amos had just taken, until she had no choice but to support the back of his neck with her entire hand, her own head moving as far away as her neck would allow, with a look of disgust on her face. But no one was comforting or encouraging her now—none of them had the patience. Nili moved the shirt over his head, Yehuda and Amos helped her with the arms, and eventually Avishay was wearing a green shirt with an illustration of a black sailboat, his head drooping forward.

"Move the sheet, will you?" Yehuda said, and Zohara hurriedly flung it off onto the floor. "Shoes," Nili said. She looked under the bed, crawled around and pulled out a pair from the other side, and put them on Avishay's feet. "These really don't match the pants, but never mind now," she commented.

"Okay, ready?" Amos said. "I'm lifting," Yehuda confirmed. They both lifted Avishay, each from an armpit, and Amos said, "My side, my side!" and they pulled him with some effort to the right side of the bed, until his rear end fell onto the carpeting. His feet were still perched on the bed, and Yehuda leaned his back on the wall and straightened up, and Amos did the same.

"Listen, we're not going to be able to do this," said Zohara, offering insights instead of effort. Yehuda said, "Yes we are, we are, open the door all the way," and he started dragging Avishay backwards, holding him by the armpits, around the bed. Amos said, "Hang on, I'll help you," but Yehuda grunted, "No need, move, move back, make room." The three of them reversed out the door and watched Yehuda's back as he dragged Avishay into the middle of the living room. He put him down on the laminate floor next to the ottoman and straightened up, sweating: "Can I get some water?" Zohara hurried to the kitchen and came back with a full glass and said apologetically, "It's tap."

Yehuda had a few sips, handed the glass back to Zohara, and said, "Right. I suggest the two of you go out to the stairwell. One go up to the third floor and one down to the ground, and if someone comes, yell, 'Yehuda!' or 'Avishay!' or something."

"What good will that do?" Nili asked. "What are you going to do with him if you're halfway down the stairs?"

"I'll sit him on the steps and hug him or something, like he's not feeling well. But who's going to be out there now anyway? It's almost midnight."

"Where's the car?" Amos asked.

"About seven houses down. We couldn't find parking. We should have thought of that before, actually, to save a spot, but never mind now. It's not very far."

"It would be better to drive it over here, just double-park outside, put the blinkers on for a couple of minutes."

"That'll block the street, it's a big vehicle."

"The question is, what's preferable? Otherwise you have to schlep him another few hundred feet. He's heavy, and also, someone might see."

"Don't worry about it, let's not make things complicated. It'll be fine. I think we should take turns—it'll look less odd for one of us to carry him on our back, like he really is drunk or injured or something, rather than both carrying him by the arms and legs. It'll attract less attention."

"Okay," Amos said. "Should I go first?"

"No, I'll start, it's okay. You two go out to the steps and leave the door open, so I can hear if you say anything."

Nili and Zohara walked out to the stairwell and Yehuda and Amos stayed in the living room.

"We'll wait for one minute, then if they're quiet we'll start," Amos said.

"Did you ever think you'd be doing something like this?" Yehuda asked him.

"To say no would be an understatement . . ."

"What a week we've ended up having, heh?"

Amos thought for a minute and then asked him, "Aren't you stressed out by it?"

"By what?"

"I don't know, aren't you worried we'll get caught?"

"How would we get caught? By who?"

"I don't know."

"Forget it, it's nonsense, believe me, the only thing—" Yehuda was interrupted by his phone ringing, its startling volume reminding them of the depth of the night. Yehuda answered quickly, to make the noise stop, and said to Amos, "It's Zohara." He listened for a moment and spoke into the phone: "Because we didn't know you were already in position. Okay, we're leaving." Then he said to Amos, "Let's go." He knelt down with his back to Avishay and said, "Hoist him onto my shoulders."

Amos bent over and tried to lift Avishay's upper body, but then he realized how it was going to end up looking. "Shouldn't he be the other way around? So his belly's against your back, not back-to-back? Do you know what I mean?"

Yehuda turned around as if straining to organize the bodies' spatial arrangement in his mind.

"It'll be more natural than having his face exposed to the street," Amos added.

"Good point. Let's turn him around." They turned Avishay over onto his face and Yehuda knelt back down with his back to him.

Amos lifted up Avishay's arms and tried to hang them over Yehuda's bowed neck, but they twisted and stretched out in an unnatural position, which would have been very painful for Avishay were he alive, and Amos instinctively pulled back. For the first time in his life he thought about the Jewish concept of the wholeness of the body, the prohibition against damaging the deceased—he wasn't sure exactly what the rules were. Sometimes they referenced it in the papers, in stories about those families who wouldn't let their loved ones be autopsied, and he always had such contempt for the prohibition and for those people. But now he felt there was something to it after all. How could they just drag Avishay like that, let him fall, twist his arms around? What if they came off? What if they pulled his arms out? So what if he was dead.

This whole week began to seem wrong. They were abusing him. There was that other Jewish prohibition, about not delaying the burial and all that—maybe that made sense, too. Avishay was decomposing, he was reeking, he was being humiliated, he was not resting. It's true that it was being done for his sake, and they only meant well, but Avishay hadn't asked for it. He was lying there helplessly while they decided for him, did this thing and not the other, invaded his home, his privacy, learned he was a father before he himself found out.

"Leave it, leave it," Yehuda said, and reached behind his back with both arms. "Just give me the hands."

Amos gently lifted Avishay's hands and moved them closer to Yehuda's. The moment the fingers touched one another, Yehuda's hands gripped Avishay's strongly, and in one surprising motion he stood up, pulling Avishay off the floor as he did so, and started carrying him off on his back.

Amos watched Yehuda take one step, then another. Avishay was obviously heavy, and Amos wondered when his turn would come and whether he'd be able to do it.

Nili came downstairs. "Give me the car keys, I'll start the engine."

"They're in my pocket, take them," Yehuda said, and he stood still so Nili could dig through his left pocket, then the right one, until she finally pulled out the keys. "It's a black Seat Alhambra, outside Bar Kochva ten," he told her.

"Is there a code?" Amos asked.

"Forty-three, thirteen, asterisk." There, he had contributed something after all.

Nili passed them and went out onto the street, Yehuda walked behind her with Avishay on his back, and Amos brought up the rear. Yehuda didn't stop: without saying a word, he exited the building. Amos imagined him saying: If I stop and have to start over, it'll only be harder. He was going to take him all the way, that was clear, and probably had been for a while. Amos watched him carrying this man who weighed as much as he did, struggling but managing, his body entirely alert, necessary; not like him, Amos, part of whose body was in vain, a weed. It's because of the food, the food and the exercise, and the cigarettes that Yehuda had quit, and it seemed to him both fair and unfair at the same time: fair because that's how it went, that was the deal, there was no big secret, everyone knew it, you eat well and don't smoke and in return you live well and look good. Yet unfair for the same exact reason: because it was so simple yet so impossible, like waving hello for a man with an amputated arm.

He reminded himself that he did not envy Yehuda, and that helped a little. If anything, he pitied him slightly. That was what enabled their friendship, tightened them into one mass—because, after all, Amos was no idiot: he knew that Yehuda pitied him, too. He supported Amos wholeheartedly, the way only someone who pities can be supportive. Because Amos made do with his life, or something like that. It didn't bother Amos, in fact it amused him, he'd long ago stopped trying to persuade Yehuda that he actually had a fairly glamorous life, for an academic. In return, he pitied Yehuda because of the book, which nothing was going to come of, and because of all the things that nothing was ever going to come of. And so they pitied each other and they were true friends, without any resentment.

══════

Up against a stone wall, hidden from the empty street, three twenty-somethings stood smoking. Yehuda sped up but Amos's gaze was captured by their curious ones, and he took one step back toward them, feeling he had no choice, obliged to satisfy their curiosity.

"He's not feeling well," he explained.

"Do you need help?" the woman asked.

"No, no, our car's right here, but thanks."

"Good luck."

"Thanks," Amos said.

One young man said, "Good night."

Amos felt ridiculous. Those kids were polite but they were still going to talk about him; that's how young they were and how strange he was. He felt like telling them what they were really doing, just to surprise them, to shake things up a bit: *You're not just young and I'm not just old. No.*

He caught up with Yehuda and they moved along as quickly as Avishay's weight would allow. They kept their eyes on the ground, stealing frequent glances around. Yehuda stopped, rearranged the weight on his shoulders, and resumed walking, Avishay's torso now dangling in front of him, on his chest. A murky liquid suddenly dribbled out of Avishay's lips, as though in an instant he'd become alive and drunk. Yehuda was so startled, or disgusted, that he dropped Avishay to the sidewalk without a second thought, like a man finding a cockroach on his sweater. Amos just had time to think: He's alive, he's obviously alive, that makes so much more sense, an embarrassing little mistake, a story for the grandkids, a sweet ending for this whole farce. But when they went closer to Avishay—Yehuda said it first: "Avishay?" and saved Amos the humiliation, then shook him gently, as if to compensate him for being dropped—Avishay did not expel fluid from his lungs like a drowning man pulled ashore and did not move and did not say anything. Amos thought the drop might have been enough to crack his skull and kill him all over again, even if he had been resurrected. That's classic, he thought: now we really will be guilty of something. Real murderers. That's what happens with good intentions.

"I'm calling Nili," he said, and the sentence cost him a great deal of effort, as though he were briefly dead or paralyzed himself. A long moment later he pulled out his cell phone from his pocket.

"Where are you?" Nili said.

"He threw up. Avishay threw up. There was vomit coming out of his mouth," Amos stammered.

"What?"

"He's lying here on the sidewalk, he had this kind of vomit coming from his mouth."

"Lying there dead . . ." Nili said.

"I think so, yes."

"Oh, I was confused for a minute. It's his gut. It's the contents of his stomach, it must have come out because of the angle."

"What he ate? Is that what you mean?" Amos asked.

"I think so, yes. Or maybe it's actually decomposition fluids."

"Is that normal?"

"How should I know? Normal is when you bury a man two hours later, not carry him upside down half a block from the shopping mall. But it makes sense, I suppose."

At that very moment Amos was rattled by a whirlwind that touched his arm, and he looked up just in time to see a biker screeching to a stop and Yehuda looking back uncomprehendingly, or perhaps comprehending a second before he did, but either way it was too late: the biker had run over Avishay. Run him over with his electric bike.

The biker looked back, and Amos thought: He's going to ride away. Leave, ride away, just keep going, hit and run like a normal person. But the guy jumped off his bike and pulled his helmet off and threw it down and leaned over Avishay's body. "I killed him . . ." he said. "I killed him!" His voice was full of terror—perhaps that was what real grief sounded like. Amos and Yehuda looked at each other and just stood there, stunned, and Amos thought this was the time, this was his uber-moment, to save their skin, his skin. But he couldn't take his eyes off this young man, who kept saying, "I killed him," with his hands on Avishay in a sort of theoretical resuscitation position but without moving, his eyes pinned on Amos and Yehuda. "I killed him." Amos felt sorry for him. He was maybe twenty-five, or even twenty. What does a twenty-year-old know? Who knows what a twenty-year-old knows? Is this going to be easy or impossible? As Amos continued to invest far too much thought in the wrong things, Yehuda said to the guy, "No, no, who are you calling?" And then Amos saw that the biker was on his cell phone, saying, "Ambulance." Yehuda said, "We've called. We've already called them." The guy said, "When?" and Yehuda repeated, like a robot, "We've called, we've called them." Meanwhile, the operator had answered and the guy said, "Yes, one minute," and Yehuda motioned to him: *Hang up!* "We've called them, we've called them, they get angry if you call twice," Yehuda insisted. The guy said into the phone, "They've already called an ambulance. Goodbye, then," wanting to stretch out the moment before he went back to his new, terrible life. He put his phone down on the sidewalk and looked back at Avishay. "We have to cut an air hole."

It occurred to Amos that they weren't upset at all: their friend was dead, or injured, certainly run over, and they weren't moving. He leaned down next to the man, touched his arm as if to make way, and then examined Avishay and touched him, on his arms and stomach and face. With his other hand he tried to swat away a couple of flies. "He's completely alive," he said, and glanced at Yehuda, who looked confused: Was this good or bad, whatever Amos was doing down there? It wasn't clear yet.

"Really?" the biker asked, with doubt in his voice but also a hint of happiness.

"What's your name?" Amos asked him.

"Mine?"

"Yes, yours. With whom do I have the pleasure?" This was his moment to be an annoying uncle. His avuncular nature was his strong suit, the only possible defense.

"Gidi."

"Gidi," Amos repeated. "Gidi. Well, first of all, he's alive, so you can calm down."

"He's alive?" Gidi asked.

"Totally alive."

"But look at him."

"He was lying here long before you came along, there was no way you could have seen him," Amos said.

"He was lying here?"

Amos nodded, as if a nod was something he could more easily retract.

"Why?"

"Why?"

"Why was he lying here?"

Yehuda chimed in: "Because he's drunk, that's why."

"He's drunk?" Gidi asked dubiously.

"Drunk as a skunk, you'd be surprised—even seventy-year-olds get drunk sometimes," Amos insisted.

"But he's not breathing," Gidi pointed out.

"Not breathing? Can't you smell the whiskey?" He put his mouth up to Avishay's, then his ear, suddenly unable to remember what he was looking for and what to find it with.

"But I ran him over."

"There's no argument there," Amos said, "but he was in exactly this condition ten minutes ago."

Gidi looked back at them. "He did throw up."

"What?" Amos said.

"Oh yeah, he threw up, he threw up," Yehuda confirmed, and then Amos realized they had stupidly failed to play their winning card: the man was lying in a puddle of his own vomit, in the decomposition juices or stomach bile or whatever it was. A textbook drunk.

"He does smell pretty bad," Gidi acknowledged.

"He stinks. It's okay, you can say it," Amos said.

"Have you seen him in this state before? Is this normal for him?"

"We've been friends for fifty years," Yehuda replied, "so let's just say I've seen him in this state maybe five hundred times."

"So he's been lying here for ten minutes?"

"We were carrying him on our back and he fell."

"Oh, man," Gidi exclaimed.

"What can you do," Yehuda continued, "we've had a few ourselves, too."

"But we'll pick him up again soon," Amos added, "it's no big deal."

"Okay, well, the ambulance will probably take him," Gidi said, and Amos realized there was supposed to be an ambulance arriving.

"I think they'll take one look at him and let him go," Yehuda said.

"More alive than this, he's not going to be," Amos added, and Yehuda gave him a scolding look, as if to say, *Don't get carried away.*

"Well," Gidi said, "in the meantime, let's exchange contact info until they get here."

=====

The three of them sat next to Avishay, shivering with cold, waiting for the ambulance. Amos was overcome with weakness, as though the disaster had relieved him of any obligation to make an effort. For a moment he imagined it was the police who were on their way—the body, after all, was right there.

He suddenly realized what they should have said: they should have reprimanded Gidi. They should have got angry, lost their temper. Right from the start. That's what they should have done. How dumb of them. Instead of just acting like people act, they'd made the number one mistake made by criminals and liars: defense instead of offense. Maybe because they weren't real criminals, not even aspiring ones.

He considered changing tactics, it might not be too late, but much as he tried he could not imagine himself standing up now and starting to yell at this Gidi: *You ruined his life! You've destroyed a whole life! Speeding down the middle of a busy sidewalk like a lunatic! Who brought you up, I'd like to know! You and all your friends, you think the street belongs to you! Get out of here and don't stand next to my friend who you just ran over! At least pay him that respect.*

He'd had enough sense to give him Avishay's phone number and address, not one of theirs. They had Avishay's phone anyway, and his apartment was empty. He'd considered making something up, which would have been the safest option. But from the minute Gidi had Avishay's number—"I'll call him now, so he'll have mine," Gidi said—he was afraid to lie. What's more, he had discovered that he was simply incapable of telling an absolute, arbitrary lie.

But what difference did it make now? None. A drop in the ocean. Their lives would be over that night; they already were. He'd moved a body in the middle of the night. This would all be in the papers tomorrow.

The flies kept buzzing around Avishay's eyes, or maybe his nose, and it occurred to Amos that they were there for a reason: it was him, the smell, the decomposition. These were no ordinary Tel Aviv flies, they were corpse flies. Or was that the same thing? Anyway, they might multiply, attract more and more flies as he lay there, to do who knows what else. Larva. Nili had said something about larva. Amos felt nauseated, and the nausea displaced the panic.

He took his phone out to send a message to Yehuda, who was sitting right next to him: "What do we do?" But when he looked up to focus his eyes, because he didn't have the right glasses on, he suddenly saw a woman appearing out of the darkness: Nili. And then he remembered: Nili! He'd hung up on her in the middle of the call, she'd probably called and called but everyone's phones were silenced. She spread her arms out and said, "What's going on—" But before she could say "with you?" or "why aren't you answering?" she noticed Gidi, or maybe he noticed her, and he said, "Are you the paramedic?" Nili said, "No," and Amos thought: Shit. She's not *that* smart. Yehuda said, "Everything's okay, ma'am, it's just that this young man accidentally ran over our friend with his electric bike and we're waiting for the ambulance. I called them ages ago, I don't know why they're not here yet." Amos wasn't sure if he was imagining it or if Yehuda had said that last bit very loudly, accentuating, as if trying to send her a subconscious message. Yehuda continued: "He's totally fine, but this young man here is acting responsibly, he wants to wait for the ambulance, and rightly so." Nili listened and Amos couldn't decipher her expression, but then she said, "I know, I know, they're very busy, they sent me over. We're a subcontractor for Magen David Adom, they have a huge shortage of medics, especially on weekends." She's a genius, Amos thought. And Nili said, "Please let me through."

She leaned over Avishay and lifted up his shirt, but the minute his body was exposed she remembered what was hiding there, the early

stages of discoloration, splotches crawling up from the back, things
that should be hidden, and she bunched the shirt fabric around his
chest. There was a tire-shaped mark on Avishay's body, and there
were lacerations, with no blood. He looked like an ET, or a zombie.
Amos didn't know the lingo, but he looked odd, unnatural.

Nili started working on his chest in what looked to Amos like an
imitation of a first-aid class on a TV show, but maybe that's how it always looked, to the point where he wondered if she wasn't exaggerating, giving this Gidi too much time to wise up. Or was she waiting
for them to do something? Maybe they had a role here too?

"He's had a few drinks," Yehuda said.

Nili looked at him reproachfully: "A few?"

"That doesn't mean he deserves to get run over by a bike."

"Did he ingest anything else?" Nili asked.

"Of course not!" Amos said. "What do you mean, anything else?
Like drugs?"

"I don't know—drugs, pills, anything."

"Maybe half a Vaben before bed."

"I don't care about that," Nili said.

"Definitely not drugs."

Nili stood up and said, "You're extremely lucky." Then she looked
at Gidi like a teacher: "You are an extremely lucky young man."

"What? What?" Yehuda said.

"Tomorrow morning he'll be as good as new," she proclaimed.

"So nothing's wrong with him?" Gidi asked.

"But that doesn't mean you shouldn't throw that bike away. You
got lucky today—tomorrow it could end with a dead child and a
prison sentence." Then she said to Yehuda: "Do you have a way to
get him home or should I tell them to send the ambulance after all?"

"We can get him home," Amos said, "thank you very much."

But Gidi intervened: "No, tell them to send it, I'll pay for it."

Good God, Amos thought, *what a pain in the neck*. "You've already done enough," he said to Gidi, and felt like a bully kicking the poor guy when he was down.

Yehuda seemed a little surprised, as did Gidi.

Nili said, "Do you need anything else from me?"

"Thank you very much, really," Yehuda said.

"Shouldn't you write a report?" Gidi asked. "Some kind of report? For the insurance?"

"It's all done by email now, with the info you gave when you called," Nili explained.

Amos could see Gidi was not satisfied: he wanted to ask something else but he was too afraid.

Nili closed up her bag and said, "And tell your friend it's not good to drink that much. He's not twenty anymore."

"We'll tell him," Yehuda said, "thank you."

"Good night, and be more careful," Nili said, and she walked away.

Gidi said, "Come on, I'll help you carry him."

Yehuda reached out a hand to shake his. "My friend," he said, as Gidi put his weak hand in Yehuda's and listened, "this is where we part ways."

"Please be in touch with me tomorrow. Let me know everything's okay, yeah? Or I'll call you, I just don't want to be a bother."

"Everything will be fine. Bye."

Gidi walked to his bike, held the handlebars, and started slowly wheeling the bike away. Amos thought: *He is never going to leave.*

Hearing the silence, Amos turned around and found Yehuda staring at Avishay with a frozen, unnatural look, as if remembering too late to hold a vigil for the dead. Yehuda's shirt had vomit on it; pieces of it had stopped halfway down and were clinging to the fabric. Amos began to consider how strong the smell was, as though Gidi were carrying away their panic on his bike, making way for other things. "Do you think maybe you should take your shirt off?"

Yehuda gave him a baffled look.

Amos jerked his chin at Yehuda's shirt, and Yehuda looked down, seemingly surprised to discover the filth. He grabbed his cuffs, the right one in his left hand and the left in his right, in preparation for disrobing. But when he started lifting up the shirt, pieces dropped into its folds like into a sack, and its imminent contact with his forehead was intolerable, even in theory. Yehuda let the shirt drop with his arms spread alongside his body, as though he wanted to fly out of it. He pinned his desperate eyes on Amos, like a toddler having trouble with his pajamas.

"Do it in one go, just pull it off," Amos said encouragingly.

"Okay." Yehuda scrunched his eyes in preparation, then leaned over to the sidewalk and vomited repeatedly.

———

When they got to the van, the engine was running and Nili was at the wheel. *It was like a heist*, Amos thought. Zohara stood outside and symbolically leaned over as Yehuda tried to lay Avishay gently on his back in the rear seat, like a baby. Amos wasn't the only one around here not doing anything useful.

He stepped onto the road, opened the other door, and started pulling Avishay by his shoulders until his head reached the edge of the seat.

"What was all that about? What do we do now?" Nili asked.

"Never mind that now, let's finish with this," Yehuda said. "We'll talk about everything later."

Two thirds of Avishay's legs were sticking out of the van, like a bridge to the sidewalk, and Yehuda tried to shove them in diagonally onto the floor. "Turn him, turn him onto his side."

Amos tilted Avishay as far as he could from one side of the van, and Yehuda from the other side, tilting and pushing at the same time, until Avishay was finally squeezed in. "I'm shutting the door," Amos said, and he pushed the door shut, too weakly at first, afraid of Avishay's skull, and then again, hard: they didn't want the door to come open in the middle of the drive. Yehuda shut his side and the door pushed Avishay's feet a little farther in.

Amos looked at Avishay through the window. His body created a triangle: one point was his rear end on its side, up against the backrest of the seat; the second was his feet behind the driver's seat, and the third and final point was his head, suspended in midair between the back seat and the passenger seat. Not at all fetal, not as he'd expected, for some reason.

He looked away and walked back to the sidewalk. Yehuda had switched with Nili in the driver's seat, and she sat next to him. Amos and Zohara, the useless ones, stood on the sidewalk. Nili poked her head out through the window: "Meet us there?"

"Yes, see you there," Zohara answered.

Yehuda signaled and they pulled out.

"Now will you tell me what happened?" Zohara said.

Amos replied wearily, "I'll tell you in the car."

=====

Zohara was rattled. "So what do we do?"

"I don't know. We'll all talk about it together soon."

"Is he injured? Does he have wounds on his body? Did anything break?"

"I don't know. From what I saw, he has scrapes on his stomach, sort of little rips, but I only saw a little. I don't know what else is under his clothes."

"So what are we going to do?"

"I don't know," Amos repeated.

"How are we going to explain it? There's no way to explain it, that's it, we're finished, he didn't die of a heart attack in bed now."

"I don't understand," Amos said. He was tired. So tired.

"If he died in bed," Zohara explained, "then how exactly did he get cut and injured and I don't know what?"

Amos was astonished to realize he'd never even thought of that because he'd been so busy worrying about the phones—the biker had Avishay's number, there was a loose end, it was all unraveling. But Zohara was right.

=====

He wondered if Yehuda was driving faster, in light of the circumstances, or slower. But when they got there they could already see him opening the front door. Amos could only guess that Avishay was lying there beneath him, outside their field of vision, on the doorstep, like a newspaper. They waited in the car, on the driveway outside the gate. Someone needed to open it for them but they would wait patiently, of course, and the fact that meanwhile they were blocking the road—even though no one was going to be pushing a stroller past at 1:15 a.m.—seemed like a good enough excuse to stay in the car and not get out to help.

They sat quietly for a while, and then Zohara said, "So Varda doesn't know anything, heh?"

It was such a non sequitur that he felt like she was punishing him for something, perhaps his lack of cooperation. "It's just until after the . . . I don't know what to call it, the Nobel yes-or-no. It's not like I would hide something like this from her, God forbid, you know?"

"But won't she be hurt that you didn't tell her?"

"I don't think so, I think she'll understand that it was for her own good."

"That you didn't tell her Avishay was dead for a week and a half? She'll understand? Really?"

"She won't have much choice," Amos said. Then he pounced on the slight lull in the conversation and said, "Go find out what's happening, I think they forgot about us."

Zohara opened the door, walked up the front path, rang the bell, and disappeared into the house.

He had a feeling they'd be stuck there for a long time; courtesy didn't seem like a high priority right now. But a moment later Yehuda appeared and opened the gate. He waited for Amos to park and they both went inside.

Avishay lay on his side on the big green couch, with his head sticking out past the armrest and lolling back, as if he were gazing at the ceiling. One foot was on the floor, touching the table leg. His shirt was so tattered that it barely stayed on his chest. Now, in the light, Amos could clearly see the lacerations, inviting a gaze into the flesh, with tire marks that covered them only at first glance. He looked as if he'd been dropped, and Amos assumed Yehuda had simply collapsed onto the couch with him and then not moved him, the way you don't play around with a body at a crime scene, however strangely it may be positioned.

On the two matching armchairs on either side of the big couch sat Nili and Zohara, like hosts on a bizarre talk show, or perhaps like the guests. With Yehuda's attractive house in the background—large open-plan kitchen, Afghan rugs, bottle chandelier, oversized chairs that made even Nili look small—the three of them brought to his mind a little harem where something had gone horribly wrong.

Sunday

Zohara

17

She chose the left side of the closet for herself. At first she was tempted to sort things according to her own tastes, the way she hadn't been able to do when he was still alive. But that might take a long time, and she didn't know how much time she had. Or rather, she knew how much time she had, she knew all too well, but she wasn't sure what else she needed to get done. Move the clothes, that was first. She thought that was it, that was the main thing, but everything was so new, so go figure. She had to build in a margin of error.

When she was finished, the bed was piled with suits and linens, button-down shirts and belts and scarves, towels and blankets of various weights. She went into the kitchen and opened a few drawers, and finally found a roll of trash bags under the sink. She pulled several off, mechanically stabbing each one with the bag opener hanging under the cabinet, and took them back to the bedroom. She started filling them gleefully, shoving things in without worrying about neatly folding the fine fabrics.

She thought back, unwillingly, to last night. She felt exponentially more sinful now, sneaking around behind the sneakers-around, committing the crime in full daylight and of sound mind.

She wondered whether to pile all the bags by the door and then take them out to the car, or take the first two out now. She settled on the latter. She made sure the key was in her pocket—the last thing she needed now was to get locked out of Avishay's apartment. But when she opened her trunk, the car alarm started wailing, as if to snitch on its owner. She pressed the remote buttons frantically until it finally fell silent for no particular reason. She loaded the two bags and slammed the trunk door shut on them. She felt like leaning on the car for a moment, but was afraid the alarm would go off again. She wished she could sit down, but there was nowhere to sit. So she just stood there, exhausted, fueling her exhaustion by thinking about the hike back to the third floor.

There was no choice.

———

Zohara had never felt as lonely as she had that morning, roaming through the countless Google results for "family lawyer." People like her didn't look for a lawyer on Google—they asked around, they got referrals. But she had no one to ask, because she couldn't tell anyone about this. And once again she sensed the anger that had increasingly filled her these past few days, at Avishay, who had imposed a secret on her that she was not allowed to tell, terrorizing her in his own charming way, leaving her muffled with the secret, trapped inside it, pushed away, isolated from the whole world. Like a battered woman—that phrase kept coming to her, even though it was completely overblown, because of course she wasn't a battered woman. And yet, wasn't that what people said about them? About those women in the papers? How the man would gradually isolate them, seal off their outlets for advice, for escape, until they were entirely dependent on him? Avishay hadn't wanted her to be dependent on him, that was true. He'd never asked her to cling to him or to look only to him; quite the opposite—he could never be accused of that. But for twenty years he'd been ashamed of her, he'd kept her gagged in the dark. So what else could you call it?

Eventually she chose one based on her name: Attorney Ada Porat. She wanted a female lawyer. When they met, Attorney Porat asked a few questions (marital status: single; children: none) and then said, "All right, Zohara, tell me why you're here."

Zohara wanted to start talking, but she couldn't. The lawyer's eyes were pinned on her and she had a friendly expression. Zohara summoned all her concentration, all her energy, and tried to focus on the lower half of the lawyer's face, but the battle was already lost: tears began streaming from her eyes.

Ada Porat did not say a word. She was younger than her name implied, barely forty. She was pretty, not just well-groomed in that lawyerly way that you could look down on. Married, or "in a relationship," of that there was no doubt, but Zohara wasn't sure about kids.

She reached out for a box of tissues in an attractive fabric holder, which sat on Ada's side of the table. Ada quickly pushed it toward her, and Zohara blew her nose. She was thirsty. She wished Ada would offer her some water, but she didn't. She blew her nose again, emptying the final remnants of her folly into the tissue. "I want your advice about a relationship I'm in," she said finally. She looked at Ada, hoping her face might help her decide what to say, but Ada only sat there listening quietly. Originally she'd planned to say very little, just to make a theoretical enquiry into the relevant legalities. At most, she would disclose the very barest of facts. But sitting there in front of this woman, she felt herself melt into the role of patient, bestowing absolute trust on her. Only for formality's sake did she ask, "Everything we say here is confidential, right?"

Ada replied, "Of course, unless you're about to commit a murder or something," with a smile, and Zohara had to remind herself of the nature of the crime she'd just come from: they'd transported a body but they hadn't murdered anyone.

"Okay," she said, "so this is the situation. I've been in a relationship with a man, he's around my age, for twenty years now."

"He's unmarried?"

"Yes."

Ada wrote something down on a piece of paper. "A romantic relationship?"

"You could say so, yes. We've been very, very good friends for decades, and at some point it became romantic, intimate."

"More intimate than romantic?"

"I would say both," Zohara replied, even though that wasn't entirely true.

"Okay."

"And now he's died."

"I'm sorry."

"Thank you."

"Suddenly?"

"Very. It was cardiac arrest," she said, stubbornly ignoring Nili's explanations about how "Avishay didn't die of a cardiac arrest. You need to understand: everyone dies of cardiac arrest in the end, even someone who has cancer. It was probably myocardial infarction or an arrhythmia or something."

"Oh my," Ada said.

"The question is, what has to occur in order for me to be considered his common-law wife? I mean, for a court to recognize that."

"I understand you never signed an agreement or declared yourselves common-law spouses?"

"What do you mean, declared?"

"In a legal affidavit, say, for some bureaucratic procedure."

"No," Zohara said.

"Does he have a will?"

"I have no idea. I don't think so." Then she remembered: "No, he doesn't." She happened to know that. Yehuda had tried to convince Avishay, and all of them, to have a will made when he'd done it himself. He'd tried so hard that Nili had finally told him, "Why do you keep going on about this? Is there a group discount or something?" But Nili already had one anyway, since the divorce, she said it was crucial when you got divorced, and Avishay said that if you didn't have kids it wasn't critical, and Yehuda said, "That's not true at all, the lawyer explained it to me, that is a major misconception," and Zohara had wondered what would happen to her apartment after she died, but then she'd forgotten about it. "I just remembered—he doesn't have one."

"Okay, and you live together?"

"No. I mean, I spend a lot of time there, but I have my own apartment too, in Kiryat Ono."

"What do you mean 'a lot'? Do you keep up the apartment in Kiryat Ono just in case, or do you live in that apartment and stay at his place occasionally?"

"No, I live in my apartment, it's not vacant or anything."

"And I gather you want to be recognized as his common-law spouse for purposes of inheritance?"

"I don't even know yet if I want to, you know, I'm just making inquiries." Zohara could see Ada's eyes staring at her, impervious, politely traversing the emotional vacillations that are none of a lawyer's business, but Zohara had to say it, so people would know she was reasonable, so Ada would know too, so she herself would know. But Ada was waiting for an answer and Zohara said, "It's not just the inheritance. In fact it's hardly about that at all. I want to be recognized as his partner, as his widow, if you could call it that."

"I see," Ada said, "but you have to understand that the posthumous implications are primarily financial. In fact, I might say solely financial. It's not just the inheritance, it's also next-of-kin rights, pensions, that sort of thing. I understand he has an apartment—he owns it?"

"Yes."

"Are there other assets?"

"He's expected to receive a sum of money."

"From what source?"

"He's a candidate for a prize, and he may get it. An academic prize, for academic achievements."

"And he can receive it even though he's deceased? It's an award given posthumously?"

"Um, yes. It's supposed to happen any day now, the decision."

"And it's a significant sum, I understand?"

"Very significant. The question is whether I'm entitled to that money. Or part of it."

"Does he have any living relatives?"

"He has a mother, she's very elderly, and she has advanced dementia. And a sister. His father is dead."

"And no children."

"No," Zohara confirmed. And then she remembered.

—————

Since he'd died she hadn't been able to fall asleep except when she was forced to, at dawn. She'd been concocting a parallel scheme at nights, a darker one than their scheme of the past few days.

She kept picturing the hours after his death was made public. That was where it all started. She imagined herself at the funeral, a regular mourner, lacking rights or status, crying discreetly like all the other grievers. And then in the farther future, being eaten away by her unrecognized status, growing old into it like a prideful baroness appointed by a kingdom that no longer existed. And when she imagined, with all her powers, the nights that would look like that, and the days, she was not saddened but tortured: the future she saw was one of actual physical suffering, scraping her skin and grating on her soul, until finally she would push the images away, sometimes physically, by actually turning her head aside, so that she could stop enduring it.

In one of those episodes, a new thought entered her mind: he's going to win. Avishay might win a Nobel Prize. And when he does, the funeral will be the last of her problems. There will not be a single newspaper, in Israel or in the world, that won't write about him. They'll be looking for material, quotes, stories, anecdotes, they'll probably get to her, too, and to Amos and Nili and Yehuda. Every acquaintance and relative will eulogize him. And the ceremony! Someone will go to the ceremony. Someone will accept the prize on his behalf.

It should have been her. All of that should have been hers, just as he should have been hers. And now she would not only miss out on the stamp of normalcy that she'd been deprived of for so many years, but also on being in a relationship with a Nobel laureate—the definitive, final confirmation.

And that's how it suddenly came to her: What if she presented herself as his loved one?

The thought singed her like a leaping flame, and she pulled back yet woke up at the same time, as if to make sure no one was listening before she went on. Would it do any harm? To whom? Not to him, that's for sure. He already had his glorious headstone. And he owed her.

Not that she would really do it. For lots of reasons, not least of which was that there were plenty of people who could testify to her and Avishay's real relationship. Plenty of people who would get up and say, *Hold on, this woman was never his partner.* But who, in fact? Yehuda, Nili, and Amos, his mother and sister, colleagues from the university maybe. If he'd had a partner, they would have known. But who would ask them? So really it was Yehuda, Nili, and Amos. All the others were solvable.

What would they actually need to do? First she would tell them, of course, about all those years, about their relationship. She might embellish a little. And they'd just have to say that yes, there was no question about it, they were a couple, they'd done almost everything together, they'd come to events together, to friends' houses. That was true: When was the last time they hadn't sat together at a briss or a wedding or a bar mitzvah? Even to ceremonies where Avishay was getting an award they usually all came, certainly to the big ones. Zohara always came, if she was invited. So what if he didn't thank her in his speeches? That meant nothing. He didn't thank anyone.

And that was all. This would not involve any bodies or decomposition or forging text messages and emails and secrets and lies. It was much simpler, there was no doubt about that, much less demanding. And in return they would change the life of a living woman, not a dead man.

Then she had a funny idea: she could claim that *she* hadn't wanted it to come out. That she hadn't allowed Avishay to say anything, maybe because she preferred things that way, noncommittal. And now? Now that he was dead, she had a guilty conscience. It would be her gift to him, she decided, a gift after death. But who would believe that?

Someone would bring up the money. Probably Amos, who was anxious about the whole thing already. *It's not all that simple and romantic, Zohara,* he'd say. *With all due respect, this has far-reaching financial consequences. The man could come into a fortune next week, and you are now claiming a right to that money—or am I misunderstanding? Well then, seriously, it's enough, there's only so far we can go. We're just decent people who tried to do a good deed, and next thing we know we're slipping into criminality.*

There was the question of money, that was true. She hadn't thought about it immediately; in fact she hadn't thought about it at all. But while the thoughts drilled through her mind, while she sailed away on them for experimental purposes, there was that term bobbing along on the current: *common-law spouses.* It had been buried on the outskirts of her consciousness, one of those things that you know exists but you're never sure exactly what it is, and Zohara easily got out of bed, which she'd only got into with some effort, as wide awake as a child forced to go to bed, and went to the computer and in ten minutes knew more or less everything there was to know about common-law spouses.

She wasn't able to ascertain what would become of the prize and whether she would be entitled to it—that wasn't exactly a recurrent question on the family-law FAQs ("My common-law husband died and a week later he got a Nobel Prize: what should I do?")—but she would be entitled to half of all his property, including pension funds and savings. She hadn't thought of that: she could argue good faith on that account. But if she was going to do this, then why not? Who would that money go to—Ruthi? Did Ruthi deserve it more than she did? What had Ruthi ever done for him? If Yehuda, who'd practically been one of the family growing up, who knew the two siblings better than anyone else did, was so bitter because of how Ruthi treated Avishay, then what more did they need?

Whereas she, Zohara, could use that money to change her life, to compensate herself for all the bad years. She wouldn't sell Avishay's apartment, she'd simply move in. In one fell swoop she'd put an end to the futile search that had already become a joke. She'd live in Tel Aviv and she'd live well. Maybe she'd meet someone. Maybe that's what she needed in order to meet someone: to change her skin, to step out of it, to do something extreme but still reasonable, something sanctioned by human compassion—if not by law. What was all this if not the chance of a lifetime, her ticket to normalcy? She would be his widow, and it would be the revenge he'd always had coming; it would be his recompense. Even if he didn't win the prize. Even if he didn't—that's what she now realized. She needed it. Maybe it would even be better if he didn't win. Yes, that would be best. So it wouldn't attract so much attention, so she could get what she deserved quietly.

This was her moment to break free. Someone else had killed him for her, because she hadn't been able to do it herself. It occurred to her that it wasn't an entry ticket she was seeking, but an exit one, a pardon: she'd been serving a life sentence, and her foolish attempts at freedom had been repeatedly made a mockery of. It was a life sentence that could end only in death. And here it was: death.

It was the same thing. The exact same thing. They'd have no choice but to go along, because she'd caught them. Every argument they'd made in favor of hiding Avishay's death was valid here, too. The case was already made: it's fun, it's an experience, it's a little bit exhilarating. Why not start? Let's start, we can always stop later. And if they get caught? So they get caught. Who's going to do anything to a professor of economics, a retired pediatrician, and an inventor?

But what if they did object? What if they brought up other arguments, ones she hadn't considered? What if she didn't have the wherewithal to argue?

She would say: I never wanted it to come to this, but you're forcing me into it, and all it does is show you up as bad friends, not me. If I'm not important to you as your friend, then I'm going to break the rules over Avishay. I'm certain you can understand that.

—————

She wondered if it was essential information. After all, it was only a fetus—who could even say if there'd ever be a child? As Zohara vacillated, even though she knew the answer was yes, Ada had already moved on: "So in fact we have three potential heirs—the mother, the sister, and you."

Zohara was forced to expound: "There's also a woman who claims she's pregnant by him."

Ada's expression lapsed into surprise mixed with reproach, whether at Avishay and his lechery, or at Zohara for only mentioning this now. "What do you mean 'claims'? Does he deny it? I mean, did he deny it?"

"He doesn't know about it. She popped up after he died."

"Was she in a relationship with him? Were they having intercourse while you were in a relationship?"

Zohara could feel the feathers being plucked off her story one by one, and so easily—how little it took to expose her pathetic case. "That's what she's claiming," she finally said.

"Okay, look. Your story is slightly complicated. At this stage, I can tell you two essential things about this whole business of common-law spouses. The first thing is that there are no rules. The whole area is subject to a lot of interpretation, and all sorts of couples and relationships can be awarded that definition. There are two parameters that enter the picture here, which are considered essential: one is the question of a shared household, and that—we don't have. Which is a problem. Two—and this is the really essential parameter for us—is the issue of 'common,' meaning, proving that you were commonly known as a couple. So people around you, on your side but mostly on his side, would have to attest that you were a couple and a family unit for all intents and purposes. The question is whether we have that. The mother and the sister, would they testify that you were his partner?" Before Zohara could answer, she continued: "Because you have to take into account that it would be completely opposed to their best interests. If you are not recognized as his partner, the mother and the sister inherit his estate fifty-fifty, that's assuming of course there's no child, because if there's a child then he inherits everything."

"He inherits everything even if I am his partner?"

"No, if you're recognized as his partner, then the child gets half and you get half, and then the mother and the sister get nothing. So in other words it's in their best interest for there to be no partner and no child. By the way, do you know how far along she is?"

"No."

"Because this child must be born no more than three hundred days after the father's death, otherwise he won't be entitled to anything."

Zohara made a quick calculation and suddenly saw this child as a monstrous creature, plotting against her in his mother's belly for three-hundred-and-something days. "Well, it's impossible to get to three hundred days."

"Not if it's from someone else," Ada pointed out. "The question is, basically, what will the mother and the sister say."

"I don't think the mother is capable of testifying to anything. She remembers less and less, I'm not sure how much longer she'll even be alive. And the sister isn't all there either. She'll want the money for herself, or for herself and the mother, of that I have no doubt, she's broke. But she's semi-unhinged, I don't think it'll—"

"What do you mean, unhinged? Is she institutionalized? Is she mentally ill?"

"I don't know if she's officially recognized as mentally ill, but she's extremely unstable and she has a history of getting into trouble. She's not exactly the most reliable thing you could put on a stand, especially if it came to her word against ours."

"The question is, who is *ours*? Who do we have who's going to stand in a court and declare: This woman and this man were a couple. A family unit, for all intents and purposes."

"We have people. We do."

18

By the time she got into bed it was almost four. There was a tired taste in her mouth, but she already knew it would lead to nothing. She'd spent enough sleepless nights in her life: it would send her to bed, crawl up the tunnels of her nose and irritate and tickle her, but sleep? That wasn't going to happen.

When had he slept with her? When had he met her? And where? Online? She imagined this girl, Liat, sitting at home, in her apartment, obviously in Tel Aviv, not even knowing that there was an Avishay, that this man was going to like her, and then to sleep with her in his comfortable apartment, where it was so fun to go to sleep and wake up in the middle of the night. All this seemed desperately, torturously unfair to Zohara—this colossal and unexpected happiness directed at the wrong person.

She imagined Liat's body without a face, the way one really should not imagine anyone. She imagined a crude, almost pornographic image. She imagined Avishay and his dick with her. Liat's body was smooth in her imagination, and she tried as hard as she could to wrinkle it a little, or maybe enlarge it, give her stomach a few folds. After all, she wasn't twenty, probably closer to forty, but she wasn't sure about the whole middle region, between twenty and seventy—who could remember what a thirty-eight-year-old body looked like?—and in her mind's eye Liat's body alternated between smooth and wrinkled, like unreliable "before" and "after" pictures.

Maybe they'd met for the child. To make him. Maybe Avishay had gone looking for a woman for that purpose, not for love. Maybe they hadn't even slept together, maybe she was inseminated, or injected, or whatever it was called. That thought brought Zohara some relief, but it was a warped relief, of limited scope, because this Liat was still lurking on the horizon with her fetus and her story, and they had yet to find out what had happened.

She thought about the child, who was half-Liat. A girl named Liat, thirty-eight years old, whom Avishay had known for maybe a month or two, six at most. No more than that. An ordinary passerby, one of several, in the life of a grown man who had waited long enough for this child, too long to have it with Liat.

He should have had it with her. He could have had it with her. They'd known each other since their twenties. So many years had gone by, in which they could have considered, debated, examined, pondered, and decided, and changed their minds and done it all over again. But Avishay had dozed off, he'd dozed off in the indulgent manner of men who are wanted, men who can do anything, even now, even afterward. Men who think they're the only ones in the world.

———

A hundred times she'd almost told them. A hundred times since he died, she'd almost opened her mouth and said, *I was having an affair with Avishay.* Or, *Did you know we were sleeping together?* But all the moments had seemed wrong, designed for higher purposes, if not for decisions then simply for sorrow, drops of which sometimes trickled through the gaps in the arrangements.

She felt like dropping this bomb on them. She felt like, for once, being the person who had shocking news. After decades of everyone else's *I'm getting married* and *I'm pregnant* and *We're getting divorced,* she felt like throwing out a new piece of information that she'd elegantly safeguarded all these years, like a detail that emerges at the end of a book to shed new light on the whole plot. But she didn't trust them to be sufficiently impressed. They would be amazed, that was for sure. But very quickly the headline in their minds would be broken down into its many familiar components: Avishay, and Avishay's life, and Zohara, and how bad she was at relationships, and the timing of the whole announcement. They were no fools. They'd continue to express amazement and wonder and ask questions, but slowly the words and questions would hollow out, like empty candy wrappers thrown at a bride by her own request, and Zohara would be left—once again—with nothing but pity.

The plan turned up in her mind again, uninvited, ready and awaiting instructions. She thought about Liat and the baby. For the time being they were only a name and a noun, without faces or tangibility, but that wouldn't be the case for much longer. That needed to be taken into account.

Let's say there was a woman and a baby in the picture. It was a baby boy in Zohara's mind, not a girl. A little Avishay who had also inherited something of his father's mean streak, which had remained small even when he got big. And so now she'd be taking money from the child, not just from Ruthi. There was no question about it: the child deserved the money. And even if Avishay didn't win, he deserved the apartment, the insurance, the savings. He deserved them according to the law, it turned out, and he deserved them according to logic, according to justice: he still had his whole life ahead of him.

But the more she tried to forgo her plan in favor of the new development, to nobly shelve it in the name of a latent maternal instinct, the more she had to admit that what really bothered her about Liat was not her imminent maternity but her youth, her stability. She wasn't crazy Ruthi or senile Penina, who could simply be written off. She was young and sane, by all appearances. She was normal and fully functioning—at least as much as Zohara herself was. If Liat said things—for example, that she was Avishay's partner, or that she'd never seen any trace of Zohara in his apartment—they would have to be taken seriously.

Zohara tried to consider the balance of power matter-of-factly: a thirty-eight-year-old pregnant single woman against four people in their late sixties, university professors and professionals, well-off family people. Even if the baby was his, it wasn't a lost cause. She could still be the common-law wife of a man who'd made a mistake, and the money, or at least half of it, would be hers.

But that sounded so cold. Unlike her. She tried hard to imagine the baby in his cradle, and then she took him out and put him on a rug, sitting with a toy, the way she'd seen in endless pictures of grandchildren. The rug was wine red and the apartment was standard issue, a little dark maybe. Behind him Zohara saw his faceless mother with her brown hair tied back in a ponytail, and she looked basically happy. It wasn't easy to be a single mother, but she was managing.

What did Zohara know about her? Maybe at the age of thirty-eight she was wealthier than Zohara, more settled, with a sound future? Maybe she'd remarry—or rather, she'd marry, later on, when the baby was older. She also had her whole life ahead of her, not just the baby. But why were this baby's first twenty years more important than Zohara's last twenty? Why did he deserve it and she didn't? He wasn't alone in this world. Someone was protecting him.

She asked herself if she was insane. She replied to herself that she was. Ergo, she wasn't.

In her years alone she'd developed a custom: every night before going to bed, she checked behind every door in her apartment, including closet doors. She didn't know what she was looking for, whether a mouse or a murderer, and she never found anything. But despite that, she stuck to the ritual, or perhaps not despite but *be-*

cause of that, because if she abandoned it she would be summoning the opposite result.

It was remarkable how far a person could sail away from normalcy while unwatched, under the cover of loneliness. And after all, that was what she wanted, not money. She wanted to be normal. She wanted everyone to know. She wanted a seal of approval stamped on the back of her hand, and then she could move on and not think about it anymore. And for this she was willing to commit the most abnormal act conceivable. Perhaps that was what really motivated human beings: not sex or money, just a simple desire to not be abnormal.

Then she had a realization: If that's not an inferiority complex, what is? What had she been feeling all these years if not inferior to those who were loved, more defective than them? Maybe Yehuda was right. Simple disappointment spread through her limbs, like someone who discovers, after dedicating their life to solving a riddle, that the riddle itself was more interesting than the solution. She didn't feel like thinking about it.

She turned over to consider things from a fresh angle. Was she really going to do it? Go on a public, aggressive crusade against a pregnant woman who hadn't done anything wrong? She would never do that. And yet it was that realization which began to somehow imbue this plan with reasonableness: its total lack of reasonableness, its clash with everything Zohara was made of, the nonexistent chance that it would ever see the light of day. The plan was protected by its unreasonableness, and inside that bubble Zohara was free to devise its details, to advance it further and further.

She turned back over, unconvinced. If everything was floating in the air, if everything was so unreasonable, then why did she keep trying to tie down the tiny threads, to paint something ridiculous in shades of gray until its reluctant, impossible image finally merged with a picture one could imagine?

What if she talked to Liat? What if she suggested they arrange everything privately? That would make it easier for both of them, save them both from any awkwardness. They could share the money—they didn't need it all anyway. And whatever was left after Zohara's death, she'd leave for Liat, including the apartment in Kiryat Ono. She didn't care.

She fell asleep.

19

By Saturday night, once they'd finally landed in Yehuda's living room and were resting unrestfully on the comfortable armchairs, Zohara was silently bidding it farewell and preparing a burial: it was enough to have hatched the plan, to have taken her imaginary revenge on him. There were some things she was never going to do in this lifetime.

"So what do we do?" Amos asked.

"What do we do in what sense?" Nili questioned him.

"What do we do with Avishay? Zohara's right—he can't have had a heart attack now. We can't say it was a heart attack, because he's injured."

Upon hearing her name, Zohara roused herself with some effort, even though all she wanted to do was hide.

"Well, obviously," Nili said.

"I admit that to me it wasn't obvious," Amos said. "I didn't get that at all."

"The question is whether it really does create a conflict," Yehuda mused. "I mean, injured people die of heart attacks, too. So he got injured before he died—I don't see why it's all that critical."

"But what if there's an autopsy?" Zohara wondered.

"Why would there be an autopsy?" said Nili.

"Exactly," Yehuda said.

"What reason in the world is there for them to do an autopsy?"

"Look at him," Amos said, pointing to Avishay, who was lying next to the TV console. But there was nothing to see, they'd covered him with a sheet. "Something happened to him—what happened? That's a question any first-year paramedic is going to ask himself."

Yehuda asked, "Even if we take him back home and put him back in bed, just like we found him?"

"You can't be serious," Zohara said.

"I'm asking a question."

"You're going to take him back to his place now?" Nili asked.

"Besides, what good will that do? So they'll find him injured at home instead of finding him injured here," Amos added.

Yehuda explained: "First of all, it looks more natural—"

"How does it look more natural? You could put him in bed here just as easily," Nili interrupted.

"It looks more natural because it's in his bed, in his home, and also it has nothing to do with us. If he's here, I have to start telling stories about where I found him and who and what."

"That's a different problem, you're talking about how they're not going to connect us with it," Nili said.

"That too. All of the above."

Zohara was getting worried: "Come on, do you really think they're going to connect us to it?"

"This surprises you?" said Amos.

"No one's going to connect us to anything," Nili declared. "You're getting carried away. What have we done to him that's so bad? Even if they find out everything—let's just assume for a moment that they find out everything. We didn't do anything to him, all we did is just move him a little."

"Let's just agree that none of us is particularly interested in be-ing on the news tomorrow because we 'just' moved a body," Amos countered.

"You're not going to be on the news, trust me. We're not as impor-tant as we think we are."

Zohara felt suddenly tired out. All this talking was getting to her. She wanted to be done with it, with Avishay and this whole adventure, and with the demand to make a decision. Was she or wasn't she capable of it, had she lost her mind or was she completely rational. She wanted to be rescued from this, for it to no longer be an option. They should bury Avishay and that's that. "The way I see it," she finally said, "there doesn't seem to be much choice. But whatever you think."

"What do you mean, no choice?" Yehuda asked.

"I mean, we have to call an ambulance. A real ambulance, tell them he died, and sad as it is, we have to be done with this. No one could accuse us of not making a super-genuine effort."

"But what are you going to say? What happened to him? What caused all this?" Nili asked.

"I'll say he fell down the stairs. Or I don't know what. That he must have had a heart attack while he was working here in the house and he fell down the steps or something. I don't know."

"Those aren't injuries from falling down steps, I'm sorry to tell you," said Amos. "Those are injuries from getting hit by a bike."

Zohara wondered when they'd all become such experts at death and bodies, positions and bruises. They suddenly seemed like silly children, dwelling on trivialities, missing the point, standing on the other side of a chasm that had opened up between her and them, although she wasn't sure when.

Nili said, "He's right, we can't say that."

"We can just say we don't know," Zohara offered.

"We don't know? That's it, just like that, we came home and found him?" Yehuda asked.

"Why not? That's what we were going to say from the get-go."

"Yes, but that was before he got run over."

Nili said, "Saying 'We don't know' is the worst option. If we say that, he goes straight to an autopsy. We're better off coming up with some explanation, even if it only half makes sense. I'm telling you, that's enough, no one's interested in doing any unnecessary autopsies, especially not when it comes to people like us."

"Again with the people like us. Honestly!" Zohara felt like she was getting angry at the wrong thing, but Nili suddenly seemed insufferable, indulging in minuscule nuisances as if to thereby affirm a fundamental happiness.

"Well, what can I say. I know it's not PC, so it's a good thing nobody can hear us, but yes, we are a group of white professionals, and if we say that our friend died of a heart attack then he died of a heart attack."

"And we're pushing seventy," Yehuda added, "I think that's the salient part. Why would a bunch of seventy-year-olds get mixed up in something?"

"I don't know," Zohara said, "maybe because when I consider all the stories I've heard in my life, 'white people' doesn't seem significant to me. White people murder and rape, too, including their own daughters."

"Oh, thank you for explaining to me that white people also murder and rape their daughters. Do you honestly think I didn't know that?"

Zohara looked at Nili. *How broad was the wingspan of normalcy,* she thought. As broad as Nili. So much could shelter in its shade, be swallowed up in its folds. There was a reason, apparently, why normalcy imbued its possessors with such confidence, such arrogance. She burned with envy and an urge to spoil things. She felt like hurling her plan at them all, using it like a crowbar to beat their self-satisfaction out of them: Let's see if your normalcy can stand up to that.

Amos said, "I just want to clarify something: for us to come forward now and tell the truth, I mean about what really happened, is not an option, okay? It's either we pull it off and he gets the prize, and then great, or it fails, but it fails without questions. There's no middle option, whether it's fessing up or getting caught. Okay?"

"You're really being hysterical, Amos," Nili observed.

"I'm not being hysterical, I just can't be as blasé as you are."

Zohara wondered if she was the only one who saw through Amos, who saw how much he was dying to get this over with.

"I'm not blasé, I'm realistic."

"All right, then, let's agree that we differ on terminology. Because my realism tells me that we are a very small distance, if any, from having this whole thing blown wide open, which to me, at least, would be a total disaster."

Nili rolled her eyes.

"Yes, a disaster, Nili, don't give me that look. Losing my career and Varda's trust and I don't even know what else, maybe Varda's bar admission. You know what? Maybe it seemed ridiculous to begin with, but now it's not. This is a criminal act, what we're doing, and Varda would be upset and rightly so. So you know what? Yes: it would be a disaster."

"Come on, Amos, don't get so angry at me. I'm sorry, okay?"

Amos gave a slight nod to indicate that it was all right, but Zohara could see the tension on his face, diminishing his eyes as if they were storing their energy for the next outburst. She felt that same mixture of pride and disappointment again, which she always felt when her friends seemed too easy to read. She often had the sense that she was perceiving their innermost feelings as they made their way out, catching embryonic signs of sorrow or anger even before it was clear whether they'd be birthed or aborted.

Nili said, "Look, you're all on some . . . I don't even know what to call it. Ego trip. You're acting like the whole world is just waiting to solve the mystery of Avishay Sar-Shalom's death. Anyone would think he was Yasser Arafat! You're of no interest to anyone, don't you get that? And neither, I'm sorry to say, is Avishay. He's dead, and that's that, may he rest in peace. Next. No one here has the slightest interest in him or in us."

"If that's the case, then why are you even trying? What are we doing all this for if it's so simple? Why didn't we just leave him dead in his bed?" asked Amos.

"Come on, you know what I mean."

"Actually, I don't. I'm really having trouble understanding how you can decide what's suspicious and what isn't. It's a little inconsistent, your whole line of thinking."

"To me it seems very clear. It's a matter of common sense."

Zohara looked at Nili, who was now moving around the kitchen, talking to them from there, opening and shutting cabinets, maybe making coffee. Why was this so important to her? Why had she even agreed to this whole thing? The question surprised Zohara, as though it had come late to the party, arriving out of breath but now demanding an answer. Nili wasn't Avishay's partner, she had her own boyfriend. Why did she need this? But then again, Zohara herself wasn't Avishay's partner either, as far as they were concerned. She was just one of his friends. So they could ask the same question about her. But she wasn't like Nili, and she did have a reason, even though she was suddenly unable to remember what it was. The exercise had confused her, the reasons had been tossed around inside the maze and fallen on their backs, unable to flip over.

Nili came back with a box of fruity Cheerios. For a brief moment she looked like a little girl, stripped of all her life events, and then Zohara thought she knew why Nili was doing this, or was about to find out. Nili held out the white plastic bag, which contained only a bottom layer of Cheerio crumbs, as if she were offering the answer. And Zohara thought: *Who eats Cheerios in this house? Why does Avishay have kids' cereal?* And all at once she forgot what she'd been thinking about. "I want to understand something," she said. "Right now the situation is that we can't back out of this, even if we want to. Right?"

"We can back out," Amos said, "we just have to either tell everything, and I mean everything, or make up a pretty impressive lie."

"I'm kind of in shock, I have to tell you."

"Why?" Yehuda asked.

"I don't know, up until two hours ago it was still sort of half-real, I was under the impression we could change our minds at any time, and now all of a sudden it's not so dependent on us anymore."

"Either way, I think we have to think very carefully about the lie," Amos said. "I'm telling you again, for me it would be extremely difficult to come clean about everything we've done. Not now and not on Wednesday and not on any other day."

"Me too. That's all I need," Zohara agreed.

"Then let's just say that Gidi guy really did kill him. I don't think he'd object," Nili suggested.

"So what are we actually trying to figure out now? How he got all those bruises?" Yehuda asked.

"How he got all those bruises after he was already dead, if anything," Amos answered. "What happened to his body after he had the heart attack, how did he get to this state." Then he asked Nili, "Apart from the lacerations, is there anything else?"

"I think there are some fractured ribs, from what I could tell when I felt around, but you can't see that anyway. There may be a broken leg, too, I'm not sure."

"He has to have fallen off something, there's no way around that. A fall could explain a lot of things."

"Again with the steps?"

"For all I care, he can fall off something else."

"Like what?"

"I don't know, I don't think steps are such a bad idea. He was working upstairs in the study. That makes sense. He had a heart attack, he tried to get downstairs and he tumbled down. There's nothing unconvincing about that."

"And then what? You're putting him at the bottom of the staircase? That's how we found him?"

"I don't know, yes, we would have had to find him somewhere, so why not by the stairs?"

"The only way it'll look like someone fell down the stairs is if you really push him down the stairs," Nili said. "Both in terms of the injuries and in terms of the position. You can't stage something like that."

"Then we'll push him down," Yehuda said simply.

Zohara felt like a sleepy observer who'd suddenly been woken up, caught in her laziness, in her idleness, and was now being tested only to be rebuked when she failed. "You're joking, right?" she said to Yehuda.

"I'm not sure. Not necessarily."

"He's right," Amos said, "the only way it's going to look like he fell is if we push him down."

"It's me who was right," Nili said, "I was the one who said that."

"Then Nili's right," Amos conceded.

Zohara wanted to say something, she had to object, but she wasn't proficient in this material, and before she could organize her thoughts, Nili said, "I'm not pushing him off anything, I can tell you that right now."

"Why not?" Yehuda asked.

"Why not? Because I'm not. Because I'm not pushing Avishay's body down the staircase in your house, that's why."

"Out of respect for the dead, or what? I really want to understand."

"Out of what? Out of the fact that I don't think it's necessary, I think it's mad, I think it's superfluous, and that's it, I should hope that's enough reasons. No one's going to come checking on us, I keep telling you. This could happen for a thousand reasons, this kind of injury."

"And what if you're wrong?" Amos pressed her. "I understand that you're never wrong, but if you just happen to be wrong this one time . . ."

Zohara could feel the factions arranging themselves on either side of the tension—Amos and Yehuda on one side, Nili on the other. And what about her? Not yet.

Nili said, "If I'm wrong then we'll deal with it. Again—what have we done wrong? What are they going to do to us?"

"See, here's where we differ," Amos said.

"Where?"

"I can't allow myself to risk that, don't you see? I just can't. My whole career would go down the drain. This isn't a joke, Nili, maybe you can afford it but we're in a different situation."

"I can afford it? What exactly can I afford?"

"Even if they don't do anything to us, we have relationships that we can lose."

"And I don't have a relationship?"

"Of course you do, but it's not the same, it just isn't."

Zohara could see where this was going but she didn't have the strength to step in, to take a bullet for someone else's emotional well-being.

"So basically we're back to the same issue," Nili said, "which is that no one takes Nathan or my relationship with him seriously."

Zohara intervened after all, wearily, mechanically: "That's not what they mean, Nili. In fact, I think it's the opposite: you're a new enough couple to withstand something like this, that's all, it wouldn't be a horrible betrayal of trust or anything like that."

"Oh, please," Nili said.

Zohara felt like telling her to go fuck herself, and Amos said, "I don't understand why I should apologize for thinking you can't compare a decades-old relationship to a five-minute one, I'm sorry."

"You're right, Amos, there's no comparison," Nili said. "I would have told Nathan ages ago if you hadn't stopped me, because I don't keep secrets from him. Not like you and Yehuda, chasing down adventures like two children, *let's throw him down the stairs, heh-heh-heh, look at how not-old we are*, and at the same time hiding the whole thing from your wives like some I-don't-know-whats."

"I'm chasing adventures? I'm childish?"

"She's talking about me, Amos, I'm the child," Yehuda said.

"Yes, a little," Nili confirmed.

"That's fine, I take it as a compliment," Yehuda said.

"Will Idit take it as a compliment, too?" Nili asked him.

"What did you say?"

"I asked if Idit would also take it as a compliment," Nili repeated.

"Yes, I heard you the first time. Nili, just be thankful that I feel sorry for you and so I'm not going to get into your quote-unquote 'relationships' here."

"*Quote-unquote*? Whoa . . ."

Zohara intervened again: "That's enough, Yehuda."

But Nili wasn't done: "Look at Zohara—she doesn't have a relationship either."

Zohara felt like murdering her—could she enlist them for that, too?

"What do you think she's got to lose, then?" Nili pressed Yehuda.

"Maybe my career?" Zohara said.

Nili looked at her for a moment and said, "And I don't have a career?"

"Well, not anymore," Zohara said.

Nili looked at them and they looked at her and no one said anything. Finally, Nili got up and said, "Throw him down the stairs, throw him off the roof, throw him of Azrieli Towers for all I care. I wish you the best of luck."

Zohara felt she should get up and run after her, but she didn't feel like it, and so as it turned out, no one said anything.

Nili walked to the door and muttered, "Where's my bag?" She found it on the floor next to the kitchen island and said, "Here it is." Zohara felt her time running out, but suddenly Amos said, "Wait a sec," and Nili looked up and her eyes were heartrendingly full of anticipation, and Zohara was so happy that someone else was doing it, but Amos said, "The phone." Nili furrowed her brow and glanced at the living room table and said, "I took it." Amos said, "I mean Avishay's phone, leave it here." Nili looked at him for a moment, as if committed to not moving until the insult was fully absorbed, and then she pulled Avishay's phone out of her bag, slammed it on the coffee table, opened the door, and shut it behind her.

———

"We have to wash him first," Yehuda said.

"But wait, what about Nili?" Zohara asked.

"What about her?"

"Shouldn't we go after her?"

"I'm not going to. You can do whatever you want."

"Why are you annoyed at *me*?"

"I'm not," Yehuda replied, "I'm just generally annoyed."

"Then don't take it out on me."

"Okay, sorry."

Amos piped up: "First things first: let's get this over with. Then we can call Nili or whatever we decide to do. Let's just get this over with already."

"But what if she's going to the police?" Zohara asked.

"Are you crazy? She's not going to go to the police."

"The police, the emergency services, I don't know. His sister."

"She'd never do that," Amos insisted. "How could you think that? The only person she'd be screwing over by doing that is herself."

"Come on, let's get it over with," Yehuda said.

"What am I supposed to do?" Zohara asked.

The answer should have been: Nothing at all, you just sit there and keep watch. Or even: You just think about what to tell Nili afterward. But Yehuda lifted the sheet off Avishay, pointed to the tire marks streaked across his stomach, and said, "We have to clean that off somehow."

"And I'm supposed to clean it? Why, because I'm a woman?"

"Would you rather carry him upstairs and push him down?" Amos said. "Be my guest."

"But what am I supposed to use?"

"I think just water or something."

Zohara went to the kitchen and picked up a dingy pink cloth from the sink. "Is there a new one somewhere?"

"Look under the sink," Yehuda said.

Zohara opened the cabinet under the sink but there were no cloths. She pulled out a bottle from behind the trash can: "Sano Javel Super Gel Cleaning Cream. All-purpose household cleaner. Removes stains and stubborn dirt without leaving scratches. Antibacterial." That looked suitable—certainly more so than the toilet-bowl cleaner. She straightened up and started opening drawers in the kitchen, searching for sponges. Yehuda was clueless anyway. She finally found them in a deep bottom drawer: an unopened container of disposable cleaning wipes, three hundred and fifty of them. If that wasn't enough, she'd have to give up. She took the wipes and the Sano Javel, walked back to the living room, and knelt down next to Avishay.

She looked at Yehuda and Amos standing over her, seeking approval, and Yehuda blinked at her to go on and hurry up. She felt humiliated. This was her moment, this was her time, Avishay was dead, she had all the power now, yet still she was obeying him even after death, continuing to bend over backwards just so he would be happy. "I'll try a little bit and if it doesn't come off then I don't know what," she said, without making much of an impression on them.

She pulled out a wipe and placed it gently over the marks, holding her face away from the body with revulsion. Then she considered the spectacle: she wasn't really disgusted anymore. Avishay had become an accessory, a sort of thing that was there, that they had to remember to take, that sometimes you used, like a magician's handkerchief. He was essential for the magic trick, but without the magician and the trick he would simply be nothing.

She gently rubbed the tire mark. The mark faded, like pencil being erased. She rubbed harder, and a little piece of skin came off. She stopped and looked at Yehuda. "It's like what happened when we changed his shirt," she observed.

"Then be gentler," Amos said.

"Gentler than this?" she exclaimed, although the truth was that she could have been gentler.

"Why don't you put some of that stuff on first?" Yehuda said. "What is that, anyway?"

"All-purpose cleaner. But should I just pour it on his body? What if it causes a chemical reaction and his whole skin gets burned?"

"I don't think they'd approve a product that burns people's skin," Amos said.

"There's no way of knowing. It's not like a normal body now," Yehuda offered.

"It's human skin, it's not one substance that suddenly turns into another substance."

Zohara said, "You know what they do with clothes in these cases?"

"What cases?" Amos asked.

"Cleaning solutions always say to test a hidden corner of the clothing first, to make sure."

"Then what are you suggesting? That we pour some on the bottom of his foot or something?"

"Yehuda, I was joking," she said.

"Oh."

"Nothing's going to happen to him, I'm telling you," Amos insisted. "Just put a little on your finger and then maybe you really should rub it between his toes or something, just to be on the safe side."

"Are you serious?" Zohara said.

"Why not?"

"I don't see why not either," Yehuda added.

"Okay, if you think it's all right."

She poured a drop onto her finger, but the lip let out too much and a little puddle of Sano Javel pooled near Avishay's head; like blood in a normal body, she thought. She quickly moved her finger to his feet—Yehuda bent over and removed his sock—and landed it deep between the big toe and the next one. She remembered that Avishay had a scar there, a strange mark that he was proud of, as though it indicated that its owner was incapable of even a banal injury. It was a souvenir from a fall he once took, in the middle of the night, off a bunk bed in a youth hostel in Belgium, straight onto the pointed toe of a pair of clogs. Zohara sort of wished she hadn't remembered that. Or was it on the other foot?

She separated the toes, as if to examine the effect of the solution on the body, but she was searching for the scar: she suddenly had to know if it was on this foot or the right one. The scar wasn't there. She stared at the smooth pad of skin, which was now orange. She'd forgotten how ugly his toes were. "Looks like it's just dripping down the skin," she observed.

"Fine, then," Amos said, "just wipe it off."

Zohara had an urge to protest, she felt a little bit like the maid, but she decided to be forgiving, thanks to the inexplicable emergence of a good mood. She wiped the Sano Javel off with her finger and spread the rest of it on his stomach. Then she added a little more along the tire tracks, tore off a few more wipes and ran them gently over it, trying not to rub too hard.

———

Yehuda stood upstairs, holding Avishay by the waist with his upper body slumped to the floor.

"Should I hold him up?" Amos asked.

"I don't think it matters, as long as it's from a standing position, don't you think?" Yehuda said.

"All right."

"So do I just throw him? Push him? I don't know how to do this," Yehuda admitted.

"Just let go. Take your hands off his waist and let him fall however he falls, naturally."

"Right, because this is all so natural . . ."

"Go on," Amos urged.

"Wait a second. It's not as easy as it looks."

Zohara thought of offering to wait outside, or in another room— she wasn't contributing anything here anyway, and Avishay didn't need a welcoming line at the bottom. But somehow she felt that if she suggested that she'd be pushing the envelope, so she just took a few steps back to give him space to fall.

They were throwing Avishay down the steps. They were actually throwing his body down a staircase. Could they really refuse to put in a few words for her, some of which were true? But as she settled with herself that they would agree to do it, it occurred to her that she'd missed the point: it wasn't the limits of their audacity that they were outlining for her, but her own. Whatever she was planning couldn't possibly be worse than this.

Yehuda said, "I'm letting go," and after a long moment he dropped Avishay and quickly put his hands against his own body, fists clenched against his stomach. Avishay tumbled face-first and stopped, upside down, his legs at the top of the stairs and his head in the middle.

"Pull him," Yehuda said, and before Zohara could say anything, Amos kicked Avishay's feet, then prodded them a little to the right with his shoe, as if trying to wake the body from its slumber. But instead of falling farther down the steps, Avishay's head got pushed up against the banister, his face and neck peculiarly stretched. His back was arched, and he was hanging on the staircase like an elderly rubber boy.

Zohara looked at Avishay sprawled there, looking ridiculous, bruised, peeled, unburied. To honor him—that's what they'd wanted. She asked herself if he deserved this, and she replied to herself that he did.

20

She walked out of the apartment, stood on the landing for a minute like an idiot, then opened the door and walked back in, so that she could judge with fresh eyes. It was a good thing Avishay wasn't here, that their shifts were over, that the apartment was all hers. They'd agreed that someone would stop in once a day, to check his Gmail account, which was open on his computer, and the Outlook account from his university, and to pick up his mail and make sure everything was okay. Zohara had quickly volunteered: she needed the apartment. She'd also gladly picked up Avishay's iPhone, abandoned by Nili, but she'd accidentally left it at Amos's.

She walked through the rooms, but everything seemed the same. That's how she wanted it: reversible, subject to regret. That's how she wanted herself: potentially brave, for two or three days. The possibility of another woman, right up to the last minute.

She opened the bedroom closets and felt she'd done an excellent job. She'd never lived with a man, but this was how the shared closet of a husband and wife was supposed to look—or the shared closet of common-law spouses, whatever. She had to get used to saying that.

Her clothes looked completely natural in there. She'd even turned a few hangers the wrong way, to make it look authentic. And there were lots of his clothes, pushed into the edges and the high shelves, the inconvenient ones. That looked right to her, that's how it usually was. She was pretty sure.

She had taken into account that it was dangerous. The more of his clothes she replaced with hers, the harder it would be to put things back if she changed her mind. And the whole process had taken her ages.

She moved on to the bathroom. She put her pills in the medicine cabinet—she was here every day anyway—and two tubes, one facial moisturizer and one body lotion. In the big cabinet at the bottom she propped two bottles of shampoo and two tubes of purple conditioner—the kind she used was white and didn't create the right effect, and pink seemed over the top. She left the shelf in the shower as it was. It would only take her a second to put one conditioner and one shampoo there, if necessary.

=====

At five to eight she sat down in front of the television. Svetlana Alexievich had won the Nobel Prize in Literature. Zohara hadn't read anything she'd written; truth be told, she'd never heard of her. But she watched the news item, riveted. They showed Alexievich hugging someone, Zohara didn't catch who it was, and she looked very joyful in an unliterary way: just normal joy. She imagined them for a moment, herself and Yehuda and Nili and Amos, getting the news on Wednesday, and Avishay's absence suddenly seemed intolerable, as though it took the point out of everything. It would be the most depressing Nobel party ever, particularly because the whole world would be shocked by the news of his death—not like them, who'd had time to get used to it.

And what about them? What would they do with their happiness? If they cheered and jumped up and down it would be at home, quietly, not in public, and it would be thanks to their success, not his—she had to admit that. Would she be happy? It seemed to her now that she wouldn't, that it would leave her cold. Perhaps because there was another mission ahead of her, and in that one she was completely on her own.

The minute they'd left her alone, she'd attacked the apartment shamelessly: rummaging and digging, unpacking decades of politely drawn borders into the drawers, practically pissing on the place because she wanted so badly to make it hers. He had a bounty of drawers, they were in every room, promising almost endless pleasures. And that had distracted her on the first day, when they'd sat in the living room debating whether or not to undertake the whole escapade. Much as she'd tried to concentrate and contribute to the discussion, to consider things rationally, she'd felt guided by the blinding force of those drawers to a completely idiotic decision, too easily convinced only so that she could eventually be alone with them.

The drawers were organized by topic, she soon realized, with the top document on each pile responsibly indicating everything beneath it, so no need to waste time or energy. Pension statements, bills, product warranties, even instruction manuals, which had their own drawer. She perked up a little when she came across an X-ray of Avishay's knee, but underneath were only ancient blood test results—some going back to 1995—and a few medical insurance policies.

She wasn't very familiar with his work, and wasn't all that interested, even though of course she'd watched the lecture on YouTube. She knew how to recite the main points, pretending to simplify things for other people's benefit: at the end of the day, being powerful wasn't worth it, because the most powerful ones finished last. That was the gist of it, although of course it was obviously much more complicated. Only one thing was really ingrained in her consciousness: the class king. He had something about the class king, and with every passing year the phrase moved further away in her mind from the model, from the theory, from economics, from academics, and closer to Avishay himself, to the real Avishay, the Avishay she knew. She was dating the class king. She was sleeping with the class king, childish as that may sound, and now she had the opportunity to peek into his dirty, unsmoothed edges, to slightly tone down the awe. She hoped to discover the earthly Avishay, the inner Avishay, the Avishay of under the fridge and behind the toilet bowl. But the man who emerged seemed like the perfect product of an economic theory, a walking bestseller: streamlined to the point of sterility, calling up all his utility companies every three months to haggle, switching providers in pursuit of the best offer. Nothing in this home looked like it had just been forgotten there, tossed into a corner unintentionally. It was so extreme that at times she saw Avishay himself, not his meticulously sorted paperwork, staring back at her defiantly from every drawer: *What do you want? What exactly are you looking for?*

Her spirits fell. She'd searched frantically but drawn a blank. Then she realized that what she'd found made him seem accessible, assailable. Mortal.

In the bottom drawer of his desk, which she opened perfunctorily, sliding it out and back in just to make sure, she found a little bit of disorder: pictures piled on top of pictures, strewn around without any order. She gathered up a few dozen of them. They all showed a younger Avishay, usually overseas, on his own, with a canal or the Duomo in the background, or in restaurants, smiling, with his arms around various people. Pictures from the days when pictures were taken with cameras, when it was still acceptable to strike a pose in front of monuments, before that was considered tacky.

She raked another pile into her lap and spotted herself with the group. It was her and Amos and Yehuda and Avishay, and she immediately recognized their trip to Wales, where she'd been sick for ten days and had a horrible time. She dug around the drawer some more, but there were loads of pictures and nothing of interest. Many of the pictures were bad, with dark spots, or no one in them, just more and more different angles of the Duomo. A drawer of duds. She had one of those too, the place where you dumped all the photos that hadn't passed selection, an alternate history rustling in the thick of the cabinets, threatening to snitch on the rest of the trip, on all the non-fun.

The recent pictures were probably on the computer, if he even had any. But why would he? He had no grandchildren, he didn't hang around maternity wards. Why would he have his picture taken? She tried to think about whether she ever had hers taken. She didn't think so, but still she did have hundreds of pictures on her phone.

She'd been postponing that a little, the matter of Avishay's computer, mainly because she was afraid it might be too much to bite off. She knew the basics—Word, email, all that—but to really dig deep required more, she felt.

She touched the mouse and the desktop sprang to life. There were a few files with names in English, only one of which looked a little suspicious, but when she opened it she realized it was a research proposal or a seminar paper and she closed it without saving.

There were three PDF files: "NiceIce1," "NiceIce2," and "NiceIce4." NiceIce 3 was missing. Zohara opened up "NiceIce1" but all it contained was an ad for vegan ice cream, probably from somewhere he liked to order from, and 2 and 4 looked exactly the same.

She wondered where to go from there, and ended up clicking back to his Gmail. No new messages. He got dozens of messages every day, mostly group ones, and the individual ones were respectable missives peppered with a sort of academic familiarity that meant nothing. In vain she searched for Liat, but he hadn't corresponded with any Liats, except a representative from a furniture manufacturer who had once sent him a price quote, and she was quickly disqualified as his lover after a brief Google search. He had a few messages

from her, from Amos, Yehuda, and Nili, mostly YouTube clips they
sent one another, and the occasional petition or Drop Box link. If
they had anything to say to one another, they said it in person.

She felt like calling Nili, but she remembered that she wasn't allowed to tell her anything about all this, she wasn't supposed to be
digging around. Not that Nili would be all that upset, and Zohara
reached for her phone but then she remembered they weren't talking.
Or something. She felt gloomy. Who could she talk to?

She closed out the windows and documents she'd opened, x, x, x,
distracted, looking for something to do with her finger. The desktop
gleamed again. She went into My Computer. My Pictures. Now she'd
see if he had any of himself. She flicked through the photos. There
were publicity shots she knew well, book covers, that sort of thing.
Her gaze fell on a series of old pictures, of him as a soldier and maybe
even a high schooler, probably scanned from old albums. She enlarged
them. She hadn't known him back then. In one he was sitting on a
windowsill, looking at the camera as though he were good-looking.
But he wasn't, not really, his face was a little round, his clothes were
horrendous, even for the fifties. She enlarged a shot of him in his army
uniform, to cancel out the effect of the hideous clothing, and Avishay
did look different, more like himself. Maybe it was just because a few
years had gone by between the two pictures. She wished she could
flip them over and read the dates on the back.

She scrolled down. This time she enlarged a series of almost identical pictures, in all of which Avishay was with people she didn't
know, in an industrial-looking kitchen, wearing an apron, and they
all looked very cheerful. She looked at their faces, mostly at the two
women in the group, but they didn't look threatening. One of the
men, on the other hand, looked very familiar, but she couldn't get
a good angle. In some of them you could see his profile, and in another he was laughing out loud, to the point of metamorphosing
into another person, and Zohara wasn't sure anymore.

At the bottom of the folder were the newest pictures: a tiny Avishay, probably at some conference, photographed from afar. Then Avishay with a woman of roughly his age and two kids, all hugging in a family scene that looked so wrong for him, practically alien on his computer. Zohara enlarged one of them: Ruthi. It was Ruthi. It had been so many years since she'd seen her. Those must be her grandchildren.

She looked at their faces. They could have been hers, if she'd had any. Hers and Avishay's. She examined their expressions and checked in to see if she was sad. But they meant nothing to her: two boys, maybe ten, or eight, just kids, their futures already permeating their faces.

She was an expert by now: she needed children to grow up fast, to skip ahead to the fully grown people stage, hiding away the remnants of their childhood, everything that had once put them in people's hearts. She needed that so that she wouldn't be sorry, so that the pain would be bearable. She looked forward to those years, she thought it would be easier: the children around her would decrease in number, replaced by human beings. But the world remained strewn with kids, and Zohara hung on to the habit as hard as she could, polishing it like a mantra: there are no kids, there's no such thing, every kid is destined to grow up.

She looked at Avishay grinning. What was he so happy about? She found it irritating. She checked the date: last Saturday. So Ruthi really did come visit him on weekends. With the grandchildren? Since when? She tried to remember the last time they'd done anything together on a Saturday. Maybe it really had been a long time.

Perhaps Avishay wanted to practice. Maybe because of the pregnancy. And who'd taken that picture anyway? Liat? She felt like deleting it, as if she would thereby also sabotage his happiness. But she didn't have the guts.

She suddenly realized that his entire home, the physical one, with its deep drawers and three-dimensionality, had no meaning. Home was an archaic concept. The whole place was frozen in 2000 or 2005 or even 199-something, frozen along with a younger version of its owner. The living, current Avishay now existed solely between the walls of the computer, and in that life of his, the current one, there was no trace of her.

She went into My Documents. There were three files floating around outside the folders: "Review after revisions to send," "Netvision," and "December 1957." She opened the latter one. "Foreword. In December 1957, I was fourteen years old." It was his foreword for Yehuda's book. She knew it. Only Avishay could use those words to introduce someone else's book.

She'd read it maybe five times already, in various drafts, trying to use her talents to rescue Avishay, who was in a total panic. She was actually somewhat on Yehuda's side in this whole thing: Avishay deserved it a little, Yehuda was teaching him a lesson. Yehuda had given him the book to read and asked for his honest opinion, and only when Avishay told him the book was simply wonderful, original, funny, fluid, and God knows what else, only then had Yehuda said, "I'm glad you think so, because I'd be very happy if you would write a foreword. I just didn't want to put you in an uncomfortable position, so I didn't let you know ahead of time. I wanted to make sure you really liked the book first."

Avishay had tried to wriggle out of it, of course. Upon Zohara's advice, he told Yehuda that he'd gladly write the foreword but he thought it was a mistake, because it would draw attention away from Yehuda and the book. This book has to stand front and center, he claimed, and a foreword by Avishay Sar-Shalom will project lack of confidence. But of course that didn't work. Avishay couldn't get out of it, not without telling Yehuda the truth, which would have killed their friendship, quite simply. Not that the thought didn't enter his mind: he was that terrified of having his name anywhere near the thing. But he wouldn't do it, of course, he told Zohara with a certain bitterness, although he did shoot her a hopeful glance, just to make sure.

At least Avishay had died before the book came out, saving him that grief. Because Yehuda was planning to go to town on it, that was clear to Zohara from the start, whether Avishay was dead or alive. And if he won the Nobel, then all the more so. She suddenly had an amusing thought: What if this was why Yehuda was doing the whole thing? So that Avishay would win the Nobel and generate even more publicity for his book. That could be a great idea for a novel, or a comedy sketch. She wished, once again, that she wasn't alone, that she had someone to share this stroke of genius with.

She sat looking at the open file, unsatisfied, and imagined Yehuda in the lead role, in a movie or maybe a short story. That was why she wasn't the one who should write it, that was exactly why she wasn't an author. Because she could only imagine the real Yehuda. She knew how to write, but she had no imagination. She wasn't even ashamed of it. She had lots of other talents.

She tried to banish Yehuda, to lop off his head in favor of someone else—maybe Jack Nicholson? But Yehuda popped up again like a Weeble, and looked at her gravely. What do you want me to do now? Tell me, what?

Why, though, did she think it was funny? Why didn't she think it was true? She tried to organize her thoughts: What was the actual notion here? That what? That Yehuda had conceived the whole idea so that Avishay would get the Nobel? They knew that already. But why did he want him to get the Nobel? That was the question. Not for him—meaning, not for Avishay, for posterity and all that, but rather for Yehuda's book, so he'd have a foreword by a Nobel laureate.

It seemed preposterous. All this to-do for that? So that instead of just a professor, he'd have a Nobel laureate's name on his book? But she had to think like Yehuda, not like a normal person. Was Yehuda capable of doing such a thing? This book meant everything to him. At this point in time, it meant everything. He'd had no qualms about ruining his relationship with her for the book. And then it became

crystal clear to her: that's why he'd done it. How could she not have
seen it?

She felt like Agatha Christie at the moment when she cracks a
case. She wanted to convene all the suspects in a room and recount
the sordid details with a knowing look, terrifying them all, each with
their own dirty secrets. She would get to Yehuda last. *Yehuda, Ye-
huda, Yehuda*, she would say. *Yehuda, Yehuda, Yehuda*. She imagined
him saying: *If I were you, Zohara, I would not say another word*. And
she knew he'd be right.

———

She got up from the desk as if to shake off the burden of secrets, hers
and Avishay's. And now there was this one, too. What did people die
for if not so that their secrets could finally expire? But they'd pile up
more and more of them on her, even after death, more secrets and
fewer people to keep them company.

How was she going to talk to him now? How could she go on with
this whole thing?

She felt angry, but not about this. Then what? Or maybe it wasn't
anger but something else: she was angry instead of being sorry. Who
had she been trying to please this whole week, if not Yehuda? Avishay, after all, was dead. She was doing this to remind him that he
loved her, to extricate what must still be there, somewhere, hidden.
Like parents and children, it was a love you could not divorce.

She sat down again, hoping the sharp movement might scare
away the flock of thoughts. But instead of Avishay's rows of Gmail
messages, which had appeared every time she'd opened the tab, she
suddenly got the log-in page: "Password?"

She didn't know it. They didn't know the password. The account had been open on his computer when he'd died, and it had

been open ever since. "Need help?" Gmail asked. *Yes, definitely*, she thought. *Thank you.*

She clicked on "Forgot Password?" and Gmail offered to send a code to her cell phone. "Send?" She thought about it for a moment: Amos had the phone. Yes, send.

But a different voice answered the phone, surrounded by background noises: "Zohara?"

"Who is this? Yehuda? Oh, I accidentally called you, I need Amos."

"Hang on, I'm moving away," Yehuda said.

"No, Yehuda, I have to hang up, I need to talk to Amos, he's about to get a message on Avishay's phone and he won't know what it is."

But Yehuda couldn't hear her, and a moment later he said, "Zohara? Can you hear me?"

"Yehuda, I'll call you back in a few minutes, okay?" She had no intention of calling—the sound of his voice was enough to unravel all her decisions, to bring to her mouth the taste of all the scoldings he'd given her all week: You're not doing enough, you don't care enough. Yeah, some friend *he* was.

Yehuda said, "No, no, listen, I have to talk to you, you're not going to believe what happened, I'm dying here."

"What happened?"

"I've been trying to slip away for hours to call you guys, I don't know what to do."

"What? What is it?"

"Idit and the girls ambushed me—I'm up here at a surprise seventieth birthday party."

"Oh, right. Happy birthday."

"Zohara—do you understand what I'm telling you?"

"Wait, isn't Idit overseas?"

"That's my point! She's not. No. She told me she was going abroad and instead they put on this whole production for me in

some godforsaken village up in the Galilee. Alonei Aba, it's called.
There's a B and B and a dinner and a whole to-do, the entire family's
here, maybe fifty people, and we're coming home tomorrow."

"So?"

"So?!"

"Oh. Oh no!"

"Zohara, you have to get him out of there. We're checking out at
one tomorrow, we'll be home by four at the latest."

"Not even that, it doesn't take more than a couple of hours. Tirzah
lives there, I know the route."

"Yes, I know, that's exactly how they got me up here. They pre-
tended Tirzah wanted to talk to me about the book," Yehuda said.

"What?"

"Never mind, Idit's gone off the deep end. Anyway, you have to
get him out of there. Someone has to come up here this evening and
get the key to my house."

"But where are we going to take him?" Zohara asked.

"To Amos, there's no choice, it has to be a private residence, it's
already starting to smell."

"He'll never agree, Yehuda, there's no chance."

"He'll have to. I can't come home with Idit to a house with
Avishay waiting inside. You must understand that. It would be
one thing if I'd told her before. But like this? She goes overseas
and I put a dead body in her house? No way. Amos will have to
talk to Varda and . . . That's that. The whole stuff about her being
a lawyer is nonsense anyway, that's not a real reason, it's just an
excuse."

"Then talk to Amos," Zohara said.

"You talk to him, I can't, I have to get back, I think there's some
activity going on now."

"He's going to kill me. He's going to kill you."

"Talk to him, go on, forget about all that, just talk. Solve the problem. And if I don't pick up, send me a WhatsApp message, I'll call you back as soon as I can."

———

Amos said, "Why crazy? I think it's nice of her."

"Okay, it's very nice, but what do we do now?" Zohara said.

"Listen, it's not just the thing with Varda. Can you see us now, me, you, and Yehuda, transporting Avishay again? Actually, it'll be without Yehuda. Without Nili and without Yehuda."

"I don't know," Zohara said, "if we have no choice . . ."

"Oh, come on, who's going to move him? Me? You? Give me a break. Besides, I don't have it in me. I'm telling you honestly, I can't go through that again."

"Me neither," Zohara admitted.

"Listen, there are lots of possibilities along the continuum. Yehuda's just being a little hysterical so he can't see them."

"Okay, will you talk to him, then? If he doesn't answer, text him or WhatsApp him, that's best."

"Do me a favor, you talk to him, I'm here with Varda."

Zohara puffed impatiently, hung up, and called Yehuda.

———

"Did you talk to Amos?" Yehuda asked. "He needs to be psychologically prepared for moving him to his place, I told him that."

"Who, Avishay?" Zohara asked.

"They want to say happy birthday, what can I do?"

"What?"

"One sec," Yehuda said, "Idit wants to talk to you."

A second later Idit came on: "So! What do you say?"

"What a great thing you've done, really," Zohara gushed.

"If you had any idea what we went through to make it happen . . . Yehuda, what are you all stressed out about? Let me talk to her for a minute. He is so stressed out, I don't get it. Hang on, hang on, he wants to talk to you."

Yehuda came back on: "I have to hang up, Zohara. Talk to him, okay? Bye."

═══════

"He's counting on us moving him to you," Zohara said.

"Yes, I know that," Amos said, "I know that and I'm ignoring it. He can keep counting on it. Idiot. How could he not realize they were planning a surprise party for him? What exactly did he think they were going to do up in the Galilee on the day of a big birthday?"

"She told him Tirzah Bar-Ness wanted to meet him, to talk about the book or something."

"Then he really is an idiot. And by the way, if we're going to move him, I'd move him back home."

"What home?" Zohara asked.

"His home."

"And who's going to move him? The two of us? Five seconds ago you said there was no way."

"No, actually there isn't. I forgot that someone has to move him. Hang on, I have another call." He came back a moment later: "They hung up."

Then Zohara had a call coming in. She looked at the screen. "It's Yehuda. He must be trying to get hold of us. Call him back?"

"He's already on call waiting; you answer."

"All right, all right. I'll call you back."

"Are you listening, Zohara? There's no time to waste. Talk to Amos. Either we move Avishay to his place, or . . ."

"But why can't *you* talk to him?" Zohara insisted. "Why does it have to go through me?"

"Because he listens to you more. He won't listen to me now."

"What do you mean, he listens to me more? What difference does it make, Yehuda, it's not going to happen, I'm telling you, he's not moving Avishay to his place."

"I get that, okay, then listen. If that's the case, then please ask Sir Amos to go online and book a flight for tomorrow, for Idit and her sister, last-minute booking, doesn't matter where, tell him to do it. There's no choice, we'll just get them out of the country, that's the safest thing."

"I'm not following . . ." Zohara said.

"So they won't be here," Yehuda explained. "Actually that's a better idea anyway, better than moving Avishay now. I've been thinking about it."

"But why? How will you explain suddenly sending her overseas?"

"I know," Yehuda said, "we'll pretend I'm surprising her back to thank her for what she did. Giving her the trip she gave up for me, or whatever, I'll make something up, she's not going to say no if the tickets are already booked."

"If we're doing that, then why don't *you* go with her? Why would she go with her sister?"

"Why don't I go with her? Because I have to be here, don't you think? Or would you rather I be in Rome on Wednesday?"

"Okay, but from her point of view it's a little weird for you to send her away with her sister for your birthday."

"Zohara, just talk to Amos, okay? I really can't talk now, the grandchildren will be here any minute. Talk to Amos."

Amos said, "I don't understand—you want me to put down two thousand dollars for a couple of tickets online now?"

"I'm sure he'll pay you back," Zohara said.

"That's not the point, the point is that it's a dumb idea. Honestly, how far can you go?"

"Listen, talk to Yehuda. Talk to him, I don't know what to say."

"Wait, hang on, maybe that's him calling." A moment later: "*Oy vey*, it's that biker, Gidi."

Zohara could hear Avishay's phone ringing in the background, loudly, demanding. "Don't answer it."

"What if he calls again?"

"Then answer it, say you're Avishay. Yes, that's better, actually. Answer it, go on, tell him everything's fine and we'll get it over with."

"I thought we weren't answering his phone calls anymore. He's supposed to be dead."

"For Gidi he's supposed to be alive."

"I silenced it." A moment later: "Do you know why he's doing this?"

"Who? Doing what? What are you talking about?"

"Yehuda. With the tickets and all that."

"Why?"

"Because he's mad at me for refusing to move Avishay to my place."

"Could be."

"And I'll tell you something else: he's mad that I wouldn't move him to my place right from the start. That's why he's mad. He doesn't really care about sending Idit abroad and all that bullshit, he's not an idiot, he just wants to give me a task, to punish me."

"You're getting a little carried away," Zohara said.

"Why should I book the flights? Why can't you? And if he wants me to do it so badly, why can't he call me?"

"You think I know how to book tickets online? Yeah, right. He just wants me to soften you up, he's afraid of you."

"Rightly so. Okay, I'll talk to him. Is he free now?"

———

The living room was silent. Zohara felt she was supposed to be on alert, to keep calling until a solution was found. But more than the thought of Idit coming home and finding Avishay dead in the living room, what bothered her was the fact that Yehuda was in Alonei Aba, two feet away from Tirzah Bar-Ness's house.

Although, what could happen, really? She tried to think about it rationally. He could go to her house, knock politely, and ask if it was a good time. He was a good friend of Zohara's, and Tirzah would ask him in, of course, and she'd be very friendly. He was here for his seventieth birthday, a surprise party his family had thrown for him, and he wondered if he might take advantage of the opportunity to discuss that critique she'd given him. "What critique?" she'd ask, and he'd say, "About *The Courage to Invent*, remember? Zohara gave you the manuscript and you wrote me a very detailed letter, which I really appreciated, by the way, I should say that first of all."

How long would it take before he figured it out? Maybe three minutes. And then what would happen? He would never talk to her again, that was for starters. He wouldn't go along with her plan—she could definitely forget about that. He would not forgive her. She wouldn't have either.

Did she regret it? She'd only regret it if she got caught. Even now she could feel at the roots of her tongue, and under her ears, the taste of the insult that had driven her to do it: to write an insulting evaluation of his book in Tirzah Bar-Ness's name.

It wasn't just his fault. There were lots of factors sitting in that spot, she didn't even feel like enumerating them all. But Yehuda had refused to be impressed by her. It had always been that way, she'd always had to force him: Be impressed, I have a big client, I deserve your kudos, look what they said about me. Things that people, friends, should know how to do without being told. But not him. Not with her. He'd always found her work pathetic—commissioned books, ghostwritten memoirs. That was the truth, even though he didn't say it, and no accomplishment of hers managed to scratch out of him what she needed.

When he'd asked for her help with the book, it had sounded like an apology, finally. Like an admission of something. As she'd listened to him, her body had already felt the intoxicating sensation of justice about to be restored. And then along came Tirzah Bar-Ness: Could she ask Tirzah Bar-Ness to read it?

When she made excuses to herself, later, she found comfort in one particular argument: he hadn't even considered apologizing. It had never occurred to him to say, *Of course I thought about you, I thought about you first, but we're too close.* Or: *I didn't want to put you in that position.* No, he'd treated her like a mortgage adviser or a sales clerk or a haberdasher—Zohara had always been crazy about that word—not like a woman who works with words every single day of her life, for her living and for her pleasure. As if he hadn't heard a word she'd told him for the past fifty years.

Beside, everything she'd written in that letter was true. It was all true, and what's more, it was phrased with a tenderness that made Zohara sometimes feel positively martyr-like—she wondered if she was being too tender, too delicate, because it really was not a good book. If anything, she was protecting Yehuda, doing a big favor for him and for Tirzah, who had enough on her plate.

Maybe she should call Tirzah now and prepare her: *I didn't want to bother you with a friend's advice book, and I knew you'd feel bad saying no, so I plonked out a few words in your name. It's just that he's in*

Alonei Aba now, at a B&B, and I'm afraid he might suddenly turn up at
your house. So I want you to be mentally prepared.

That sounded all right. Or did it?

She considered the new information she'd acquired: Yehuda was
not doing this for Avishay, but for himself. But it was both invalu-
able and worthless, because Yehuda would deny everything. He'd
arranged himself a crime with no evidence.

Was there really a chance he'd turn up and knock on her door?
He hated the letter, he hated Tirzah for it, he'd been really insulted.
If there was one thing you could count on, it was Yehuda's injured
pride. So that was that, she would just forget about it. Worst-case
scenario, everyone's feelings got hurt. What could she do about it?

———

"So?" she said.

Amos said, "I can't get hold of him. But listen, I thought of something else."

"What?"

"You know what we were planning to say on Wednesday? We
could just tell Idit that now."

"Tell her what?" Zohara asked. "I don't get it."

"Yehuda tells Idit that he gave Avishay the key to their house for a
few days, to work in their guest room while Idit was away. And then
he just died there, at some point during those days. And when they
come back, they find him. So they find him dead tomorrow instead
of Wednesday, that can't be helped."

Zohara said, "But the whole idea was that Idit can't know
about it."

"The whole idea was that Idit can't know what Yehuda did. Or
is doing."

"Yes . . . ?"

"So she doesn't have to know anything. It's like they just find him dead, together. The only thing that has to happen is that Yehuda goes inside a few minutes before she does, to take the sheet off him."

"Okay," Zohara said.

"It's a good idea, isn't it? For them to just come home and find him?" Amos insisted.

"I don't know, I guess so. Honestly, my brain hurts from all this, I can barely keep up."

"I'm going to try Yehuda again, I'll get back to you."

"Amos, Amos, hold on, just see if you got a text message with a code on Avishay's phone."

"Do me a favor, get this phone away from me already," Amos said.

"Okay, but just check."

"Hang on, I'll get it."

And then Zohara said, "You know why it's not a good idea?"

"What isn't?"

"Because you still have to get to Wednesday, you have to pretend the idea comes up tomorrow, to restage the whole show and hope Idit goes along with it. And she won't."

"Of course she won't!" Amos said. "Are you crazy? Why would we bring Idit in on it?"

"Then I don't get it, I thought you meant we'd suggest the idea from scratch and just bring her in."

"What for? So she can say no and then it'll just be planted in her mind and she'll tell Varda and I don't know who else?"

Zohara was confused. "So he and Idit find him and they call the police, the ambulance, all that?"

"Yes, if there's no choice," Amos confirmed.

"And what do we say? The truth?"

"Are you out of your mind? We say what we just said: he was working at Yehuda's house, he had a heart attack, he fell down the steps."

"Yehuda is really not going to like this," Zohara said.

"Too bad."

"You talk to him."

"I'll talk to him, fine," Amos said, and a moment later, "Your Google Verification Code?"

"What?" Zohara said.

"Your Google Verification Code," he repeated, "is that what you needed?"

"Yes, yes, that's it."

"Should I read it out?"

"Hang on, I'll go to the computer." As she walked to the office, she explained, "I got logged out of his Gmail."

"Avishay's?"

"Yes, don't ask. But I figured it out—they just send a code to your cell phone that lets you back in. Okay, read it out."

"Eight one two, five eight zero."

"Great, thanks, don't erase it for now, just in case."

"I won't erase anything," Amos promised.

———

"Eight, one, two, five, eight, zero."

"New Password?"

Zohara typed: "Z, O, H, A, R, A."

Gmail warned her, in red letters: "Weak Password."

Monday

Yehuda

21

He looked up: the climbing wall loomed more than fifty feet high and was on a challenging incline. It was 9:10 a.m. and his belly contained a chicory smoothie, a beet greens salad, and four slices of plain sourdough bread. Yehuda asked himself whether he had arrived in hell—perhaps instead of Avishay.

About twenty of his relatives were standing around the wall. They were the ones who had spent the night—his and Idit's family, and his brother Shuki's—and Yehuda searched in vain for a comrade-in-despair, a pair of supportive eyes. But they were all surprisingly wakeful and upbeat. Well, of course they were: they'd had coffee. Vegan, my ass, he thought: in the confines of their own rooms, everyone did what they felt like.

The matter with Avishay remained as unsolved as it had been last night. Amos would try to find something online and Yehuda would try to delay their departure from the B&B. That's what they'd agreed; they would talk first thing this morning. And now Yehuda was trapped on a climbing wall. This was his family. This was his life. A seventy-year-old man with a birthday in Alonei Aba, and one final chance to divert his destiny off its course.

He tried to make good use of the time. It was the first quiet moment he'd had since arriving, so it was a time to think, a time to find a solution. Because there was one, there always was, even if nothing was going to come of Amos or any of the others. It was like in the movies: time was short and the murderer was closing in, but there still was a way out. All it took was proper initiative.

In one of their endless talks about the book, Idit had told him: "But is that how you want your fame? Thanks to Avishay?" Yehuda hadn't understood what she was talking about—who thought that? He spent a whole day dwelling on what she'd said, wanting to dismiss it, until finally he came up with the answer: "It's not a question of becoming famous thanks to Avishay. Avishay's foreword and the radio ads and all that are just doing justice to the book, that's all. Giving it the chance to compete. And then either it does or it doesn't."

He looked around for his daughters. At the far end of the room he recognized Daria's back. She wasn't like everyone, that girl, and Yehuda never pressured her. Maybe, in return for her bachelorhood, she would do something great one day.

She had a closet-organizing business now. At first he'd tried to console himself with the thought that it was a business, his daughter was a businesswoman, and when it came to business the sky was the limit—who knew that better than him? But she wasn't making much money, nor was she trying hard enough to, in his opinion, and he'd learned to live with the idea that his daughter was an organizer. That's what she did and maybe she was happy that way. Organizing other people's closets. How had it happened? Somehow. She'd studied political science, then worked in IT for a while, then done some traveling and come back home, then studied coaching and opened the business. That's how.

He thought about Idit at her age. How could you even compare? But that's how it was now: they had so many opportunities, they were so talented—all of them, born talented whether they wanted to or not, compelled by their addresses and their parents and their generation. These days in Tel Aviv you'd have to try really hard to emerge from your mother's belly untalented. And in the end they did nothing. Apart from making babies, that is.

Daria was going to get pregnant now, too. Yesterday, after they had sex, Idit had told him that Daria was starting to meet men for that sole purpose, being very concrete about it. Yehuda asked where she met them and Idit said, "I don't know, I didn't ask, I didn't want to pry. She can tell us however much she wants to."

That had put a damper on his mood, too. The thought of Daria and Avishay sailing through the same world, at the same time, looking for the same thing: someone to have a child with. He wasn't really sure about Avishay, though. After Nili found out about the pregnant girl, he'd tried to believe it was an accident. But as the days went by, perhaps because of the effort this whole week had demanded of him and the resulting grudge mounting inside him against his will, he became convinced that Avishay had wanted a child. He'd wanted a child and hadn't told him. And from the moment that secret became conceivable, an entire universe of possible secrets unfurled. He knew this was irrational and a little perverted, but still—what if Daria and Avishay had gotten together? These things happened. Characters in books had crushes on Daddy's friend—and sometimes characters outside of books did, too.

Avishay had never taken an interest in Yehuda's daughters. It was as if they didn't even exist. And once they stopped being helplessly affixed to their parents, he saw them every few years at best. Now that would only make things easier for him instead of him being punished for it, as he should be.

Suddenly Yehuda was glad Avishay was dead. It put an end to that possibility.

At least the sex had gone off without a hitch. He hated having sex away from home, in settings meant for sex and frequently devoted to it, like vacations and hotels. The date was always scheduled so far in advance, the preparations dragged on so long, that the pressure became intolerable. Maybe that was how a gigolo felt, he thought, when he starts his workday. Then he realized maybe he was flattering himself a little.

He was actually still attracted to Idit, and sometimes he did have the urge. But he liked it when the urge arose unpredictably, when she fell asleep in the car or asked him to bring her a box of panty liners from the top drawer in the hallway bureau. He liked to guess whether she was in the mood too, he liked to be in suspense. Maybe that's what had saved them yesterday: she fell asleep on the bed before they had time to do anything, and when she woke up to brush her teeth he wasn't sure if she was awake enough.

Was it possible that Daria was like that because of him? But he was a completely normal dad. Or was he? Was there something that everyone except him could see? He already had one daughter who'd fallen in with an older man. He looked down at Daniella, with her cute little pregnant belly, sitting with her back to the wall playing with her iPhone. He'd been suspicious of the whole feminist story for years, precisely because he had girls: he saw all the opportunities they had, and how capable they were, and he saw how they themselves disparaged what was out there, what was available, and how they made small choices. But now that Daria was seeking out men who were too old, who were not good enough, simply because she was thirty-eight, while Avishay could afford to suddenly wake up at the age of seventy and pursue fatherhood with intolerable ease—now Yehuda was filled with fury and a dismal sense of injustice. He felt like snitching, like calling the police: *You're not going to believe what's happening here! Outrageous inequity!* But at the same time he was embarrassed, like someone who gets the punch line long after the joke was told.

He considered the possibility that there were other things in his life about which he was unjustly adamant. He was a good father, of that he was certain. He behaved the way a father should, and much more than that. But when—very infrequently—he replayed the girls' childhood, his memory bumped around between the walls of age three and age twenty, after which they turned into different creatures, real people. He saw them often, but knew little about the lives they led in between their meetings. Or about their thoughts, which used to burst out of them within an hour or two at most, still unripe but impossible to contain. Whereas now those thoughts were watered and watered, until they grew and struck roots, and no one ever picked them. Certainly not the parents. What had they thought about him these past twenty years? What was he doing in their minds? He didn't know why, but he had the dim sense that his standing in there was not as good as Idit's.

He would do something about it. He would do it as soon as this week was over, before he died, too. But what? He imagined himself asking Daria out for coffee. That would be strange. Without Idit? Without Daniella? He felt like giving her something. Not money, something else. But what? He didn't know what she needed.

Daniella was five months pregnant. She measured things by weeks, and Idit translated for him after they left. She was going to take at least a year off after the baby was born, she'd already told the university and they were fine with it. Daniella was a math prodigy, thirty-six years old and already a tenure-track lecturer at Ben Gurion University. But Yehuda had a bad feeling about it. She would take a year off, but she wouldn't want to put the baby in daycare when he was only a year old, so she'd take more time off, and then she might get pregnant again. Granted, it was Nili who'd put that idea into his head, she said that's how they were these days, and Yehuda had told her she was wrong, it was nonsense. But as time went by he had less confidence in himself and in Daniella and the job and the university, and certainly in Yossi.

For the past few years he'd been obsessively consuming articles and news items about people who'd become extremely successful at a late age. Writers who suddenly flourish at sixty, earning six-figure advances, gifted chefs who'd hidden their talents under a veneer of ordinariness until their late blooming. Idit always said: "You made your mark early, at twenty-nine—what more do you want? Don't you understand that's what people dream of? That kind of early success?" But Yehuda found it annoying, and he refused to recognize his success, refused to have it count—it wasn't fair for that to be it, for that to have been his moment. There had to be a statute of limitations. He had the right to compete again.

He was in a horrible mood, he realized now. The irritations and insults clambered over one another like worms, but Yehuda felt like wallowing. There were fewer and fewer of those articles that managed to raise his spirits. Authors with bestsellers at age fifty-something he could still occasionally read about, but at seventy?

His daughters weren't going to do anything big either. Not at this point. It just wasn't going to happen, because that's how life was. Daria would keep organizing closets or something, and Daniella would give up on things, because you couldn't do everything. So she wouldn't get a Nobel Prize. She'd be a professor—wasn't that good enough anymore? There were plenty of respectable professors. She'd work at the university, and when she turned seventy someone would throw her a birthday at Alonei Aba. Then she'd die. Or maybe not? That's what he'd thought about Avishay, too, for many years. He'd thought economics was not something worth devoting one's life to, he'd looked down on Avishay for choosing a bourgeois, drab profession, until suddenly the Nobel came into the picture—when had that started? Five years ago, maybe seven. And then all of Yehuda's synapses had suddenly lit up: the Nobel was a big deal, the Nobel was a dream, and his respect for Avishay ballooned. The whole subject of economics suddenly became of great interest to him, all the details and the chances and the probabilities. He could already see the five of them taking a road trip in Sweden to accept the prize and have a grand old time. So why couldn't it happen to his daughter?

Or maybe that Yossi guy would win it. Or maybe nobody would. That was the most likely scenario. His memory flitted over the events of the past week, and they all seemed so foolish, so pointless. What were they doing? And for what? Avishay wasn't going to win the Nobel. People didn't just win Nobel Prizes. His children would die, everyone would die, they'd just die without anything. He'd probably die that way, too.

He felt himself swallowing down the anger. Disgusting, pent-up anger, the kind you couldn't brandish or spit out. Having no choice, he aimed it at the dead. It was Avishay who'd put the whole Nobel thing in his mind. Worse, in fact: he'd planted the idea that there could be a different life. That's what he'd put in Yehuda's mind. That you should expect something out of life. That's how it had always been, ever since they were little. Not a single hope was superfluous, and when something didn't come to fruition, you simply had to be disappointed. Avishay offered no consolation. No reprieve, not even at seventy.

Yehuda imagined Avishay in his room, in his bed, lying there, dead, but then he quickly updated the scene to the floor of his own house—he was there now, after all. But that made him feel bad and he went back to the picture he'd imagined in the days that now seemed almost peaceful, back when Avishay had lain dead in his own bed, before everything got totally screwed up. Even that way, horizontal, resting, he was still making them all work, denying them even a final moment of grace. They were following his presumed will when he hadn't even bothered to scribble it on a piece of paper. They were worshipping his memory without asking questions, like parents of a son fallen in battle—or a saint.

Before he could assess his anger and decide whether to stick with it, the pictures broke free and started flipping back wildly, and the next thing he knew he was looking at Avishay the boy. Yehuda tried to stop the reel from spinning, hurling the whole weight of his body on it, summoning Avishay as an artillery officer, Avishay on their trip to London. But it was no good. Avishay was a boy, it was final, as if he'd spent most of his life as a child and his maturation was merely a technical malfunction. Yehuda sensed that Avishai would never go back to being anything else again, not even in his own imagination.

He remembered that time in elementary school when they'd built the Shoah out of cardboard boxes in Avishay's living room: this is the ghetto, that's the SS command. Then Avishay's cat peed on the Gestapo, and they weren't sure if they were allowed to laugh. Was Avishay really going to get the Nobel Prize? Yehuda suddenly had the urge to protect Avishay from the unfair burden of growing up. He wanted to protect his daughters, too, and himself, and everyone he'd known as a child, everyone who'd ever proved to him beyond a doubt that he'd been a child. It occurred to him that perhaps that was the essential difference between childhood friends and everyone who joined in later, the ones who were born into your life as adults and were therefore fair prey.

In every interview Avishay gave, over and over again, he was asked if he himself had been the "class king"—was that where his inspiration had come from? And Avishay would always say, "Me? Class king? No way. It was my dear friend Yehuda Harlap who was the king of the class. Yehuda Harlap of the bag opener, yes, yes, google him." And every time, Yehuda would swell with gratitude that never faded, amazed at Avishay's generosity, which was rather uncharacteristic and therefore testified all the more sincerely to the depths of their friendship.

He really had been the class king, that was true. Avishay wasn't even his deputy, but he was protected by virtue of their friendship and his good grades—those had counted for something back then. How had they even become friends? Yehuda found himself wondering. Was it because of their parents? But the thought confused him and he quickly replaced it with a different one: he liked to think of himself as the original class king. In some sense he was a shareholder in the model. Wasn't it their chance, then, to do something great? Both of them? Something great and collaborative, a worthy finale for a lifetime of friendship?

His book cover flickered in his mind like a lighthouse. The proper cover, not truncated or trimmed or autopsied, the God-given cover: "With a Foreword by Nobel Laureate Avishay Sar-Shalom." The image brought him comfort and excitement: only two days to wait. But then it wandered off, getting further and further away, with a little pang of guilt that trailed behind it for just a moment too long.

Six days was a long time. Six days during which he had whispered fiery defenses as he lay in bed, repelled the charges with a horror that had now become authentic, and fallen dishonorably into an insult-laden slumber. Yehuda discovered, to his relief, that time had the power to dilute, to blur solid lines of separation, to reeducate one's memory: of all his friends, he was the only one who had come up with the idea of doing something so grandiose, so demanding, so altruistic. He was the one who had fought for his dead friend, even when he'd been absolved of the friendship by all rights.

He reached the top of the climbing wall. From up there, everyone down below looked the same. He shouted: "I made it! What now?" And the coach yelled up: "Now come down."

═══

He had an unanswered call and two text messages from Amos: "Get back to me" and "Where are you?" Yehuda texted back: "Can't talk, text me. Did you get tix?" Amos wrote: "Call me when you can," and Yehuda realized there were no tickets. Amos was getting on his nerves.

If not for Avishay, would Yehuda be enjoying himself? He tried to imagine the events of the past day and night, minus Avishay: driving to Alonei Aba, stopping off at the Pancake House, having one of his funnest drives ever, filled with anticipation, driving toward something—but doing it all in a different week, when Avishay was still alive, or already buried. But the whole thing seemed simply impossible. He almost had the feeling that Avishay had never been alive, but also that he could never be dead, and he had to admit that it wasn't troubling him all that much. That wasn't it. It wasn't Avishay who was ruining his birthday.

While they were packing that morning, Yehuda had found an unexpected patch of quiet, and he'd used it to pick up the bricks of thought that had sat at the bottom of his mind last night until he fell asleep, too exhausted to erect them into anything.

What had Idit actually done? A seventieth birthday party, a lavish production, built on the ruins of the thing he cherished most: his book, his future, his one chance in this world. Had there really been no other way to get him to Alonei Aba, other than posing as Tirzah Bar-Ness? What were they thinking—that it was funny? That the joy of a family gathering and the birthday excitement would make him forget?

He remembered Idit's response after he hung up the phone and proudly informed her that he was going to meet Tirzah. "I just hope you don't get disappointed," she'd said, "you don't really know what she wants." Although the events were long over, he couldn't help redeciphering them with hindsight, having cracked the mystery. At the time he'd been angry: "You're always belittling, always mocking. Why can't you just be supportive for once?" But now he realized Idit was worried—the prank had gone better than she'd expected.

He was thrilled that Tirzah Bar-Ness wanted to meet him, and she was afraid he'd be disappointed. She was afraid that instead of doing something good, she was doing something bad. Did she deserve his forgiveness?

The anger mounted again, impervious, with no way out. How could he forgive her, when he hadn't even been given the chance to be angry? She might have thought of it that day, after the phone call, but they'd been here for a whole day and night, and his disappointment and sadness and futility were all buried under an avalanche of cheer and festivities and an unimpeachable claim: *Look at this party we've thrown you, hey? Hey?*

⸻

He'd reached Alonei Aba without any trouble. At the gate outside the village he told the guard he had a meeting on Ha'haruv Street, and was waved in. He reached a big dirt lot, parked, and got out of the car without his bag, just to make sure it was the right place. He walked carefully up a gravel path to the stone house on the corner, his head trying to get ahead of his feet, his eyes rushing forward. He entered through a narrow opening that led to a lawn, and his ears were suddenly assailed: "Happy Birthday!!!!!!"

His heart thumped violently in his chest—this must be how it feels when you get a stent inserted if the anesthetic doesn't work properly—and his eyes dashed after his ears in confusion, trying to parse out the clump on the lawn into something coherent. The first one he identified, for some reason, was Mika, Shuki's oldest daughter. Then he saw the kids, and that reassured him a little. Then Shuki, and next to him Idit, who emerged from the clump and walked toward him. Everyone was there: Shuki's girls, including Lihi from the US, the husbands, the grandchildren, and of course

Shuki's wife, Yemima, and Idit and Daria and Daniella and Yossi, and Miki, Idit's sister, with her partner and the kids, hers and his. So many kids. A familiar panic warmed his body, climbing up from the soles of his feet, threatening to light him on fire: Had he been invited to this thing? Had he forgotten? Idit kissed him and they all clapped and cheered excessively, and suddenly Yehuda had a horrifying thought: This had better not be a renewal of vows.

Idit called out: "I hope you're hungry!" Yehuda stammered: "Aren't you overseas?" and everyone burst out laughing. Only then did his eyes recognize two men and a woman in white uniforms on the lawn, bustling around a structure with smoke billowing up from its center. He wanted to say: I have a meeting with Tirzah Bar-Ness in seven minutes, but he was afraid everyone would laugh again. Still, he wasn't sure and couldn't leave the doubt unresolved: What if there really was a meeting? What if this was something else, in the same place, using the perfect excuse to get him there? He whispered in Idit's ear: "Is there a meeting with Tirzah Bar-Ness?" Idit said, "What do you think?" Yehuda wasn't sure what that meant and how to read her voice. Was it a *Yes, what do you think* or a *No, what do you think*? "No?" he tried. And she simply repeated, "What do you think?" Yehuda said, "So you just asked her to call for no reason?" Idit said, "Do you really think that was *her* on the phone?" "Then who was it?" he mumbled. "Later, I'll tell you later," Idit said, and she turned to the many kissers and huggers who had surrounded them both, as though they were of equal status at this event.

Shuki hugged Yehuda. "What a party she's thrown you! I'm really impressed." Then he shouted, "Okay, can we start eating now?"

Idit said, "Of course, of course! I guarantee you won't be eating alone!"

One after the other, the greeters drifted over to the food tables, and Idit and Yehuda stood alone on the lawn, the first moment of communion for the new couple. Idit was emotional, gushing with details and secrets she longed to share: "We've been here since Saturday! Daria and I spent the night, and Daniella and Yossi came this morning. You won't believe how long we've been working on this! I'm telling you, you won't believe it, it was like a military operation. You thought I was overseas? God, no! And I put so much thought into what to tell you." After each revelation, instead of breathing or pausing, she said, "So you really didn't know? Nothing, right? You bought it!"

He touched her lightly on the back, with what might have been an affectionate pat or might have been a shove. It worked, and they both walked over to the food. The pancakes were still humming in his stomach, but with great concentration he managed to make room in his mind for some grilled meat; it was a different stomach anyway. Then he remembered that he was supposed to be vegan and his spirits fell. He would simply die if he couldn't eat meat now; the whole event would be irredeemable. *Oh, what the hell*! he'd say: it was his seventieth birthday, he'd give himself a pass just this one evening. But as he began fending off imaginary attacks—*Oh, so suddenly you don't find it disgusting? I thought meat was a piece of cancer between two slices of bread!*—Idit said, "Shimrit Ackerman did the catering." Yehuda said vaguely, "She's a chef or something, right?" Idit said, "What's the matter with you? She wrote *First Nature*. Do you know how hard it was to get her? Do you know how much they charge?" Yehuda looked at the colorful dishes smiling back at him like bimbos on a candid camera show, and even before he looked at the menu, he knew the answer to his question: "Oh, so is everything here vegan?"

There was roasted kohlrabi stuffed with freekeh; pearl barley salad with figs and raisins; cabbage confit on a bed of quince and lentils; eggplant tabouleh; radish momo; green-bean-cuffed leek bundles; mung-fava-lupine bean mash; black-eyed peas with pineapple jackets; seitan Benedict; konnyaku-stuffed Swiss chard; avocado chips; Jerusalem artichoke on a bed of heirloom lettuce; soy, oat, and cherry loaf; quinoa steak with citrus velouté; mac-'n'-no-cheese; millet kebabs; mushroom "schnitzel"; spiced millet "fish" with nigella seeds; poached not-salmon; tofurkey breast; fennel, broccoli, beet, and watercress "shawarma"; vegan wings; adzuki-bean pizza; Japanese pumpkin and spelt falafel; flaxseed kibbeh; four-cauliflower lasagna; guava chocolate milk; kale mousse; and spelt Toblerone.

=====

A picture of the girls flickered on a white screen hanging near the tables, and once it stabilized he identified the setting: his backyard at home. When had that been taken? When he was asleep? He was seized with fear. He tried to use logic to calm himself: these were his relatives, they wanted the best for him. But then his thoughts brought new forms of panic: What if this whole week had all been part of the ruse? Had his best friends conspired with his family to organize an unforgettable surprise party? But Avishay was dead. Avishay was really dead. He looked at Idit sitting next to him. He wanted to ask her: Is Avishay dead? But he was afraid she'd say, "What do you think?"

Daniella sprung alive on the screen. "Hi, Dad," she said, and her always-childish voice reassured him at once, caressing him as he sat in his chair, reminding him of who he was. "We know you're stressed out, so don't worry, we haven't put together an evening of eulogies." Then the voice changed. It was Daria: "Instead, we asked the people closest to you to tell the worst, most terrible, most humiliating story about you they can come up with. This is going to be the roast of all roasts, Dad, so you should probably have a drink. I mean, another drink..." Everyone laughed and Yehuda looked around: They weren't there. Avishay, Nili, Zohara, and Amos, they weren't there. Of course. Avishay was dead. Everything was okay.

First came Shuki. He told the lemonade story, which everyone had heard a million times before, but he still managed to ruin it. Then came Idit. She told the story about that time when they were on their way home from Eilat and they stopped to drop her dad off at the station for his bus to Ashkelon. When Idit got out of the car to move up to the passenger seat after her dad got out, Yehuda drove off and left her on the side of the road. There were no cell phones back then, and Yehuda noticed and turned back only an hour later. Idit stood there that whole time, convinced he'd come back any minute.

He wondered if he would have enjoyed it some other time. If there existed a Yehuda who was capable of laughing at something like this. But before he could find the answer, he heard a familiar, deep voice, which he recognized even before he identified the face, although he had not taken his eyes off the screen for a minute. He felt his jaw drop the way a jaw can drop only in books: Avishay. It was Avishay, filling the giant screen, almost vulgar in his vitality and his dimensions. And Avishay said, "Remember, Yehuda, that evening with the youth group, in sixth grade?" Yehuda felt like saying, *No, I don't remember*. He felt like taking Avishay aside and asking him to tell the story privately. But Avishay went on: "It was an activity meant to build trust. So they split us up into pairs, with one kid in each pair blindfolded, and the seeing one had to lead the blind one through the streets of Tel Aviv, hand in hand. So I blindfold myself, and I hold my best friend Yehuda's hand, and not two minutes later—bang! Yehuda kept walking and I slammed straight into a utility pole. I swear, it was just like a cartoon." Yehuda looked up at the screen like a little boy sitting with his classmates around the teacher at circle time. How does it end, Avishay? He had to hear how the story was resolved, but the on-screen Avishay got up and walked away, and Yehuda remembered all of a sudden how tall he was, how much space he took up in the world, and Avishay walked over to a concrete post in his apartment and banged his head on it and said, "Bang!" Everyone laughed out loud, and Idit said, "Oh, he's so cute! He's really excited," and Yehuda realized he was crying.

22

Yehuda tried to take advantage of Idit being focused on the poorly paved road and send a WhatsApp message while she was driving, but the letters got jumbled every time they hit a pothole, the autocorrect went wild, and after sending Amos a message that said, "Lacing bow," he gave up.

When they finally got on the highway, Idit said, "So? How was it? It was great, wasn't it?"

"So great. Really, really great," Yehuda answered. At the same time, he typed:

We're on our way. What's happening?

"Come on, give me something more than that."

"Something more?" Yehuda repeated. Amos wrote back:

You go in together, you find him dead together. No choice.

"Do you think Shuki and Yemima are okay?" Idit wondered. Another message came in from Amos:

She'll be happy he's dead, trust me.

"What's going on? Who are you texting so furiously with?" she asked.

"With Amos and everyone. I'm telling them about the birthday."

"Well, what do they say?"

Amos again:

What else do you suggest? We either get him out, which is no
longer feasible, or we tell her, and then we're finished.

Yehuda said, "They're super-excited, of course. They're really excited." And he wrote:

I suggest you call a locksmith NOW!!!! Get him out of there.
Make a real effort to find a solution.

"They aren't offended that we didn't invite them, are they? Did
you explain that we made a decision early on to limit it to family?
I hope they aren't insulted that they weren't in the film, it's just
that we had to keep it short. Make sure they understand, okay?
Tell them we decided we'd only use people who knew you from
childhood."

Amos:

We have nowhere to move him, remember?

Yehuda wanted to write back but he could see that Amos was still
typing, so he took advantage of the pause to say, "Shuki and Yemima
seem fine to me. Why? Did you notice anything? I was just kind of
on a high from the whole thing."

Amos:

We're not going to carry a body out in the middle of the day.
And we don't have Nili, ok? It's just me and Zohara.

Then another message:

Meaning, just me.

Before Yehuda could answer, there was another one:

I understand you're angry, even though I'm not sure why, but think about it rationally.

"Didn't you pick up that weird vibe at dinner, when she came over to take a bite of his food and he kind of pushed her away? It was really strange, even for them."
Amos sent another message:

When exactly did I not make a real effort? When I stayed up till 2 a.m. looking for flight deals?

Yehuda said, "I didn't see that at all, but is that it? Is that why you ask, or did you see something else?" and he wrote:

It's inconceivable to me that on a Sun. night you can't find 2 tickets to somewhere for Mon. It doesn't make sense.

Idit said, "I don't know, Daniella saw the thing at dinner, too, and she said it was bizarre, so it's not just my imagination."
"What happened exactly? Tell me again? He wouldn't let her taste his food?"
"She came over and reached her fork out for a piece of the pumpkin falafel or whatever, and he kind of moved his plate away so she couldn't reach it, like a little kid."
"Sounds like he was just joking around," Yehuda said.

Amos wrote:

I don't know when you last booked next-day tix online, but it's
not as easy as you think. I drove Hagar crazy getting her help,
the two of us were online all night. So why do I deserve this?

"It wasn't a joke," Idit said, "it was really unpleasant, and it
looked like it was the continuation of a fight or something. Daria
and Einat were sitting right there, it was really embarrassing. She
just got up demonstratively—Yehuda, can you be with me for a
second?"

"I'm with you the whole time, but Amos is having a crisis," Yehuda said.

"What happened?"

"It's just that Wednesday is the Nobel, so he's stressed out," Yehuda replied, pleased with himself for coming up with a story that
was both smart and, basically, true.

"So Amos is worried Avishay's going to get the prize?"

Yehuda touched the blank box in preparation for typing a message and said, "Not worried, but you know, it's an awkward situation. Much as you want to be a good friend, you're also a human
being." He was about to type but then he saw another message coming in from Amos:

Also, I kind of feel like you've fallen in love with all the action,
you're forgetting that we have a goal, which is to keep Avishay
under the radar till Wed. with the least possible drama, not to
rack up adventures before you croak.

Idit said, "I'd like to go on record as saying that I'm in favor of
Amos."

Yehuda typed:

I'm looking for adventures before I croak?? How exactly? By keeping Avishay at my house while you all get a pass?

Idit said, "If there's any justice in the world . . ."

"If there's any justice in the world then what?" Yehuda asked.

"Then Amos will win. But there isn't."

"Neither of them will probably win."

"I'd rather neither of them do than Avishay."

"Oh, really? What a surprise."

"Did he even call you?" she asked.

"Call me about what?"

"About what?" she repeated in disbelief.

"Oh, to say happy birthday? Yes. He did."

"Very nice of him."

"Stop it, Idit."

Amos wrote:

You've done a lot. More than all of us, no one's disputing that. But you sometimes forget that there's a simple way.

"Stop what?" Idit said. "I don't recall him ever remembering your birthday."

"So what. You think I always remember his? We've spent sixty years not making a big deal out of birthdays." Amos sent a smiley face, and Yehuda almost snapped.

Idit said, "But come on, it's your seventieth."

Yehuda wrote:

Don't patronize me.

And said, "But I'm telling you he did call, what more do you want?"

"Okay, why are you getting so angry?"

Amos wrote:

Who's patronizing?

Yehuda wrote back:

The lengths you'll go to, to get out of doing something, it's unbelievable.

"Was he happy we threw the party for you?" Idit asked.

"You're starting again?" Yehuda said.

"What? What did I say wrong?"

"Why wouldn't he be happy? Seriously, what sort of a dumb question is that?"

Amos wrote:

I'm warning you, I'm getting sick of this.

"All right, I was just wondering what he said about the party, that's all. I can't say anything to you anymore."

"Why aren't you asking if Nili was happy? If Zohara was happy? Why wouldn't Avishay be happy for me? What sort of a notion is that? Can't you see what an annoying question that is?"

"All right," Idit said.

"All right what? What does that mean? Come on, let's hear it."

"It doesn't mean anything. Let's stop this. I'm done talking."

Yehuda rode her declaration out a little and wrote:

All these machinations—for what? So you won't have to take

initiative on anything, god forbid? Or move something and take a risk, god forbid?

Nothing from Amos.
Yehuda typed on:

Yehuda can take care of the body, Yehuda can carry the body, Yehuda's wife can get mad the day after she throws him a surprise party, it can all come crashing down, so long as Amos Barzani doesn't have to do anything.

No answer. Idit said nothing.
Amos wrote:

Then suggest something else.

Yehuda wrote:

Find a solution. Solve the problem. And not a solution where I get screwed again.

He reread what he'd written and added:

Let someone else get screwed a bit too. He's not just my friend, he's yours. You want him to win, don't you?

Amos didn't answer. Yehuda continued:

Or maybe you don't.

But he didn't send it.

He waited a little, but Amos still didn't answer.

He added a question mark and hit "Send."

———

On ordinary days, this was exactly the reason Yehuda liked Amos: he was the only one of the five of them who looked and acted his age, and did so openly without apologizing, as if it were the most natural thing in the world. Yehuda loved that about him, almost the way you love a child. And he viewed himself as a mentor of sorts, a guide or a big brother, whose job was to extricate everything that was hidden inside Amos. First of all, academically. Not that Yehuda knew much about it, but happiness economics was a controversial field, he did know that, both from Amos and from Avishay. It was the *enfant terrible* of economics, if he was reading the picture correctly. It was not a field for geeks; Amos just needed a little more self-confidence.

Generally speaking, Yehuda had the feeling that all of Amos's hard work, all the modesty with which he labored over god-knows-what like some lab rat, was destined for greatness: Amos would walk out of that lab one day with a cure for cancer. Or the economic equivalent of one. Something that would really turn the tables, both the economists' and Amos's. He only hoped it would materialize before he died.

But things were happening to Amos outside of academia, too, which he seemed to be trying to push away. His kids, for example. Yehuda had always been interested in parents and children, in the way parents treated their children, in the whole mess, probably because he himself was debating what to do, how to think about it all, and was plagued by a constant sense of having missed something. With so much money, there had to be a way to crack the secret of life, of success, of happiness, if not his then at least theirs. And when he listened to Amos, he marveled at him. Okay, he had Hagar, whom he was worried about, and rightly so; she was never going to be a musician, that was embarrassingly obvious. But he also had Achinoam, the older son, who was always being written up in the financial papers. He owned a chain of six DIY furniture stores, and the media loved him. He was the wunderkind giving hell to the big chains.

And now there was the way Amos was carrying on about Varda's bar exam. As if she really needed to behave herself so she could be a lawyer, rather than exactly the opposite. As if anyone in the bar association, or for that matter in the whole world, cared what Varda did.

Yehuda usually found it amusing. At most it aroused in him a paternal urge to shake Amos up, to spur him on, to push him out of his comfort zone. But when it came to this escapade with Avishay, it was getting on his nerves. Amos had seriously offered both Idit's bar exam and Achinoam's position in the hotly competitive furniture market as excuses for why he couldn't have a body in his house or even get into a tiny bit of trouble. It made things difficult for all of them, especially him, but it also depicted Yehuda as the one with the more boring life, the one whose sins were uninteresting. And that was unforgivable.

———

He looked at the screen and couldn't decide whether he wanted Amos to answer or not. It would have been nice for Zohara to show some interest, too. Maybe she'd talked with Amos.

The truth was, he wouldn't have gone home in any case, even without Idit. At five a.m. on Sunday morning he'd checked in to a hotel, like a criminal on the run or a man involved in some sexual intrigue. But the desk clerk was well-trained and courteous, and Yehuda reminded himself that sometimes ordinary people arrive from overseas early in the morning. Not without luggage, however. Either way, he'd booked a room for five nights, just in case.

He'd been alone with Avishay for maybe ten minutes, the time it took Amos and Zohara to walk down the path and get into a cab and get far enough away—in his estimation—and even that was too much. For most of those ten minutes, he stood by the narrow crack he left open in the door, his mouth and nose peeking out, defying Nili's instruction to leave the doors and windows shut. He felt as though Avishay were drawing all the oxygen in the house to himself.

He wasn't cut out for this—that was the truth. Being with Avishay when the rest of them were there was tolerable. Even carrying his body was doable. It's not that the body disgusted him. It didn't at all, or not especially, at least as long as he wasn't vomiting, and the disgust it did provoke simply motivated him to carry Avishay faster, it revved up his engines. But staying with him alone—he couldn't do that.

He'd realized this immediately, on the first day, when he'd gone into Avishay's room to look for the A/C remote control. That was the real problem with this plan; the only problem, as far as he was concerned: he couldn't stay alone with the body. He would have to get around it somehow, to make up for it by showing up in other ways.

It's true that he was supposed to watch over Avishay until Wednesday. But what could he do? He was donating his house, that was the most he could do. He had donated it knowing he wouldn't be there. It's not like anyone was going to come visit anyway—who would come over? Only he and Idit and the girls had keys, and the girls would never just turn up. And if they did, they did. If that's what ended up toppling the whole plan, he would pay that price.

It surprised him, because he was nothing if not a rationalist. A rationalist and an atheist. Avishay was dead and that was it—other than worms, there was nothing. He was convinced of this before Avishay had died and he was still convinced of it now, but it made no difference: it was a body, a dead body of a dead man, and it was lying there unburied. And unreported, which, oddly, bothered him in particular. Avishay had died off the record; the lack of supervision meant that this dead man might suddenly rise up.

———

Idit drove on in silence. They'd be home in forty minutes.

"Why don't we go somewhere?" Yehuda suggested.

"I thought you were mad at me."

"I don't like the way you dislike Avishay, the way you don't even respect my love for him."

"I respect the fact that you love him, I just don't respect him."

"Same difference. If you don't respect him, you can't respect the fact that I love him. It's impossible."

"Look," Idit explained, "even if I ignore all his qualities that don't have anything to do with other people and don't hurt them, right?"

"I understand it's a pretty long list, is it?"

"Look . . ."

"What do you mean by 'qualities that don't have anything to do with other people'?"

"I don't know, like the fact that he's arrogant. Okay, so he's arrogant. And by the way, it's not that success changed him—he was arrogant before that, too. Okay, so you're arrogant too, and I'm also a little arrogant. Let's say that all of you are pretty arrogant and that's fine, that's how you should be at this age. Not that it comes close to Avishay's level, but fine, he can be pleased with himself, it doesn't hurt anyone. That's what I'm talking about, for example."

"I'm arrogant?" Yehuda said.

"I'm arrogant too, I said so. I have good reasons to be, so I'm arrogant. Never mind that now."

"Okay, so . . ."

"But I am talking, let's say, about the way he treats other people.
And not his PhD students—"

"He treats his PhD students better than anyone, they love him,"
Yehuda pointed out.

"I have no idea if they love him or not, maybe they do. But I'm
talking about his best friends, which is how a man is measured."

"How exactly does he treat us badly?"

"Take Zohara," Idit said. "The poor woman has been in love with
him for I don't know how long, and he pays no attention, he has no
empathy, not even a minimal sensitivity to a person who—okay, so
you're not in love with her, but she's such a good friend of yours, for
so many years, not to mention that you're sleeping with her, right?
So really, I mean . . ."

"First of all, I don't think Zohara's in love with him. Maybe. Maybe
she was once, but you're talking about something that was relevant
eons ago, maybe thirty years," Yehuda countered.

"Do me a favor, Yehuda, she's obviously in love with him. Helen
Keller could see that. Seriously."

"You know what? You really are arrogant. Apparently you don't
even entertain the possibility that I know these people slightly better
than you do, that I spend maybe four thousand times more time with
them than you do, partly because you have no interest in spending
time with them."

"You want to know the truth?"

"Go on," Yehuda said.

"Never mind."

"What?"

"There's no possibility that you know these people better."

"Are you serious?" Yehuda exclaimed.

"I mean, I suppose that in some ways you do, but you're all in each other's business so much that you can't see anything anymore. I'm telling you for real, if you can't see that Zohara is in love with Avishay, then seriously, it's like, I don't even know what to tell you. Ask Nili, you know what? Don't take my word for it."

"Okay," Yehuda said, "so let's say she is in love with him. What do you expect him to do about it? What has he done wrong? I don't understand. He shouldn't sleep with her, is that it?"

"Firstly, yes, it wouldn't be a bad thing for him to stop sleeping with her. It just confuses her and deludes her and it's just horrible of him," Idit replied.

"Oh, come on, this really kills me—he's supposed to decide for her that it's better for her if he doesn't sleep with her, even though she wants to sleep with him and is sleeping with him of her own free will and apparently thinks it is a good idea? Is that some kind of feminism?"

"It has nothing to do with feminism, it's just behaving like a decent human being."

"Oh, I thought everything had to do with feminism."

"What is going on here?" Idit snapped. "I'm trying to talk with you about your friend."

"Fine, then I'm asking you, what did he do wrong? Is it that he's sleeping with her?"

"What did he do wrong? He shoves his girlfriends and his stories and his business in her face like he's . . . I don't know . . . Without any sensitivity, like he's not even aware of it, and he is very much aware of it, believe me, he just wants her to know her place. In general he likes people around him to know their place."

"I don't get it: if he has a girlfriend, a partner, is he supposed to not bring her along? Is he supposed to hide her, so Zohara won't get her feelings hurt?"

"He doesn't have to hide her and Zohara's a big girl, but I've been at thousands of those dinners, and Avishay really likes to be in the role of the older man playing the field, who hasn't settled into middle-class conventionality like the rest of us. He really likes to wave that around in your faces. By the way, the whole thing about not having kids, too, I have no problem with him not having kids, you know me, I honestly don't think everyone has to be a parent, but the way he treats all of your kids, I've never seen such a thing."

"All right, you don't have to get so worked up, that's just who he is," Yehuda protested.

"That's who he is—that's exactly my point. And by the way, I'm the last person you can accuse of getting worked up. Except for that one time, which was an anomaly, I admit it, and I still haven't forgotten what he said."

"What, the thing with the screwed-up kids?"

"Damaged. Please be accurate: your kids are damaged," Idit corrected him.

"He didn't say our kids were damaged, what rubbish."

"I'll tell you exactly what he said, word for word, because I will take that to my grave. You were arguing with Daniella about the apartment on Mivtza Kadesh, she stormed off into her bedroom, and Avishay said, 'That's the fun thing about watching older kids: it's like watching people who are already damaged, it totally kills your motivation to make them.'"

"So you think he was saying Daniella is damaged? What nonsense, you don't really believe that, he wouldn't have spoken like that unless it was obvious that it was just talk."

"Yehuda, that is a very ugly thing to say, very violent, and it was said during an extremely difficult, extremely tense moment. But forget it, we've already had this argument a thousand times. I can't be bothered. The point is, the guy's made a career out of talking about the class king? What a joke! The man hasn't seen a kid for sixty years."

This was the moment to tell her. They'd be home in eleven minutes. *Avishay's dead, did you know that? I didn't want to tell you before, so as not to ruin the amazing birthday party.* He said: "Let's go away, Idit, I'm serious. Take the exit to the airport, just the way we are, fly out of here to somewhere."

"What's the matter with you, Yehuda? Overseas? Are you crazy?"

"I don't know, I just feel like stretching this birthday out a little longer. The minute I walk in the front door, it's over."

"You want us to go away, fine, we'll go away."

"Thank you."

"But not now, Yehuda!"

"Okay, forget overseas, let's go to a hotel, let's go to a hotel in Tel Aviv, the Hilton or I don't know what, like a couple in their twenties. Look how great it is when we talk, look at us talking now."

"I actually found this conversation about Avishay pretty excruciating, I have to tell you. I hate these kind of talks, I always come out like I'm the one who doesn't know what I'm talking about, the bad one."

"Nonsense. I'm putting the Hilton in the GPS." He canceled the navigation from the B&B, which they didn't need any more anyway; it said they would arrive in eight minutes.

"Okay, okay, we'll go, but would you mind waiting till, I don't know, tomorrow?"

"Yes, I would mind, I really would—you're missing the point. Once we get home, the momentum is gone."

"But I don't have anything on me."

"What do you need? Go into the convenience store and buy a six-pack of underwear."

"The convenience store? I haven't been home since Saturday, I don't even have enough medication with me."

Yehuda looked around: from here it was on foot. On foot and by car, same time. "Idit, I'm begging you, stop the car. Stop driving for a second."

"Yehuda, what's the matter with you? We're a block from the house!"

"Idit, pull over, I'm not joking. Stop the car, I can't go back there. I have this tightness in my chest, this whole seventieth birthday is stressing me out, I can't go home, I can't go back there."

"Does your chest really feel tight?"

"Terribly, Idit."

"Should we go to the ER?! Is it that bad?"

"Yes!" Yehuda practically shouted.

"I'm taking you there now. Text Daria to stop at the house and get my pills."

"No!"

"What do you mean, no?" Idit cried.

"Don't go to the hospital, Idit. Stop the car for a minute, I'm begging you. Just pull over."

She drove onto the sidewalk on Pinkas, near the butcher. "Okay, I've stopped."

Yehuda said, "Avishay is dead, Idit. And I'm not a vegan. And I want a divorce."

23

He felt his pulse beating in new spots, testifying to his vitality—or perhaps his imminent death. Maybe his heart was about to explode, whether because of the conversation with Idit (if you could call it a conversation: "I'm going to my sister's, get your stuff out of the house by tomorrow," she'd snapped. And he'd somehow found the courage to haggle: "Give me till the end of the week, okay? I need time to make things right with the girls," he'd said, even though that was meaningless, because what did the girls have to do with anything? But it had worked. She was as weak as she was furious) or because of Avishay waiting for him there, dead, like a welcome mat.

He thought there was a little stain on the door, but as he got closer it took on color and volume, and it wasn't a stain, it was a note, stuck between the doorway and the door. Yehuda didn't have to read what it said to know that this was it, this was the moment his body had been preparing itself for this whole time. This was the great forgetfulness, the great catastrophe: the cleaner. It was the cleaner's day.

He pulled out the note as if clutching at his final chance, and prayed it would say: *I forgot the key, I will come tomorrow. The key doesn't work, I will come tomorrow. I will come another time, ok? I saw the dead person, don't worry, ok? Ok?*

But what Victor had written was: "Please buy more Sano Javel, finished." And his letters were as large and festive as usual.

Yehuda stuck the key in the lock but didn't turn it, as though from the moment the latch slid out of its slot he would be doomed to enter, beyond the point of no return.

He thought: I'll turn him in, I'll call immigration on him, he knows I will, it's not worth it for him. But what if Victor had already called the police? He wouldn't—who would believe him? A foreign laborer from the Ivory Coast, an illegal alien? They'd think he'd killed Avishay himself. Yehuda almost calmed down, because yes, that was right, of course, no one would believe him, they'd never believe him, what sane foreign laborer would report a wealthy white man's body in another wealthy white man's home? And you could see on Avishay that he was wealthy, dead or alive, like fingerprints or teeth, you couldn't hide that. So if it came down to the Ivory Coastian or the billionaire—which one of them had killed him? Yehuda also thought it was a good thing they'd covered Avishay, so larvae wouldn't set in, and so Yehuda would somehow be able to live there, because otherwise Victor might have thought he was saving someone's life, he might have called Idit: *Was an accident, come, come,* whereas this way it was obvious that he was there intentionally, someone had put him there, someone had forgotten him, someone had murdered him—oh, good lord! Yehuda suddenly realized he had no idea what this Victor guy might do, or what he'd already done, how he would behave, what sort of person he was. But he *was* a person, too, and how would Yehuda explain to him what had happened? Had he even heard of the Nobel Prize? Did he even know what a prize was? Maybe it was best if he did think it was a murder, because then he'd be scared, and suddenly there were footsteps behind him and he turned his head around fearfully, but it was just Idit. It was Idit. Idit was behind him and now she was next to him.

=====

"Are you going to open it?" she asked.

Yehuda stared at her questioningly.

"I need my pills."

He looked at her and at the door, and Idit waited a moment and then moved toward the door with the impatience of someone who has to do everything herself, and she flung it open and walked inside, and said, "What's going on here? It's freezing, and it stinks, we have to air this place out."

Yehuda followed her in, his burning hot head blasted by the chill of the house that had frozen along with Avishay at sixty degrees, his thoughts about the Ivory Coastian marching in behind him, polluting the polished house like shoes that stepped in shit, and the living room floor was gleamingly clean and there was no sign of Avishay.

Tuesday

Nili

24

S he sat at the kitchen island. He loaded the dishwasher. He held a plate up and said, "This is the third time I've put this in without using it. It keeps coming out dirty."

Nili thought he was about to throw it on the floor as punishment. "Maybe you need to replace the filter? It's free if you have appliance insurance."

Nathan said, "You have insurance on your dishwasher?"

"Doesn't everyone?"

He gently put the plate back into its slot in the dishwasher, giving it a temporary stay of execution, and said, "You lead a fascinating life."

"You ain't seen nothing yet," Nili replied.

That line made her a little horny, and strangely so did the whole exchange, but there was something that suddenly became very urgent, and she decided to put the horniness on hold, like carrying the one in long addition, and even though her temples were pulsing with danger, she heard herself say, "Do you know that Avishay got some woman pregnant?"

"Which Avishay? Your Avishay?"

Nili started mapping out all the possible permutations of this conversation—what was the worst thing that could happen?—but she abandoned the task sloppily, lazily, and indulgently gave in to the line that had already been crossed: "Yes, of course my Avishay."

"When?"

"Recently. We only just found out."

"How old is he?"

"Sixty-nine, seventy," Nili said, swallowing down the "about my age" just in time.

"Whoa . . . Fertile guy!"

"Turns out."

"And is he into it? Is this what he wants?"

"Unclear," she said, and thought it was a pretty accurate answer.

Nathan asked, "How can it be unclear?" at the exact same moment as Nili asked, "Have you ever gotten someone pregnant?" Her question overrode his, and he said, "Have I? Not that I know of."

"Never?"

"Why are you so surprised?"

"I'm not, it's just that, you know, fifty years of sex . . ."

"Fifty? I wish. Barely forty."

Nili calculated. "Really?"

"I swear."

She resisted asking, So when was it? I mean, how old were you? But the horniness had passed.

"For all I know, I might be sterile."

"You might," Nili said, and wondered if she was supposed to comfort him if that was true. But he didn't want kids.

"So is he happy at least?" Nathan asked. "Avishay."

"I have to tell you something," she said, and when Nathan turned to her with anticipatory anger on his face, she quickly added, "It's not about us."

"Okay. Should I sit down?"

"You can sit down. Yes."

———

Two days had passed since the last time she'd talked to them, since she'd stormed out of Yehuda's house. She'd left without a plan, only partially determined, unsure of her anger. But the more they didn't run after her and seek her forgiveness, the greater her insult grew, establishing itself and filling her with the addictive pleasure of a mortal wounding.

She'd spent forty years preparing for this moment, conducting secret rehearsals, so secret that even she wasn't usually aware of them occurring somewhere on the outskirts of her consciousness. And when the moment came she did not have the courage to open her mouth and say: Enough about Nathan! Six months, sixty months— what is this bullshit? It's *me*. I'm the one you don't take seriously, not Nathan. We've been together for forty years, you guys and me, not six months and not two years. So what more do you want?

On Monday afternoon Yehuda had called. She'd looked at his name flashing on the screen and struggled to let go of the hurt feelings. When she finally decided to answer, it had stopped ringing. She decided she would pick up immediately, on the first ring, when he called again, but he didn't. And the more time went by without him calling, the deeper her forgiveness was buried under the insult, and the insult under the anger. He'd only called so that he could get away with the bare minimum; he should have really wanted it, he should have tried harder.

She thought she'd made a mistake but she wasn't sure where. As she replayed the past week's events, her decisions always seemed logical and unchangeable: if not for her, this whole thing wouldn't have happened. She was proud of it, the way a parent is proud of a child. She developed a strange sense of ownership, as though the child's father were trying to kidnap him from her and take him to another country. And what would happen to him when he was far away from her? If they retreated now, it would all go down the drain—all the solutions and the little strokes of brilliance and the tribulations and the slightly heroic acts, even the idea itself, which did not deserve to be buried. It deserved to come to light, and they deserved to get credit. But then Nili remembered that the plan would come to light only if the whole thing failed.

What would happen if it failed? Now that they'd abandoned her, she felt they deserved to fail. Yet she found that the possibility made her truly despondent, as though if the plan failed, Avishay's death would become final, irredeemable: another death in a series of standard deaths. Perhaps that was where she'd gone wrong. She'd replaced the sadness too quickly, parsed it into activity with distasteful speed.

On Saturday night, when they'd stood around his bed and Zohara had asked Nili if she'd cried, she was astonished to discover that she hadn't; she hadn't even thought about it. It was as if she'd completely erased that aspect of death, the one that had to do with sadness. And when she remembered that other possibility, it suddenly sprawled out before her in all its awfulness. They had fled from it into the arms of a peculiar adventure, accustomed themselves to a preposterous scheme, but there it still was: sadness, more sadness, respectable sadness, unsatisfying sadness, mature sadness, the kind she knew so well—all the more so because the deceased was at a reasonable age, so it was his right to die, or it was death's right to take him, and they had no right to complain.

Yehuda began to seem like a charlatan, one of those swindlers that pop up in people's lives at moments of crisis and exploit their weaknesses. He had offered them an anti-dying potion, like anti-aging except it delayed death instead of wrinkles: *He doesn't really have to die! So what if he's dead!* Nili knew he was a bit of a charlatan, albeit a charming one, yet she hadn't been able to resist.

No, she didn't want the plan to fail, with or without her. Still, it increasingly and unwillingly took on a fantastical veneer, like a flashback scene in a lousy movie. The week grew less concrete, life seeped in, Avishay seemed to have been dead for a very long time. They could start getting used to it. They could also start getting used to the fact that he wouldn't win the Nobel. And he could be dead just the same, without it.

"To tell you the truth," she said to Nathan, "I don't really know how to tell you this."

"Now I'm scared."

"You won't tell anyone, will you? If I ask you not to?"

"I don't know what to say. What's this about?"

She didn't answer for a while, and Nathan must have interpreted her silence as a condition, because a moment later he said, "I won't say anything."

"It's Avishay. He had a heart attack. Or something."

"When?" Nathan asked.

"A week ago."

"A week ago? Why didn't you tell me? Where is he—in hospital?"

"No, he's not in hospital. He . . . He died."

"You're pulling my leg," Nathan said.

Nili gave him a long look, as if to say: Does it look like I am?

"Avishay is dead?"

"Yes," Nili said.

"I'm in shock. You just told me he got some woman pregnant . . ."

"He did get some woman pregnant. Before he died."

"Yes, I figured that out." He paused. "When did you find out?"

"A week ago. That's the thing."

"Okay . . ." Nathan said.

"I'm afraid this is going to sound dumb," Nili said.

"Try me."

"You know how Avishay was a candidate for the Nobel? Not a candidate, but, you know, he had a serious chance of winning this year?"

"I didn't know that. Good for him. For all that kindergarten stuff?"

"King of the class," Nili corrected him.

"Right."

"So anyway, he had a really good chance, an excellent chance, in fact. Basically, it was supposed to be his year. Again, as far as anyone can estimate these things, right?"

"Okay."

"So long story short, the announcement is tomorrow."

"The Nobel announcement?" Nathan asked.

"In economics, yes."

"Okay."

"And in order to win, you have to be alive. Meaning, the award committee has to declare in good faith and full knowledge that you are alive, in order for it to count. Even if you've died two days earlier. It's valid as long as they don't know that."

"Okay . . ."

"Bottom line, no one knows that Avishay's dead."

"Apart from you?"

"Apart from me, Yehuda, Amos, and Zohara. And now you. Yes."

"I don't understand. You're hiding the fact that he's dead?"

"Basically, yes. Yes."

"And why is that? Explain this to me again. So that he wins the Nobel Prize tomorrow?"

"So that he has a chance of winning. No one's promising that he's going to win, but so that he at least has a chance. If he doesn't win, then we just 'find' him dead, and then he's dead, end of story. Even if he does win, he's dead, right? But then at least he dies a Nobel laureate."

"And why is it a good thing for him to die a Nobel laureate?" Nathan wondered. "Sorry if I'm missing something here."

"Why is it a good thing? I don't know, if you had the choice of dying a Nobel laureate or not a Nobel laureate, which would you prefer?"

"I don't know. If I were dead and I didn't know that I'd died a Nobel laureate, I'm not really convinced it would make much difference to me."

"Okay, but that's because you just don't care, the Nobel Prize doesn't interest you."

"What do you mean, doesn't interest me? It interests me theoretically, but to tell you that it's the reason I do what I do, that it's why I do my research . . . ?"

"It's not the reason Avishay does his research either," Nili countered, "but you know, from the minute it becomes somehow relevant, I guess it's hard to let go of. It starts to become, I don't know, almost an obsession."

"I find it hard to see how something that happens after death could be considered a dream coming true, or an accomplishment."

"Well, never mind. If you knew how much we'd debated this, then . . . Anyway, this is what we decided to do, because this is what we think Avishay would have wanted, and that's the situation right now."

Nathan thought for a moment. "You realize this is absurd, right?"

"What's absurd?"

"A man dies, he's done with the follies of this world, right? Finally. But no, even in death he continues to chase respect."

"He's not the one chasing respect, it's us chasing it for him, on his behalf. He didn't ask for it."

"But if it comes out, everyone will think he did ask you, that's obvious. No one's going to think it was your idea—I mean, it's a totally wacky idea. They'll think he was so intent on getting the honor that he asked you to do this. So you guys are so intent on doing the right thing that you'll end up destroying his reputation. This is going to make him look really bad."

"That's what people will think? That he left instructions to get him
the Nobel if he happened to die a week before the announcement?
Does that strike you as reasonable?"

Nathan said, "You know what? Even if he didn't 'leave instructions,' let's just say that this thing has his fingerprints all over it. That
at the very least, he gave you the impression that this is what he
would have wanted you to do."

"No one's going to think that, come on, that's a twisted idea. It's
totally dismissing the value of friendship."

"*That's* the twisted idea? You're the ones hiding a body. You started
it, to put it bluntly. And you know what?"

"What?"

"I'll tell you something else: there is something to it." Then he repeated
his words, accentuating each one: "There is something to it. There's a
reason he won't come out of it not looking good, even if he really didn't
ask you to do it. Because you wouldn't do this for just anyone. You said
so yourself. You're doing it because you know he's that kind of person.
He really is chasing respect, even from the grave. Whether he asked for it
or not, that doesn't matter at all. Or hardly matters."

"Nathan."

"Nili."

"Enough. No one's going to think that."

"If you say so. Anyway, where is he? At home?"

"He's at Yehuda's."

"At Yehuda's? Is that where he had the heart attack?"

"He had the heart attack at home, but we decided to move him.
His sister turned up all of a sudden. Never mind all that."

"So his sister doesn't know either? You didn't tell his own sister?"

"I'm telling you, we didn't tell anyone."

"But wait, I don't understand—how did you move him? Did you
get an ambulance or something?"

"An ambulance?! Do you think we could have called an ambulance?"

"Then how?"

"You don't want to know," Nili said.

"Oh, come on."

"Yehuda carried him to the car, over his shoulders, in the middle
of the night."

"Nili, you're pulling my leg, right? You're pulling my leg."

"I swear I'm not."

"Okay, you're pulling my leg. Now I know for sure you are."

"Nathan, I swear to you on my kids, I am not pulling your leg.
What do you think I am, twelve years old? You think I could make
something like this up?"

"You guys did not do that. No chance. I've been with you all week."

"Not all week," Nili pointed out.

"Whatever, you were in a great mood."

And that was what made Nili regret telling him: because she saw
herself caught red-handed, not sad enough, allowing herself to act
that way because Nathan didn't know anyway. "I wasn't in a great
mood, I was in some kind of trance. I'm telling you the truth, and I'm
only giving you the tip of the iceberg about what went on this whole
week. We had a whole mess on the way to Yehuda's, never mind, it
was this kind of adrenaline rush, I didn't have time to even stop and
think, to grieve."

Nathan looked at her. "If you're pulling my leg, this is it. Do you
understand that?"

"Do you really think I would make something like this up?"

"Is it even legal?" Nathan asked.

"Let's say it's a gray area, but it's not . . . It's a calculated risk, let's
put it that way."

"I'm in shock, Nili, I'm really in shock. How could you not tell me something like this? I'm not saying that as a complaint, but how did you hold it in?"

"What could I do? We agreed we wouldn't even tell spouses, so I couldn't. And believe me, I wanted to."

"I'm stunned. I'm just absolutely stunned. The lot of you are insane."

"*I'm stunned, I'm stunned*—what else do you have?"

"What else? What else could I have?"

"I don't know. What do you think about the idea?"

Nathan thought for a moment. "Was it your idea?"

"No. Yehuda's. But it doesn't matter, tell me what you really think, tell me honestly, I'm interested."

"Yehuda's?"

"What difference does it make?"

"No, it's just that I'm surprised a person with kids would propose such an idea."

"What does that have to do with it?"

"I don't know, aren't you bothered by what your kids will say? What they'll think about this whole thing? What it'll do to them?"

"Why would they say anything? What does this have to do with them? Why would they even find out? Let's start with that."

"Well, you can't count on that. Or maybe you can, I don't know. Correct me if I'm wrong—I'm not a parent."

She paused for a moment. "And if they do find out . . . ?"

"I don't know, you tell me."

"They're grown-ups."

"I'm not worried about them, don't get me wrong, I'm worried about you."

"That what? They'll be mad at me?"

"They'll be mad, they'll be horrified, they'll be disappointed—I don't know. There are lots of possible emotions here, you know? Their mother is hiding a body, messing around with a body, moving it, transferring it, I don't know what else. And I'm not even talking about cheating, or lying. I mean, this is a pretty extreme thing to do, Nili, it's not . . . Let's just say that my mom and dad did not do this sort of thing, and that if they had, it would have been . . . I don't know what to say. It would have changed everything I think about them, from start to finish, everything between me and them for our whole lives, even if I'd found out at age sixty. I can tell you that unequivocally."

She felt an urge to object: *It's not true.* But what if he was right? What if he was right and her protestations only buried her maternal nature even deeper, made it harder for her to extricate it later, to convince him that she was a good mother.

She tried to imagine her kids finding out. Maybe at Friday dinner. The way you announce a divorce. Would that be better or worse? For some reason it had seemed better, much better, but now she wasn't sure anymore. She'd been deep inside this story from the beginning, watched it from up close as it took on more and more twists and turns, grew without even trying, from its own sheer momentum, and she had protected it as much as she could, making decisions that all seemed normal, suitable for the moment, obeying an internal logic that they had formulated solely for the purpose of this issue and which would never be of any use in any other context. Like a fourth child. And now she was blind to its defects and could not see the totality—nor did she want to.

She was ashamed that she hadn't thought of it herself, and even more ashamed that she was cunningly hanging on to his nonparenthood for her defense, out of fear, reciting: *It's true, you're not a parent, Nathan, you really are not a parent.*

She became increasingly alarmed. It was too late. Not only did he not know her as a parent, he didn't know her at all—what was six months? They were right, she was out of her mind, he wasn't Zohara and he wasn't Amos, he could still change his mind, he hadn't signed off on the absolute truth that asserted that she was normal, that she was wonderful, that she was allowed to do something like this and nothing would change.

"What's going through your mind, Nili?"

"What's going through yours, Nathan?"

"I'm worried about you, Nili. That's all I care about, I'm telling you. I've met Avishay exactly twice, with all due respect, so to tell you that I really care whether or not he gets the Nobel?"

"Never mind me, tell me what you think about the idea."

"What do I really think?"

"Absolutely."

"I don't know. If you're really doing it, then I think it's not a good idea. That's the truth."

"Not good? Why?" Nili asked.

Nathan seemed to be thinking out loud: "I don't know, I just don't believe it'll work."

"Why not?"

"Because you're not liars, that's why. You're not people who lie, that's a basic fact."

"What exactly does that mean, 'people who lie'? We've been lying left and right for a whole week."

"You're not lying, you're playing, there's a difference. You're doing something that entertains you, you're answering his text messages, okay, but what happens when you really have to lie? When you have to—I don't know—face the police and lie?"

"Police? Why? Why would you bring up the police?"

"Never mind, then—a hospital, a doctor. You know what? Forget that—the Nobel committee. You will have to lie to the Nobel Prize committee, won't you? I can't even believe I'm having this conversation. Just imagining you talking with someone from the committee sounds preposterous to me, and now you're going to lie to them? I can't understand how you don't see this. Such a smart woman, so down to earth."

"That's exactly why. If I'm telling you I'm going to do this thing, it's not like you're talking to some schemer."

"Well, I guess we'll find out."

"I guess we will. And anyway he probably won't even win, so all of this is, you know . . ."

"One never knows." He sat quietly for a moment, then reconsidered: "No, I'm sorry, you guys are not going to lie to five or seven or however many Swedish professors are on the Nobel Prize committee. I mean, are you going to lie to them in English? Just picture it for a moment, Nili, picture the four of you getting up on stage in Stockholm, with cameras from all over the world on you, journalists, every newspaper in the world, all the Israeli press, and imagine yourselves taking that prize in your hands, okay? Taking the plaque or whatever it is, the medal, the check, okay? Imagine that for one second."

Nili thought: He's right. And the thought comforted her, like finding out that a terminally ill parent has died, and she realized it didn't really matter anymore. That was the truth: she didn't care anymore, she'd lost interest. She loved Avishay but she no longer cared about the Nobel. She was alive and she had her own problems, she needed her strength for something else, for Nathan instead of for Avishay, for a far more urgent and more crucial test.

"So what's the story with Yehuda?" Nathan asked.

"What story with Yehuda?"

"Before you said there was some story on the way to Yehuda's."

Expertly and swiftly, out of habit, Nili scanned the area they were about to enter, like a scout preferring to step on a land mine himself, alone. But she stopped her inspection midway, even though the area wasn't clear—precisely because of that. Because she felt like shocking him, like putting him to the test. This was it, this was their test. And she said: "Do you know what decomposition fluids are?"

━━━━

Nathan said, "So now he's lying at Yehuda's house, run over? Is that the situation?"

"Yes," Nili said. She debated again, but decided to save him the whole staircase episode after all, as though if she tugged a piece of truth out of that, the whole lie would unravel. She also thought it better not to mention the fight, not at this point, as if fearing she might be left entirely alone in the world, just her against Nathan, with no backup, no friend. But now it was time for a new lie, a complete lie, and what would she say? Why on earth did she need his help in this matter? She thought quickly and was in such a panic that she looked around as if seeking salvation from the floor tiles, the glistening floor tiles that no child had ever soiled, and suddenly she felt like making a mess, stinking up this whole house irredeemably, unrecognizably, leaving a stench that could never be cleansed, not even if they polished it and aired the place out: she would brand him with a mark of Cain, to earn his loyalty, his true love. And so she said, "The problem is that now his girls want to come over."

"Whose girls?"

"Yehuda's. Their mom's overseas so they're worried about him, they want to stop by."

"Okay," Nathan said.

"So anyway, we have to find another private residence to move him to."

"Remind me why it has to be a private residence?"

"Because of the smell, the smell of the . . . of Avishay. We're afraid he'll smell."

"But why didn't you consult with me? I do have some knowledge about these things, after all."

Nili angrily remembered the restrictions they'd imposed on her, and suddenly her idea seemed even more logical: she would prove something, to herself and to them. "It doesn't matter, we can't move him to my place or Zohara's anyway."

"What's wrong with your place?" Nathan asked.

"My grandchildren. The kids. My house is wide open."

"And Zohara?"

Nili could feel her lies running out—this was probably the last one she'd be able to enlist: "She's having her house painted, or A/C installed, I'm not sure exactly what, but there are workmen there all week." She felt she'd gone too far, the lie was too deep, it was doomed to be found out. But it didn't make any difference, not in the universe she was now inhabiting.

"What a mess," Nathan remarked.

"Although, now that I'm here, I'm starting to think..." She stopped for a moment, with a real, unplanned pause.

"Now that you're here you're starting to think...?" His voice disclosed a certain possibility of playing innocent. He got it, he wasn't dumb, he was just waiting for her to say it.

"That maybe we could just bring Avishay to your place," Nili said.

"My place?"

"Here, to your house. Just till tomorrow."

He looked at her wide-eyed, his tongue traveling around his mouth. She had no idea what that expression meant. She felt as if she didn't know him, this random hostage she'd trapped for an experiment. "Where would you put him?" he finally asked.

"I don't know, wherever you say. Or wherever we decide, if you'd rather not know. Not in your bed. It could even be on the floor."

Nathan looked at the dark gray granite tiles, as if trying to picture it.

"Or not, of course, if you're not up for it," she added, and at the last moment she avoided saying: I'll completely understand.

"Okay," Nathan said.

"Really?"

"Yes, but I won't be here, and by this time tomorrow evening he won't be either."

Nili suddenly wished she'd asked for longer, for a week, at least till Friday, to magnify the accomplishment, to polish off her certificate of excellence in her relationship with Nathan a little more: *Your wives wouldn't do it, but my man would, six months or not six months. What do you have to say about that?* There was no real reason for her request anyway, it was nonsense, the girls weren't coming to Yehuda's and no one was going to move a body to Nathan's. But he'd agreed, and she would be bringing that loot to them, hanging off her belt.

While she composed imaginary scenarios in her mind, her infantile cheerfulness was suddenly invaded by his face hanging on hers, right now, here, in this house, waiting for something, perhaps for a prize in the form of a lot of emotion, and for one brief moment she knew that he loved her.

25

She stood impatiently at a stop sign. She was late. She'd been planning to cancel it, that was the truth. Smadar had arranged this date back in August—her son Aviv was getting a best-teacher award at the democratic school and she wanted to take advantage of her visit to Tel Aviv to meet up. Nili had gladly and generously agreed—back then, October had seemed like an eternity away. But when Smadar had called on Saturday, she'd sounded like a message from another planet—from the pre-Nobel era, or the pre-mortem era—and the very suggestion that they meet seemed impertinent.

"Wow, I'm actually not sure at all," she'd told Smadar, blaming it on the kids and some vague medical situation, "but let's talk on Tuesday, I'll see if I can shift things around." When Smadar called on Tuesday, with heartbreaking obedience—she really did want to meet Nili, she wasn't pretending—Nili had to confess that there was not a single thing she needed to do, she was not making any con-tribution to humanity at that particular moment. There was never going to be a more convenient time or a better opportunity to get it over with; if she wriggled out now, she'd pay the price later.

She gazed up at the billboards along the left side of the street, looking for reading material to pass the time, when her eyes fell on five fingers painted with fluorescent green nail polish very much like the kind Avishay's Liat had worn. Nili was always surprised when she had any notions of her own to do with fashion, but that color seemed so incongruent—fluorescent green, of all things? Fluorescent anything, for that matter.

The fingers were holding a cup of ice cream, which was also bright green, but a paler shade. The caption said: "You don't have to be pregnant to crave pickle ice cream." And below that: "*Nice Ice*—Israel's first vegan ice cream. 15 Yehuda Maccabi St. Custom flavors available." She realized it was an ad for Ram's ice cream place, it was finally open. She was excited for a moment, as if out of habit, and the strip of world visible through her window revealed more and more bright green fingernails, all the way to the horizon, and Nili thought: That must have cost them a fortune. As she calculated, her eyes fell on the next ad. In this one, the green fingers weren't holding ice cream but rather a little plastic stick with two stripes in a window. Nili couldn't understand what she was seeing, and her eyes kept roaming down the boulevard of columns, as though the plot was guaranteed to develop. But the ads only repeated themselves cyclically, alternating between fingers holding a stick, without any caption at all, and fingers holding ice cream: "You don't have to be pregnant to crave pickle ice cream." She rifled through her bag for Avishay's phone, to look at the picture Liat had sent. But she didn't have the phone anymore. She looked back at the ad: that was definitely it. That was the picture. It wasn't a pregnancy test, it was an ice cream advertising campaign. But what was it doing on Avishay's phone? She turned the wheel sharply to the right, as if she were in a movie car chase, but she ran into a dense cluster of cars and there was a horrible honking sound as her hood swerved into the next lane, and there she sat, waiting, like an idiot.

26

She knocked on the door and immediately rang the bell without waiting. "Just a minute," a female voice called from inside, slowly, lazily, not getting the hint. Nili preemptively lost her patience as she imagined sleepy sweatpants and a tank top, reeking of sex. Meeting her ex-husband's new girlfriend, having to be nice? That was all she needed now.

The door opened. It took Nili a minute, and she recognized the panic on her face even before she recognized the girl herself: Liat. Avishay's Liat. Nili found herself looking to the fingernails—green or not?—as if this would solve the mystery. But they were polish-free, and Liat said "Hi," and without taking her eyes off Nili, shouted, "Ram!" Nili was startled. Everything seemed so strange and lacking context. A woman stands close to her and suddenly raises her voice to a scream, like in a horror film—was there a murderer lurking behind her? Was she herself the murderer? But then Ram appeared from inside and Nili realized that Liat had just been calling him, that's all. Ram looked suddenly old, which Nili found somewhat encouraging, even though she wasn't sure what sort of encouragement she needed at this point. "Nili!" he said, with some surprise, and then, "Come in. Tul-Tul, this is Nili. Nili, Tul-Tul." Liat said, "We've met," and Nili remembered her "WTF is up with that?!" That's what she'd written about her, about Nili. *WTF is up with that?* More than any other line, that one was imprinted in her memory—not just her memory but her personality, the way a different line had once been imprinted, when she was a child: "She disgusts me," someone had written about her in his diary, someone who'd actually been a friend of hers, but he meant it sexually, explaining to himself why she was only a friend, and it was his right because it was his diary, and she'd never told him she'd read those words, and she'd never told anyone else either, not even therapists, even though she'd spent years and wasted a fortune pointlessly racing around those words. That, she learned, was how you recognized the truly important lines: you could repeat them only to yourself.

Ram's eyebrows furrowed into a question and Liat said, "At Avishay's," and his face fell when he understood, when he remembered. Liat said, "I'll be right back," and abandoned him under the guise of politeness. Ram said, "Okay," and Nili said, "Is that your girlfriend?" It was the first thing she'd said since walking in.

Ram answered, "Yes, come in, come in."

"Then what was she doing at Avishay's?" Nili asked.

"Come on, come in, why are you . . ." But he didn't finish his sentence.

Nili walked in gingerly, as if fearing that more discoveries might leap out at her. She sat down stiffly on the couch.

"Coffee?" Ram asked.

"No."

"Wait a second, then, I'm making some for myself."

Nili said nothing, just imagined him escaping out the kitchen window. But a moment later he came back with a cup of coffee. "So I understand you met Tul-Tul."

"What was she doing at Avishay's?"

"Okay, it's a bit of a long story," Ram replied.

"Go on."

"Basically, Avishay invested in our gelateria. It's just money, he's not a partner in any other sense at all."

Nili didn't understand why he said that—what was the difference?

"He's a silent partner," Ram continued. "I mean, he brought Ruthi in as a culinary adviser, she's advising us about the sugar issue. But he himself is completely removed from the substance, he has nothing to do with it."

"Why would Avishay have any interest in your gelateria?" Nili asked.

"You know he connects with the whole vegan thing, so it's through that, I think, and also through Ruthi."

"But how did he even know you were opening a gelateria?"

"He heard about it, that's not so strange."

"What do you mean, heard about it? Where did he hear about it? From you?"

"Yes," Ram said.

"So you and Avishay are in touch?"

"A little, yes."

"Since when?"

"I don't know, a while."

"You mean, since then?" Nili asked.

"Since when?"

"Since we separated?"

"More or less, yeah."

"That's a long time."

"A pretty long time," Ram admitted.

"But I thought it was over. No, I didn't just think—you told me, you said you didn't connect with each other or something like that. Avishay told me that, I think."

"Okay, but in the end we did connect."

"I don't understand. You've been in touch for six years and you never told me?"

"It's not like we lied to you."

"'We didn't connect' isn't a lie?"

"At first it really was faltering along . . ."

"Rami, would you mind cutting the bullshit?"

"I'm not bullshitting you, Nili, I'm embarrassed about this, too."

"So you and Avishay have been friends since we broke up?"

"Yes," Ram said.

"But why didn't you tell me? I don't understand. Why did you think I'd care?"

"I don't know, we just had the feeling you would."

"How? Based on what?" Nili demanded. "I was always so supportive."

Ram shook his head in a sort of dubious gesture and said, "Nili, never mind, the fact is that both of us, Avishay and I, not just me, had the impression that you preferred to have Avishay to yourself and me to yourself. A separation of powers, you could say."

"I prefer Avishay to myself? What nonsense. I share him with at least three other close friends, in case you've forgotten."

"I don't know, I don't go poking around in your group's business, I just know for myself that I didn't feel comfortable telling you about my friendship with Avishay."

"If you didn't feel comfortable, that's your problem. What can I do? So what, it's my fault too?"

"No, of course not! I don't know how I would feel if the situation were reversed, I'm telling you honestly."

"Then why do I deserve to be punished for this?"

"Punished? Who's punishing anyone?"

"My best friend and my ex-husband are hiding something like this from me, actively. What else would you call it?" Nili said.

"I'm telling you honestly, Nili, we never said a word about you. Never. If anything, it was only good things."

Nili quickly wondered whether she believed him and, if she did, whether that comforted her. Having no choice, she also pondered all the things they did discuss—women, women, women, sex, and dating—what else could there be? The same things he talked to her about, except with a man. With a friend. She suddenly needed to know if Avishay had told him that he did want kids, and she wondered how she could find out. But other pieces of thoughts pounded between her temples and scattered about: Liat is Tul-Tul. So actually, she's Ram's girlfriend, not Avishay's. Then who wanted kids? Avishay didn't want kids. She perked up her head in surprise at the discovery: "Wait, so it's just an ad? That picture she sent Avishay?"

"What, the gelateria ad?"

"Yes."

"What else would it be?" And a moment later he asked, "Where did you see it?"

Nili ignored the question, even though she didn't care at this point—if he asked again, she would say something. The whole No-bel/Avishay business seemed like a relic from another era now. But Ram's status in this conversation was wobbly, so he let it go, and Nili said, whether to herself or to him or to no one: "So no one's pregnant."

But Ram did not say "No" or "Not as far as I know."

So just to make sure, Nili said, "Right?"

And Ram said, "The truth is, Tul-Tul actually does happen to be pregnant."

Nili quickly referred to the legend she'd put together in the past few minutes—who was Tul-Tul again? And she said, "Liat is pregnant?"

"Yes," Ram said, with a smile on his face that was both proud and embarrassed.

"By you?" Nili asked.

He shook his head again, this time throwing it back, as if to say: Who else?

She hated Jaffa and she hated Smadar, who was waiting for her so conscientiously. She felt she was meeting the dead in the wrong order—she should be meeting Avishay, not Smadar, who was still there.

When she saw her, sitting in a chic café adorned with lettering in Hebrew and Arabic, she suddenly got frightened: she looked like a cancer patient, one of those cases about whom there is no doubt at all. Smadar compensated for her bald head with chunky jewelry that her delicate frame could barely carry. Waitresses with asymmetrical hairdos hovered among the tables, soft and slender, and Smadar looked as though she were unintentionally mocking them, sending regards from the future. Nili hadn't seen her for a month or two, which now seemed like a very long time. Wondrously long. How had Smadar carried all this, day after day, without dying on the way?

"Is everything okay with the girls?" Smadar asked.

"Why wouldn't it be?" Nili said.

"Oh, I don't know, you said there was an emergency."

Nili remembered that that was supposedly why she was late, very late, an excuse pulled out offhandedly, irresponsibly and uncaringly—for all she'd cared, Smadar could have canceled. "Oh, yes, everything's fine," she said.

She looked at Smadar. There she was: one thing that was worse than what had happened to her. Much worse. This was what proportions looked like—right in front of her nose. What more could she ask for? Nili thought about Avishay. Avishay was dead, too. Perhaps this was her punishment for refusing to get it. Perhaps they would keep dying until she got it. Until she recognized that she had a beautiful life, or something like that, and that everything was good. But when Avishay rose up in her imagination, it only served to ignite the anger again, and the insult. Kicking him out, she asked Smadar, "How was it?"

"It was wonderful," Smadar said. "Really, an extraordinary event. The democratic school is so different, it's hard to believe. You walk in the front gates and you can feel it right away."

"That's so great," Nili said. Smadar looked a little disappointed, and Nili quickly reviewed the etiquette: What else was she supposed to ask? "Did you take pictures?" she finally said.

"They took some, I'll send them to you."

"Send me everything, I'm so sorry I missed it."

"It really is a shame."

"So, how are you feeling?" Nili asked.

"Well. I'm feeling well."

Her tone was already grating on Nili's nerves, canceling out all her determination from just moments ago. "What do you mean, well? What's the status?"

"It's the same."

"What does that mean?"

"There's illness, yes, but you know, as far as I'm concerned, it's a chronic disease. For all intents and purposes I'm no sicker than you or anyone else. It's just that, unlike other people, I know exactly what I have, that's all."

"What do you mean, you're no sicker than anyone else? You have cancer."

"That's true, I do have cancer," Smadar said. "I also have an allergy to cat dander. What do you have?"

"I'm not following."

"What do you have? What do you feel in your body?"

"I have high cholesterol," Nili said.

"And what are you doing about it?"

"What am I doing about it? I'm taking pills, that's what I'm doing about it. What are you doing about it?"

"About the cancer?" Smadar asked. "You can say it: *cancer*."

Nili felt like she was losing her mind, as if she was some old-fashioned aunt who wouldn't dare say the word cancer out loud. What nonsense. She felt like telling Smadar that Avishay was dead, throwing a real death at her. *Avishay's dead, you know?* So she'd know that people died in the world. She wouldn't live long enough to tell anyone anyway.

"About the cancer, yes," Nili said. "And about the death. What are you doing to not die?" She was furious and felt she had the right to say it. It was in her life too, now. Death. They were acquainted.

Smadar pulled back slightly. "I'm living, just like you. Living and hoping for the best, and eating well." She steadied her grip on the reins of the interaction. "Better than you, Nili, if we're on the topic."

Nili scanned her side of the table in a panic—had she distractedly ordered something? Had she gone wrong? But there was nothing except a cup of herbal tea. She felt trapped in this conversation, which had no purpose and from which there was no escape. And which did not interest her—that was the truth. What are you doing about it, what are you not doing about it—what difference did it make? What did it matter? It was meaningless, just conversation filler, like that crumpled paper they put inside new shoes. Conscripted eagerness designed to cover up the futility. Smadar was going to die, whether or not she had chemo. What did Nili want of her?

She was seized by an awful, urgent fear. There was not going to be another opportunity. She simply had to open her mouth and talk to

Smadar, talk to her like a sister: like a confessional, like in the movies, like in a dream. She had to say everything, for once, about Ram and Avishay and Liat and the pregnancy, and Nathan and the dates, the humiliations, all the humiliations. She had to talk about herself, to tell her everything. What was the worst that could happen? Why shouldn't she? Smadar would be so happy, and they'd hug, and she'd die happier. And who else could she tell, anyway? Whatever she said would live outside of Nili for such a short while, Smadar would know these things for a few weeks at most. She suddenly forgave Zohara, and she forgave Yehuda and Amos. She almost pitied them. All they were doing was being skeptical where she was not, being protective where she was not. Because they didn't know, because she didn't tell them. She told them she had no patience for her granddaughters instead of saying she was afraid they'd be like her: fat. She rewrote her dates with men, she told fictions. And she suddenly felt sad for herself, and sad for Avishay, but Avishay was dead and she wasn't. She looked at Smadar looking back at her questioningly. But no, not yet, she couldn't do it yet. It couldn't come out of her mouth now. But she would tell Yehuda and Zohara and Amos, she would tell them everything, as compensation, soon. She wanted to give something to Smadar, too, and so she said, "To tell you the truth, you do look good."

Smadar looked at her uncomprehendingly.

"Really," Nili said, "I should do something like that, too."

"We can do it together, if you'd like," Smadar said. "Once a week we'll weigh ourselves and update each other. I have to *gain* weight, of course," she added with a smile.

"We'll do it," Nili said.

28

She found a miraculous parking spot on Mazeh Street and walked the short distance. Half an hour earlier, when she'd stood outside the apartment, ringing and ringing the doorbell—she'd seen the lights on from the street corner—he'd finally answered when she phoned: "I'm not at home, I'm at a hotel," he'd said. She'd said, "But the lights are on," and he'd repeated that he was at a hotel.

As she walked, she wondered who was at home, then. If it was Idit, that meant everything was over.

She entered through the glass doors, nodded at the front desk clerk with the confidence of a guest, and took the elevator up to the second floor. She found room 12 and knocked fearfully, and a moment later, more forcefully.

The door opened. Yehuda was wearing shorts and a white Fruit of the Loom T-shirt. "Nili," he said, like an officer counting his cadets.

"What's going on," she said, without a question mark.

He held the door open wide and she walked in. Chinese food take-out cartons were scattered around the floor, with remnants of his meal on the desk. She spotted a few uneaten ribs, some sort of beef dish, and sesame chicken nuggets.

"How could you leave me with those two bozos?" Yehuda rebuked her. "I'll never forgive you for that. Sit down. Want some ribs?"

Wednesday

Amos

29

The news did nothing to cheer Amos up, and he felt old, as though his comprehension had finally caught up with his chronological age. So Varda was going to be a lawyer.

He felt like suggesting they go somewhere, perhaps inspired by Yehuda and his dumb ideas. They should go away, just the two of them, to celebrate her success instead of waking up the next morning at home, for the first day of who knew how many more of his life. Maybe that was how he'd live from now on, from one delay to the next: one week with Avishay, the next week in Rome, and the next week they'd figure something out. Maybe someone else would die by then, God forbid.

Otherwise, he was alone. Avishay was dead, having generously cleared the arena for him, pulled out the rug of excuses from under his feet. Now it was all up to him to finally get justice after twenty, thirty years. To achieve a proper verdict, to bring triumph to the unsexy, to the small-talk-challenged of the world. And if not in economics, where could that triumph occur?

And if he won? Who would see it? If a man wins a race in the middle of the forest . . . But he didn't know how to finish the metaphor.

Avishay was dead. Dead too soon. One minute he was alive, and the next he was dead, like someone who'd taken an unfair shortcut, dropped out as soon as he had the upper hand. Amos wished Avishay could come back for a while, perhaps to die slowly. *You have seven months left. Three months left.* He needed more time.

He imagined Avishay living again. What would Amos do? He imagined himself coming clean. He'd come clean, and so would Avishay. *You were jealous of me? But I was jealous of you! What on earth were you jealous of me for?* And Avishay would say, *What for? Do I lack for reasons?* He thought he might have seen a movie like that once, with Bette Middler.

Maybe Avishay really should have been ill. Very ill. If he'd been deathly ill, it would have woken them up in time. But someone had pressed the button too hard, too much poison was injected, and now he was dead instead.

He tried to think about other people in his life who might die instead of getting ill, instead of living—people who might skip a stage. Varda. Hagar. He brushed away the exercise.

He tried shutting his eyes but the thoughts prickled his eyelids from inside, bounced them out of their sockets.

He deserved some rest.

———

They'd been sitting at Avishay's since that morning. Zohara, who'd slept there, was setting the table with a surprisingly welcoming meal, considering that the home was uninhabited: sliced vegetables, some dips and bread, warm pasta salad. They ate hungrily and fast, as if in a hurry to make way for the occasion.

They would call. They always made the announcement by phone. Amos knew that, but still he found himself tensing up in all directions, as though there were no telling where it might come from: a phone ringing or a knock on the door, a chirping cell phone or a dinging inbox. So many voices and openings. The apartment seemed completely breachable, and his ears and eyes and heart did not know what to prepare for, where to aim their weapons. It might even come from the window, he thought. A man in ridiculous clothing might come swinging through the window into the living room on a rope: *Hear ye, hear ye! Avishay has won the Nobel Prize!* Perhaps with a trumpet.

Zohara turned on the TV, but as soon as the sound invaded the apartment they realized how idiotic it was: there was no "Breaking News" or "Live from Sweden," just a morning talk show. She switched to a different channel and Yehuda said, "Stop, turn it off. If anything, it'll be on Facebook."

Zohara climbed up the channels to the untouristed high numbers of the box, where it was all Russian and English and other languages. "Facebook? That's where they'll announce it?"

"That's not where they'll announce it," Nili said, "but maybe it'll show up on our feed. That's how I always find out who won the literature Nobel."

"And the economics one?" Zohara asked.

"Actually, no," Nili admitted.

"If anything, it'll be on Amos's," Yehuda said.

"I'm not sure at all." Amos took his cell phone out and scrolled through his Facebook page for a while. "Nothing yet. Anyway, you understand that if it's on Facebook or Sky News then it's a no, right? It would just be to get it off our plate, to know that it's someone else. It's not like we're going to find out on Google that Avishay won."

"Why? Doesn't it ever happen that they can't get hold of the candidate and he finds out on TV or something?" Nili wondered. "That's what happened with Alice Munro, that time. They couldn't get hold of her."

"Not when the candidate is sitting at home next to his phones, landline and cell," Amos said.

"I wonder how long they wait to publicize it. How long can we just sit around here doing nothing?" Nili said.

"It's immediate—they call and a second later it's on the radio, or CNN," Amos asserted.

"You seem to be an expert," Zohara observed.

"You think I don't know people who've won the Nobel? And more than that—you think people who've won the Nobel talk about anything else? Especially in economics."

"But not in chemistry?" Zohara wondered.

"I don't know."

"Well, there's nothing at the moment," Nili summed up.

"Did you look for Nobel winner in economics, no quotes?" Yehuda asked.

"Not 'winner,' they use a different word," Nili said.

"Laureate," Amos said. "Nobel laureate."

"There's nothing, and we set up a Google Alert."

Yehuda typed something on his phone—Amos knew he didn't trust their searches and was embarrassed to ask how to spell *laureate*. Nili looked at him and was apparently thinking the exact same thing, her tongue clucking against her teeth to indicate unspoken dissatisfaction, and she said, "Well, anyway, there's no point sitting around obsessively. Let's decide to check every hour, say, otherwise we'll go crazy."

Yehuda stared at his phone.

"Yehuda?" Nili said.

"Just a second," he said.

"Did you hear me?"

Yehuda tapped a few more times with his thumb, in regular intervals, probably *Back, Back*, then he looked up at Nili and said, "I heard you. Every word."

=====

Yehuda had called him on Monday afternoon. Amos had inhaled deeply, preparing to be magnanimous, taking in a forgiving breath, but Yehuda had sounded unlike himself: "Amos, they took Avishay," he said in a trembling voice, as though he were notifying him of Avishay's death. Then he said, "You have to come over."

"Who took him?" Amos asked.

"I don't know. My cleaner maybe. The Nigerians. I don't know, he's not here, Amos, what do I do?"

"Your cleaner took Avishay? Took him where?"

"I came home and he was gone, and that was after the cleaner came, I forgot it was his day."

"But before that he was there?"

"Who?"

"Avishay."

"Of course he was."

"And when you came in he wasn't?" Amos asked.

"Amos, just come over, okay?"

"Where are you?"

"At home. Outside the house."

"Did you call him? Did you call the cleaner?"

"Why would I do that?"

"You didn't call him? Call him, find out what happened."

Yehuda said, "You're telling me to call my cleaner and ask if he saw a body?"

"No, but . . . I don't know . . . Call and see if he says anything."

"Amos, just come over, okay? I'm standing outside here."

"Why are you outside?"

"I can't be inside," Yehuda said.

"Okay, I'm coming. I'm leaving Herzliya now."

=====

He found Yehuda sitting on the front path smoking a cigarette. It took Amos a moment, like a "spot the difference" game, and when he

finally got it—Yehuda was smoking, he'd taken up smoking again—
his happiness momentarily annulled everything else.

"Come on, let's go inside," he said.

"I can't go in there, Amos," Yehuda pleaded.

"What are you afraid is going to happen?"

"I don't know, I'm afraid they're waiting for me in there, I don't
know, that they're going to blackmail me, I don't know, I'm totally
freaked out."

"Who's waiting for you in there? The Nigerians?"

"I don't know. Yes, the Ivory Coastians—he's from the Ivory
Coast. Not waiting for me in there, but you know. Maybe they did
something to his body. I don't know."

"Do you want to give me the key?"

Yehuda quickly said "Yes," as though that's what he'd been planning. He held out the key.

Amos took it and said, "Okay. I'll be right back."

He put the key into the lock and carefully opened the door. Avishay's smell was still in the air, undoubtedly, but Avishay was gone.
Amos was afraid. Yehuda's house was big. But at the same time he
felt a little bit like Superman. Or SuperGeek. Surely they had that
now? He'd pulled off the whole bike incident and saved everyone
with his lecture. He wasn't who they'd thought he was. He was doing
everything he could for Avishay. And it was no coincidence that Yehuda had called him first, despite their fight, despite everything. He
was filled with a profound sense of justice, the kind one usually does
not get: in the very end, when all was said and done, he had won.
There was heroism in logic.

"Hello?" he called out. He scanned his surroundings. The floor
under the staircase looked wide open, like a chasm, trying to shout
something at him. He was loath to go any farther. If this had been
a movie, the audience would look away now. But it wasn't a movie,

and there was no one there. He glanced at the living room but it was empty. He peered under the couches, bending over strenuously but quickly, trying to reduce the duration of embarrassment. He opened the door to the guest bathroom with a sharp, surprising motion, but there was no one there either, including behind the shower curtain. He shut the door and plodded up the steps, almost on his tiptoes, nauseated by the sight.

The smell got worse. Now he was following it, playing hot-or-cold, walking down the long corridor. A swarm of flies was buzzing around the guest room door like an arrow; he swatted them away and opened the door. But no one was lurking there either, and why would there be? It wasn't rational, but Yehuda had put that thought into his head, the kind of thing that could be revoked only by uttering it out loud.

Only then, once his heart stopped pounding and his eyes grew accustomed to the nothing, to the everything's fine, did the stench finally hit his nostrils after patiently waiting its turn. And Amos saw him: Avishay, or the outline of Avishay, covered with a sheet as though he'd wandered in with it from the living room like an upside-down flying carpet, cargo beneath carrier. Above him, the flies circled like hired mourners.

He moved a walking frame aside and went closer to the bed, pinching his nostrils with his fingers. He lifted up one corner of the sheet, peeked underneath, and quickly let it fall: it was the most disgusting thing he had ever seen in his life.

He rushed out of the room and shut the door, strode quickly across the living room, and stepped outside with relief, shutting the door behind him, as though having escaped the dead. Yehuda turned his head to Amos questioningly.

"He's there," Amos said, "upstairs, in the room."

"Avishay is?" Yehuda asked with hesitant relief.

"He's in the guest room, the room with the walker. Your guy must have moved him so he could clean. He must have put him somewhere he thought made more sense."

"Is he okay?"

"Okay . . . ? I wouldn't use that word."

"Like yesterday, I mean?"

"Give me a cigarette," Amos said.

═══

They sat in Avishay's living room. "Have you heard from Idit?" Nili asked.

Yehuda said, "I texted with Miki."

"Is she staying with her?"

"For the time being," Yehuda said.

Amos had the feeling he'd skipped a chapter: something had happened and he wasn't up to date. He was briefly insulted. He had stood by Yehuda's side, come to his aid at the crucial moment, yet still things had happened that he didn't know about—things had very definitely happened in his absence. "Miki her sister?" he asked.

"Idit's staying there for now," Zohara explained.

"For now, meaning until we move Avishay?" Amos asked.

"Doesn't he know?" Nili inquired.

And then Yehuda said: "We're getting divorced."

Amos was stunned, but he didn't want to say anything stupid. He flipped through a few possible responses, all of which sounded like he was consoling a distant relative after a rather unmoving death.

Zohara asked, "Are you sad, Yehuda?" and Amos looked at her with gratitude and astonishment: what a logical question.

"Am I sad?" Yehuda repeated.

"Of course he's sad," Nili said, "it's a horribly sad thing, even if it's the right thing to do and everything's the way it should be, it's still sad."

"Yes, I am sad," Yehuda said.

Amos finally came up with his own question, which was whether this had anything to do with Avishay, but it sounded insipid now.

"Do you even want to talk about it, or should we change the subject?" Zohara asked.

"I don't mind talking about it, but I'm not sure if there's all that much to say."

Nili stepped in: "Am I allowed to tell them how I found you last night?"

"How did you find me last night?"

"With the takeaway boxes?"

"Go ahead, tell them," Yehuda said.

"He's gone back to eating meat," she announced.

"No way!" Amos exclaimed, fished from the depths of a torturous topic back onto solid ground, although he wasn't particularly surprised. After all, Yehuda had also taken up smoking again.

"But do me a favor," Yehuda pleaded, "just don't be all horrified, I can't deal with that. That's why I didn't tell you before."

Amos could tell that they'd all skipped a chapter this time: What did he mean "before"? But everyone kept quiet, so as not to seem horrified. "Congratulations, Yehuda," he said, "welcome back into the fold of the artery-cloggers."

"Thank you kindly, it's good to be back."

Amos felt he was riding a wave, but he wasn't sure what else to say.

Yehuda said, "Hey, you guys want to hear a great story?"

Nili said, "If you're telling a great story, I have to go to the bathroom first. Wait for me, don't start." She got up and started walking toward the bathroom.

Yehuda went on: "I can't believe I didn't tell you. It's just that it happened right in the middle of all the stress about what to do with Avishay."

"Wait for me!" Nili said.

"We're waiting, I'm just giving background." When she'd disappeared into the bathroom, he went on: "Such a crazy couple of days."

"But was it nice, too? The whole birthday, and the B and B? Or was the whole thing ruined?" Amos asked.

"How could it be nice? Do you have any idea what they made me do? A climbing wall."

"What is that?" Zohara asked.

"You know those walls where you have to climb up while you're tied to equipment?"

"Go on."

"Well, there's this whole area with those walls, and I had to climb up fifty feet, first thing in the morning."

"Wow. Okay, wait for Nili if this is going to be funny, you promised."

"Okay," Yehuda said.

They waited in exaggerated silence, which might have expressed both respect and mockery. Amos wondered if it would ever be fixed, this business with Nili, which had not been discussed. She'd clearly made up with Yehuda, in his role as ambassador, and she'd come back to sit there with them as though nothing had happened. Maybe she thought they'd apologized and maybe they thought she had, which was convenient for everyone. But now they all conveyed a certain overstated cheerfulness, and Amos wondered whether it would die down to its normal proportions—or whether their friendship would.

Nili came out after much too long, with the guilty look of someone who'd just pooped, and said, "Do you have any idea what's going on in his cabinet? The whole thing's full of shampoos and lotions."

"Which cabinet? The bathroom one?" Zohara asked.

"It's quite the selection he has in there."

"Why are you snooping around his cabinets?"

"He's dead," Nili said.

"So what?"

"What do you mean, so what? So what does he care?"

"What does he care if he gets the Nobel?" Zohara shot back.

"Not exactly the same thing."

"Would you like people to go snooping around your cabinets after you're dead?"

"I wouldn't care, to be honest. They'd be snooping in worse things than my cabinets, and the most shocking thing they'd find would be condoms."

"You use condoms?" Yehuda asked.

"Not now, but we used to."

"Good for him," Yehuda said.

"Why good for him? Why not good for me?"

"Good for both of you. So d'you want to hear the story?" Yehuda pressed.

"Maybe they're his sister's?" Zohara posited.

"Zohara," Nili said, "it's okay to acknowledge that there have been other women here once in a while. It doesn't make you any less important."

"What do you mean?" Zohara demanded.

"Nothing."

"No, you meant something."

"I'm just saying that you were important in Avishay's life. That's all."

Zohara looked like she was deliberating, unsatisfied, but Nili had already moved on. She said to Yehuda, "You were going to tell a joke, weren't you?"

"A story," Yehuda corrected.

"We were all important in Avishay's life," Zohara said.

"Zohara, don't push it," Nili said.

Amos suddenly found her impertinent, and extremely annoying. He thought she deserved to be punished. What about the whole false pregnancy and all that? They hadn't even talked about it. Wasn't that slightly her fault? How could she torture Zohara like this, so arrogantly, when she herself had turned out to be not much of a genius at all, stressing them all out because of something that had never even happened, getting them off course. "Nili, stop it," he said.

"What?" Zohara asked.

"Stop it, this is ridiculous," Yehuda said, "the man is going to be buried in a few hours, I think the secret is over."

"In a few hours? How is that going to happen?" Nili said.

"In a few hours, whether he wins or not, we bury him. I mean you're not going to keep hiding the fact that he died, either way."

"I didn't think about that. I didn't even grasp that at all. Wow. My heart is suddenly pounding," Nili admitted.

Zohara said, almost to herself, "I'm in shock," perhaps continuing a different conversation.

Amos put his hand on her shoulder but wasn't sure what to do with it.

Yehuda asked Nili, "Are you okay? Do you want a drink?"

"I don't know what happened," Nili said, "I just suddenly got anxious."

"About what?" Yehuda asked.

"I don't know, it suddenly seems real."

Amos thought Zohara might be about to cry, and he tightened his grip on her shoulder, but it came out like a pinch.

"*Now* it seems real?" Yehuda asked Nili. "The whole thing is behind us now."

"Exactly the opposite—it's all still ahead of us. The whole thing of going public, and the lying," Nili countered.

"We won't be lying more than we already have," Amos said. "Now we just have to say he's dead, which is the truth. Think about it that way."

"That's not exactly the way it is," Nili argued, in a tone that said, *And you know that.*

"Not exactly, but you can think about it like that," Amos said.

"I don't know. Nathan says . . ." But Nili stopped midway.

"Nathan says . . . ?" Zohara asked.

"No, it's just that he always says I'm a terrible liar."

"You didn't tell him, did you?" Amos asked.

"Are you crazy?"

"Are you sure?"

"Your phone is ringing," Nili said to Yehuda.

"It's not mine."

They all concentrated, as if trying to identify the sound of their own child crying, until Nili said, "It's the landline."

═══

Nili got up quickly and followed the ring. Zohara said, "I think the phone's in the bedroom," and Nili disappeared and came back with the ringing phone, holding it out. Yehuda said, "Answer it," and Nili pushed the phone at him. Yehuda took it and put on his glasses and held it away from his eyes and said, "Unlisted." Then he answered it: "Hello?" with a hint of a British accent, or a business accent, and they all looked at him while he listened, until he hung up and said, "Tele-marketer."

═══

Amos said, "You know that when they call, they have someone else on the line, someone you know, so you won't think it's a joke."

"What do you mean, someone you know? A relative?" Nili asked.

"A professor whose voice you recognize, someone from the committee who you've met, it doesn't matter, just so you believe it's a legitimate call."

"Are you telling me people play practical jokes on each other about this?" Zohara asked incredulously.

"Apparently."

"I don't think professors in their eighties prank call each other, do you?" Yehuda said. "But it could be that people simply don't believe it, that you can't convince them it's real. That makes more sense."

"Yes, that's true," Amos conceded. He had a question on the tip of his tongue but he had trouble imagining how it would sound if he were to really ask it, whether it would come off as defiant or reasonable. He was too curious, though, and time was pressing, so he said, "Do you think he's going to get it?"

"There's no way to tell," Yehuda said.

"I don't think he is," Zohara said.

"No?"

"No."

"Why not?" Nili asked.

"I don't know, I just don't. Can you really see that phone ringing now and Avishay getting the Nobel Prize?"

"That's how it always happens," Nili pointed out, "it's not like anyone's used to getting that kind of call, or expecting it. If anything, we're relatively prepared for it, we're anticipating it. Maybe that's the reason he won't get it, actually, because we're too expectant."

"I have to say that I have no hunch either way. I really have no clue. It could be a yes and it could be a no," Yehuda said.

"I think he will, for some reason. I don't know, at least for most of the week I've thought so," Nili said. "But now I'm all stressed out, I don't trust my own judgment anymore."

Amos listened, fascinated, as though he were watching a court-room drama, trying to decide which side to believe.

"You know why I don't think he will?" Zohara asked Nili.

"Well?"

"It's too much of a happy ending. It's not realistic, this is not what happens in real life."

"I get what you're saying, but you know what sorts that out for me? That it's not happening in our reality, it's not something good happening to me or you, you know what I mean? If you told me this was going to happen to me, I'd say, this isn't something that could happen in my life, it can't be, it's like winning an Oscar. But in Avishay's life? Why not? It still leaves space for jealousy, you see? It's still something that happens in someone else's life, and I can say, Goddammit, why can't these things happen to me."

"Think about it like a novel."

"Okay," Nili said.

"And the whole novel, you're like, will he get it or won't he get it? Will he or won't he? And at the very end, ready, set—he gets it! You'd say it was a bad book, that it was a cheap happy ending."

"Not necessarily," Yehuda opened, "it depends how it's written. You're not saying a happy ending is automatically a bad book, are you?"

Amos wondered when was the last time Yehuda had read a book—after all, he only wrote.

"Basically, yes," Zohara replied.

"Nonsense, that's not true at all, that's a really superficial thing to say," Nili countered.

"You know what? Not a bad book, but you must agree that there's a certain lack of sophistication in happy endings. It's like good against evil, and good wins. And in real life that doesn't happen."

"Why doesn't it happen?" Yehuda said. "Don't good things happen in life? Are you saying that's unrealistic?" He accentuated the *unrealistic* with exaggerated refinement, and Amos felt a little sorry for him being trapped in this discussion, as though it were not Avishay or his Nobel that he was trying to protect, but himself: his book, not the book they were now in.

Zohara said, "In real life things are usually more complex, that's all. Good things happen and bad things happen, but most of the things that happen are neither one or the other, they're somewhere in between. And even the good and bad things that happen are usually not absolutely good or bad."

"Okay, but the fact that something good happens in the end doesn't mean bad things haven't happened too, or complicated things," Yehuda said. "If Avishay wins the Nobel it's not exactly a happy ending—the man is dead, after all."

"Well, it's a matter of taste," Zohara pressed on. "For me, when I read a novel with a happy ending, I'm disappointed. Unless it's a book from a very particular genre and that's what I'm expecting to begin with."

Nili said, "And if it's not a happy end but a sad end? Think about it the other way around for a minute: the whole book is will he or won't he get it, tension, action, and in the end—he didn't get it, goodbye, the end. That's also an annoying ending. Wouldn't that annoy you? Wouldn't it leave you kind of, I don't know, like: so what? What was the point of all that?"

"I wouldn't find it annoying, but I guess I'm looking for different things," Zohara said.

"Well, it's not a book, so this whole discussion is somewhat irrelevant, fascinating as it may be," Amos intervened. "There's a committee here, and it makes the decision—or already has, actually, it's just us who don't know it yet."

"Oh, do you have something better than conducting pointless debates to do at the moment?" Zohara asked.

"Do you want to hear my story already?" Yehuda piped up.

"Okay, Yehuda's story. Go on, let's hear it."

Yehuda began: "So anyway, I get to Alonei Aba—on Sunday, I mean—and I find the surprise party there, right? And then I think, Well, okay, at least I'll get some good food, right?"

They all looked at him expectantly.

"Now, what would you have guessed they'd serve at my birthday dinner?"

"Go on," Nili urged him.

"Right, I will now read to you the menu from my seventieth birthday party, okay? Seventieth, mind you!" He waved his iPhone and read out loud: "Roasted kohlrabi stuffed with freekeh. I'm starting with the hors d'oeuvres, yes? This is just the hors d'oeuvres. Okay, so roasted kohlrabi stuffed with freekeh, pearl barley salad with figs and raisins, cabbage confit on a bed of quince and lentils, eggplant tabouleh . . ."

Amos looked around to see if he was missing something—what was this drivel?

Yehuda continued: "Radish momo, green-bean-cuffed leek bundles."

"What is that?" Nili asked.

"Excellent question," said Yehuda.

And then Nili said, "Wait, listen. Can you hear that?"

"It's me, it's me, it's my phone," Zohara said, and she took out her phone, which had gone silent by then, and said, "I set a reminder to go off every hour. Check Google, let's see what's new."

━━━

He didn't want Avishay to win. He wanted him not to win. He was sitting there waiting, and for what? For this. Sitting here hoping. At first he'd been ashamed; then he'd been angry at Avishay for making him ashamed. Not any longer. This whole affair had been designed purely to dig a dark truth out of the bottom of his soul: You could never be happy because of a friend's happiness. You could be happy *for* him, that might be true. You could be happy next to him, happy with him, happy when you were present in that happiness, in its environs. But true happiness, the kind that leaves its mark on your soul, that sticks to your soul and walks out the door with it? There was a reason that idiom had come into being, that distinction: happy *for* someone, not happy because they were happy. It was a happiness that sat on your skin like clothing, which you took off when you were alone and put back on in company. It was a happiness that left you cold. It was not yours.

That was natural, wasn't it? It had to be. He couldn't be the only one, the sole villain. But how could he be sure? After all, he couldn't say it out loud, it could never be uttered. Not even privately. If it flew out of his mouth and reared its ugly head over the swamp of his hidden thoughts, how could he ever look himself in the mirror? And so it was destined to remain shameful, nonexistent, even though it was true, always true, true for everyone. He was convinced of that. Or almost convinced. And perhaps it was that "almost" that kept the world safe: no one was sure. It was always possible that someone else was better than you. That was how the dynasty was maintained, that was how there could be friendships, that was how it was viable. Even though there was a horrible secret in the foundations, a universal lie that was never revealed.

A crude, violent ring of the doorbell dispelled his thoughts. They looked at one another questioningly. Amos remembered something Varda always said: People on TV and in the movies were always shocked when the doorbell rang. What were they so shocked about? He suddenly understood those people, and he missed Varda.

Yehuda walked to the door. They heard him say, "Yes?" And then, "From where?" They couldn't hear the answers but Yehuda opened the door.

Amos stood up and went to the door, unable to contain himself. Yehuda was barely holding an almost tastelessly large bouquet of flowers, propping a piece of paper on the delivery guy's helmet and trying to sign it. When he saw Amos out of the corner of his eye, he asked, "Do you have ten shekels?" Amos pulled out his wallet and fished out seven.

Zohara appeared behind him with a twenty-shekel note, and Amos kept holding his coins out, to clarify that he was still willing to offer them. To his surprise, Yehuda took the coins, too, and gave the delivery guy twenty-seven shekels. He said goodbye cheerfully and shut the door.

He stood in the living room doorway with the bouquet in his arms and said, "I think this is it."

"Really?" Nili said.

"This is what?" Zohara asked.

"I think he got it. He won," Yehuda said.

"Open the card," Amos urged him.

"But wait, how could someone know before him?" Nili wondered.

"That doesn't make sense to me either," Zohara concurred.

While Yehuda struggled with the envelope, which was attached to the cellophane with too many staples, Amos said, "You never know." He was doing his best to maintain an excited expression. "Look at the size of that thing—what else could it be for?"

"I can't get it open," Yehuda said, "hold this for a second." He plunked the enormous bouquet in Amos's hands and finally ripped off the envelope, tore it open, and read the card. Then he threw it on the table. "I am seriously going to kill that guy."

Zohara picked up the card and read it out loud: "Dear Avishay:

Since you are unavailable (and maybe do not want to talk to me, which is understandable), at least allow me to apologize. I feel terrible, and if there's anything I can do to make it easier for you, or to take responsibility—from daily necessities through insurance/medical forms, etc.—please let me know. I hope you still feel well, and my apologies again. Yours, Gidi Nachman." Then she added, "He wrote his phone number." She examined the picture on the card and waved it at them in amusement: a sick rabbit with a thermometer in its mouth, lying in bed, with a big caption at the top: "Get well soon."

Amos looked at the bouquet lying on the dining table. The first of many, he thought. It occurred to him that this Gidi was going to blame himself for Avishay's death when he found out, when he read it in the papers. It was like in those stories you always heard, when you thought nothing was wrong and then someone died from internal bleeding or concussion. *It wasn't a victimless crime*, he thought; this crime did have a victim, and the victim was Gidi. What if he confessed? What if Gidi decided to confess? It was not just a philosophical contemplation, he realized. "What if this Gidi guy reads that Avishay is dead and thinks it's his fault? Because of what happened on Saturday? It's kind of a coincidence for a guy to die three days after he gets hit by a bike, isn't it?"

"You're right," Zohara said.

"How will he know he's dead?" Yehuda said. "If he doesn't win, he'll never find out. Even if he does, it's highly doubtful."

"But even if he doesn't think he killed him, he could just come out and say: How could he have been dead for a week? I ran him over three days ago," Nili pointed out.

"Believe me, if the papers say he died of a heart attack, he'll be very happy to accept that. At most he'll feel a little guilty. He's already scared of us," Amos said.

"I hope so," Nili said. "I'm exhausted from all this."

Years earlier, maybe a decade ago, he'd been at Zohara's when she'd been getting ready to go out on a date she'd been looking forward to for weeks or even months. It was a long time ago, when people hardly ever put their pictures online, and Zohara certainly didn't, especially since she viewed herself as a sort of public figure because of her profession. Zohara would draw out those correspondences forever, and then the phone calls, until she was finally convinced that the candidate was intelligent and articulate, and that was what mattered, after all.

Amos would accompany her through all the milestones: *There's something about him, definitely.* And then: *I think we're totally in love, it's mutual, I'm positive, you should have heard him on the phone, I think we're going to meet next week.* That Thursday, he'd sat in her living room waiting for her to come out, dressed and made up, and when she did she looked quite beautiful, but she looked her age. She sat down and they waited together.

He had to go but she asked him to stay: "I'll go out when he gets here, and you leave two minutes later. Just shut the door behind you. I don't feel like waiting alone."

The guy arrived on time and Zohara leaped to the door. Amos heard murmurs in the doorway. A moment later she came back, alone: "He's looking for a proper parking spot and then we're going to walk."

"So?" Amos asked.

"He looks lovely. But considering everything I know about him, he'd have to be a real gorilla to ruin things now."

"That's great!" Amos said.

Zohara stood for a while longer and then sat down. She was in high spirits.

Amos remembered that moment, a mass of tumbling time that suddenly fell on his heart like a rock, only moments before it fell on hers: he wasn't coming back. That man was never coming back. Worst of all, perhaps, were those moments while he waited for her to be buried under the landslide too, helpless in the face of disaster.

And now he sat here with his friends, the hours killed and the Google searches run, and all of a sudden, in one moment that was in no way different from the previous ones, he knew that Avishay had not won the Nobel.

He looked into their faces with slight dread. Perhaps the truth had been revealed to them all at the same time? He feared the unpredictability and timing of their responses. But nothing had changed in the room. He looked at Google, surreptitiously ran a search that provided no answers, glanced at his email, and then put the phone aside. Maybe he was wrong?

———

At eight minutes past twelve—Amos was sitting with his phone in his lap, glancing and glancing and glancing at the time, as if surprised by how late the announcers were running, imprinted by the time as though it marked a little birth—Yehuda said, "Well, it's a no."

Amos kept sitting there silently, with the guilt of one who bears a secret.

Nili said, "It's a no?"

Yehuda, with his face still in his phone, said, "Angus Deaton won."

"No!" Zohara said.

"Fuck," Yehuda said.

"What a strange feeling," Nili said.

"Well," Amos said, "it wasn't unexpected. Deaton."

"If it was so expected, what did we do all this for?" Yehuda asked.

Amos resisted saying: Good question.

Nili said, "Well, okay, we knew it was an option, there's nothing we can do about it. That's the game."

"That's the game, yes," Yehuda repeated resentfully.

"What's your problem?" Nili asked him.

"What's my problem?"

"Who exactly are you mad at? I don't understand."

"I'm not mad at anyone."

"Because it sounds like you're mad at us, for some reason."

"I'm mad at the situation—aren't I allowed to be?"

"Yes, you're allowed."

"You're allowed to be mad," Zohara said, "but no one owes you anything, you know."

"I don't understand what that means."

"It's not like we deserve a prize for making an effort. It's possible that this Angus guy deserves it more than Avishay does. What can you do. We're grown-ups."

"But I'm not a friend of Angus," Yehuda said, "I'm a friend of Avishay."

"A good friend, there's no question about that," Zohara said.

They sat quietly for a while. Finally, Yehuda said, "Well, we have to start moving things. I'll let Ruthi know, she'll tell their mom."

"Wait, wait, let it sink in," Nili said. "Let me process things for a while. Ruthi can wait half an hour."

"We really should have the funeral today," Yehuda said, "we've dragged it out as it is. Let's try to narrow down the field of questions, not open it up."

"I just want to let you know that I have to be out of here at twelve thirty. I'm picking up Varda from the convention center, she has her bar exam today," Amos announced.

"Okay, then let's stay with Amos for the next fifteen minutes, and when he leaves we'll start the whole shebang," Zohara suggested.

"No problem," Yehuda said. "So, what do you want to talk about?"

"What do we want to talk about, Zohara?" Nili asked.

"Actually," Zohara said, "if no one has anything else, then I do have something I want to talk to you about. Or rather, ask you for."

"Shoot," Nili said.

The five of them walked in a cluster: Varda and Amos brought up the rear, a fortified wall behind the snaking backs of the other three, where Zohara was slightly behind one minute, and Yehuda and Nili the next. For a moment he thought it might be their last time together: by separating from Idit, Yehuda had sentenced Amos to exile from their company, purged the last of the group who was still part of a couple.

They walked roughly in the middle of the procession, perhaps at the end of the first third of the numerous mourners, none of whom Amos recognized. Nor did he attempt to mingle, keeping his eyes on the ground, as the others were also doing. When he looked up it was for Varda's sake, as she walked there, free of any sins, occasionally wanting to say something. Amos was slightly glad to be sheltered by a funeral, where everyone was as strange as he was, and he was protected from her sagacity for at least a few more hours.

She was in an excellent mood but was forced to bury it. Amos could picture her impatiently squeezing into her rain boots, gleefully aiming at the grave site and beyond, out of Yarkon Cemetery, just longing to be sitting alone in the car already so she could let all that happiness out. He felt guilty. *For what?* she would surely ask; *You don't control when people die.*

She'd passed the bar. There were no results yet, but it had gone extremely well. She'd definitely passed and she might even have done more than that, maybe much more, "But never mind, there's no point in just talking, the main thing is I'm done with it. Amos, can you believe it? Finally!" He'd kissed her and sat there without starting the car, and then he'd said, "Avishay is dead." Up until the second the words left his mouth, he'd still been planning what to say: *I'm so happy for you, but I have to ruin it for you, Varda, I have something to tell you.* That was too dramatic. *We'll have to postpone the celebration for a day or two.* Maybe something like that. But when the moment came, he suddenly found that his strength had run out and he simply said it.

She was stunned, just as she should have been. Given her cheerful mood, she suspected he was joking at first, but a moment later the sadness filled the car and banished the jollity through the shut windows, and Amos remembered that she'd loved Avishay. Not only because she'd loved Amos: he'd been a real presence in her life. A wellspring of sadness began seeping up from his heart, as though her eyes had drilled through the layers of the passing days and the detriment, a primeval sadness that had been prematurely buried before its object had.

They drove home in silence, a strange few minutes during which he lost his gauge of the closeness between them, which seemed to be casually rocking back and forth between the yellow lights and the turns. Were they completely alienated or were they one single soul? What was he allowed to say and what was he not?

═══

Amos didn't know what had happened after twelve thirty, when he'd left Avishay's apartment to pick up Varda. Who had they called, what had they said, which version and in which order, how had people responded. Varda's presence had protected him from the details, and he preferred it that way, summed up in a one-line message over WhatsApp: "Funeral at six thirty at Yarkon."

As he'd waited in the car for her to come out of the exam, he'd been riddled with guilt, which he substituted with irritation—at his friends, the dead and the living, who'd sent him that message without bothering him with the details, and at Varda, whose exam he'd forgotten to worry about at all. And then he remembered, with some surprise, that there was this escape called the internet.

He had no new email messages. He surfed a few news sites, without knowing what he was looking for—whether they'd written about the newly minted Nobel laureate, or whether they'd already reported Avishay's death. He found the Nobel laureate buried in the depths of the financial news.

He thought about Avishay's Wikipedia entry. Soon it would be frozen in time.

He opened up the page: "Avishay Sar-Shalom (Born December 23, 1943)." That would change soon, he thought: "Avishay Sar-Shalom, 1943–2015."

How would his own entry end? The one he didn't have? 2015? 2016? 2030? 2040? There was no question: he was alive.

He scrolled down the page but everything was still the same, including the line that said, "Considered a leading candidate to win the Nobel Prize in Economics," which leaped out at Amos like a star pupil, volunteering to save him any unnecessary reading.

How long would it take until they noticed? Hours? Minutes? Things moved quickly in that mysterious entity, Wikipedia. And what would happen when they did notice? What would they write instead? Or would they just erase the line? It was superfluous now, irrelevant. They'd remove the inaccuracies.

He roamed up and to the right with his thumb, like someone who'd been fantasizing about that movement all his life. His thick thumb barely homed in on the little tab marked "Edit," but the page finally opened up and he moved the cursor all the way down to "Considered." He highlighted it, changed the uppercase "C" to a

lowercase "c" and inserted "Was": "Was considered a leading candidate to win the Nobel Prize in Economics."

No one would erase that.

=====

From a distance, he spotted Avishay's mother, supported by a man
he didn't know. Maybe it was someone from the old-age home. He
hadn't seen her for years, and she'd grown so old that it was hard to
isolate the sorrow from her face. If they'd wronged anyone, it was
her. But then he remembered that she was senile, as Zohara had reminded them: "His mother is senile, it doesn't matter to her anyway,
five minutes this way or that. Wait another five minutes. I want to ask
you for something."

For some reason, Amos was convinced she was going to bring
up money. What else could she ask for? He was already working
on a possible defense when Zohara said, "I want to meet someone."
Amos couldn't understand what she was saying; it lacked all context.
At first he thought she was making a criminal request: introduce me
to someone who does that sort of thing. That was how far this week
had gone in disrupting his settings. But Nili said, "You mean, meet a
guy? Like, a partner? Meet someone romantically?"

Zohara said, "Yes, I want you to help me."

He didn't know what to say. It was so peculiar.

"Help you how?" Yehuda asked.

"I don't know. I want you to think about whether you know someone right for me. Ask around. Just have it in your minds. Put some
effort into it."

"Do you think if we had someone we wouldn't have introduced
you ages ago?" Yehuda said. "You think we'd hide him?"

"Not that you'd hide him, but there's a difference between wanting my well-being hypothetically and actually working toward it. I want us to decide that one year from today, I'm with someone. I'm living with someone."

Nili said, "Works for me."

Yehuda said, "Me, too, I just don't understand. I mean, the timing."

"No? You really don't understand?" Nili asked him.

"No, okay, I'm just asking, is it urgent to do this before Avishay's funeral?"

"It's not urgent to do it before Avishay's funeral, Yehuda, calm down, I'm not expecting you to set me up with the undertaker," Zohara quipped.

"Okay, I just didn't get it, I thought it was connected somehow."

"Good for you, Zohara, that's the right way to do things. I'll think about it. I'll think about it and I'll ask around," Nili declared.

The rabbi was saying something, or singing, and Amos strained to concentrate, not on the rabbi but on the moment, for Avishay. Here they were, burying Avishay, no questions asked. They'd come prepared, on alert, with so many lies at the ready, and then nothing. It was a little insulting, he realized. It put all of their efforts in a pitiful light.

Even the fact that they were burying Avishay with a rabbi was unbelievable. An ordinary funeral in an ordinary cemetery, as if the whole thing were designed to emphasize their failure to elevate Avishay above the masses. They'd been so crazy all week that they didn't have the energy left to invest in a slightly more appropriate, secular burial, a burial more suited to Avishay. Or maybe that didn't matter anymore? Amos amused himself with the idea until he was forced to acknowledge that it actually would have mattered to Avishay. There was no life after death—only a void. But there were principles. Looking at the covered body lying beside the grave, he wondered if Avishay had relinquished them.

They stood in a row next to one another, but no one touched anyone else; not even Varda touched Amos, perhaps so as not to draw attention. He sought out their eyes but instead found hands: Yehuda's hands next to his body, like a high schooler at a Memorial Day ceremony; Nili's crossed behind her back. A moment later she moved them forward, like Zohara's.

Avishay vanished into the depths of the grave. From where they stood, they could no longer see him. And with him went the past eight days, as if they had never existed.

A Note from the Translator

Getting into someone else's mind is what translators do. If we're doing our job well, we are closely attuned to the author's thoughts, perspective, ideas—to their psyche. But often the mind we get into is already rather crowded, because all the characters' minds are in there, too—or rather, the author is in theirs. This results in an Escherian interplay of psyches and their representations on the page, and it can make for a delightfully cacophonous conversation.

Noa Yedlin, perhaps more than any other writer I've translated, gets into her characters' minds. She tracks their every thought and second thought, their regrets and doubts, their visceral responses to things other characters say and do, even the way they tamp down and modulate those responses before they speak—or, in some cases, the way they fail to. She does so with such virtuosity and fluency that it's easy to forget that the characters on the page are fictional. Because as far as I'm concerned, I know these people. I've met them. I've seen them and heard them all around Tel Aviv: gossiping in cafés, griping in supermarket checkout lines, honking at each other in traffic jams. I love the noisy, nosy, sarcastic, kind-hearted, selfish, passionate, brutally honest way they move through the world and treat each other. They are the contradiction that is Israel.

How, then, can they exist in English? Because although the themes of *Stockholm* are universal, and the plot could occur anywhere, there is nevertheless something about the characters—who are the back-bone of Yedlin's writing—that is uniquely Israeli and very difficult to transpose to a culture that tends to be less forgiving of messy contradictoriness, of people who can be exasperating and beloved at the same time.

These questions point to a larger conundrum that underpins all translations, and indeed the act of translation itself: if a person (and by extension, a character) is in part defined by the language she speaks, is she still the same person when she speaks an entirely different language? Rather than transposing a story that takes place in Tel Aviv to, say, London, New York, or Melbourne, I prefer to locate the characters in a setting that perhaps exists only in my imagination—a sort of bizarro world in which they are still Israelis, with all their uniquely Israeli charms and faults, and they are still in Israel, but they can now miraculously speak fluent, idiomatic English, as can everyone they interact with. It's an act of faith on the part of the author to allow me into her mind and into her characters' minds, and that faith is what allows me to abduct those characters and transport them into my own mind, where they are reenvisioned for an English-speaking world.

—Jessica Cohen

Here ends Noa Yedlin's
Stockholm.

The first edition of this book was printed
and bound at Lakeside Book Company in
Harrisonburg, Virginia, in October 2023.

A NOTE ON THE TYPE

Named after the Florentine River, Arno draws on the
warmth and readability of early humanist typefaces
popularized during the Italian Renaissance. Designed
for Adobe by Robert Slimbach, Arno honors fonts of
the past but is thoroughly modern in style and function. An Adobe favorite, it offers extensive European
language support, including Cyrillic and polytonic
Greek. The font family also features five optical size
ranges, many italic sets, and small capitals for all supported languages.

HARPERVIA

An imprint dedicated to publishing international voices,
offering readers a chance to encounter other lives and other
points of view via the language of the imagination.